Praise for Th

"In *The First Night*, love is ...gerous, exhilarating adventure, which brings together science, fantasy, police intrigue, and journeys across the world in a narrative written by a great admirer of Jules Verne."

Télé 7 Jours

"Marc Levy's latest novel, *The First Night*, takes the reader around the globe... a second fantastic adventure novel [following *The First Day*], which combines an action-driven, fast-paced narrative with a love story."

Le Parisien

Praise for *The First Day*

"Over the years, Marc Levy has seduced millions of readers. What's his secret? He writes about quintessential themes, such as love, friendship, and the mysteries of life, in an accessible way."

Paris Match

"Marc Levy's latest novel, *The First Day*, is the most epic yet in scope, a page-turning adventure story."

Nice Matin

"A wonderful read."

Le Parisien

Also by Marc Levy
Available from McArthur & Company

All Those Things We Never Said
The First Day

Visit Marc Levy online at
www.marclevy.info

THE FIRST NIGHT

A novel

Marc Levy

Translated from the French by
Lakshmi Ramakrishnan Iyer and Kate Bignold

McArthur & Company
Toronto

First published in English in Canada in 2011 by
McArthur & Company
322 King Street West, Suite 402
Toronto, Ontario
M5V 1J2
www.mcarthur-co.com

First published in French as *La première nuit*
by Éditions Robert Laffont

Library and Archives Canada Cataloguing in Publication

Levy, Marc, 1961-
The first night / Marc Levy ; translated from the French
by Kate Bignold & Lakshmi Ramakrishnan Iyer.

Translation of: La première nuit.
ISBN 978-1-55278-984-1

I. Bignold, Kate II. Iyer, Lakshmi Ramakrishnan III. Title.

PQ2672.E9488P7413 2011   843'.92   C2011-904292-4

Cover photographs: © Michael Hanson/Aurora Photos/Corbis;
© Ron Nickel/Design Pics/Corbis
Maps: Alain Brion
Typeset by Kendra Martin
Author photograph: © Jean Daniel Lorieux

Printed and bound in Canada by Trigraphik LBF

10 9 8 7 6 5 4 3 2 1

JAN 1 7 2012

For Pauline and Louis.
And for Rafaël.

"We all have a little of the Robinson Crusoe in us,
with a new world to discover and a
Man Friday to meet."
ELÉONORE WOOLFIELD

"This story is entirely true,
since I made it up."
BORIS VIAN

My name is Walter Glencorse. I'm the administrator of the Royal Academy of Science in London. I met Adrian a little under a year ago when he was rushed back to England after suffering altitude sickness at the Atacama astronomical observatory site in Chile, where he was exploring the skies in search of the original star. Adrian is a highly talented astrophysicist and over the months we became firm friends.

Because all he dreamed of was continuing his work on the origins of the universe, and because I found myself in a thorny situation at work – I'd proven hopeless at balancing the books – I convinced him to compete for a generous grant being offered by a scientific foundation in London.

We spent weeks and weeks writing his project presentation and during that time got to know each other very well. But I've already told you we were friends, haven't I?

We didn't win the competition. The prize was awarded to an impetuous and determined young woman archaeologist. She had been leading a dig in the Omo Valley in

Ethiopia when a sandstorm destroyed her site and forced her to return to France.

The evening everything began, she was also in London hoping to win the grant and leave for Africa again to pursue her research on the origins of humanity. By one of life's strange coincidences, Adrian had already crossed paths with Keira, the young archaeologist. They'd had a summer romance years before, but not seen each other since.

They spent that night in London together, Keira celebrating her success and Adrian nursing his failure. When Keira disappeared the next morning, she left Adrian not only with the hope of rekindling their romance, but also with a strange, stone-like pendant she had brought back from Ethiopia. Hari, a local orphan boy she'd taken under her wing and become deeply attached to, had found the object in the crater of a dormant volcano.

One stormy night, Adrian discovered that the pendant had astonishing properties. When a powerful light source – lightning for example – shone through it, it projected millions of luminous dots.

Adrian didn't take long to understand what it was. As incredible as it may sound, the dots corresponded to a map of the stars. But not any old map; it showed a portion of the sky filled with the stars that appeared over Earth four hundred million years ago.

Adrian left straightaway for the Omo Valley to inform Keira of his extraordinary discovery. Unfortunately they weren't the only people interested in this strange object. On a trip to see her sister in Paris, Keira had met an elderly ethnology professor named Ivory. This man contacted me and ended up persuading me, in the most contemptible way, it must be said, to encourage Adrian to pursue his research.

In exchange for my services, Ivory gave me a small sum of money and promised to make a generous donation to the Academy if Adrian and Keira succeeded in their work. I accepted the deal. Little did I know that Adrian and Keira were being tailed by a secret organisation that, unlike Ivory, on no account wanted them to achieve their goal of discovering other fragments. You see, Keira and Adrian had learned from the old professor that the object found in the volcano wasn't the only one of its kind: there were four or five similar ones in various parts of the world. They decided to try and find them.

Their search took them from Africa to Germany to England to the Tibetan border, then on a clandestine flight over Burma to the Narcondam Island in the Bay of Bengal, where Keira unearthed a second object resembling hers.

As soon as the two fragments were united, a strange phenomenon occurred: they pulled towards each other like magnets, turned an incredible shade of blue and began sparkling brilliantly. Even more encouraged by this latest discovery, Adrian and Keira set off for China, despite warnings and threats from the secret organisation.

One of its members (all of whom are named after a major city), an English lord called Sir Ashley, decided to break away from the others and put an end to Keira and Adrian's travels any which way.

What was I thinking of when I persuaded them to continue? Why didn't I get the message when a priest was murdered before our very eyes? Why didn't I see how serious the situation was and tell Professor Ivory to manage without me? Why didn't I warn Adrian he was being manipulated by the old man? And by me, his so-called friend?

Just before they left China, Adrian and Keira were the victims of an appalling murder attempt. A car pushed their 4x4 off a mountain road into a ravine, where it sank to the bottom of the Yellow River. Adrian was saved from drowning by some monks who happened to be on the riverbank, but Keira's body wasn't found.

After his convalescence in China, Adrian was sent home to London but refused to return to work. Devastated by Keira's death, he sought refuge in his childhood home on the small Greek island of Hydra (Adrian's father is English and his mother is Greek).

Three months went by. While he suffered from the absence of the woman he loved, I waited impatiently, racked with guilt. Then one day an anonymous parcel from China arrived at the Academy, addressed to his attention. Inside were belongings that Keira and he had left behind in a monastery and a series of photographs in which I immediately recognised Keira. She had a strange scar on her forehead – a scar I'd never seen before. I informed Ivory, who ended up convincing me that it was perhaps proof that Keira had survived.

I told myself a hundred times not to say anything, to leave Adrian in peace, but how could I possibly hide something like that? So I went to Hydra, and – once again because of me – Adrian took a flight to Beijing, full of hope.

I'm writing these lines with the intention of giving them to Adrian one day as a confession of my guilt. I pray every night that he will read them and forgive me for all the harm I've done him.

Walter Glencorse
Administrator, Royal Academy of Science
25 September, Athens

Adrian's Notebook

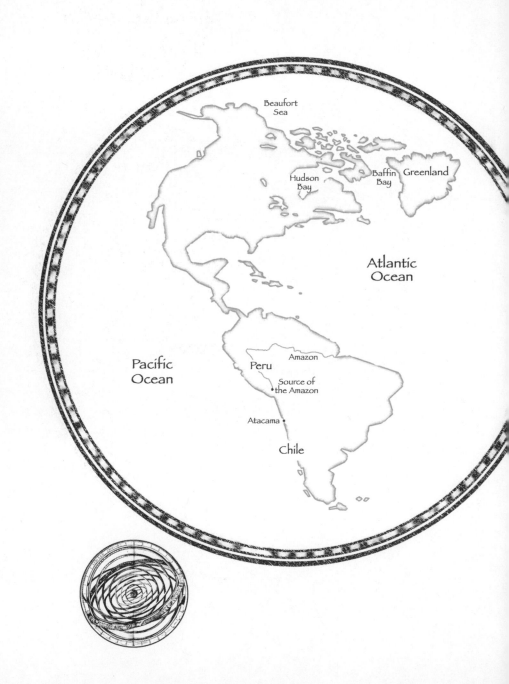

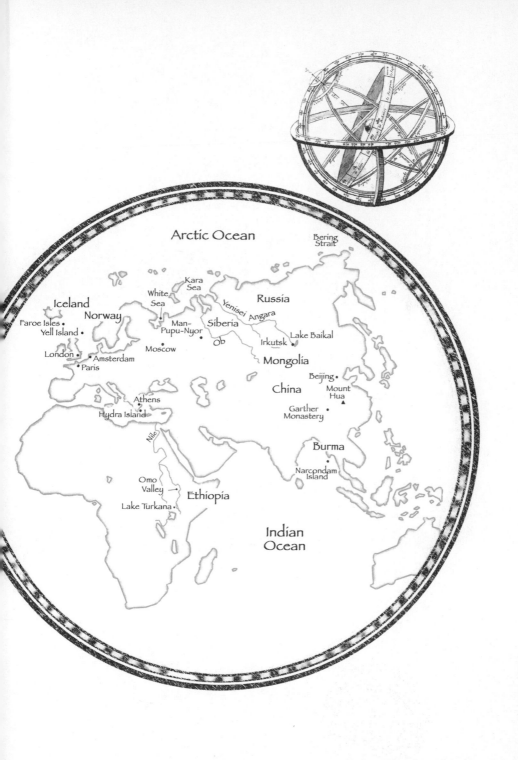

Room 307. The first time I slept in here I paid no attention to the view – I was happy back then and happiness makes you distracted. I'm sitting at a small desk facing the window with Beijing spread out before me. I've never felt so lost in all my life. The mere thought of turning round to look at the bed is unbearable. Your absencc has entered my body and is eating me alive, tunnelling through me like a mole. I tried to anaesthetise the pain by washing down my breakfast with plenty of *baijiu*, but even that potent wheat liquor hasn't helped.

I've had a ten-hour flight with no sleep. I must get some before setting out. All I'm asking for is a few moments of unconsciousness, to stop my mind incessantly replaying images of what we experienced here.

Are you there?

You asked me that question through this very bathroom door a few months back. All I can hear now is the steady drip of water from a leaky old tap into a stained ceramic washbasin.

I push the chair back, put my coat on and leave the hotel.

A taxi drops me off at Jingshan Park. I walk through the rose garden and over the stone bridge spanning a pond.

I'm happy to be here.

I was too. If only I'd known what we were racing towards, oblivious and hungry for discoveries. *If I could freeze time, I'd stop it at this precise moment. If you could rewind the clock, this is where I'd come back to.*

I've returned to the spot where I expressed that wish, by this white rose bush in Jingshan Park. But time hasn't stopped.

I enter the Forbidden City through the north gate and make my way along the alleyways with memories of you as my only guide.

I'm looking for a stone bench near a large tree – a bench – that was occupied not so long ago by a very elderly Chinese couple. If I can find them again, perhaps it'll give me a little peace of mind. I thought I'd read in their smiles the promise of a future for the two of us. Perhaps they'd just been laughing at the fate that awaited us.

I've finally found the bench, but it's empty. I lie down on it. The branches of a weeping willow are swaying in the breeze and their languid dance is making me drowsy. I close my eyes and picture your unscarred face. I fall asleep.

I'm woken by a policeman asking me to leave. Night is falling and visitors are no longer welcome here.

I return to the hotel and go back up to my room. The city lights dispel the darkness. I've pulled the blanket off the bed, spread it on the floor and am lying curled up on it. The headlights of passing cars are making strange patterns on the ceiling. There's no point wasting any more time here – I won't be able to fall asleep again.

I pack my bag, go down to the reception to pay my bill and collect my car from the car park.

The GPS directs me towards Xi'an. Night fades momentarily as I drive through the industrial towns, then plunges me into darkness again in the countryside.

I stop in Shijiazhuang to fill up on gas but I don't buy any food. You'd have called me a coward. Perhaps you'd have been right. But I'm not hungry, so why tempt fate?

A hundred kilometres later, I spot the deserted little village at the top of a hill. I walk up the dirt path to watch the sun rise over the valley. It's said that places hold the memories of time spent there by lovers. A crazy idea perhaps, but this morning I need to believe it.

I walk up and down the empty lanes and past the drinking trough on the main square. The bowl you found in the ruins of the Confucian temple has disappeared. You'd said it would. Someone must have taken it away to use as they saw fit.

I sit down on a rock on the edge of the cliff and watch the day gradually dawn, tremendous. Then I set off again.

Driving through Linfen is as nauseating as the first time we were here. The acrid, polluted air burns my throat. I take out of my pocket the piece of material you made into makeshift masks for us. I found it among the things posted on to me in Greece. There's no trace of your perfume left on it, but as I put it on over my mouth I vividly picture you doing the same.

It smells revolting, you complained as we crossed Linfen. You were always moaning about this, that and the other. How I'd like to hear your grumbling again right now.

It was as we were driving through here that you pricked your finger while rummaging in your bag and discovered a hidden microphone. I should've made the decision to turn back that evening; we weren't prepared for what lay in store – we weren't adventurers, just two scientists behaving like reckless kids.

The visibility is as poor as ever and I have to chase these negative thoughts from my mind to concentrate on the road.

I remember pulling up along the verge as we were leaving Linfen and just throwing the microphone away without giving any thought to the danger it represented, concerned only about the intrusion on our privacy. It was there that I admitted I wanted you, and refused to tell you everything I liked about you, out of awkwardness rather than as a game.

I'm approaching the place where the accident happened, where those murderers pushed us into a ravine. My hands are shaking.

You should let him overtake us.

Beads of sweat are forming on my forehead.

Slow down, Adrian, please!

My eyes are smarting.

I don't believe it, they're actually after us.

Have you got your seatbelt on?

And you said "yes" in reply to the question I barked out like an order. The first jolt propelled us forward. I can still see you gripping the door strap so hard your knuckles went white. I lost count of the number of times the car rammed our bumper before our wheels scraped the parapet and we plunged into the precipice.

I kissed you as we were sinking under the water of the Yellow River. I kept my eyes riveted to yours as we drowned. I stayed with you until the very last moment, my love.

My driving's edgy as I take the bends of the winding road; I have to concentrate to keep the car steady. Have I already passed the junction where a little track leads to the monastery? Since I left for China, this place has been in my thoughts constantly. The lama who hosted us there is my only acquaintance in this foreign land. Who else could provide me with a lead for finding you, or give me information to back up the faint hope that you're alive? A photo of you with a scar on your forehead isn't much to go on – a little scrap of paper I pull out of my pocket a hundred times a day. I recognise the path on my right seconds after I've passed it. I brake hard, the car skids and I reverse.

The wheels of the 4x4 sink into the autumn mud. It's rained all night. I park by the entrance to a wood and continue on foot. If my memory serves me right, I'll have to cross a ford and climb the slope of a second hill, then at the top I'll see the monastery roof.

It takes me just under an hour to get there. In this season, the stream is much fuller and crossing it is no easy task: the big round stones are slippery, standing barely clear of the rushing water. If you were here watching my less-than-graceful attempts to keep my balance, I know you'd make fun of me. That thought gives me the courage to continue.

The sludge on the ground sticks to my shoes and I feel

as if I'm walking backwards rather than forwards. It's a real struggle to reach the top. I arrive soaking wet and covered in mud, wondering what kind of reception I'll get from the three monks who come out to meet me – I must look like a tramp.

Without saying a word they bid me to follow them. We reach the door of the monastery and the monk who kept turning around on the way to check I hadn't sneaked off takes me into a small room. It looks like the one we slept in. He asks me to sit down, fills a bowl with clean water, kneels in front of me and washes my hands, feet and face. Then he hands me some linen trousers and a clean shirt, and leaves the room. I won't see him again for the rest of the afternoon.

A little later, another monk brings me something to eat. He lays a mat on the floor and I realise this will also be my room for the night.

I watch the sun setting. As its golden glow disappears behind the skyline, the monk I came here to meet arrives at last.

"I do not know what brings you here, but unless you tell me you've come on a retreat, I would be grateful if you could leave tomorrow. We have had enough trouble because of you as it is."

"Have you had any news about Keira, the young woman who was with me? Have you seen her?" I ask anxiously.

"I am sorry about what happened to you both, but if someone has led you to believe that your friend survived that terrible accident, it is a lie. I do not claim to know everything that goes on in the region, but believe me, that I would know."

"It wasn't an accident! You explained to us how your religion forbids lying, so I'll ask you my question again: do you know for certain that Keira is dead?"

"It is pointless raising your voice here – it will have no effect on me, or the disciples. No, I do not know for certain. How could I? The river did not return your friend's body; that is all I know. Given the speed of the current and the depth of the water, that is not in the least surprising. Sorry to mention those details; I imagine they must be painful to hear, but you did ask."

"And did they find the car?"

"If the answer really matters to you, you must ask the authorities – although I strongly advise you not to."

"Why?"

"I told you we had had trouble, but you do not seem very concerned."

"What kind of trouble?"

"Do you think there were no repercussions from your accident? The special police carried out an investigation. The death of a foreigner in China is no trivial matter. And as the authorities are not very keen on our monasteries, they treated us to some rather unpleasant visits. Our monks were interrogated aggressively and as we are forbidden to lie we admitted that we had lodged you. You will understand why our disciples do not look very favourably on you being here again."

"Keira is alive. You have to believe me and help me."

"That is your heart talking. I understand your need to hold on to that hope, but by refusing to face reality you are only holding on to your suffering, and it will eat away at you. If your friend had survived, she would have reappeared somewhere and we would have been informed. It's impossible to keep a secret in these mountains. I fear the river kept her prisoner; I am sincerely sorry and share your sadness. I see now why you've embarked on this journey and I apologise for being the one who has to make you see sense. It is difficult to mourn your loss when there is no body to bury and no grave to visit, but your friend's soul is always near you and will remain close as long as you cherish her."

"Oh please, spare me the rubbish! I don't believe in God, or in a somewhere else better than here."

"That is your most basic right; but for a non-believer, you spend a lot of time in monasteries."

"If your God existed, none of this would have happened."

"If you had listened when I advised you not to undertake the trip to Mount Hua, you would have avoided the tragedy you are facing today. As you have not come here on a retreat, there is no point continuing your stay. You may sleep here tonight, and then you must leave. I am not chasing you away, that is not in my power, but I would be grateful if you did not take advantage of our hospitality."

"If she survived, where could she be?"

"Go home!"

The monk leaves.

I spend nearly the whole night lying wide awake trying to find a solution. That photo can't be a lie. I didn't stop looking at it on my ten-hour flight from Athens to Beijing, and I carry on now by candlelight. I want to believe that scar on your forehead is irrefutable evidence. Unable to sleep, I get up without making a sound and slide open the panel door made of rice paper. Guided by a faint light, I walk along a corridor and through a room where six monks are sleeping. One of them must have felt my presence because he turns over and draws a deep breath. Luckily he doesn't wake up. I continue on, stepping quietly over the bodies lying on the floor, until I reach the monastery courtyard. I sit down on the edge of a well at the centre. The moon is two-thirds full tonight.

A noise makes me jump, then a hand covers my mouth to stop me speaking. I recognise the lama I talked to earlier. He beckons me to follow him. We leave the monastery and walk through the fields until we come to a large weeping willow.

I show him the photograph of Keira.

"When will you understand that you are putting us all in danger, yourself most of all? You must leave; you have done enough harm already."

"What harm?"

"Did you not tell me yourself that your accident was not an accident? Why do you think I have led you away from the monastery? I can no longer trust anyone. The people who attacked you will not miss the second time if you give them the chance. You are not very discreet and I fear that your presence here has already been noticed. It would be a miracle if it had not. Let's hope you have enough time to get back to Beijing and take a plane home."

"I won't go anywhere before finding Keira."

"It was before that she needed protecting; it's too late now. I do not know what you and your friend discovered, and I do not want to know, but once again I beg you to leave here!"

"Give me a clue, even a tiny one, a lead to follow; and I promise I'll be gone at daybreak."

The monk stares at me without answering, turns round and sets off for the monastery again. I follow him. From the courtyard, he walks me back to my room in silence.

It's already broad daylight when I awake; jet lag and travel fatigue must have got the better of me. I guess it's around midday when the lama comes into the room carrying a bowl of rice and some broth on a small wooden tray.

"If anyone caught me serving you food in bed I would be accused of wanting to turn this place of prayer into a bed and breakfast," he said, smiling. "Here is something to eat for the road. You are leaving today, are you not?"

I nod. There's no point insisting, I won't get anything else out of him.

"Have a good journey back," the lama says, then leaves the room.

As I lift up the bowl of broth, I discover a piece of paper folded in four under it. I slip it instinctively into my palm and put it discreetly into my pocket. As soon as I finish my meal, I get dressed and walk out of the room. I'm dying to read what the lama has written but two disciples are waiting for me by my door to escort me back to the edge of the wood.

As they leave, they hand me a parcel wrapped in brown paper and tied with hemp string. Back in my car, I wait for them to be out of sight before reading the note.

If you decide to ignore my advice, I have heard that a young monk entered Garther Monastery a few weeks after your accident. Perhaps this is not related to your search, but it is quite rare for that temple to welcome new disciples. It has come to my attention that this person does not appear to be happy with his retreat. Nobody can tell me who he is. If you decide to persist with this unreasonable investigation, drive to Chengdu. Once you get there, I advise you to abandon your vehicle as the region you will be continuing on to is very poor and your 4x4 might attract unwanted attention. In Chengdu, change into the clothes I have asked you to be given – they will help you blend in better among the inhabitants of the valley. Take a coach to Mount Yala. I cannot advise you what to do after that. It is impossible for a foreigner to enter Garther Monastery, but who knows, perhaps luck will smile on you.

Be careful, you're not alone. Most importantly, burn this note after you have read it.

I'm eight hundred kilometres from Chengdu; it'll take me nine hours to get there.

The lama's message doesn't leave me with much hope. He could easily have written it with the sole aim of sending me far away, but I don't think he's capable of such cruelty. The question will no doubt plague me all the way to Chengdu.

The road I'm driving along crosses a plain from east to west. To my left, a mountain range casts eerie shadows over the dusty grey valley. Two chimney stacks loom up ahead. A dark sky hangs over Liuzhizhen's intensely sad landscape of open-air quarries, mining fields and the remains of disused factories.

It hasn't stopped raining. The windscreen wipers are struggling to cope with the steady stream of water. The road is slippery. When I overtake a lorry, the driver looks at me strangely. I don't think many tourists visit this area.

Two hundred kilometres behind me; six more hours of driving. I'd like to call Walter and ask him to join me. I'm feeling oppressed by the loneliness – I can't bear it anymore. I lost the selfishness of my youth in the turbulent waters of the Yellow River. I catch sight of myself in the rear-view mirror, my face has changed. Walter would say it's tiredness, but I know it's because I've reached the point of no return. I wish I'd known Keira earlier, not wasted all those years believing that happiness came from what I was accomplishing. Happiness is much simpler than that – it comes from the other.

A barrier of mountains cordons off the far end of the plain I'm driving through. A sign indicates in Western script that Chengdu is still six hundred kilometres away. A tunnel takes the motorway through the rock; the radio fades, but I don't mind, I find these Asian pop tunes excruciating. Bridges spanning deep canyons mark the landscape for the next two hundred and fifty kilometres. I stop at a service station in Guangyuan.

The coffee isn't that bad and I set off again with a packet of biscuits beside me.

Every narrow little valley I drive through is occupied by tiny hamlets. It's past 8pm when I reach Mianyang, a city of science and high technology that is strikingly modern in comparison, with tall glass and steel towers

rising up alongside a river. Night falls and I'm overcome
with tiredness. I should stop for some sleep, to get my
strength back. I study the map. Once I get to Chengdu,
it'll take several hours to reach Garther Monastery by
coach. Even with the best will in the world, I won't make
it there this evening.

I've found a hotel and parked my car. I'm walking along
the cement riverside promenade. The rain has stopped. A
few restaurants are serving dinner on wet terraces heated
by gas lamps, but the food is a bit too greasy for my liking.

In the distance, a plane takes off with a deafening
sound, climbs over the city and banks south. Probably
the last flight of the evening. I wonder where the passengers sitting at the lit-up portholes are heading. London
and Hydra are so far away. I suddenly feel dejected. If
Keira really is alive, why the silence? Why wouldn't she
have contacted me yet? What has happened to her to justify disappearing like this? Perhaps the monk is right, I
must be mad to keep up this illusion. The lack of sleep
exacerbates my dark thoughts. The blackness of the night
takes hold of me. My palms are clammy. My whole body
breaks out in a sweat. I shiver and flush hot and cold. The
waiter comes over and I guess he's asking if everything's
all right. I want to answer, but can't utter a single word.
I keep on dabbing the back of my neck with a napkin;
my back's dripping with perspiration. The waiter's voice
fades further and further away. The light on the terrace
becomes translucent, my head starts spinning, then I
black out.

*

The eclipse gradually passes and daylight returns. I hear voices – two, three? They speak to me in a language I don't understand. Something cool is put on my face. I must open my eyes.

I make out the features of an elderly lady. She strokes my cheek and makes it clear the worst is over. She moistens my lips and murmurs words that sound comforting.

I feel a tingling sensation; blood's flowing through my veins again. I must have fainted; from tiredness, an illness brewing or something I shouldn't have eaten – I'm too tired to think. They've laid me on a leatherette sofa in the back of the restaurant. A man has joined the old lady who's looking after me – her husband. He smiles at me too. His face is even more wrinkled than hers.

I try to talk. I'd like to thank them.

The old man lifts a cup to my mouth and forces me to drink. It tastes bitter, but I've heard of the healing properties of Chinese medicine, so I let them carry on.

This couple looks so like the one Keira and I crossed paths with one day in Jingshan Park, you'd think they were twins. I find the resemblance reassuring.

My eyelids close and I feel sleep washing over me.

Regaining my strength is my best option right now, so I just lie there and wait.

Paris

Ivory paced up and down his living room. The game of chess wasn't going in his favour and Vackeers had just moved his knight, putting Ivory's queen in danger. He went over to the window, drew back the curtain and watched a bateau-mouche tourist boat cruising down the Seine.

"Do you want to tell me about it?" asked Vackeers.

"About what?" replied Ivory.

"About what's worrying you so much."

"Do I look worried?"

"The way you're playing leads me to believe you are, unless of course you're letting me win on purpose; in which case, the blatantly obvious way you're handing me victory is almost insulting. I'd rather you told me what's bothering you."

"Nothing, I just didn't sleep much last night. To think I used to be able to go two nights without sleeping in the old days. What have we done to God to deserve a punishment as cruel as old age?"

"No flattery intended, but I think God's been rather lenient with us."

"I hope you won't mind my saying it might be better if we brought this evening to a close. Anyway, you'd have checkmated me in four moves."

"Three! You're more preoccupied than I thought, I don't want to force your hand. I'm your friend; you'll tell me what's worrying you when the time seems right."

Vackeers got up and went over to the hall. He put on his raincoat and turned round to find Ivory still looking out of the window.

"I'm going back to Amsterdam tomorrow. Come and spend a few days there – the cool canal air might help you sleep better. You'll be my guest."

"I thought it was better we weren't seen together."

"The case is closed, there's no need for us to play those complicated games anymore. Stop feeling guilty, you're not responsible. We should have guessed Sir Ashley would take matters into his own hands. I'm as sorry as you are about how that business ended, but you can't do anything else about it."

"They all suspected Sir Ashley would intervene sooner or later, and the hypocrisy suited everyone. You know that as well as I do."

"I promise you, Ivory, if I'd had any idea about his jump-the-gun approach, I'd have done everything in my power to stop him."

"And what was it in your power to do?"

Vackeers looked Ivory straight in the eyes, then lowered his gaze.

"Your invitation to Amsterdam still stands; come whenever you want. One last thing: I'd prefer this evening's game not be entered on our scoreboard. Goodnight, Ivory."

Ivory didn't reply. Vackeers shut the apartment door behind him, got into the lift and pressed the button for the ground floor. His footsteps resounded on the cobblestones as he crossed the courtyard. He pulled the heavy main door and walked across the road.

The night was mild. Vackeers began making his way along Quai d'Orléans, then turned back to look at the building he had just left. He saw the lights in Ivory's fifth-floor living-room window go out. He shrugged and carried on walking. As he turned into Rue le Regrattier, a set of headlights flashed at him twice. Vackeers approached the Citroën parked alongside the pavement, opened the passenger door and got in. The driver reached for the key in the ignition but Vackeers held him back.

"Let's wait a few moments, if you don't mind."

The two men sat in silence. The driver took a packet of cigarettes out of his pocket, lifted one to his lips and struck a match.

"What's so interesting that you want us to stay here?"

"That phone booth right opposite us."

"What are you talking about? There aren't any phone booths on these embankments."

"Be so kind as to put out that cigarette."

"Bothered by tobacco now, are you?"

"No, by the glowing end."

A man walked along the embankment, stopped and leaned on the parapet.

"Is that Ivory?" asked Vackeers' driver.

"No, it's the Pope!"

"Is he talking to himself?"

"He's making a phone call."

"Who to?"

"Are you being stupid on purpose? If he leaves his home in the middle of the night to make a call from the riverbank, it's probably so nobody knows who he's speaking to."

"So what's the use of us doing surveillance if we can't hear his conversation?"

"To check a hunch."

"And can we go now you've checked your hunch?"

"No. What's going to happen afterwards interests me too."

"Because you know what's going to happen afterwards?"

"You do prattle on, Lorenzo! As soon as he's hung up, he'll take the SIM card out of his mobile and throw it into the Seine."

"And you're planning to dive into the river to get it, are you?"

"You really are a poor fool."

"Instead of insulting me, why don't you explain what we're waiting for?"

"You'll find out in a minute."

London

The telephone rang in a small flat on Old Brompton Road. Walter got out of bed, put on his dressing gown and went into the living room.

"All right, all right, I'm coming," he growled as he approached the side table to answer it.

He recognised the voice at the other end immediately.

"Still nothing?"

"No, sir. I got back from Athens late this afternoon. He's only been there four days. I hope we'll have some good news soon."

"I hope so too, but I can't help worrying. I haven't slept a wink all night. I feel powerless and I absolutely hate that."

"To be honest, I haven't been able to sleep much lately either."

"Do you think he's at risk?"

"I'm told not, and that we just have to be patient. But it's hard to see him in this state. The prognosis is uncertain. He had a very close brush with death."

"I want to know if someone's behind all this. I'm looking into it. When are you going back to Athens?"

"Tomorrow evening, or the day after tomorrow at the latest if I haven't managed to finish everything I've got to do at the Academy."

"Call me as soon as you get there. And try to get some rest before you go."

"You too, sir. Hope to be in touch again tomorrow."

Paris

Ivory got rid of his SIM card and retraced his steps. Vackeers and his driver automatically ducked down in their seats, but at this distance it was unlikely the man they were observing could see them. Ivory disappeared around the corner.

"Can we go now?" asked Lorenzo. "I've been cooped up here all evening and I'm hungry."

"No, not yet."

Vackeers heard the hum of an engine starting up. Two headlights swept over the embankment and a car stopped at the spot where Ivory had stood a few moments earlier. A man got out and went up to the parapet. He leaned over to look at the riverbank below, shrugged his shoulders, then climbed back into the vehicle. The tires screeched as the car sped off.

"How did you know?" asked Lorenzo.

"A nasty feeling. And now I've seen the car's number plates, it's even worse."

"What about the number plates?"

"Are you saying that deliberately to entertain me? That

car belongs to the British diplomatic corps; do you need me to spell it out for you?"

"Sir Ashley's having Ivory followed?"

"I think I've seen and heard enough for tonight; would you be so kind as to drive me back to my hotel?"

"Hey, Vackeers, that's enough; I'm not your chauffeur. You asked me to do a stake-out in this car, explaining it was an important mission. I sat here freezing for two hours while you were up there nice and warm sipping your cognac, and all I saw was your friend going and throwing a SIM card into the Seine – I still have absolutely no idea why – then a car from Her Majesty's consular services spying on him doing it. So either you walk back to your hotel, or you tell me what's going on."

"Given that you appear to be completely in the dark, my dear Rome, I'll try to enlighten you! If Ivory goes to the trouble of leaving his place at midnight to make a phone call, it means he's taking certain precautions. If the British are staking him out outside his apartment building, it means the affair we've been dealing with these past few months isn't as closed as we all wanted to assume. Do you follow me so far?"

"Don't take me to be stupider than I am," said Lorenzo, starting the engine.

He drove along the embankment and over the Pont Marie bridge.

"Ivory's being so cautious means he's one step ahead," continued Vackeers. "And there I was believing I'd won tonight's game. He'll clearly never cease to surprise me."

"What are you planning to do?"

"Nothing for now. And, please, not a word about what

you've found out tonight. It's too early. If we tell the others, they'll each start scheming away on their own and no one will trust anyone else anymore, like in the past. I know I can count on Madrid. And you, Rome, what side will you be on?"

"Right now, I appear to be just to your left. That should partly answer your question, shouldn't it?"

"We must locate the astrophysicist as soon as possible. I bet he's no longer in Greece."

"Go back and interrogate your friend. If you needle him, perhaps he'll spill the beans."

"I suspect he doesn't know much more than us and must have lost his trail. His mind was elsewhere this evening. I've known him for too long to be fooled; he's plotting something. Are you still in touch with your contacts in China? Can you approach them?"

"It all depends what we're expecting of them and what we're prepared to give them in exchange."

"Try and find out if Adrian has recently landed in Beijing, if he's rented a vehicle and if by chance he's used his credit card to withdraw money, pay a hotel bill or whatever."

They drove on in silence. Paris was deserted. Ten minutes later, Lorenzo dropped Vackeers off in front of the Hôtel Montalembert.

"I'll do my best with the Chinese, but it'll be on condition that we return the favour," he said as he parked.

"Let's wait and see the results before you present me with the bill, my dear Rome. See you soon and thanks for the drive."

Vackeers got out of the Citroën and went into the hotel.

He asked the receptionist for the key. With it, he was handed an envelope.

"Someone left this for you, sir."

"How long ago?" asked Vackeers, surprised.

"A taxi driver dropped it off just a few minutes ago."

Vackeers was intrigued. He walked over to the lift and waited until he was in his suite on the fourth floor to open the letter.

My dear friend,

Unfortunately, I fear I will be unable to accept your delightful invitation to join you in Amsterdam. Not because I don't want to come or because I don't want to make up for my poor performance at chess this evening, but as you suspected I have some business to deal with in Paris.

Nevertheless, I hope to see you again very soon. In fact I'm quite sure I will.

Your devoted friend,

Ivory

PS Regarding my night-time stroll – I was used to you being more discreet. Who was that smoking next to you in that beautiful black, or was it navy blue, Citroën? My eyesight gets weaker every day.

Vackeers folded the letter and couldn't help smiling. The monotony of his days was getting him down. He knew this operation would probably be the last of his career, and the idea that Ivory had found a way – whatever way that was – to reopen the case pleased him immensely.

Vackeers sat down at the small desk in his suite, picked up the telephone and dialled a number in Spain. He apologised to Isabel for disturbing her so late at night, but he had every reason to believe that there had been a new development, and what he had to tell her couldn't wait until morning.

Mianyang, China

I'm up at the crack of dawn. The old lady is dozing in a
nearby armchair – she must have watched over me all
night. I push back the blanket she's covered me with and
sit up. She opens her eyes and gazes benevolently at me,
putting a shushing finger to her lips. Then she gets up and
goes to fill a teapot sitting on a cast-iron stove. A folding
partition separates this room from the restaurant. Looking
around me, I see the rest of her family lying asleep on
makeshift bedding. Two thirtyish men are stretched out
on mattresses on the floor under the only window; I recognise the man who served me dinner last night and his
brother, who'd been hard at work in the kitchen. Their
sister, who looks around twenty, is fast asleep on a cot
near the stove, while my providential landlord is lying
on a table, still wearing his sweater and thick woollen
jacket, with a pillow tucked under his head and a blanket
pulled up to his shoulders. I'd been given the sofa bed the
couple opens out to sleep on at night. They moved a few
tables every night to turn one end of the restaurant into
the family bedroom. I'm feeling horribly embarrassed

about encroaching on their privacy – such as it is. I can't imagine any of my neighbours in London giving up their bed to a perfect stranger the way these people have.

The old lady pours a cup of smoky tea and hands it to me. We can't use anything but sign language to talk to each other. I tiptoe out of the bedroom into the restaurant with my tea and she slides the partition closed behind me.

The promenade is deserted. I walk as far as the parapet overlooking the river and stand watching its westward flow. The water is shrouded in early morning mist. A small junk glides slowly past. A boatman waves at me from the deck, and I wave back.

I'm cold. I shove my hands into my pockets, feeling Keira's photo between my fingers.

For some reason the memory of our evening in Nebra resurfaces at this precise moment. My thoughts wander back to our night there – the eventful night that brought us so much closer together.

I'll be leaving shortly for Garther Monastery. I don't know how long it'll take me to get there, or how I'll get into it once I arrive, but it doesn't matter. It's the only lead I have so far to try and find you. If you're still alive…

Why am I feeling so weak?

There's a kitschy, Seventies-style phone booth a few yards away. I want to hear Walter's voice. The phone accepts credit cards, but I hear a busy signal as soon as I start tapping numbers in. I suppose this phone isn't equipped to make international calls. I try again a couple of times then give up.

It's time I went to thank my hosts and pay them for last

night's dinner so I can hit the road again. They refuse to let me pay. I thank them profusely, and leave.

It's late morning by the time I finally reach Chengdu. It's a polluted, bustling, aggressive city, though there are still a few small houses with peeling facades wedged in between the skyscrapers and mammoth housing blocks. Looking for the bus station, I make my way to Jinli Street, a popular tourist spot where I might bump into a Westerner who can give me directions.

The flowers are in full bloom in Nanjiao Park, where boats from a bygone era sail peacefully along a lake lined with melancholy willows. I spot a young couple and guess they're American from the way they're dressed. It turns out they're university students staying in Chengdu as part of an exchange programme. They're thrilled to hear someone speak to them in English, and tell me the bus station is all the way across town. The young woman pulls a writing pad out of her rucksack, scribbles a note on it, tears it off and hands it to me. Her Chinese calligraphy looks perfect. I ask her to add the words "Garther Monastery."

I'd left the car in an outdoor parking lot. I go back to it, change into the clothes the lama gave me and stuff a sweater and a few other necessities into a bag. I decide to leave the 4x4 in the car park and take a taxi.

I show the note to the driver, who drops me off at Wu Gui Qiao bus station half an hour later. Still clutching my precious note, I go up to a counter. The employee hands me a ticket in exchange for twenty yuan and points to platform 12, flapping a hand to indicate I should hurry up if I don't want to miss my bus.

The vehicle looks as if it's seen better days. I'm the last person to get on, and the only place I can find is all the way at the back, squeezed in-between a corpulent woman and a bamboo cage occupied by three extremely well fed ducks. The poor things will probably be roasted Peking-style as soon as they reach their destination, but I don't see how I can warn them about their sad fate.

We cross a bridge spanning the Funan River and the driver swerves into the fast lane with a noisy shifting of the gears. The bus stops at Ya'an and a passenger gets off. I don't know how long this trip is going to take – it already seems interminable. I show my fellow traveller the calligraphed note and point at my watch. She taps the six o'clock hand on the dial. So it'll be evening by the time I arrive. Where am I going to sleep tonight? No idea.

The road snakes its way towards a mountain range. If Garther is situated at high altitude, it'll be freezing cold at night. I'd better find a place to stay as soon as possible.

The more arid the landscape becomes, the more I find myself plagued by doubt. What on earth could have made Keira want to disappear into such a forsaken spot? It must be the search for some fossil that's brought her all the way out here to the ends of the earth – I can't think of any other reason.

Twenty kilometres on, the bus comes to a halt in front of a wooden bridge suspended from a couple of steel cables that look very much the worse for wear. The driver orders all the passengers off the bus; he's got to make it as light as possible. I peer out of the window at the sheer drop under the bridge and laud his wisdom.

I'm sitting on the seat furthest back, so I'll be the last

one to get off. The bus is practically empty when I stand up. As I pass the cage in which the ducks are bustling about, left to their own devices, I kick away the little bamboo rod holding shut the door. Freedom awaits them at the far end of the aisle, on the right. They can even take a short cut to the door by going under the seats. It's up to them to decide. The three ducks happily follow close on my heels. Each one picks a different route – the first one waddles along the aisle, the second dives under the row of seats on the right and the third cuts across to the left. I just hope they let me get off first, or I'll be accused of aiding and abetting their escape. Not that anyone's paying any attention. Their owner's already on the bridge, clutching the handrail and creeping forward, eyes half-closed to ward off vertigo.

I cross the bridge equally fearfully. Now they're all safely on the other side, the passengers have taken it upon themselves to encourage our brave driver with shouts and gesticulations as he steers the bus gingerly across the unsteady wooden slats. There's an ominous creaking sound; the cables squeal and the bridge sways dangerously as the bus inches across, but it holds, and all the passengers are back in their original seats after less than fifteen minutes, except for me – I've seized the opportunity to plonk myself on a free seat in the second row. Two of the ducks are found to be missing when the bus starts up. The third one pops up in the middle of the aisle and waddles its way straight back to its owner, the stupid thing. I can't help smiling at the sight of my former seatmate crawling around the bus on all fours in a fruitless hunt for her feathered runaways as we drive through Dashencun. She gets off at Duogong with a face like thunder, and who could blame her.

The languorous journey passes through a succession of towns and villages with names like Shabacun and Tianquan. The road runs alongside a river as the bus continues its climb to dizzying heights. I find myself shivering constantly – I must not be fully recovered. Lulled by the steady throb of the engine, I manage to drop off from time to time, until a jolt jerks me awake again.

To our left, Hailuogou's glaciers brush the clouds. We're nearing the famous Zheduo Pass – the last stop. At nearly four thousand three hundred metres altitude, I can feel my temples pounding; my migraine is back. I think back to the Atacama and wonder what's become of my friend Erwin. It's been so long since I've had any news of him. If I hadn't collapsed in Chile a few months back, if I hadn't disobeyed the safety instructions we'd been given, if I'd listened to Erwin, I wouldn't be here now, and Keira wouldn't have disappeared into the murky depths of the Yellow River.

I remember the words my mother said to console me when I was grieving for you back in Hydra: *It's terrible to lose someone you love, but even worse never to have met them.* She must have been thinking of my father when she said that; but it's completely different when you feel responsible for the death of the woman you love.

The snow-capped mountains are reflected on the tranquil surface of Lake Mugecuo. The bus picks up a bit of speed as the road slopes steeply down again into the Xinduqiao Valley. There's lush vegetation as far as the eye can see – it's a far cry from the Atacama Desert. Herds of yaks graze on succulent grass. Elms and silver birches meld gracefully in this expanse of grassland enclosed by mountains. We've dropped back below four thousand metres, and my migraine has vanished.

The bus comes to a sudden halt and the driver turns around to look at me. It's time to get off. The only other road of sorts, as far as I can see, is a stony pathway leading off in the direction of Mount Gongga. The driver gesticulates at me and grunts a few words. I gather he's telling me to do my thinking on the other side of the folding door he's just opened, letting in a blast of icy air.

Standing on the roadside with my pack at my feet, my cheeks numb with cold, I watch, shivering, as my bus gets further and further away until it disappears altogether around a bend in the distance. I'm all alone on this boundless plain with the wind howling down from the hills. In this timeless landscape the ground has taken on the colour of husked barley and sand. There's no sign of the monastery I'm looking for, and sleeping under the stars is out of the question – I'll freeze to death. I have to walk, but where to? I haven't a clue. All I can do is keep going to stave off the numbing cold. I start running in short bursts from one slope to the next, towards the setting sun, with some absurd hope of fleeing the night.

And then I catch sight of a black nomad's tent in the distance. Salvation. I see a Tibetan child making her way towards me across the immense expanse. She can't be more than three years old, four at most – a little scrap of a thing with cheeks as red as apples and sparkling eyes. She doesn't seem in the least afraid of me – a stranger – and no one's hovering anxiously over her; she's free to go wherever she wants. She bursts out laughing when she gets close enough to see how different-looking I am, and her laughter fills the valley. She starts running in my direction, arms outstretched, only to stop a few metres away and race back to her family. A man emerges from the tent and comes towards me. I hold out my hand, but he brings his together, bows and gestures for me to follow him.

The tent is made up of large patches of black canvas held up by wooden pegs. It's huge inside. Crackling flames leap up from the dry branches on the stone hearth over which a woman is cooking some kind of stew; its hearty aroma fills the air. The man beckons me to sit down and hands me a jar of rice wine. We take swigs from it in turn.

I share the nomad family's meal in a silence broken only by the little apple-cheeked girl's laughter. She finally falls asleep, snuggled up against her mother.

At nightfall, the nomad leads me out of the tent. He sits down on a rock, rolls a cigarette and offers it to me. We stay there looking at the sky together. It's been a long time since I've contemplated the sky like this. I spot one of the loveliest autumn constellations, to the east of Andromeda. I point a finger at the stars and name it for my host. "Perseus," I tell him. The man follows my gaze. "Perseus," he repeats. His laughter rings out, sounding exactly like his daughter's – as bright as the stars that light up the night sky above our heads.

I've slept in their tent, sheltered from the wind and the cold. The next morning, I show my host my scrap of paper. He brushes it aside – he can't read. Day is breaking, and he has a lot to be getting on with.

As I help him to gather kindling, I try saying "Garther" to him several times, pronouncing it differently each time, in the hope one or the other pronunciation will get a reaction from him. No such luck. His face remains expressionless.

Once we've finished gathering wood, we're on water duty. The nomad hands me an empty goatskin and slings another one over his shoulder, showing me how to carry it. We set off on a path leading south.

We've been walking for at least two hours when, from the top of a hill, I see below us a river flowing through tall grasses. The nomad gets there well before me. When I catch up with him he's already in the water, bathing. I take off my shirt and jump in. The temperature of the water comes as a shock – the source of the river must be one of the glaciers I can see in the distance.

The nomad holds his goatskin under the water and I do likewise. The pouches swell up, and I find myself struggling to lug mine all the way to the riverbank.

Back on solid ground, he tears off a bunch of tall grasses and rubs himself vigorously with it. When he's dried off, he puts his clothes back on and sits down for a rest. "Perseus," he chuckles, pointing at the sky. Then he indicates a bend in the river a few hundred metres upstream, where around twenty men are bathing. Another forty or so of them are ploughing the soil, each one making long, perfectly straight furrows with his plough. I take one look at their clothing and realise who they are.

"Garther!" my travel companion whispers.

Thanking him, I scramble to my feet, but the nomad grabs my arm, his face suddenly sombre. He shakes his head, telling me not to go. Pulling at my sleeve, he points to the path we took to come here. I see the look of fear on his face and obey, following him back up the slope. When we reach the top, I turn to take another look at the monks. The bathers have put their robes back on and are hard at work ploughing furrows in an odd-looking pattern resembling the peaks and troughs of an ECG. I lose sight of them as we start walking downhill. I decide I'm going to give my host the slip and return to this valley as soon as I can.

Nomad tradition dictates that I'm welcome to stay with them as long as I'm willing to earn my daily ration of food. The woman comes out of the tent and leads me to a herd of yaks grazing in a field. I take no notice of the bucket she's swinging as she walks along, humming to herself, until I see her kneel in front of one of the strange four-legged beasts and start to milk it. She gestures for me to take her place a few seconds later, having evidently decided the lesson's gone on long enough. She leaves me there on my own, her parting glance at the bucket making it clear I'm not to return until I've well filled it.

This proves not half as simple as she thinks. Either because of my nervousness or because of the wilful character of this damned Asian cow who obviously has no intention of letting some passing stranger fiddle with her teats, each time I reach for her udders the yak either moves forward or steps back, remaining supremely indifferent to all my tactics – wheedling, hectoring, pleading, shouting and sulking.

To my everlasting shame, I'm rescued by a four-year-old. The little girl with cheeks as round and red as apples suddenly pops up in the middle of the field. I get the feeling she's been hiding there for a while, enjoying the show and struggling to keep back the peals of laughter that have alerted me to her presence. She comes up and gives me a light whack on my shoulder, as if to apologise for making fun of me, then grabs the yak's teat in one fast movement and laughs good-naturedly when the milk starts flowing into the bucket. So it really is that simple. She's pushing me closer to the yak, throwing me a silent challenge I've got to take up. She watches as I kneel next to the yak, and claps when I've finally managed to get a few drops of milk into the bucket. She settles back on the grass, arms crossed, to supervise my work. There's something reassuring about having this little tyke for company. We spend a peaceful, carefree afternoon together.

When I return to the camp with my pint-sized chaperone, another two tents have been pitched next to the one I slept in last night, and there are three families sitting around the big fire. The men come up to us, and my host gestures at me to keep going; the women are waiting for me. As for the men, they're off to round up the cattle. I obey, feeling miffed about being excluded from a task that's surely more masculine than the one I'm going to be assigned.

The light is fading, and I gauge from the position of the sun that it can't be more than an hour to nightfall. I'm wondering how I can sneak away from my nomad friends to go and spy on what's happening in the valley below. I want to follow those monks to their monastery. But my host's return interrupts my plotting. He embraces his wife, picks up his daughter and hugs her, then goes into the tent to wash up. When he comes out a few minutes later, he catches me staring fixedly at the horizon. He squats besides me and offers me one of his cigarettes, which I politely refuse. He lights up and silently turns his own gaze to the hilltop. I suddenly feel the urge to show him what you look like. I'm missing you so badly, and it's an excuse to look at your photo again. It's the most precious thing I can offer to share with him.

I take the photo out of my pocket and show it to him. He glances at it, smiling as he hands it back. Then he takes one long, last puff, crushes out his cigarette between his fingers and gets up to leave.

At nightfall we share our stew with the other two families. The little girl sits beside me. Her parents don't seem bothered by our closeness. Her mother pats her head and tells me she's called Rhitar. I'll learn later on that it's the name given to a child whose elder brother or sister has died, to ward off the evil eye. When Rhitar's clear laugh rings out, does it wipe out the sadness of a tragedy that struck before she was born? Does it remind her parents that she's brought happiness back into their household? The little girl nods off on her mother's knees; she's still smiling, even though she's sound asleep.

After dinner the men change into baggy trousers while the women unbutton the tight sleeves of their tunics, letting them flap in the wind. They join hands in a circle with the men on one side and the women on the other. They burst into song, the women waving their sleeves in time to the rhythm. The singing stops and the dancers shout out as one; then the circle sets off in the opposite direction and the tempo picks up. The dancers carry on running, jumping, shouting and singing until they're exhausted. I'm pulled into the joyful circle and let myself go, drunk on rice wine and the rhythms of a Tibetan round dance.

Someone's shaking my shoulder. I open my eyes and make out my nomad friend's face in the half-light. He beckons me to follow him outside the tent. The vast plain is bathed in the ashy glow of the dying night. My host has hoisted my pack over his shoulder. I'm not sure what he means to do, but I guess he's taking me to a place where we will each go our separate ways. We set off on the path we took the previous day. We tramp along for at least an hour without him uttering a single word. He turns right when we reach the top of the highest hill, leading me into a forest of elm and hazel. He seems to know every single path and slope of it like the back of his hand.

Day hasn't yet dawned when we emerge from the woods. My guide lies flat on the ground, pulling me down beside him, and shows me how to conceal myself under a layer of dead leaves and branches. We lie there in silence, watching and waiting. I've no idea what we're supposed to be watching for. Is he a poacher? We're not carrying any weapons though, so what animal are we supposed to be hunting? Or maybe he's come to check his snares.

I'm completely off the mark, as it turns out, but I have to wait for another hour, until sunrise, to find out why he's brought me here. When dawn finally breaks, the boundary wall of a monastery so huge it's practically a fortified town looms up before our eyes. "Garther," the nomad murmurs. It's the second time he's said the word. I'd offered him the name of a star in the sky above his plain one night. This morning, he's returning the favour by naming the place I've been searching for more desperately than I've ever searched for any star in the whole immense universe.

My companion shakes his head, warning me not to budge. He seems terrified we'll be seen. I can't tell why he's so worried. The monastery is more than a hundred metres away. But as my eyes grow accustomed to the pale dawn light, I make out the shapes of men in robes patrolling the ramparts. What danger could they be watching for? Are they afraid of a possible attack by Chinese soldiers – would they really come all the way to this isolated place to persecute them? I'm not an enemy. If it were up to me, I'd get up right now and run towards them. But my guide places a restraining hand on my arm.

I watch as the monastery doors open and a column of worker monks files out onto a path leading to the fruit orchards to the east. The heavy doors close slowly behind them. The nomad gets to his feet and beckons me into the shelter of the woods. He hands me my pack once we're hidden behind the great elms, and I realise he's bidding me farewell. I take his hands in mine and clasp them. The affectionate gesture makes him smile. He holds my gaze for a moment before turning and walking away.

I've never felt lonelier than I did the other evening, when I got off the bus from Chengdu in the middle of these high-lying plains and started running in an attempt to flee the cold and the onset of night. There are times when a look, a presence or a gesture is all it takes for a friendship to be born, despite the differences that frighten us and hold us back. A helping hand in a time of need is all it takes for a face to be imprinted on our memory, never to fade. I know I'll carry the image of the Tibetan nomad and his little apple-cheeked daughter around with me until I die.

Creeping along at a safe distance just behind the treeline, I follow the procession of about sixty monks walking towards the bottom of the valley. I can spy on them quite comfortably from my vantage point. As on the previous day, they start by undressing and bathing in the crystal-clear waters of the river before getting down to work.

I watch them all morning. The sun has climbed high in the sky, but I'm starting to feel really cold and my back is getting horribly clammy. My body's trembling uncontrollably. I rummage in my pack and find a bag of dried meat – a gift from my nomad friend. I gnaw at it, finishing about half and leaving the rest for my evening meal. I'll dash down to the river for a drink of water once the monks have left, but for now I'll just have to put up with the raging thirst the salted meat has given me. This journey seems to be heightening every bodily sensation – hunger, cold, heat and tiredness. I blame the altitude. I spend the rest of the afternoon plotting ways to get inside the monastery. My head is full of wild imaginings; am I going mad, I wonder?

At six in the evening, the monks stop work and start climbing back uphill to the monastery. I leave my hiding place and rush across the fields to the river as soon as they've disappeared over the top of the ridge. I strip off and jump in to drink my fill. My thirst quenched, I sit back on the bank and think about where to spend the night. The idea of sleeping in the woods doesn't appeal to me in the slightest. Going back to my nomad friends on the plain would mean admitting defeat. Even worse, I'd be exploiting their generosity. It must have been hard enough for them to scrape together enough food to feed me two days in a row.

Spotting a cleft in the hillside, I decide I'll burrow into it and sleep there. I'm sure I'll be able to survive the night-time temperature with my pack over me. I finish the rest of the salted meat as I wait for the sky to darken, watching for the first star to appear as keenly as you'd wait for a friend to come along and cheer you up when you're feeling down.

Night falls. Despite the violent shivers racking my body, I manage to fall asleep in my chosen spot. I'm woken some time later by a rustling sound. I don't know how long I've been asleep. Something's creeping its way towards me. I try to keep my fear under control. If it's a wild animal out hunting, I'll stand more of a chance of escaping undetected by staying in my burrow rather than crashing blindly through the darkness. But it's hard to follow my wise advice when my heart is thudding out of control. What wild beast could it be? And what the hell am I doing huddled in a muddy hole thousands of kilometres from home, filthy and frozen, my nose running? Why on earth am I lost in this foreign land, chasing the ghost of a woman I'm crazy about who didn't mean anything to me six months ago? I wish I was back in the Atacama with Erwin, or in my comfy little home and the streets of London – anywhere but here, in imminent danger of having my entrails ripped apart by a bloodthirsty wolf. *Don't move*, I tell myself. *Don't tremble; don't breathe; lower your eyelids so the light of the moon won't be reflected in the whites of your eyes*. But it's impossible to follow my wise advice when fear's grabbing me by the scruff of the neck and shaking me brutally. I'm feeling as defenceless and insecure as a twelve-year-old boy.

I see the glimmer of a torch through my half-closed lids. Maybe it's just a thief who's after my meagre possessions. Anyway, I'm perfectly capable of defending myself, aren't I? I should get out of this hole, out of the dark, and face the danger. I haven't come all this way to be fleeced by a robber or torn to pieces like a hapless pheasant. I open my eyes. The torch is moving towards the river. Whoever's holding it up at arm's-length knows exactly where he's going; he's striding along confidently, unconcerned about tripping or getting his foot caught in a snare. I can make out two shadows in the torch's glow, one slightly thinner than the other – teenagers, if the shape of their bodies is any clue. One of them stops at the bank, while the other takes off his robe and slips into the water. My apprehension gives way to a feeling of hope. Perhaps these two monks have broken the rules and sneaked out for a night-time swim. These truants might be able to help get me inside the fortifications. I scramble through the grass towards them. I'm nearly at the river when I see something that makes me catch my breath.

I know every inch of that slender body. The shape of those legs, the roundness of that bottom, the curve of that back; that stomach, those shoulders, the back of that neck, that proudly tilted head. It's you. You're the person bathing naked in a river like the one in which I watched you drown. Your body is like a vision by moonlight. I'd have recognised you in a crowd of thousands. There you are, only a few metres away, but I can't go up to you. You wouldn't recognise me in my bedraggled state; I'd scare you, and you'd scream and give the alert.

You're up to your hips in the water, cupping handfuls of it to pour over your face. I move forward until I've reached the bank, and splash my face with the fast-flowing water to clean off all the mud. The monk accompanying you takes no notice; he's turned his back on you and is standing some distance away, probably not wanting to look at your naked body. I can feel my heart pounding and my vision getting blurry as I move closer. You start wading back to shore, coming straight towards me. When you catch sight of me you stop for a moment, tilt your head to one side and stare at me. Then you pass me and carry on walking as if I didn't exist.

It was such an empty stare. It wasn't really you looking at me. You put your robe back on in total silence, as if you'd been robbed of the power of speech, and turn to the monk who brought you here. Your companion picks up his flashlight and the two of you start climbing back up the path. I follow you, careful not to betray my presence, except once, when a stone rolls away from under my foot and the monk glances over his shoulder, but the two of you keep going. When you reach the monastery you walk along the wall and through the great doors, and I see your shapes disappearing into a trench. The flashlight flame flickers and dies. I stand there waiting, chilled to the bone. Then I approach the recess into which you disappeared, hoping to find a way in. All I can see is a small wooden door. It's firmly shut. I crouch down next to it for a while until I've got a grip on myself. Then I make my way back to my burrow at the edge of the woods.

Later in the night, a suffocating feeling rouses me from my torpor. The temperature has plummeted, and my arms and legs have gone numb. I can't even move my fingers to undo the knot keeping my pack closed and take out something to cover myself with. Exhaustion slows the slightest movement. The stories I've heard about the mountains lulling climbers into a sense of security and then putting them to sleep forever come flooding back into my mind. This place is four thousand metres above sea level – how could I have airily thought I'd survive the night? I'm going to die in these woods of elm and hazel on the wrong side of a wall only a few metres away from you. They say that when you're about to die, you see a dark tunnel opening up in front of you, with a bright light at the far end. I can't see anything of the sort. My glimpse of you bathing in the river will have to be my light.

I'm floating in and out of consciousness. I feel hands taking hold of me and lifting me out of my hole. I'm being held up under my arms and dragged along a path. I can't seem to manage to stand upright, or raise my head to see who's pulling me along. I can feel myself slipping into oblivion from time to time. The last thing I remember is the boundary wall and a big door opening up. Maybe you're dead, and I'm finally about to join you.

Athens

"You wouldn't have taken the risk of coming all the way here if you hadn't been so worried. And don't tell me you invited me to dinner because you were dreading the prospect of spending the evening on your own. I'm sure room service at the King George is far better than this Chinese restaurant. It's quite tactless of you to have picked this place, actually, in the circumstances."

Ivory contemplated Walter. He picked up a piece of candied ginger and offered it to his guest. "I'm starting to find time dragging too. And the worst part is not being able to do anything."

"Do you know for a fact that Ashley's behind all this?"

"I can't be sure. I find it hard to believe he'd go that far. Keira disappearing should have been enough for him. Unless he'd found out about Adrian's trip and decided to take matters into his own hands. It's a miracle he didn't achieve his aim."

"He nearly did," Walter muttered. "Do you think the lama told Ashley about Keira? Why would he do that though? He wouldn't have sent Keira's things back if he didn't want to help Adrian find her."

"There's no definite proof that it was the lama who sent that little gift. Somebody around him could have stolen the camera, photographed our archaeologist friend bathing in the river and put everything back in its place without anyone being the wiser."

"So who's this messenger, and why would he take such a risk?"

"What if just one monk in the community saw her bathing and refused to betray the precepts he's sworn to follow? That's all it would take."

"What precepts?"

"Never telling a lie, for one thing. But perhaps our lama encouraged one of his monks to play messenger because he himself is sworn to secrecy."

"You've lost me, sir."

"You should learn to play chess, Walter. It's not enough to be one move ahead if you want to win – you have to be three or four moves ahead. Anticipating your opponent's game is the prerequisite for victory. As for our lama, perhaps he's torn between two principles that could be incompatible in a particular situation – not telling a lie, and not doing anything to harm any living thing. Let's say Keira's survival depended on everyone thinking she's dead, that would put our wise man in a fix. If he told the truth, he would put her life in danger, and go against the belief he holds most sacred. If, on the other hand, he lied and allowed everyone to think she was dead, even though she's alive, he would be violating another precept. Awkward, isn't it? It's what you'd call a stalemate in chess. My friend Vackeers hates a stalemate."

"I can't imagine how your parents managed to give

birth to such a twisted mind," said Walter, fishing in the bowl for another piece of candied ginger.

"I'm afraid my parents had nothing to do with it. I should like to give them credit for it, but I never actually met them. I'll tell you about my childhood some other day, if you don't mind. I'm not the one we're talking about at the moment."

"So you think that, faced with a dilemma, our lama encouraged one of his disciples to reveal the truth while he protected Keira's life by keeping quiet?"

"The lama is irrelevant for the purposes of our argument. I do hope you realise that."

Walter's grimace made his answer abundantly clear. He hadn't the faintest idea what Ivory meant.

"You're pathetic, my dear fellow," said the elderly professor.

"I might be pathetic, but I'm the one who noticed that detail on the photo they'd put on top of her pile of belongings. I'm the one who compared it to the other photos and deduced what we all now know."

"I'll allow you that. But, as you've just said, the photograph was on top of the pile!"

"I should have kept my mouth shut, like your lama. If I had, we wouldn't be here now waiting anxiously for news of Adrian and praying he's still in a condition to give it to us."

"I repeat – that photograph was on the top of the pile. It's hard to believe it was a mere coincidence. It was certainly a message. What we don't know is whether Ashley managed to find out about it when we did."

"Or maybe we desperately *wanted* to see it as a

message! We'd have seen it as a message if we'd read it in our coffee grounds. Who's to say *you* haven't brought Keira back to life to get Adrian to carry on your work?"

"Oh, please, don't be crass!" Ivory said, his voice rising. "Would you rather he had kept moping about his island in the pitiful state we saw him in, and wasting his talent? Do you really think I'd be cruel enough to send him off to look for his girlfriend if I didn't honestly believe she was alive? Do you take me for a monster?"

"That's not what I meant," Walter said equally vehemently.

Their brief argument had attracted the attention of the people at the next table. Walter lowered his voice. "You said it isn't the lama we're interested in. Who else, then?"

"The person who put Adrian's life in danger. The person who's worried he'll find Keira, and who wouldn't stop at anything if he did. Anyone come to mind?"

"There's no need to be so condescending. I'm not your lackey."

"It's costing a fortune to reroof the Academy. I do think the generous benefactor who's miraculously balanced your budget and made sure your employers don't find out about your poor management deserves a little respect, don't you?"

"All right, I get the message. So you're accusing Sir Ashley!"

"Does he know Keira is alive? Possibly. Has he decided he doesn't want to run the slightest risk? Probably. I have to admit that if this line of thinking had occurred to me earlier, I wouldn't have sent Adrian to the frontline. Now it's not Keira I'm most worried about; it's him."

Ivory paid the bill and got up to leave. Walter took their coats off the rack and joined him in the street outside.

"Here's your raincoat. You were about to leave it behind."

"I'll pay him a visit tomorrow," said Ivory, hailing a taxi.

"Is that wise?"

"I've already come all the way here. Besides, I feel responsible. I have to see him. When can we expect the next test results?"

"They come in every morning. The results are improving – it looks as if the worst is behind us. But there's always the risk of a relapse."

"Call me at my hotel when you know. Make sure you don't use your mobile – go to a telephone booth."

"Do you really think they've tapped my phone?"

"I wouldn't know, my dear Walter. Goodnight."

Ivory climbed into his taxi. Water decided to walk back. It was a mild late autumn night, and a slight breeze was blowing over Athens. A bit of fresh air would help him to put his thoughts in order.

When Ivory reached his hotel, he asked the concierge to have the chess set in the bar sent up to his room. He doubted any of the other clients would use it at this time of night.

An hour later, Ivory abandoned the game he was playing against himself in the small sitting room of his suite and went to bed. Lying with his arms crossed behind his head, he mentally reviewed all the contacts he had made in China in the course of his career. The list of names was a long one, but the annoying thing about this rather odd inventory was that none of the people he could remember was still alive. The old man switched on his bedside lamp and pushed back the blanket. He got up and sat on the side of the bed, put on his slippers and looked at his reflection in the mirror on the closet door.

Oh, Vackeers, why aren't you here when I need you? he sighed. *Because you can't depend on anyone, you old fool*, he told himself, *because you're incapable of trusting anyone! Look where all your arrogance has got you. You're playing solo, but you still think you can call the tune.*

Ivory stood up and started pacing around the room. *You'll pay dearly if you've poisoned him, Ashley.* He swept the chess set off the table, sending the pieces flying. The realisation that it was the second time he'd lost his temper that evening gave him pause for thought. He stared at the chess pieces scattered over the carpet. The black bishop and the white bishop had landed next to each other.

At one in the morning, he decided to break a self-imposed rule. He picked up the telephone and dialled a number in Amsterdam. Vackeers picked up at the other end and heard his friend ask a question that was unusual, to say the least. Was there a poison that could provoke the symptoms of severe pneumonia?

Vackeers didn't know, but he promised to find out as soon as he could. He was too discreet – or too good a friend – to ask Ivory to explain.

Garther Monastery

Two men are holding me up while a third rubs my chest briskly. I'm sitting on a chair with my feet in a basin of warm water and have regained some of my strength – I can almost manage to stand on my own. They've taken off my damp, filthy clothes and wrapped me in a kind of sarong. My body temperature is nearly back to normal, though I still shiver occasionally. A monk enters the room and places two bowls, one filled with broth and the other with rice, on the ground in front of me. As I lift the broth to my lips I realise I'm feeling very weak. I lie down on a mat as soon as I've finished the meal and fall into a deep slumber.

Another monk wakes me in the early hours and beckons me to follow him. We make our way along an arched walkway with doors opening every thirty feet into large halls where disciples listen attentively to their masters' teachings. If I didn't know better, I'd think I was in a private school in good old England. The monk turns into another wing of the huge quadrilateral building and steps into a vast gallery. He leads me into an unfurnished room at the far end and disappears.

I'm left shut in there on my own for the rest of the morning. As a gong sounds midday, I see a strange scene through the window overlooking the inner courtyard of the monastery. A hundred-odd monks troop into the quadrangle in single file, sit down at equal distance from each other and begin to meditate. I can't help imagining Keira concealed under one of those robes. If my memories of last night's events are real, she must be hidden in this monastery and could very well be sitting among the Tibetan monks praying down there. Why is she being held here? All I can think of is finding her and taking her far away from here.

A ray of light sweeps across the floor and I turn to see a monk standing in the doorway. A disciple whose face is covered by a hood walks past him and over to me. He lifts the hood and I stare in disbelief.

There's a long scar across your forehead, but you're as beautiful as ever. Your hair is cut short and your face is unusually pale. I move to take you into my arms but you step back. Looking at you and not being allowed to touch you, having you so close and not being able to hold you tight is the cruellest punishment. You stare at me, forbidding me to get any nearer. It's as if our passionate embraces are a thing of the past; as if your life has set you on a path on which I am no longer welcome. When you speak, your words hurt even more than the distance you're forcing between us.

"You have to leave," you murmur tonelessly.

"I've come to get you."

"I didn't ask you to. You've got to go away and leave me in peace."

"Your excavations, your fragments… Give up on us if you like, but not all that!"

"It doesn't matter anymore. My pendant led me to this place, and I've found so much more here than anywhere else."

"I don't believe you. Your life isn't here, in this monastery at the ends of the Earth."

"It's all a question of perspective, isn't it? The Earth's round – you know that better than anyone. As for my life, I nearly lost it because of you. We were being reckless. There won't be a second chance. Go away, Adrian!"

"Not until I've kept the promise I made you. I swore I'd take you back to the Omo Valley."

"I've no intention of returning. Go back to London, or wherever – just make sure it's a long way from here."

You slip your hood back on, lower your head and walk slowly away. At the last minute you turn back to me, your face expressionless.

"They've washed your clothes," you say, glancing at the bag the monk has left. "You can spend the night here, but be on your way tomorrow morning."

"What about Hari? Are you giving up on Hari too?"

I see a tear glisten on your cheek and understand your silent call for help.

"That little door leading out into the trench," I ask, "the one you use to go to the river at night – where is it?"

"In the basement, just under this room. But don't go there, please."

"What time do they open it?"

"At eleven," you answer, and leave.

I spend the rest of the day shut up in this room where

I found you only to lose you again almost immediately. I spend the rest of the day pacing around the room like a maniac.

A monk comes to fetch me in the evening and leads me into the courtyard. The disciples have finished chanting the last prayer of the day, so I'm being allowed out for some fresh air. There's already quite a nip in the air, and it occurs to me that night is the real warden at this prison. I know from experience that it's impossible to cross the plain without freezing to death. But I'll have to find a way, however risky it might be.

My supervised walk around the courtyard is giving me a chance to scope out the place. The monastery is spread over two levels – three, counting the basement Keira's told me about. There are twenty-five windows overlooking the inner courtyard. High arches run the length of the ground-floor walkways, which have a spiral stone staircase at either end. I count my steps once more. It'll take me five or six minutes at most to reach one of the staircases from my cell, provided I don't run into anyone on the way.

When I've had my dinner, I stretch out on the mat and pretend to be asleep. It doesn't take long for my guard to doze off and start snoring. The door isn't locked – no one would dream of leaving this place in the middle of the night. The gallery is deserted. The monks patrolling the rooftops can't see me. It's too dark for them to be able to spot me under the arches. I move forward, keeping close to the walls.

My watch says 10.50pm. If Keira did arrange to meet

me – if I understood her message this morning correctly – I've got ten minutes to reach the basement and find the little door I'd seen from the woods the previous day.

10.55pm. I've finally reached the staircase. There's a door blocking the entrance, an iron hook keeping it firmly closed. I have to lift the hook soundlessly, given that around twenty monks are sleeping in a nearby room. The hinges squeak as I push the door ajar and slip through.

I walk down the slippery, well-worn stone steps, feeling my way cautiously in the dark. I'm finding it hard to keep my balance, and I don't know how much further it is to the basement floor. The luminous dial on my watch shows nearly 11pm. At long last my foot touches loose earth, and I make out a passage in the dim light cast by a flashlight fixed on the wall a few metres ahead. I glimpse another flashlight further into the passage, and walk towards it. There's a sudden rustling noise from behind. As I whip around to see where it's coming from, a cloud of bats begins whirling around my head, their wings brushing against me, their shadows dancing on the walls in the flickering light. I must press on. It's already five minutes past eleven; I'm late, and I still can't see the little door. Have I gone the wrong way?

There won't be a second chance, Keira had told me this morning. I can't possibly get it wrong – not now.

A hand grips my shoulder and draws me into a doorway. Keira's been hiding in an alcove. She pulls me into her arms and holds me tight. "God, how I've missed you," she whispers.

I don't reply. Instead, I take your face in my hands and kiss you. It's a long, long kiss; it tastes of soil and dust and salt and sweat. You rest your head on my chest and I stroke your hair. You're crying.

"You have to leave, Adrian. You've got to go away. You're putting both our lives in danger. They must believe I'm dead if you're to survive. If they find out you're here and that we've seen each other, they'll kill you."

"Who? The monks?"

"No," you say, sniffing. "They're our allies. They saved me from drowning in the Yellow River. They looked after me and hid me here. I mean the people who wanted to kill us, Adrian. They won't give up. I don't know what we've done or why they're after us, but they'll stop at nothing to bring our search to an end. If they know we're together again, they'll find us. The lama we met – the one who made fun of us when we were looking for the white pyramid – he's the one who got us out of trouble. And I made him a promise."

Athens

A knock on the door made Ivory start. A bellboy handed him an urgent fax. Someone had called the reception and asked for it to be brought up to him immediately. Ivory took the envelope, thanked the young man and waited until he had left before opening it.

Rome wanted him to call on a secure line as soon as possible.

Ivory dressed hastily and went down to the street. He bought a phone card at the newsstand in front of the hotel and called Lorenzo from a nearby phone booth.

"I've got some strange news."

Ivory held his breath and waited for Lorenzo to continue.

"My Chinese friends have tracked down your archaeologist."

"Is she alive?"

"Yes, but that doesn't mean she's ready to come back to Europe."

"Why not?"

"You're going to find this hard to swallow. She's been arrested and put in prison."

"That's ridiculous! What for?"

Lorenzo, alias Rome, supplied Ivory with the missing pieces of the puzzle he'd been trying to put together. The Mount Hua monks had been on the banks of the Yellow River when Adrian and Keira's 4x4 had careened into the water. Three of them had jumped into the swirling eddies to pull them free. Adrian had been taken out of the car first and rushed to hospital by workers in a passing truck. Ivory knew the rest – he'd gone to China to get Adrian out of hospital and back home.

Keira had been a different story. It had taken the monks three tries before they were able to get her out of the drifting wreck. By the time they'd hauled her back on dry land, the truck had already left. They'd carried her unconscious body to the monastery. The lama soon heard that the people behind the murder attempt were members of a local triad whose tentacles reached as far as Beijing. He hid Keira and stoically accepted the rough treatment he was given by the unsavoury characters who came asking after her a few days later. He swore that although his disciples had indeed jumped into the river to try and save the two drowning Westerners, they hadn't been able to save the young woman, who had perished. The three monks who had come to her rescue were also put through the wringer, but none of them talked. Keira remained in a coma for ten days. She had caught an infection, which slowed down her recovery, but the monks managed to nurse her back to health.

When she was fully recovered and fit to travel, the lama had her sent far away from his monastery, where people might come looking for her again. He had decided to disguise her as a monk until things had blown over.

"What happened after that?" Ivory asked.

"You're not going to believe it," Lorenzo replied. "Unfortunately, things didn't go at all as the lama had planned."

Their conversation lasted for another ten minutes. When Ivory hung up, he had used up all the minutes on his phone card. He rushed back to his hotel, packed his bags and jumped into a taxi. He rang Walter from his mobile to inform him he'd be with him shortly.

Ivory arrived half an hour later at the entrance to the large building perched on the Athens hillside. He took the lift to the third floor and walked hastily along the corridor, looking for room 307. He knocked and went in. Walter listened open-mouthed as Ivory told him the story.

"There you are, my dear Walter. You know practically everything there is to know."

"Eighteen months? But that's terrible! Do you have any idea how to get her out of prison?"

"No, not the slightest. But let's look at the positive side of things. At least now we're sure she's alive."

"I wonder how Adrian will take the news. I'm worried it'll make him feel even worse."

"I'd be happy just to know he's in a state to hear it. Any news of him?"

"None, unfortunately, except that everyone seems optimistic. They tell me it shouldn't be more than a day, perhaps even a few hours, before we can talk to him."

"Let's hope their optimism is justified. I'm going back to Paris today. I must find a way to get Keira out of this predicament. Look after Adrian, and if you're lucky enough to be able to have a word with him, don't tell him anything yet."

"I can't keep Keira's situation a secret from him. That's out of the question; he'd wring my neck if he found out."

"That's not what I meant. Don't tell him about our suspicions – it's too soon. I have my reasons. Goodbye for now, Walter. I'll be in touch."

Garther

"What did you promise that lama?"

You look at me sadly and give a small shrug. You tell me that the people who tried to kill us would take up the chase again – and mere borders wouldn't stop them – if they came to know you were still alive. And if they couldn't get hold of you, they'd take me out first. The lama had asked you to give him two years of your life in exchange for all his help. He wants you to use the two-year retreat to meditate and think about what you want to do with your life from now on. "There won't be a second chance," he'd told you. "Two years to think about a life you almost lost – that's not such a bad bargain." He's promised to find a way to get you out of the country once things have calmed down.

"Two years to save both our lives. That's all he's asked for, and I've accepted the deal. I've been able to cope because I knew you were out of danger. If only you knew how often I've pictured you going about your everyday life while I've been on this retreat. How often I've revisited all the places we went to, and imagined myself in your little house in London. I've filled up my days imagining every single one of those moments."

"I promise you…"

"Later, Adrian," you say, placing your hand over my mouth. "You're leaving tomorrow. I have another eighteen months to go. Don't worry about me. It's not so bad living here. I'm out in the fresh air, and I've got time to think – plenty of time. Don't look at me like that, as if I'm a saint, or a madwoman. And don't give yourself too much importance; I'm doing this for myself, not for you."

"For yourself? What are you getting out of it?"

"Not losing you a second time. If I hadn't told the monks about you, you'd have died in the woods last night."

"You were the one who told them I was there?"

"I wasn't going to let you freeze to death!"

"Never mind what you promised the lama. We're getting out of here. You're coming with me whether you like it or not, even if I have to knock you unconscious."

I see you smile – a genuine smile – for the first time in a long while. You put a hand on my cheek and stroke it softly.

"Fine. Let's get out of here. I couldn't bear to watch you leave, anyway. And I'd hate you for leaving me here."

"How long before your jailers realise you're not in your cell?"

"They're not my jailers. I'm free to go wherever I want."

"What about that monk who was with you at the river? Wasn't he there to keep a watch on you?"

"He was escorting me, in case anything happened to me on the way. I'm the only woman in this monastery, so

I've been going down to the river at night to bathe. Well, all summer and since autumn started, anyway. That was my last bath in the river yesterday."

I open my pack, take out the sweater and pair of trousers and hand them to you.

"What are you doing?"

"Put these on. We're leaving right now."

"Wasn't yesterday's experience enough for you? It must be zero degrees outside, and it'll be minus ten in an hour's time. There's no way we can cross that plain at night."

"And there's no way we can cross it by day without being spotted! Will we survive an hour's walk, do you think?"

"The first village is an hour away – by car! And we haven't got one."

"I'm talking about a nomads' camp, not a village."

"Your nomads could have moved on by now."

"It'll be there, and the people living in it will help us."

"All right! Let's not argue about your nomads' camp," you say, pulling the clothes on.

"Where's the damn door to get out of here?" I ask.

"Right behind you. I can see we're not going to get there anytime soon."

As soon as we're outside I pull you in the direction of the woods, but you tug my arm and lead me to the path going down to the river. "There's no point getting lost in these woods," you say. "It won't be long before the cold starts boring right through us."

You know the area better than I do, so I fall in obediently behind you. Once we get to the river, I'm sure I'll recognise the path leading uphill. It'll take us ten minutes to reach the path and another three-quarters of an hour to climb to the top of the hill and down the other side to the large valley where the camp is. We'll be home and dry in less than an hour.

The night is icier than I'd expected. I'm already shivering, and we haven't even reached the river yet. You haven't said a single word since we left – you're totally focused on finding the way. I can hardly blame you for not talking, you're probably right to conserve your energy. I can feel my strength ebbing away with each step.

By the time we reach the far end of the fields that the monks cultivate by day, I'm wondering why I dragged you into this mess. I've been trying to overcome a feeling of numbness for several minutes now.

"I'll never make it," you say, panting.

A white cloud escapes your mouth with every word. I hold you tight and start rubbing your back. I'd like to kiss you, but my lips are frozen. You push me away. "We don't have a minute to lose," you say. "We can't just stand here. You'd better lead us to your camp as fast as possible, or we'll die of hypothermia."

I'm so cold my whole body is trembling.

The hillside seems to be getting steeper as we continue our climb. *Hang in there*, I tell myself. *Keep going. Another ten minutes and we'll be at the top.* It's such a clear night – surely we'll see the tents in the distance from there, and just thinking about the warmth inside them will give us renewed strength and courage. I know that once we've reached the top of the hill, it'll take us a quarter of an hour at most to go down the other side and into the valley. And even if we can't move another step, I'll shout for help. With any luck my nomad friends will hear me cry out in the stillness of the night.

You fall down three times, and I help you up. At your fourth fall, your face has turned alarmingly pale and your lips are blue, like they were when you were drowning before my eyes in the waters of the Yellow River. I lift you up, pull your arm over my shoulder and drag you along, shouting at you to keep going, forbidding you to close your eyes.

"Stop yelling at me," you whimper. "It's hard enough as it is. I told you we shouldn't have tried this. You didn't want to listen."

A hundred metres – that's how close we are to the top of the hill. I pick up speed, and feel your weight getting lighter; you've recovered a bit of strength.

"It's my last breath," you say, "the final twitch before death." Then, catching sight of my face: "Oh, come on. Stop staring at me with that downcast look. Don't I make you laugh anymore?"

You're putting on a show of bravado – your swollen lips can barely move. And yet you straighten up, push me away, and start walking, unaided, in front of me.

"You're dawdling, Adrian, you're dawdling!"

Fifty metres. You're leaving me behind. However hard I try to put one leg in front of the other, I can't catch up. You'll get to the top well before I do.

"Well? Are you coming? Come *on*, hurry up!"

Thirty metres. The top isn't much further now – you're almost there. I have to get there before you do. I want to be the first one to see the camp that's going to save our lives.

"You won't make it if you drag your feet like that. I can't come back and get you. Get a move on, Adrian; hurry!"

Ten metres. You've reached the top of the hill and are standing there straight as a rod, hands on your hips. I watch you from behind as you survey the valley in silence.

Five metres. My lungs feel like they're about to explode. Four metres! I'm no longer merely trembling; my whole body is being racked by violent spasms. I've no more strength. I collapse. You're not paying me the slightest attention. I must get up; only two or three metres to go – but the ground beneath me feels so soft, and the sky is so beautiful on this full moon night. I can feel the breeze caressing my cheeks, lulling me.

You're leaning over me. A terrible coughing fit tears my chest apart. The night is white – so white it's as clear as day. It must be the cold that's making me feel dazzled. The light's so bright I can hardly bear it.

"Look," you say, pointing to the valley. "I told you. Your friends have left. Don't be mad at them, Adrian. They're nomads. They may be your friends, but they never stay in one place for long."

I open my eyes with difficulty, and see the buttresses of the monastery in the distance in the middle of the plain, not the camp I'd been hoping for so badly. We've gone round in circles. We've retraced our steps. It can't be possible. This isn't the same valley – I can't see the woods.

"I'm so sorry," you murmur. "Don't be angry with me. I promised, you see. And you can't break a promise. You swore you'd take me back to Addis Ababa, and you'd do it if you could, wouldn't you? Look how you're suffering because you're powerless. You must understand me. You do understand me, don't you?"

You kiss my forehead. Your lips are icy. You smile at me, and start walking away. Your steps are so confident, as if you're suddenly immune to the cold. You move forward serenely into the night, walking towards the monastery. I can't find the strength to either hold you back or join you. My body is holding me prisoner: it's simply refusing to move, as if my arms and legs were firmly bound. I'm powerless, as you pointed out before abandoning me. The huge doors of the monastery open up when you reach the boundary wall. You turn back one last time, and then you go in.

You're much too far away for me to hear you, and yet the clear sound of your voice carries all the way to where I am.

"Be patient, Adrian. Perhaps we'll find each other again. Eighteen months – that's not so terrible for two people in love. Don't be afraid; you'll survive. You've got that inner strength. And besides, someone's on his way. He's nearly here. I love you, Adrian. I love you."

The heavy doors of Garther Monastery swing slowly shut on your frail shape.

I shout out your name into the night. I howl like a wolf caught in a trap seeing certain death approach. I struggle and pull with all my strength, despite my deadened limbs. I'm crying out again and again when I hear a voice in the middle of the deserted plain. *Calm down, Adrian.* I know that voice. It's the voice of a friend. Walter repeats the phrase, which doesn't make any sense.

"Calm down, Adrian, for heaven's sake! You'll end up hurting yourself."

Athens University Hospital, Department of Pulmonary Medicine

"Calm down, Adrian, for heaven's sake! You'll end up hurting yourself."

I opened my eyes and tried to sit up, but found I was attached to the bed. Walter was standing over me, looking extremely puzzled.

"Are you really back in the land of the living, or just delirious again?"

"Where am I?" I murmured.

"First answer a quick question: who are you talking to? Who am I?"

"Have you gone soft in the head or what, Walter?"

Walter began clapping. I had no idea why he was so excited. He hurried to the door and shouted down the corridor that I'd woken up; he seemed beside himself with joy. He stood there for a while, leaning his head out, then turned to me, exasperated.

"I don't know how one lives in this country; life seems to grind to a halt at lunchtime. There's not even one nurse around – unbelievable! Oh, I promised I'd tell you where we were. On the third floor of Athens hospital, in the pulmonary medicine department, room 307. When you're able to, you should come and admire the view; you can see the harbour from your window. It's really rather pretty – not at all like your standard hospital vista. Your mother and your delightful Aunt Elena moved heaven and earth to get them to give you a private room. They badgered the admin departments until they did. Your delightful aunt and your mother are real saints, believe me."

"What am I doing here, and why am I attached to the bed?"

"The decision to strap you down wasn't taken lightly, but your fits of delirium were violent enough for them to consider it wiser to protect you from yourself. Plus the nurses had had enough of finding you on the floor in the middle of the night. You really were incredibly restless in your sleep. Right, I don't suppose I'm allowed to, but considering everyone else is having a siesta, I consider myself the only proper authority here. I'm going to unstrap you."

"Walter, are you going to tell me why I'm in a hospital room?"

"Don't you remember anything?"

"If I remembered anything, I wouldn't be asking you."

Walter went over to the window and looked out.

"I'm not sure I should," he said, pensively. "I'd rather wait until you're feeling a little stronger, then we'll talk about it, promise."

As I sat up in bed, my head started spinning. Walter rushed over to keep me from falling out.

"See what I mean? Now lie down and calm down. Your mother and your delightful aunt have been worried sick, so be so good as to be awake when they come to visit you at the end of the afternoon. Don't tire yourself out unnecessarily. That's an order! As there isn't a doctor or nurse in sight, and all of Athens is snoozing, I'm in charge."

My mouth was dry, so Walter held a glass of water to my lips.

"Gently does it, pal. You've been on a drip for a very long time. I'm not sure if you're allowed to drink. Don't be a difficult patient, please."

"Walter, I'm giving you one minute to tell me how I ended up here, otherwise I'll rip out all these tubes!"

"I should never have unstrapped you."

"Fifty seconds!"

"It's not very nice of you to blackmail me. I'm disappointed in you, Adrian."

"Forty!"

"As soon as you've seen your mother."

"Thirty!"

"Well then, as soon as the doctors have been and confirmed that you're better."

"Twenty!"

"You really are impossibly impatient! I've been watching over you for days and days – you could at least take a different tone with me."

"Ten!"

"Adrian!" yelled Walter. "Take your hand off that drip immediately! I'm warning you, Adrian, one drop of blood on these white sheets and I won't tell you a thing."

"Five!"

"All right, you win! I'll tell you everything, but I'll always hold it against you, mark my words."

"I'm all ears, Walter."

"So you don't remember anything?"

"Not a thing."

"Me coming to Hydra?"

"Yes, I do remember that."

"Us having coffee together on the terrace of the café next to your delightful aunt's shop?"

"That too."

"The photo of Keira I showed you?"

"Of course I remember that."

"That's a good sign. And what happened after that?"

"That's the vague part. I remember us taking the ferry to Athens and saying goodbye to each other at the airport. You were going back to London and I was off to China. But I don't know if that really happened, or if it was just part of a long nightmare."

"No, no, it was completely real, I assure you. You did take the plane, even if you didn't get very far on it. But let's go back to when I arrived on Hydra. Oh, and no time like the present: I've got two pieces of news to tell you."

"Start with the bad."

"That's impossible! Without knowing the good news first, the bad won't make any sense."

"Well, as I have no choice in the matter, let's go for the good news."

"Keira's alive! Not maybe, but definitely!"

I bounced up.

"So there you go. Now you know the main thing, what do you say to a little break while we wait for your mother, or the doctors, or both?"

"Walter, stop stalling; what's the bad news?"

"One thing at a time. You asked me what you were doing here, so let me explain: a 747 had to be rerouted because of you – not everyone can lay claim to that. You owe your life to an air stewardess's presence of mind. An hour after your plane took off, you lost consciousness. It's highly likely you were carrying around some bacteria or other after your lengthy dive in the Yellow River: you'd developed a ferocious lung infection. You looked as if you were sleeping peacefully in your seat, but when this hostess brought you your meal, she was struck by how pale and clammy your face looked. She tried to wake you, but couldn't. You were having trouble breathing and your pulse was very weak. Given the seriousness of the situation, the pilot turned the plane around and had you rushed here. I heard the news the day after I returned to London, so I came straight back."

"So I never got to China?"

"No, I'm afraid not."

"And Keira – where's she?"

"She was saved by the monks who'd accommodated you near the mountain whose name I forget."

"Mount Hua."

"If you say so. They nursed her back to health, but unfortunately, as soon as she was better, the authorities came to take her in for questioning. Eight days after she was arrested, she appeared in court and was tried for entering and circulating on Chinese territory without identity documents, and therefore without the government's authorisation."

"But she couldn't have had her ID on her – her papers were in the car at the bottom of the river."

"I totally agree. But the lawyer appointed by the court can't have mentioned those details during their defence speech because Keira was sentenced to eighteen months' imprisonment. She's being held at Garther, a former monastery that's been turned into a prison, in the province of Sichuan, not far from Tibet."

"Eighteen months in prison?"

"That's right. And according to our consular services, which I've been in touch with, it could have been worse."

"Worse? Eighteen months, Walter. Can you imagine what it must be like spending eighteen months in a Chinese jail?"

"A jail is a jail. But you're right, of course."

"Somebody tries to kill us and she's the one put behind bars?"

"In the eyes of the Chinese authorities, she's guilty. We'll go and plead her case at the embassies and ask for their help. We'll do everything possible. I'll help you as much as I can."

"Do you really think our embassies are going to get involved and risk compromising their economic interests to get her released?"

Walter returned to the window.

"I'm rather afraid that neither of your sorry situations will rouse anyone into action. You'll just have to be patient and pray she endures her jail sentence as well as she can. I'm really sorry, Adrian. I know how awful this situation is, but... What are you doing with your drip?"

"I'm getting out of here. I have to go to Garther Prison. I have to let her know that I'm going to fight to get her freed."

Walter rushed towards me and gripped both my arms with a strength I was powerless to resist in my weak condition.

"Listen carefully, Adrian. Your immune system was at zero when you arrived here and the infection was spreading by the hour, frighteningly fast. You were delirious for days and suffered several bouts of fever that could've killed you. The doctors were forced to put you into an artificial coma for some time, to protect your brain. Your mother, your delightful Aunt Elena and I took turns by your bedside. Your poor mother aged ten years in ten days. So stop being so childish and start behaving like an adult."

"It's OK, Walter. I hear you. You can let go of me now."

"I'm warning you: try putting your hand anywhere near that catheter and see how fast mine hits your face!"

"I promise I won't move."

"That's better. I've had it up to here with your fits of delirium recently."

"You've no idea what strange dreams I had."

"Believe me, between monitoring your temperature charts and eating the vile food in the cafeteria, I had plenty of time to listen to your gibberish. The only comfort I had in this hellish place were the cakes your delightful Aunt Elena bought me."

"Hey, Walter, what's this new way of talking about Elena?"

"I don't know what you mean."

"About my 'delightful' aunt?"

"I'm allowed to find your aunt delightful, aren't I? Her humour's delightful, her cooking's delightful, her laugh's delightful, her conversation's delightful. Where's the problem?"

"She's twenty years older than you."

"Oh, great attitude – congratulations! I didn't know you were so narrow-minded. Keira's ten years younger than you but it doesn't matter that way round, is that it? Ageist, that's what you are."

"You're not telling me you've fallen for my aunt? What about Miss Jenkins?"

"Miss Jenkins and I are still at the stage of talking about our respective vets. You have to admit that's not exactly the height of passion."

"Meaning that with my aunt, the passion is... Don't answer that. I don't want to know."

"And you don't go putting words into my mouth. Your aunt and I talk about all sorts of things, and we have a lot of fun together. You're not going to criticise us for trying to have a good time now and then, after all the trouble you've put us through? That would be too much, it really would."

"Do whatever you want. What business is it of mine anyway?"

"Pleased to hear that."

"Walter, I've got a promise to keep. I can't just stay here and do nothing. I have to go and find Keira in China and take her back to the Omo Valley. I should never have taken her away from there."

"Start by getting better, then let's see. Your doctors will be here shortly. I'm going to let you rest; I've got some shopping to do."

"Walter?"

"Yes?"

"What did I say when I was delirious?"

"You said Keira's name one thousand seven hundred and sixty-three times. Well, that's an approximate number – I must have missed a few. But you only called my name out three times; I'm quite offended. Mostly you just said incoherent things. Between two fits of convulsions, you sometimes opened your eyes and just stared into space. It was rather terrifying. Then you'd fall back into unconsciousness."

A nurse came into the room. Walter felt relieved.

"You've come round at last," she said as she changed my drip.

She stuck a thermometer into my mouth, wrapped a blood pressure cuff around my arm and noted down the readings.

"The doctors will be along to see you in a little while," she said.

Her face and stout build vaguely reminded me of someone. As she waddled out of the room, I was sure I recognised my fellow passenger from the bus I took on my way to Garther. A member of the cleaning staff was working in the corridor. As he passed my door, he flashed Walter and me a big smile. In his pullover and thick woollen jacket, he looked the spitting image of the husband of the restaurant owner I'd met in my feverish dreams.

"Did I have any visitors?"

"Your mother, your aunt and me. Why do you ask?"

"No reason. I dreamed of you."

"How dreadful! I order you never to reveal that to anyone."

"Don't be stupid. You were with an elderly professor

I once met in Paris, an acquaintance of Keira's. I can't really tell where the dreams stop and reality begins."

"Don't worry, things will gradually fall into place, you'll see. Can't offer you any explanation about the old professor, I'm afraid. But I won't breathe a word about it to your aunt – she might be offended if she found out you saw her as an old man in your dreams."

"The fever's to blame, I suppose."

"Probably, but I don't think that'd be good enough for her. Get some rest now; we've talked too much. I'll come back early evening. I'm going to phone our consulate and hassle them about Keira. I've been doing it every day at a set time."

"Walter?"

"What now?"

"Thanks."

"Really!"

Walter left the room and I got shakily out of bed. My legs wobbled at first, but by leaning on various things, first the back of the armchair near my bed, then the trolley and lastly the radiator, I managed to reach the window.

The view certainly was beautiful. The hospital clung to the hillside and overlooked the bay. I could make out Piraeus in the distance. I'd seen that port so many times since I was a child, without ever really looking at it – happiness makes you distracted. Today, from the window of room 307 in Athens hospital, I looked at it differently.

Down in the street, I saw Walter enter a telephone booth – to call the consulate no doubt.

Beneath his clumsy appearance, he's a great guy; I'm lucky to have him as a friend.

Paris, Ile St-Louis

Ivory got up and answered the telephone.

"What's the news?"

"One piece of good news, then something rather irksome."

"Tell me that first then."

"It's odd…"

"What is?"

"…how everyone always wants to know the bad news first. Well, I'm going to start with the good news; without it, the other won't make any sense. His fever subsided this morning and he's recovered his senses."

"That is indeed wonderful news. I'm quite delighted. I feel as if a great weight has been lifted from my shoulders."

"It must be a huge relief above all: without Adrian, you'd have lost all hope of seeing your research continued, wouldn't you?"

"I really was concerned about his health. Do you think I'd have risked visiting him otherwise?"

"Perhaps you shouldn't have. I'm worried we may have

talked a little too close to his bed – it appears he made out snippets of our conversation."

"He remembers what we said?" asked Ivory.

"His memories are too fuzzy for him to attach any importance to it. I convinced him he must have been delirious."

"That's an unforgivable gaffe; very careless on my part."

"You wanted to see him without being seen, and the doctors had guaranteed he was unconscious."

"Medicine is still an approximate science. Are you sure he doesn't suspect anything?"

"Rest assured – he has other things on his mind."

"Was that the irksome news you wanted to tell me?"

"No. What's worrying me is that he's made up his mind to go to China. I told you, he'll never sit idly by waiting for Keira for eighteen months. He'd prefer to spend them sitting under the window of her cell. As long as she's being held, you won't be able to interest him in anything other than her release. The moment he's discharged, he'll take a flight to Beijing."

"I doubt he'll be given a visa."

"He'd get to Garther by crossing Bhutan on foot if necessary."

"He has to go back to his research. I'll never be able to wait eighteen months."

"He said exactly the same thing about the woman he loves. I fear you'll just have to wait, like him."

"Eighteen months is a time frame that takes on a different meaning at my age – I don't know if I can boast I'll live that long."

"Come on now, you're in great shape. And anyway, in one hundred per cent of cases, life ends in death," Walter continued. "I could get run over by a bus when I leave this phone booth."

"Keep him from going at all costs. Dissuade him from undertaking anything at all over the next few days. Most importantly, don't let him contact a consulate, and certainly not the Chinese authorities."

"Why not?"

"Because the next move requires diplomacy and it can't be said he shines in that department."

"May I know what you have in mind?"

"In chess, we call it a castling. I'll tell you more in a day or two. Goodbye, Walter. And be careful crossing the road."

Walter left the phone booth and went for a walk to stretch his legs.

London, St. James's Square

The black cab stopped in front of an elegant Victorian town house. Ivory got out with his case, paid the driver, then waited for the taxi to leave. He pulled the chain hanging to the right of the wrought-iron door. He heard a bell ring, then footsteps approaching. A butler appeared and Ivory handed him his visiting card.

"Please be so kind as to inform your employer that I would like to see him. It's about a relatively urgent matter."

The butler was sorry, but his master wasn't in town and was most probably unreachable.

"I don't know whether Sir Ashley is at his house in Kent, at his hunting lodge or at the home of one of his mistresses – and to be honest, I don't give a damn. What I do know is that if I were to leave without seeing him, your 'master,' as you call him, might hold it against you for a very long time. So I'd suggest you contact him. I'm going to take a walk around this block of fine houses and when I get back and ring the doorbell again, you will give me the address where he wishes me to go and meet with him."

Ivory went down the porch steps into the street and set off on his walk, carrying his small case. Ten minutes later, as he strolled past the railings of a square, a luxury car pulled up alongside the pavement. A chauffeur got out and opened the door for him; he had been given orders to drive Ivory two hours outside London.

The English countryside that rolled past was as beautiful as in Ivory's most distant memories. Not as vast and lush as the pastures of his native New Zealand, but very pleasant indeed, he had to admit. He settled back into his comfortable seat and used the journey to rest.

It was just after noon when the sound of the tires crunching on the gravel roused him from his daydream. The car was driving down a majestic path lined with perfectly pruned eucalyptus bushes. It stopped under a columned portico overrun with climbing roses. A domestic employee showed him through the house to the small sitting room where his host was waiting.

"Cognac, bourbon, gin?"

"A glass of water will do nicely, thank you. Hello, Sir Ashley."

"Twenty years since we last saw each other?"

"Twenty-five, and don't tell me I haven't changed. Let's face facts – we're both older."

"That's not what you've come to talk about, I imagine."

"Yes it is, believe it or not. How much time do we have?"

"You tell me. You invited yourself."

"I mean how much time do we have left on this Earth? At our age, ten years at most?"

"How should I know? And anyway, I don't want to think about it."

"What a magnificent estate," continued Ivory looking at the grounds through the picture windows. "I hear your home in Kent is just as stunning."

"I'll congratulate my architects on your behalf. Was that the reason for your visit then?"

"The trouble with all these properties is that you can't take them with you to the grave. This accumulation of wealth obtained after so much effort and so many sacrifices – all in vain on your dying day. You can always park your beautiful Jaguar in front of the graveyard, but, quite frankly, what's the point of leather upholstery and wood veneer then?"

"But my friend, all these riches will be handed down to the generations that follow us, just as our fathers passed them down to us."

"And yours is certainly a wonderful legacy."

"It's not that I find your company unpleasant, but I have a very busy schedule, so perhaps you'd like to tell me what your point is."

"You see, times have changed. I was thinking that only yesterday as I read the papers. Big-time financiers are behind bars, rotting their whole lives away in tiny cells. *Goodbye* luxury hotels and opulent estates, *hello* nine square metres tops – and that's the VIP space allocation! And while they're inside, their heirs squander their cash and try to change their names to rid themselves of the shame inherited from their parents. The worst thing is nobody's safe: impunity has become a priceless luxury, even for the richest and most powerful. Heads are rolling, one after the other – it's the in thing now. You know better than I do that politicians have run out of ideas. And any ideas they do have are unacceptable. So, what better way for masking the shortcomings of their visions for society than stoking public condemnation? The extreme wealth of some is responsible for the poverty of others; everyone knows that these days."

"Have you come to my home to hassle me with your revolutionary prose and your quest for social justice?"

"Revolutionary prose? You misunderstand me. I'm as conservative as they come. But you're right to credit me with wanting justice."

"Get to the point, Ivory; you're starting to seriously bore me."

"I've got a deal to put to you – something fair and just, as you'd say. I'll give you the key to the cell where you could end your days – if I sent the *Daily Mail* or *The Observer* the file I've got on you – in exchange for a young archaeologist's freedom. Now do you understand why I'm here?"

"What file? What gives you the right to come here and threaten me?"

"Influence peddling, illegal acquisition of interest, covert financing in the House of Commons, conflicts of interest in your various companies, misuse of company property and tax evasion. You're quite something, old man; you'll stop at nothing, not even organising the murder of a harmless scientist. What type of poison did your hit man use to get rid of Adrian for you? And how did he administer it? In a drink he had at the airport or on the plane just before take-off? Or was it a contact poison? Or a quick jab while he was being searched at security? Do tell, I'm curious to know."

"You're ridiculous, my friend."

"Pulmonary embolism on a long-haul flight to China. A bit of a mouthful for a thriller title, don't you think? And it was far from the perfect crime."

"Your unfounded accusations don't scare me. Get out before I have you thrown out."

"Newspapers don't have time for fact-checking these days. Old-fashioned editorial rigour has perished on the altar of high circulation figures. You can't blame them: competition is tough in the Internet age. A lord like you under the spotlight – that'd sell one hell of a lot of papers. Don't think for a second that because of your age you wouldn't live to see an enquiry commission's findings. Real power doesn't lie in the courts or in parliaments anymore; it's the newspapers that feed trials, supply evidence and make victims testify; all judges do is deliver sentences. As for contacts, you can't rely on anyone anymore. None of the authorities would risk compromising themselves, particularly for one of their members. Corruption scares them too much. Justice is independent now. Isn't that what makes our democracies noble? Look at that American financier who was responsible for the biggest fraud of the century – the whole thing was sorted out in two or three months."

"What do you want from me, dammit?"

"Weren't you listening? I've just told you: use your power to get the young archaeologist released. I'll be kind and not say anything to the others about your plot against her and her friend, you poor fool. If I revealed to them that, not content with trying to murder him, you then had him poisoned. You'd be dismissed from the committee and replaced by someone more respectable."

"You're being completely ridiculous; I don't know what you're talking about."

"In that case I'll say goodbye, Sir Ashley. May I take advantage of your generosity again and ask if your chauffeur could drop me off, at a train station at least? I've got nothing against walking, but if something were to happen to me on my way home from visiting you, it would look very bad."

"My car is at your disposal. Have it drive you wherever you want – just leave!"

"That's very generous of you. And prompts me to be so too. I'll let you have until this evening to think about it. I'm staying at the Dorchester; don't hesitate to call me there. The documents I gave my messenger this morning will only be delivered to their recipients tomorrow, unless I have them brought back to me beforehand, of course. I assure you that my request is very reasonable, given the information they contain."

"If you think you can blackmail me in such a crude manner, you're making a serious mistake."

"Who said anything about blackmail? I'm not deriving any personal benefit from this little deal. What a beautiful day. I'll leave you to enjoy it to the full."

Ivory picked up his case and walked alone down the corridor leading to the front door. The chauffeur, who was smoking a cigarette by the roses, rushed over to the car and opened the door for his passenger.

"Take your time to finish your cigarette, my friend," said Ivory. "I'm in no hurry."

From his office window, Sir Ashley watched, seething, as Ivory climbed into the back of his Jaguar and the car moved away down the drive. A secret door in the bookshelves opened and a man stepped into the room.

"I'm speechless. I wasn't expecting that, I must admit."

"That old idiot came to threaten me in my own home! Who does he think he is?"

Sir Ashley's guest didn't reply.

"What? Why are you making that face? You're not going to start too, are you?" raged Sir Ashley. "If that senile old fool dares to accuse me publicly of anything at all, he'll be skinned alive by my lawyers. I've done absolutely nothing to be ashamed of. You do believe me, I hope?"

Sir Ashley's guest picked up a small crystal decanter, served himself a large glass of port and downed it in one go.

"Are you going to answer me or not, for God's sake?" Sir Ashley burst out angrily.

"I'd rather say 'not,' then at least our friendship will only suffer for a few days, or a few weeks at the most."

"Just leave, Vackeers. I've had enough of your arrogance."

"None was intended, I swear. I'm really sorry about what's happening to you, but in your place I wouldn't underestimate Ivory. As you said, he's a bit mad, but that's what makes him even more dangerous."

Vackeers left without saying another word.

London, Dorchester Hotel, mid-evening

The telephone rang. Ivory opened his eyes and looked at the time on the clock on the mantelpiece. The conversation was short. He waited a few moments before making a call himself, from his mobile.

"I wanted to thank you. I've just hung up after speaking to him. You've been an invaluable help."

"I didn't do much."

"On the contrary, yes you did. What would you say to a game of chess? In Amsterdam, at your place, next Thursday. Up for it?"

Once he'd finished talking to Vackeers, Ivory made one last call. Walter listened carefully to the instructions he gave him and made a point of congratulating him for his master stroke.

"Don't harbour any illusions, Walter, our troubles haven't ended yet. Even if we managed to get Keira home, it wouldn't mean she'd be out of danger. Sir Ashley won't give up. I shook him up severely, and on his territory to boot, but I had no choice. I know from experience that he'll take his revenge as soon as the opportunity arises, believe me. It's vital all this stays between us; no need to worry Adrian for now. He mustn't know anything about why he ended up in hospital."

"And what about Keira – what do I tell him?"

"Make something up. Invent a scenario for her release, and say you were behind it."

Athens, the next day

Elena and Mum had spent the morning at my bedside. They'd taken the first ferry from Hydra at seven in the morning, as they'd done every day since I was in hospital. On arriving at Piraeus at 8am, they'd run to catch the bus, which had dropped them off in front of the hospital half an hour later. They'd stopped at the cafeteria to have breakfast before coming up to my room laden with refreshments, flowers and get-well wishes from our village. As they'd done every day, they'd leave again at the end of the afternoon and take the bus back to Piraeus, where they'd board the last ferry home. Elena hadn't opened her shop since I'd been taken ill, and Mum had spent her whole time in the kitchen putting all her love and hope into preparing dishes that brightened up the days for the nurses looking after her son.

It was already midday, and I have to say I found their incessant chatting even more exhausting than the after-effects of my wretched pneumonia. But when they heard a knock at the door, they instantly fell silent. I'd never witnessed that before – it was almost as surprising as the cicadas interrupting their song in the middle of a scorching day. As Walter came in, he noticed my stunned look.

"What's wrong?" he said.

"Nothing, nothing at all."

"Yes, it is. You're making a strange face."

"Absolutely nothing's wrong. I was having a conversation with my delightful Aunt Elena and my mother when you came in, that's all."

"What were you talking about?"

"I was just saying that his illness could perhaps have some unexpected after-effects," answered my mother before anyone else could speak.

"Could it?" asked Walter, worried. "What did the doctors say?"

"Oh, them. They said he could leave next week. But his mother says her son has become a bit of a moron. That's the medical assessment in my opinion. You should go and have a coffee with my sister, Walter. I've got a few things to say to Adrian."

"I'd be happy to, but first I need to speak to him myself. Please don't take offence, but I have to talk to him man to man."

"Well, if we women aren't welcome anymore," said Elena getting up, "then off we go!"

She led my mother out, leaving Walter and me alone.

"I've got some excellent news," he said as he sat down on the edge of my bed.

"Start with the bad even so."

"We need a passport within six days and it's impossible to get one when Keira's not here."

"I don't understand what you're talking about."

"I didn't think you would, but you did ask me to start with the bad news. This systematic pessimism is getting irritating. Right, listen: when I say I've got some good news to tell you, I mean it. Had I already told you I've a few high-up contacts on the Academy's board of directors?"

Walter explained that our Academy had undertaken research and exchange programmes with some of China's major universities. He also informed me that in the course of all these foreign trips, connections had been forged at various levels of the diplomatic hierarchy. Walter told me that thanks to his contacts, he'd managed to put the wheels of a silent machine in motion. From a Chinese student about to finish her doctorate at the Academy whose father was a judge well regarded by the authorities, and some diplomats working at Her Majesty's visa service, to a consul in Turkey who'd spent most of his career in Beijing and still knew a few high-ranking officials there, the wheels had been turning from one country and continent to another until a breakthrough had finally been triggered in Sichuan province. The local authorities had recently turned compassionate, and begun wondering whether the lawyer who'd defended a young Western woman might have lacked the requisite vocabulary during the preliminary hearings leading up to her trial. Linguistic misunderstandings with his client might explain why he'd omitted to tell the judge in charge of the case that the foreign national sentenced for not having papers did in fact have a perfectly valid passport. With goodwill the order of the day and the magistrate promoted, Keira would be pardoned on condition that this new evidence was presented at the court of Chengdu without delay. All that remained to do was to go and pick her up and escort her out of the People's Republic.

"Are you serious?" I asked, jumping up and hugging Walter.

"Do I look like I'm joking? You might have had the courtesy to notice that I didn't even draw breath so as not to prolong your torture."

I was so happy that I grabbed him and whirled him round and round. We were still doing our wild dance in the middle of my hospital room when my mother arrived. She stared at us both, turned on her heel and went back out.

We heard her sigh heavily in the corridor and my Aunt Elena tell her not to start going on about me again.

My head was spinning a little so I climbed back into bed.

"So when will she be free?"

"You've forgotten the other bit of news you asked to hear first. Let me tell you again: the Chinese magistrate is willing to release Keira if we present her passport within six days. As her precious ticket out of there is currently lying at the bottom of a river, we'll need to obtain a brand new one. But in the absence of the party concerned, it'll be impossible within such a short deadline. Do you understand our problem more clearly now?"

"Six days is really all we've got?"

"If you allow one day for getting to the court in Chengdu, that leaves us only five to have a new passport issued. Short of a miracle, I don't see what we can do."

"Does the passport absolutely have to be new?"

"In case your lung infection has also contaminated your brain, I'd like to point out that I'm not in fact a customs officer. I suppose as long as the document is valid, that should do the trick. Why?"

"Because Keira has dual nationality: French and British. And as my brain is still in good health – thank you for your concern – I fully remember that we entered China with her British passport because I was the one who went to get it stamped beforehand with the visas we needed. She carried it on her the whole time. When we found the microphone in her bag, we turned the contents out and I'm sure her French passport wasn't in there."

"Great news! So where is it? I don't want to be a spoil-sport, but we have hardly any time to get hold of it."

"No idea."

"Well, at least we've made progress. I'm going to go and make a couple of calls, then come back later. Your aunt and your mother are waiting outside; I don't want them to think we're being ill-mannered."

Walter left my room and Mum and Aunt Elena came straight in. My mother sat down in the armchair, turned on the television that was fixed to the wall opposite my bed and didn't say a word to me. This made Elena smile.

"Isn't Walter charming?" she said, as she sat on the end of my bed.

I gave her an intent stare. Talking about that in front of Mum wasn't the best idea perhaps.

"And rather handsome, don't you think?" she continued, ignoring my frowns.

My mother replied in my place, without taking her eyes off the screen.

"And rather young, if you ask me. But go ahead as if I wasn't here! After a conversation between men, what could be more natural than a powwow between an aunt and her nephew? Mothers don't count! As soon as this programme's over, I'll go and chat with the nurses. Who knows, perhaps they'll have some news about my son."

"Now you understand why they call it Greek tragedy," said Elena, with a sidelong glance at my mother who was still sitting with her back to us and her eyes riveted to the TV, which she was watching with the sound turned down so as not to miss any of our conversation.

The programme was a documentary about the nomadic tribes of the high Tibetan plateaux.

"What a bore! It's at least the fifth time this has been on," Mum sighed, switching the set off. "What are you making that face for?"

"Was there a little girl in that documentary?"

"I've no idea. Perhaps. Why?"

I preferred not to tell her. Walter knocked at the door. Elena stood up and suggested they go to the cafeteria to let her sister spend some quality time alone with her son. That was her excuse anyway. Walter didn't need asking twice.

"To spend some quality time with my son – I don't think so!" exclaimed my mother as soon as they'd shut the door. "You should see her; since you fell ill and your friend arrived, she's been acting like a love-sick teenager. Ridiculous."

"There's no age limit for falling in love. Anyway, it makes her happy."

"It's not the fact she's fallen in love that makes her happy; it's that someone's courting her."

"And what about you? You could think about a new relationship, couldn't you? You've been in mourning long enough. If you let someone into your life, it doesn't mean you have to chase Dad from your heart."

"That's my son telling me that? There'll only ever be one man in my house, and that's your father. Even though he's laid to rest, I feel his presence. I talk to him when I wake up every morning; I talk to him in my kitchen, on the terrace when I'm tending the flowers, on my way down to the village, and in the evening when I go to bed. I'm not on my own just because your father isn't here anymore. It's not the same for Elena; she was never lucky enough to meet a man like my husband."

"All the more reason to let her flirt, don't you think?"

"I'm not against your aunt's happiness, but I'd prefer it if it weren't with one of my son's friends. I know I'm being old-fashioned perhaps, but I'm allowed to have faults. She should have turned her attentions to that friend of Walter's who came to visit you instead."

I sat up in bed and my mother took the opportunity to plump up my pillows.

"What friend?"

"I don't know. I saw him in the corridor a few days ago, before you'd come round. I didn't have a chance to say hello properly because he was leaving when I arrived. Anyway, he was distinguished-looking with amber-coloured skin. I thought he was very elegant. Also, instead of being twenty years younger than your aunt, he must have been at least that much older."

"And you have no idea who it was?"

"We literally passed each other, that's all. It's high time

you got some rest and your strength back. Let's change subjects; I can hear our two lovebirds cooing in the corridor. They'll be back in here any minute."

Elena had come to get Mum because it was time to leave if they didn't want to miss the last ferry to Hydra. Walter accompanied them to the lifts, then came straight back to my room.

"Your aunt told me a few stories from your childhood. She's hilarious!"

"If you say so."

"Is something bothering you, Adrian?"

"Mum told me she saw you a few days ago with a friend who she said had come to visit me. Who was it?"

"She must have made a mistake. It was probably a visitor asking me directions. Actually, now I come to think of it, it was exactly that: an elderly man looking for a relative. I sent him to the nurses' office."

"I've thought of how we might get hold of Keira's passport."

"Now that's more like it. I'm all ears."

"Maybe her sister Jeanne could help us."

"Do you know how to get in touch with her?"

"Yes. I mean no," I said, rather embarrassed.

"Yes or no?"

"I never plucked up the courage to call her about the accident."

"You haven't given Keira's sister the news? Not one call in three months?"

"I just couldn't tell her over the phone that she'd died. And I didn't have the strength to go to Paris."

"What a coward! That's appalling. Can you imagine

what a state of worry she must be in? How come she hasn't got in touch herself anyway?"

"It's not unusual for Jeanne and Keira to go a long time without giving each other news."

"Well, I think you'd better contact her as soon as possible. And I mean today."

"No, I have to go and see her."

"Don't be ridiculous. You're confined to bed and we've no time to lose," snapped Walter, handing me the phone. "Deal with your conscience and make that call now."

I dealt with it as best I could. As soon as Walter left me on my own, I found the number of the Quai Branly museum. Jeanne was in a meeting and couldn't be disturbed. I dialled the number again and again, until the switchboard operator made it clear it was pointless harassing her. I guessed Jeanne was in no hurry to speak to me because she saw me as partly to blame for Keira's silence and was cross with me for not giving her any news. I called back one last time and explained to the receptionist that I had to talk to Jeanne extremely urgently; it was a matter of life or death concerning her sister.

"Has something happened to Keira?" Jeanne asked in a trembling voice.

"Something happened to both of us," I replied, heavy-hearted. "I need your help, Jeanne, now."

I told her our story, playing down the tragic Yellow River accident and the circumstances leading up to it. I promised her that Keira was out of danger and explained that it was because of a stupid mix-up over her identity papers that she'd been arrested and held in China. I didn't mention the word prison. I could hear that each thing I said was a hard blow to Jeanne; she had to hold back the tears several times. I had to contain my emotion too. I'm no good at lying, no good at all, and Jeanne quickly realised the situation was much more worrying than I was admitting to her. She made me swear again and again that her little sister was well. I promised to bring her back safe and sound, explaining that to do so I needed to get hold of her passport as quickly as possible. Jeanne didn't know where it could be, but said she'd leave the office right away and turn her apartment upside down if necessary, then call me back as soon as she could.

As I hung up, I was overcome with the blues. Speaking to Jeanne again had revived my sorrow and my crushing feeling of emptiness in Keira's absence.

Never in her life had Jeanne driven across Paris so quickly. She zoomed her little car through three red lights on the embankments, narrowly missed hitting a van and almost swerved out of control on the Alexandre III Bridge to the sound of horns hooting. She sped down bus lanes, mounted a pavement along a congested boulevard and nearly knocked over a cyclist, but arrived back at the foot of her apartment building miraculously unscathed.

She dashed into the hallway, knocked on the concierge's door and begged her to come and give her a hand. Madame Hereira had never seen Jeanne in such a state. The lift was being used by some delivery men on the third floor so they bounded up the stairs, four at a time. Once inside the apartment, Jeanne gave Madame Hereira orders to search the sitting room and the kitchen while she did the bedrooms: nothing should be left to chance, every cupboard must be opened and every drawer emptied. They had to find Keira's passport wherever it was.

Within an hour they had ransacked the place and made a worse mess than any burglar would have. Books littered the floor and clothes were strewn here, there and everywhere. They'd upended the armchairs and unmade the bed. Jeanne was just starting to lose hope when she heard Madame Hereira shriek in the hall. She scrambled in there to see the table that served as a desk knocked over and the concierge triumphantly holding the small burgundy-covered book. Jeanne hugged her, and kissed her on both cheeks.

Walter had returned to his hotel when Jeanne called back, so I was alone in my room. We spent ages on the phone. I made her talk about Keira; I needed her to fill the void made by Keira's absence by sharing memories of their childhood. Jeanne accepted my request willingly; she missed Keira as much as I did. She promised to send the passport to me at Athens hospital by express post. Just before saying goodbye, she asked me how I was.

Two days later, the doctors spent longer than usual with me on their rounds. The head of the pulmonology department was still wondering about my case. Nobody was able to explain how such a virulent lung infection could have started without any warning signs whatsoever. I'd been in perfect health when I'd boarded the airplane. The doctor declared that if the air stewardess hadn't had the presence of mind to alert the captain and if he hadn't turned the plane around, I'd probably have died before reaching Beijing. It wasn't a virus and he'd never seen anything like it in his entire career. The essential thing, he said with a shrug, was that I'd responded well to the treatment. We'd been close to the worst, but I'd pulled through. A few more days of convalescence and I could pick up my normal life again. The department head promised to discharge me in a week or so.

He had just left my room when Keira's passport was delivered. I opened the envelope containing the precious safe conduct and found a short note from Jeanne with it: *Bring her back as quickly as possible. I'm counting on you – she's my only family.*

I folded the note back up and opened the passport. Keira looked a bit younger in the photo. I decided to get dressed.

Walter came into the room and caught me in my boxer shorts and shirt. He asked me what I was doing.

"I'm going to go and look for her. Don't try and talk me out of it – it'd be a waste of time."

Not only did he not try to, he actually helped me escape. Having repeatedly complained about the hospital being deserted during siesta time in Athens, he now turned the situation to our advantage. He kept lookout in the corridor while I gathered my things together, then escorted me towards the lifts, making sure we didn't bump into any hospital staff on the way.

As we passed the next room along, we saw a little girl standing all alone in the doorway. She was wearing ladybird pyjamas and gave Walter a little wave.

"Hello, little monkey!" he said, going up to her. "Isn't your mother here yet?"

Walter turned to me and I understood that he knew my ward neighbour well.

"She paid you the odd little visit," he told me, giving the child big knowing winks.

I kneeled down to say hello to her too. She looked at me mischievously and burst out laughing. Her cheeks were as red as apples.

Everything was going according to plan as we got to the ground floor. An orderly had shared our lift, but not paid us any particular attention. Then, as the doors opened onto the hospital foyer, we ran into my mother and Aunt Elena, and our escape attempt turned into a nightmare. Mum began shrieking, asking me what I was doing out of bed. I took her by the arm and begged her to follow me outside without making a scene. I would have had better luck asking her to dance the Sirtaki in the middle of the hospital cafeteria.

"The doctors have authorised him to go for a short walk," said Walter to reassure my mother.

"And he needs his travel bag for this short walk, does he? Perhaps you want to find me a bed in geriatrics while you're at it!" she raged.

She turned to two ambulance men who were passing and I guessed immediately that her plan was to get me taken back to my room, by force if necessary.

One look at Walter and he understood. As Mum began shouting, we sprinted towards the main door and managed to get out before security could react to her bellowing orders to catch me.

I wasn't in the best shape. When I reached the corner of the street, I felt a burning sensation in my chest; my heart was pounding and a violent coughing fit took hold of me. I had to stop to get my breath back. Walter turned round and saw two security guards running in our direction. His quick-thinking was genius: he limped over to the men and declared with a mortified look on his face that two thugs had just knocked him over and taken off into the adjacent street. As the vigilantes rushed in that direction, Walter hailed a taxi.

He didn't say a word to me on the journey. It worried me to see him suddenly so quiet and I didn't understand what had thrown him into that state.

Walter's hotel room became our headquarters for preparing my journey. The bed was big enough for us to share and Walter put a bolster down the middle as a boundary line. While I rested, he spent hours on end on the telephone. From time to time he went out to get some fresh air, he said. Those were about the only words he said; he was barely speaking to me.

I don't know by what miracle he managed it, but he got the Chinese embassy to issue me a visa within forty-eight hours. I thanked him profusely. But since our escape from hospital, he hadn't been the same.

One evening, as we were having dinner in the hotel room, Walter turned on the television, still refusing to talk to me. I picked up the remote control and switched it off.

"Why on earth are you being so sulky with me?"

Walter grabbed the remote control out of my hand and turned the TV back on.

I got up, pulled the plug out of the socket and plonked myself in front of him.

"If I've done something to upset you, let's sort it out once and for all."

Walter gave me a long look, then went and shut himself in the bathroom without saying a word. I hammered on the door in vain; he refused to open it. He reappeared a few minutes later in his pyjamas, warning me that if the checked pattern prompted the slightest bit of sarcasm from me, I'd be sleeping out on the landing. Then he slipped under the covers and turned out the light without wishing me goodnight.

"Walter," I said in the dark, "what have I done? What's going on?"

"What's going on is that, at times, helping you is rather a burden."

Silence fell again and I realised I hadn't thanked him properly for all the trouble he'd gone to for me lately. My ingratitude had most probably hurt him, so I said I was sorry. Walter replied that he couldn't care less about my apologies. But, he added, if I could find a way for us to be forgiven for our inexcusable behaviour in the hospital towards my mother and especially my aunt, he'd be very grateful. Then he turned over and stopped talking.

I switched the light back on and sat up in bed.

"What do you want now?" asked Walter.

"Do you really have a soft spot for Elena?"

"What's it to you? All you think about is Keira. All you care about is your own business. Everything revolves around you. When it's not your research and your stupid fragments, it's your health. When it's not your health, it's your archaeologist. And every time, good old Walter is called on for help. Walter this, Walter that. But if I try to confide in you, you don't give me the time of day. And don't go saying now that you're interested in my feelings

– the one time I confided in you, you made fun of me."

"I didn't mean to, I promise."

"Well, that's how it came across. Can we go to sleep now?"

"No, not until we've finished this discussion."

"What 'discussion'?" Walter snapped. "You're the one doing all the talking."

"Walter, are you really in love with my aunt?"

"I'm upset that I upset her by helping you leave hospital like that. Is that the answer you want?"

I rubbed my chin and had a think for a few moments.

"If I arranged for you to be completely exonerated and forgiven, would you stop being angry with me?"

"Do it and we'll see."

"I'll get on with it first thing tomorrow."

Walter's face softened and he even gave me a little smile before turning over and switching off the light.

Five minutes later, he switched it back on and bounced back upright.

"Why not apologize tonight?"

"You want me to call Elena at this hour?"

"It's only ten o'clock. It took me two days to get you a visa for China – surely you can get me your aunt's forgiveness in one evening."

I got back out of bed and called my mother. I listened to her reprimands for a good quarter of an hour, without being able to get a word in edgeways. When she'd run out of things to say, I asked her if, no matter what the circumstances, she'd have gone to look for my father at the ends of the earth if he'd been in danger. I heard her think. I didn't need to see her to know she was smiling.

She wished me a good trip and pleaded with me not to stay any longer than absolutely necessary. While I was away in China, she would prepare some proper dishes to welcome Keira with on our return.

She was about to hang up when I remembered the reason for my call and asked her to give Elena the phone. My aunt had already retired to bed in the guest room, but I begged my mother to go and get her.

Elena had found our escape incredibly romantic. Walter was an exceptional friend for having taken so many risks. She made me promise not to repeat what she'd just told me to my mother.

I went to join Walter who was pacing up and down the bathroom.

"Well?" he said anxiously.

"Well, I think that this weekend, while I'm flying to Beijing, you can sail to Hydra. My aunt will be waiting at the port to have dinner with you. I recommend you order moussaka for her – she's very partial to it. But that's between you and me; I haven't said a thing."

Then I turned out the light, exhausted.

On Friday of that week, Walter accompanied me to the airport. The plane took off on time. As it climbed into the sky above Athens, I watched the Aegean Sea fade into the distance below the wings and experienced a strange feeling of déjà vu. In ten hours, I'd be arriving in China.

Beijing

As soon as the customs formalities were over, I took a connecting flight to Chengdu.

A young interpreter sent by the Chinese authorities was waiting for me. He drove me through the city to the law courts. I waited for several hours on an uncomfortable bench for the judge in charge of Keira's case to see me. Every time I nodded off (I hadn't slept for about twenty hours), my companion poked me in the ribs with an elbow, sighing loudly to make me understand he found my behaviour unacceptable in a place like this. Towards the end of the afternoon, the door we'd been waiting in front of opened at last. A portly man came out of the office with a stack of files under his arm and paid me no attention whatsoever. I jumped up and ran after him, to the great displeasure of my interpreter who hurriedly gathered his things together and rushed after me.

The judge stopped and looked me up and down, as if I were a strange animal. I explained the purpose of my visit: that it had been arranged for me to come and show him Keira's passport so he could repeal her sentence and sign her release. The interpreter kept up as best he could, the tremor in his voice betraying his fear of the judge's authority. The man was impatient. I didn't have an appointment and he had no time for me. He was being transferred to Beijing the next day and still had lots of work to do.

I barred his way, my tiredness loosening my hold on my temper.

"Do you have to be cruel and indifferent to command respect? Isn't dispensing justice enough for you?" I asked him.

My interpreter's face became worryingly pale. He spluttered, refused categorically to translate my words and took me to one side.

"Are you out of your mind? Do you know who you're talking to? If I translate what you've just said, we'll be the ones sleeping in prison tonight."

I couldn't have cared less about his warnings. I pushed him out of the way and ran after the judge, who'd slipped off in the meantime. I stood in his way again.

"This evening, when you open a nice bottle of champagne to celebrate your promotion, tell your wife that you have become such a powerful, important person that the fate of an innocent woman is no longer enough to plague your conscience. While you're treating yourself to delicious after-dinner sweets, talk to your children about honour, morals, respectability and the world they will inherit from their father – a world in which innocent women sometimes rot in prison because judges have better things to do than dispense justice. Say all that to your family on my behalf; then I'll feel slightly like I'm at your party. Keira will too!"

This time my interpreter yanked me over to him and begged me to shut up. The judge watched as he lectured me, then at last addressed me: "I speak your language fluently, having studied at Oxford. Your interpreter is right, you're lacking in manners, but you've certainly got quite a nerve."

He looked at his watch.

"Give me the passport and wait here. I'll deal with you now."

I held out the document and he grabbed it from me, then hurried off towards his office. Five minutes later, two police officers suddenly appeared behind me. I'd hardly had time to realise they were there before they'd handcuffed me and begun marching me off. My interpreter, who was beside himself, followed me, vowing he'd inform my embassy the very next day. The officers ordered him to stand back, then pushed me forcibly into a van. Three hours of bumpy road later, I arrived in the courtyard of Garther Prison, which was nothing like the imposing monastery I'd imagined in my worst nightmares.

They confiscated my bag, watch and belt, took off my handcuffs and escorted me to a cell, where I met my fellow inmate. He must have been over sixty, and was completely toothless and sunken-cheeked. I'd have liked to know what crime he'd committed to be shut up here, but a conversation seemed unlikely. He was on the top bunk, so I took the bottom one; it was all the same to me – until I saw a chunky rat scuttling along the corridor. I had no idea what my fate was to be, but the thought that Keira and I were in the same building kept me going. The only star this establishment had was a red one stitched on the warders' caps.

An hour later, the door was opened and I followed my cell companion and fell in behind a long line of prisoners who were walking down the stairs to the canteen in time with each other. When we reached the vast dining room, my pale skin caused a stir among the seated convicts. I imagined the worst as they scrutinised me. But all they did was laugh at me before bending over their bowls again. The broth with rice and scraps of meat floating in it took my appetite away completely. I made the most of everyone being engrossed in their food to look at the long security grille separating us from the women's side of the canteen. My heart started beating faster; Keira must be somewhere among the rows of female prisoners eating just a few metres away from us. How could I signal my presence to her without being spotted by the guards? Talking was forbidden. My neighbour had been whacked with a rod on the back of his neck for asking the man beside him to pass the salt. I tried to imagine what punishment I'd get, but couldn't stand it any longer, so I jumped up, shouted "Keira" right in the middle of the hall, and sat straight back down again.

The clanking of cutlery died away and the inmates stopped chewing. The warders scanned the hall without moving. None of them could locate the person who'd dared break the no-talking rule. The leaden silence lasted a few moments, then I suddenly heard a familiar voice call out "Adrian."

All the male prisoners turned their heads towards the female prisoners, who in turn all looked in our direction. Even the male and female guards did the same. Both sides of the huge room stared at each other.

I stood up and started walking towards the security grille. You did the same. We passed each table in silence, getting closer and closer to each other.

The guards were so stunned they didn't move.

The male inmates shouted "Keira" in unison and the women answered "Adrian."

You were only a few metres away. You looked washed out and had tears in your eyes. I was crying too. We approached the grille feeling so elated by this eagerly awaited moment that neither of us cared about the baton that was lying in wait. We joined our hands through the bars and intertwined our fingers; we put our faces up close and your mouth kissed mine. I told you "I love you" in the canteen of a Chinese prison and you murmured that you loved me too. Then you asked me what I was doing there.

"I've come to get you out."

"From inside the prison?"

You were right; caught up in the emotion of it all, I hadn't thought about that detail. And I didn't have time to now: a whack on the back of my thighs brought me to my knees, then a second blow, to the small of my back, floored me. We screamed each other's names as they dragged us away.

Hydra

Walter apologised to Elena: the circumstances were unusual and he wouldn't have left his mobile phone switched on if he wasn't expecting information from China any minute now. Elena told him he must take the call. Walter stood up and walked away from the restaurant terrace towards the port. Ivory was asking for news.

"Still none, sir. His plane has definitely landed in Beijing though. If my calculations are right, he must have met the judge by now and be on his way to the prison. They may even already be reunited. Let's grant them some well-deserved privacy. Imagine how happy they must be to see each other again. I promise to phone you as soon as he's contacted me."

Walter hung up and returned to the table.

"Unfortunately, it was just a colleague from the Academy who needed to know something," he said to Elena.

They continued their conversation over the dessert that Elena had ordered for them.

Garther Prison

My effrontery during the meal had won me my fellow inmates' sympathy. As two guards escorted me back to my cell, I got a few friendly slaps on the back from some of the other prisoners returning to their quarters. My cellmate gave me a cigarette, which must have been a very valuable present in here. I lit it out of good grace, but my recent lung infection sent me into a coughing fit, which amused my new friend a great deal.

The wooden plank that served as a bed was covered by a straw mattress barely thicker than a blanket. The pain where I'd been whacked flared up again as I lay down, but I was so tired that I fell asleep right away. I'd seen Keira again and her face stayed with me all through the long night in that seedy cell.

The following morning, we were woken up by a gong that resounded throughout the prison building. My fellow inmate got down from his bunk and pulled on his trousers and the socks he'd hung over the bedpost.

A warder opened our door. My cellmate picked up his tin bowl and went out into the corridor. The guard ordered me to stay where I was. I realised I was being banned from the canteen because of my behaviour the previous day. I was overcome with sadness; I'd been counting the hours until I saw Keira there again. Now I'd have to wait.

As the morning passed, I worried about the punishment that lay in store for her. She was already so pale. I found myself – me, the atheist – kneeling by my bed and praying like a child to God that Keira had been spared solitary confinement.

I heard the prisoners' voices in the courtyard. It must have been exercise time. I wasn't allowed out. I stayed where I was, sick with worry about Keira's fate. I climbed on a stool and hoisted myself up to the skylight in the hope of seeing her. The prisoners were walking in rows towards a yard. I balanced on my tiptoes, slipped and fell onto the floor. By the time I'd picked myself up again, the courtyard was empty.

The sun was high in the sky; it must have been noon. Surely they weren't going to let me die of hunger just to teach me some discipline? I wasn't counting on my interpreter to get us out of here. I thought about Jeanne. I'd called her before taking off from Athens and promised to give her news today. Perhaps she'd realise something had happened to me and alert our embassies within the next few days.

I was in extremely low spirits when I heard footsteps coming along the corridor. A guard opened my cell and told me to follow him. We crossed the gangway, went down the metal stairs and into the office where my things had been confiscated the day before. I was given them back, asked to sign a form and pushed out into the courtyard without knowing what was happening. Five minutes later, the prison gates closed behind me and I was free. The door of a vehicle in the visitors' car park opened and my interpreter got out and walked towards me.

I thanked him for managing to get me out and apologised for having doubted him.

"I had nothing to do with it," he said. "After the police officers carted you off, the judge came back out of his office and asked me to come and pick you up here at twelve o'clock. He also asked me to tell you he hoped one night in prison had taught you some manners. I'm only translating what he said."

"And Keira?" I asked immediately.

"Turn around," he replied calmly.

I saw the gates open again, and you appeared. You were carrying your belongings over your shoulder. You put them down and ran towards me.

I'll never forget the moment we wrapped our arms around each other in front of Garther Prison. I hugged you so tight I almost suffocated you, but you were laughing and we spun around together, wild with joy. The interpreter coughed, stamped his feet and pleaded with us to stop, but in vain – nothing could have interrupted our embrace.

As I kissed you, I asked your forgiveness for having got you involved in this mad adventure. You put your hand over my mouth to stop me talking.

"You came; you came to look for me here," you whispered.

"I promised I'd take you back to Addis Ababa, remember?"

"I forced that promise out of you, but I'm truly happy you've kept it."

"How have you managed to keep going all this time?"

"I don't know. It was long, horribly long. But I used the time to think. That's all I could do. Listen, don't take me back to Ethiopia straightaway; I think I know where to find the next fragment, and it's not in Africa."

We climbed into the interpreter's car and he drove us to Chengdu, where all three of us took the plane.

In Beijing, you threatened our interpreter that you wouldn't leave the country if he didn't take us to a hotel where you could have a shower. He looked at his watch and gave us one hour alone, just the two of us.

Room 409. I paid no attention to the view. Like I've already told you, happiness makes you distracted. I sat at a small desk facing the window with Beijing spread out before me, but I couldn't have cared less; all I wanted to look at was you lying on the bed. From time to time, you opened your eyes and stretched. You told me you'd never realised just how good it felt to sprawl around in clean sheets. You squeezed the pillow in your arms, then threw it in my face. I wanted you again.

The interpreter must have been beside himself with rage – we'd been there for well over an hour. You got up and I watched you walk to the bathroom. You called me a voyeur and I didn't try to justify myself. I noticed the scars on your back and your legs. You turned round and I read in your eyes that you didn't want us to talk about it, not now. I heard the shower running, the sound of the water gave me my strength back and stopped you hearing my cough that kept coming back like a bad memory. Some things had changed forever. In China, I'd lost some of that indifference I used to find so reassuring. I was scared of being alone in that room, even for a few moments, even separated from you by a simple partition wall. But I was no longer afraid of admitting it to myself, or of getting up and going to join you and confiding all that to you.

At the airport, I kept another promise: as soon as our boarding cards were printed, I took you to a phone booth and we called Jeanne.

I don't know which of you two started first, but right in the middle of this huge terminal, you began crying. You were laughing and sobbing at once.

Time was ticking on and we had to go. You told Jeanne you loved her and you'd call her again as soon as you arrived in Athens.

When you hung up, you burst into tears again and I had an uphill battle trying to console you.

Our interpreter seemed more exhausted than us. We went through passport control and I saw a look of relief on his face at last. He must have been so happy to be rid of us that he didn't stop waving goodbye through the glass.

It was night-time when we boarded the plane. You leaned your head against the window and fell asleep before we'd even taken off.

As we began our descent towards Athens, we passed through some turbulence. You took my hand and squeezed it very tight, as if you were anxious about the landing. To distract you, I took out the fragment we'd discovered on Narcondam Island, leaned over and showed it to you.

"You said you had an idea where one of the other fragments was."

"Are planes really made to stand up to this much jolting?"

"There's no need to worry. So, what about the fragment?"

With your free hand – the other one was squeezing mine harder and harder – you took out your pendant. We debated whether to put them together, then abandoned the idea when we passed through an air pocket.

"Wait until we've landed for me to tell you all about it," you begged.

"Give me a clue at least."

"The Arctic, somewhere between Baffin Bay and the Beaufort Sea. That gives us a few thousand kilometres to explore. I'll explain why, but first you've got to show me round your island."

Hydra

We took a taxi in Athens and were boarding the Hydra ferry two hours later. You took a seat in the cabin, while I went to the rear deck.

"Don't tell me you get seasick," you said when you came to find me.

"I love the fresh air."

"You're shivering but you want fresh air? Why don't you just admit you get seasick? Why don't you tell me the truth?"

"Because it's almost a sin for a Greek not to be a good sailor. I don't see what's so funny."

"Somebody I know made fun of me not so very long ago because I had airsickness."

"I wasn't making fun of you," I answered, leaning over the handrail.

"You've gone an odd shade of green and you're trembling. Let's go back to the cabin, otherwise you'll end up really falling ill."

I started having another coughing fit and let you take me back inside. I could feel that the fever had returned, but I didn't want to think about it; I was happy to be bringing you to my home and didn't want anything to spoil the moment.

I waited until we arrived at the port of Piraeus before letting my mother know we were there. As the ferry docked in Hydra, I was already imagining her critical remarks. I'd begged her not to organise a party for us; we were exhausted and dreamed of just one thing: sleeping until we could sleep no more.

Mum welcomed us into her house. It was the first time I'd seen you intimidated. She thought we both looked dreadful. She prepared a light meal for us on the terrace. Aunt Elena had chosen to stay in the village to leave the three of us alone. Mum pestered you with questions at the dinner table. I glowered at her to leave you in peace, but nothing doing. You went along with her, answering enthusiastically. I was seized by another bout of coughing, which put an end to the evening. Mum showed us to my room. The sheets smelt of lavender. We fell asleep to the sound of the sea lapping against the cliffs.

You tiptoed out of bed early in the morning. Your stay in prison had made you lose your habit of lying in. I heard you leave the room but felt too weak to follow you. You were talking to my mother in the kitchen; the two of you appeared to be getting on well. I fell straight back to sleep.

I found out later that Walter had landed on the island at the end of the morning. Elena had called him the day before to tell him we were arriving and he'd taken a plane straightaway. He confided to me one day that because of all those return trips between London and Hydra, my adventures had made a serious dent in his savings.

After lunch, Walter, Elena, Keira and my mother came into my room. They looked distraught to see me laid up in bed, burning with fever. My mother applied a compress soaked in a eucalyptus leaf potion to my forehead. But that old remedy of hers did nothing to stave off the sickness that was taking hold of me. A few hours later, I received a visit from a woman I'd thought I'd never see again. But Walter was in the habit of noting everything down, and the telephone number of this doctor – and pilot when the mood took her – had slipped into the pages of his little black book. Dr. Sophie Schwarz sat down on my bed and took my hand.

"This time you're not putting it on, unfortunately; you've got a raging fever, my poor friend."

She listened to my lungs and immediately diagnosed a relapse of the infection my mother had told her about. Ideally, she'd have evacuated me to Athens straightaway, but the weather forecast wouldn't allow it. A storm was arriving, the sea was wild and her little plane wouldn't be able to take off. Anyway, I was in no condition to travel.

"We'll just have to do the best we can with what we've got," she said to Keira.

The storm lasted three days. For seventy-two hours, the powerful meltemi wind raged across the island, bending trees in its path. The house creaked loudly and tiles were blown off the roof. From my bedroom, I could hear the waves crashing against the cliffs.

Mum had put Keira in the guest bedroom, but as soon as the lights were out, she'd come to my room and lie down next to me. The few times she allowed herself to snatch some sleep, the doctor took over the watch. Walter overcame his fear and climbed the hill on a donkey twice a day to visit me. He was soaked from head to toe when he arrived in my room. He sat on a chair and told me how he thanked God for the storm; the bed and breakfast where he always stayed had had part of its roof ripped off and Elena had offered to put him up. I was furious at myself for spoiling Keira's first few days on the island, but the presence of all these people made me realise that the solitude I'd experienced on the Atacama high plateau was now a thing of the past.

On the fourth day, the meltemi subsided, and with it my fever.

Amsterdam

Vackeers was rereading a letter. There were two gentle knocks at the door. As he wasn't expecting anyone, he automatically reached into his desk drawer. Ivory came in looking solemn.

"You could have let me know you were in town – I would have sent a car to meet you at the airport."

"I took the Thalys train. I had some reading to catch up on."

"I haven't prepared anything for dinner," Vackeers continued, surreptitiously closing the drawer.

"I see you're as serene as ever," Ivory sighed.

"I receive few visitors at the palace and even fewer without notice. Let's go out to dinner. We'll have a game afterwards."

"I've come here to talk to you, not to battle it out with you over chess."

"How serious you sound. You seem very worried, my dear fellow."

"Forgive me for turning up like this unannounced, but I have my reasons and I'd like to talk to you about them."

"I know a discreet table in a restaurant not far from here; I'll take you there and we can chat while we're walking."

Vackeers put on his raincoat. They crossed the state room of the Royal Palace. As they walked over the vast planisphere engraved on the marble floor, Ivory stopped to look at the map of the world under his feet.

"The research is going to start again," he said sombrely to his friend.

"Don't tell me you're surprised. It appears you've done everything you can to make it happen."

"I hope I won't have any reason to regret it."

"Why are you looking so gloomy? I hardly recognise you; you're normally so happy to disrupt the established order. You're going to cause complete chaos – you must be in seventh heaven. I wonder what your biggest motivation is in this adventure: discovering the truth about the origins of the world or taking your revenge on certain people who have upset you in the past?"

"I suppose it was a bit of both at the start, but I'm no longer alone in this search and the people I've got involved in it have risked their lives and are still at risk."

"And that frightens you? If it does, you've aged a hell of a lot recently."

"I'm not frightened, I'm facing a dilemma."

"It's not that I don't like this sumptuous hall, dear fellow, but I think our voices carry rather too much for a conversation of this kind. Let's go out, shall we?"

Vackeers made his way to the western end of the room, opened a secret door in the stone wall and went down a staircase leading to the basement level of the Royal

Palace. He guided Ivory along the wooden walkways running above an underground canal. It was a damp place, sometimes slippery underfoot.

"Watch your step," Vackeers warned. "I wouldn't want you to fall into that cold, dirty water. Follow me," he continued, switching on a flashlight.

They passed the beam where a rivet controlled a mechanism which Vackeers switched on when he wanted to enter the IT room, but on this occasion he didn't stop.

"Nearly there," he said to Ivory, "just a little further and we'll end up in a small courtyard. I don't know if anyone saw you entering the palace, but rest assured that nobody will see you leaving."

"What a strange maze of a place. I'll never get used to it."

"We could have taken the passage towards the New Church, but it's even wetter and our feet would have got soaked."

Vackeers pushed open a door. They walked up a few steps and found themselves out in the open air. An icy wind howled around them and Ivory turned up his coat collar. The two old friends walked up Hoogstraat, a street running alongside the canal.

"Well then, what's worrying you?" Vackeers resumed.

"My two protégés have met up with each other again."

"That's rather good news. After the rotten trick we played on Sir Ashley, we ought to be celebrating, not looking dejected."

"I doubt Ashley will stop there."

"You overdid it somewhat, challenging him in his own home. I'd suggested more discretion."

"We had no time. The young archaeologist had to be

released as quickly as possible. She'd been rotting behind bars long enough."

"But at least those bars were keeping her out of Ashley's reach and protecting your astrophysicist too as a result."

"That nutcase also had a go at him."

"Do you have proof?"

"I'm certain he had him poisoned. I saw large quantities of deadly nightshade along the paths in Ashley's garden. The fruit of that plant causes serious lung complications."

"I'm sure lots of people have deadly nightshade growing outside their homes, but that doesn't make all of them serial poisoners."

"Vackeers, we both know what that man is capable of. Perhaps I reacted impetuously, but not without proper judgement. I sincerely thought…"

"You thought it was time your research began again," interrupted Vackeers. "Listen to me, Ivory. I understand your motives, but it's not safe to continue your work. If your protégés set out in search of a new fragment, I'll be obliged to inform the others. I can't indefinitely run the risk of being accused of betrayal."

"Adrian has had a bad relapse, so for the time being Keira and he are resting in Greece."

"Let's hope that lasts as long as possible."

Ivory and Vackeers crossed a bridge spanning the canal. Ivory stopped and leaned on the balustrade.

"I love it here," sighed Vackeers. "I think it's my favourite place in the whole of Amsterdam. Look at the beautiful views."

"I need your help, Vackeers. I know you're loyal and I'll never ask you to betray the group, but alliances will form sooner or later, as in the past. Sir Ashley won't have only friends."

"You'll have them too. And since you're not on the committee anymore, you'd like me to be your mouthpiece and convince the majority. That's what you're expecting of me, isn't it?"

"That and something else," murmured Ivory.

"What exactly?" asked Vackeers, surprised.

"I need to get access to resources I no longer have at my disposal."

"What kind of resources?"

"Your computer, to get on the server."

"Absolutely not. We'd be spotted straightaway and I'd be compromised."

"Not if you agreed to plug a small object in behind your terminal."

"What sort of object?"

"A device that opens a discreet, undetectable link."

"You underestimate the group. They've hired some of the finest young computer scientists to work for them – including a few big-time ex-hackers."

"You and I are better chess players than any young person today. Trust me," Ivory said, holding out a small case to Vackeers.

Vackeers looked at the object distastefully.

"You want to tap me?"

"I just want to use your code to access the network. I assure you, you don't risk a thing."

"If I'm suspected, I risk being arrested and brought to justice."

"Vackeers, can I count on you or not?"

"I'll think about it and let you have my answer as soon as I've come to a decision. Your little story has completely taken away my appetite."

"I wasn't very hungry either," Ivory told him.

"Is it all worth it? What chance do they have of succeeding, do you even know that?" Vackeers asked with a sigh.

"On their own, not much. But if I put the information I've gathered during thirty years of research at their disposal, it is possible they will discover the missing fragments."

"Do you have an idea of where they are, then?"

"You see, Vackeers, not very long ago you doubted their very existence, and now you're interested in where they're hidden."

"You haven't answered my question."

"I think I have."

"So where are they?"

"The first was discovered in the centre, the second in the south and the third in the east. I leave you to guess where the last two could be. Think about my request, Vackeers. I know it's serious and potentially damaging for you, but as I said, I need you."

Ivory said goodbye to his friend and walked away. Vackeers ran after him.

"What about our game of chess? You're not just going to leave like that, are you?"

"Could you make us a snack at your house?"

"I should have some cheese and crackers."

"That'll do the job with a nice glass of wine. Prepare to lose – it's my turn to avenge!"

Athens

Keira and I were sitting on the terrace. Thanks to Dr. Schwarz's care, I was getting my strength back and had spent my first night without coughing. The colour had returned to my cheeks, which almost reassured my mother. The doctor had taken advantage of her forced stay to examine Keira and prescribe her various plant-based remedies and vitamin supplements. Prison had taken its toll on her.

The sea was calm, the wind had dropped and our doctor's little plane could take off again today.

We all met up at the breakfast table, where Mum had prepared a meal fit for a queen in the doctor's honour. While I'd been ill, she and Dr. Schwarz had spent hours on end together in the kitchen and the living room, swapping stories and memories. Mum had been fascinated by the adventures of this flying doctor, who flew from island to island to tend to the sick at their bedsides. Before leaving, the doctor made me promise I'd spend at least a few more days convalescing before envisaging doing anything else. My mother made her repeat the advice twice in case I hadn't heard properly. She accompanied her back to the port, giving us a little time on our own at long last.

As soon as we were alone, Keira came and sat beside me.

"Hydra's a charming island, Adrian, your mum's a wonderful woman, and I adore everyone here, but…"

"Me neither, I can't stand it anymore," I interrupted. "I dream of getting out of here with you. Does that make you feel better?"

"Oh, yes!" she sighed.

"We broke out of a Chinese prison, I think we ought to manage escaping from here without too much difficulty."

Keira looked out to sea.

"What's the matter?"

"I dreamed of Hari last night."

"Do you want to go back there?"

"I want to see him again. It's not the first time I've dreamed of him; Hari often visited me at night in Garther Prison."

"Let's go back to the Omo Valley if that's what you want. I promised you I'd take you back there."

"I'm not sure I'd belong there anymore though. And besides, we've got our research to do."

"It's already cost us enough; I don't want to make you run any more risks."

"It's not as if I want to show off or anything, but I did come back from China in better shape than you. I suppose we should decide together whether to carry on though."

"You know what I think."

"Where's your fragment?"

I got up and went to find it in the drawer of my bedside

table, where I'd put it for safekeeping when I'd arrived. When I returned to the terrace, Keira took off her pendant and placed the two pieces together on the table. As soon as they touched, the phenomenon we'd witnessed on Narcondam Island happened again: the fragments turned a deep sky blue and began sparkling exceptionally brightly.

"Do you want us to call it a day?" Keira asked, staring at the objects as their sparkle faded. "If I returned to the Omo Valley without having got to the bottom of this mystery, I'd never be able to do my work properly again; I'd spend all my time wondering what this object would reveal if we put all the fragments together. Anyway, speaking of promises, you made me another one: saving me hundreds of thousands of years in my research. If you think that offer fell on deaf ears, you're wrong!"

"I know what I promised you, Keira, but that was before a priest was murdered right in front of us, before we nearly fell into a ravine, before we were catapulted from the top of a cliff into a riverbed, and before you did time in a Chinese prison. And do we have any idea which direction to go off in search of it?"

"I told you: the Arctic. Nothing very specific yet, but at least it's a lead."

"Why there and not elsewhere?"

"Because that's what I think the text written in Ge'ez suggests. I didn't stop thinking about it when I was holed up in Garther. We have to go back to London so I can do more research in the great library at the Academy. I need to look up certain books, and I must talk to Max again. I've got questions to ask him."

"You want to go and see your printer again?"

"Don't make that face, you look ridiculous. Anyway, I didn't say I wanted to go and see him, I said I needed to talk to him. He's worked on the new translation of the manuscript; if he's discovered anything at all, I need that information. Most of all, I want to check something with him."

"Let's go back then. London will give us a good reason to leave Hydra."

"If we could, I'd like to make a flying visit to Paris."

"To see Max, I suppose?"

"To see Jeanne. And to go and visit Ivory."

"I thought the old professor had left his museum and gone travelling."

"I went travelling, and now I'm back. Who knows, perhaps he is too?"

Keira went off to prepare her things, while I prepared my mother for our departure. Walter was sorry to hear we were leaving the island. He'd used up all his time off for the next two years, but was hoping to stay one more weekend in Hydra. I said he shouldn't change his plans and that I looked forward to seeing him the following week at the Academy, as I'd decided to go there too. This time I wouldn't let Keira do her research alone, especially since she'd told me she wanted to stop off in Paris first. So I bought two tickets to France.

Amsterdam

Ivory had dozed off on the sofa in the living room. Vackeers had covered him with a blanket before going to bed. He spent a great deal of the night awake, turning thoughts over in his head. His old associate was seeking his help, but doing so would mean compromising himself. The next few months would be the last of his career, and the prospect of being caught out for betrayal didn't exactly fill him with enthusiasm. He got up in the early hours and went to make breakfast. The whistling kettle woke Ivory.

"Short night, wasn't it?" he said, taking a seat at the kitchen table.

"That's an understatement. But it was worth it for such a top-quality battle," Vackeers replied.

"I didn't realise I'd fallen asleep on the sofa. It's the first time that's happened to me. Sorry to have imposed on you like that."

"It really doesn't matter. I hope that old Chesterfield hasn't done your back in too much."

"I think I must be older than it," chuckled Ivory.

"You're deluding yourself; my father left it to me."

They went silent. Ivory stared at Vackeers, drank his cup of tea, munched a melba toast and got up.

"I've abused your hospitality long enough. I'll let you start your day in peace. I have to go back to my hotel."

Vackeers said nothing and watched Ivory walk out into the hall.

"Thanks for the excellent evening, my friend," Ivory went on as he picked up his raincoat. "We both look dreadful, but I must admit we haven't played so well for a long time."

He buttoned up his coat and put his hands in his pockets. Vackeers still said nothing.

Ivory shrugged and opened the latch. As he was doing so, he noticed a note positioned prominently on the small pedestal table next to the door. Vackeers didn't take his eyes off him. Ivory hesitated, picked up the piece of paper and saw there was a sequence of numbers and letters on it. Vackeers continued to stare at him from his chair in the kitchen.

"Thank you," whispered Ivory.

"What for?" grunted Vackeers. "You're hardly going to thank me for having taken advantage of my hospitality to rummage through my drawers and steal the access code to my computer."

"No, I'm not. I wouldn't have the nerve."

"That's reassuring."

Ivory closed the door behind him. He just had time to go back to the hotel, collect his things and take the Thalys train back. He hailed a taxi in the street.

Vackeers paced around his apartment for a while, then

put his cup of tea down on the hall table and picked up the phone.

"Amsterdam here," he said as soon as the person he was calling answered. "Inform the others. We have to organise a meeting: 8pm tonight, phone conference."

"Why don't you do it yourself via the computer network, as we usually do?" asked Cairo.

"Because my computer's broken down."

Vackeers hung up and went to get ready.

Paris

Keira had hurried over to Jeanne's. I'd preferred to leave them on their own to make the most of their time together. I remembered there was an antiques dealer in the Marais who sold the most beautiful optical instruments in the French capital. I received his catalogues once a year at my house in London. Most of the pieces on display were well beyond my means, but it was free to look, and I had three hours to kill.

When I entered the shop, the elderly antiques dealer was sitting behind his desk, cleaning a magnificent astrolabe. He paid me no attention at first, until I stood transfixed in front of an exceptionally well made armillary sphere.

"The model you're looking at, young man, was made by Gualterus Arsenius. Some say his brother Regnerus worked with him to produce this little gem," declared the man, getting to his feet.

He came over to me and opened the display case to show me the precious object.

"It's one of the most beautiful pieces of work to have come out of the Flemish workshops in the sixteenth

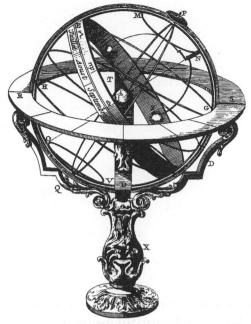

Armillary sphere

century. There were several craftsmen named Arsenius, and all they made were astrolabes and armillary spheres. Gualterus was related to the mathematician Gemma Frisius who wrote a treatise published in Antwerp in 1553 containing the oldest presentation of the principles of triangulation and a method for determining longitudes. What you're looking at is an extremely rare piece, with a price to match."

"Namely?"

"Priceless – if it had been an original, of course," the antiques dealer continued, putting the astrolabe back into its cabinet. "Unfortunately, this one is merely a copy, probably made towards the end of the eighteenth century for a rich Dutch trader anxious to impress his circle. I'm bored," he sighed. "May I offer you a cup of tea? It's been such a long time since I had the pleasure of talking to an astrophysicist."

"How do you know what I do?" I asked, astounded.

"Few people can manipulate this kind of instrument with such confidence, and you don't look like a dealer, so it doesn't take a genius to work out what you do. What sort of object did you come into my shop to look for? I do have some much more reasonably priced pieces."

"You'll probably be disappointed, but I'm only interested in vintage camera bodies."

"What a strange idea, but it's never too late to start a new collection. I know, let me show you something. I'm sure it'll fascinate you."

The elderly antiques dealer went over to a bookcase and took out a large leather-bound book. He put it on his desk, adjusted his glasses and turned the pages with the utmost care.

"Here we are," he said. "Look, this is a drawing of a remarkably well made armillary sphere. It's attributed to Erasmus Habermel, Emperor Rudolph II's mathematical instrument manufacturer."

I bent over the engraving and was surprised to see a reproduction that looked just like the one Keira and I had found under the stone lion's paw on the top of Mount Hua. I sat down on the chair the antiques dealer was offering me and studied the amazing drawing more closely.

"Note the astonishing precision of the work," he said, leaning over my shoulder. "What's always fascinated me with armillary spheres," he added, "is not so much that they enable us to establish the position of the stars in the sky at any given time, but rather what they don't show – which we can nevertheless guess."

I lifted my head out of his precious book and looked at him, curious to hear what he was going to tell me.

"The void and its friend time!" he concluded cheerfully. "What a strange notion the void is. The void is filled with things that are invisible to us. As for time that passes and changes everything, it alters the course of the stars and rocks the cosmos in perpetual motion. It's time that keeps the gigantic spider of life walking across the web of the universe. Time, which we know nothing about, is an intriguing dimension, don't you think? It's very nice of you to look so surprised by these trifles I'm saying; I'd like to offer you the book at the price it cost me."

The antiques dealer whispered the sum he hoped to get for it in my ear. I was missing Keira, so I bought it.

"Come back and see me," he said as he accompanied me to the door. "I've got other marvels to show you. It won't be a waste of time, I assure you," he said cheerily.

He locked the door behind me. Through the shop window, I watched him disappear into the back of his shop.

Here I was out in the street again with the big book under my arm, wondering why I'd actually bought it. My mobile phone vibrated in my pocket. I answered it and heard Keira's voice. She suggested I come to meet her later at Jeanne's, who'd be delighted to have us to stay for the evening and the night. I'd sleep on the sofa in the sitting room, and the two sisters would share the bed. And as if that plan wasn't enough to brighten up the end of my day, she also announced she was off to visit Max. As his print works wasn't far from Jeanne's, it'd only take her ten minutes to walk there. She added that she was very keen to check something with him and promised she'd call me back as soon as she'd done so.

I didn't react, just said I was thrilled about tonight's dinner together. Then we hung up.

When I got to the corner of Rue des Lions-Saint-Paul, I didn't know what to do or where to go.

How many times have I grumbled about having to grab minutes when I can, of never being allowed a moment of leisure time? This particular late afternoon, walking along the banks of the Seine, I had the strange and unpleasant sensation I was caught between two moments of the day that refused to come together. People who like going for a wander must know what to do. I've often seen them sitting on benches, reading or daydreaming. I've caught sight of them as I've passed a park or a square, without ever wondering about their lot. I'd have liked to send Keira a message, but I didn't let myself. Walter would have strongly advised me against it. I'd have liked to join her at Max's print works. Then we could have gone to Jeanne's together and bought her some flowers on the way. That's what I was dreaming about as my feet led me towards the Ile Saint-Louis. But as simple as it was to make that dream come true, it would have been taken the wrong way; Keira would have accused me of being jealous, and that's not like me. At least not usually.

I took a seat under the canopy of a small café on the corner of Rue des Deux-Ponts. I opened my book and immersed myself in it, checking my watch every so often. A taxi stopped in front of me and a man got out. He was wearing a raincoat and carrying a small suitcase in his hand. He hurried off along Quai d'Orléans. I was sure I'd already seen his face, but I couldn't remember where.

I watched him disappear through an entrance into a courtyard.

*

Keira had perched on the corner of the desk.

"The chair's more comfortable," Max said, lifting his eyes from the document he was studying.

"I've got out of the habit of sitting soft these last few months."

"You really spent three months in prison?"

"I've already told you I did, Max. Concentrate on the text and tell me what you think."

"I think that since you've been hanging out with that guy – your so-called colleague – your life has been turned upside down. I don't understand why you're still seeing him after what's happened to you. Damn it, Keira, he's ruined your research, not to mention the grant you were awarded for your work. You don't get that kind of present twice. And you seem to think it's all perfectly normal."

"Max, spare me the lecture – I've already got a sister who's an expert at it and I can assure you she's head and shoulders above you, so don't waste your time. What do you think of my theory?"

"And if I answer, what will you do? Go and explore the depths of the Mediterranean in Crete? Swim all the way to Syria? You're doing any old thing, any old how. You risked your neck in China, you're being completely reckless."

"Yes, completely, but as you can see, my neck's still in one piece, if a little more wrinkled than before!"

"Don't be impertinent, please."

"Mmmm, my Max. I like it when you take your professor's tone of voice with me. I think that's what attracted me to you the most when I was your student. But I'm not your student anymore. You know nothing about Adrian and nothing about the journey we went on. So if this little favour I'm asking is too much of a pain for you, it doesn't matter. Just give me the piece of paper back and I'll be off."

"Look me straight in the eyes and explain how this text is in any way going to help you with the research you've been doing for all these years?"

"Max, weren't you an archaeology professor once? How many years did you devote to becoming a researcher, then a teacher, before becoming a printer? Can you look me straight in the eyes and explain how your new job has any connection with what you accomplished in the past? Life is full of surprises, Max. I got kicked out of the Omo Valley twice. Maybe it was time for me to start rethinking my future."

"You must be absolutely besotted with that guy to be talking such nonsense."

"That guy, as you call him, may have loads of faults – he's absent-minded, sometimes dreamy, and incredibly clumsy – but he has something I've never experienced before: he captivates me, Max. Since I've met him my life has been turned upside down, you're right, but he makes me laugh, he moves me, he provokes me and he reassures me."

"It's worse than I thought. You're in love with him."

"Don't put words into my mouth."

"I'm not. You've said it yourself, and if you don't even realise you have, then you really are incredibly stupid."

Keira got off the desk and walked over to the glass wall overlooking the printing presses. She watched the paper spinning around the rollers at a furious pace and listened to the staccato sounds emanating from the folding machines. Suddenly they stopped and silence fell in the workshop as it closed for the night.

"Does that bother you?" Max went on. "And what about your beloved freedom?"

"Can you study this text or not?" she whispered.

"I've pored over your text a hundred times since your last visit. It was my way of thinking about you when you weren't here."

"Please don't, Max."

"Don't what? Have feelings for you anymore? What do you care? It's my problem, not yours."

Keira walked to the office door and turned the handle.

"Stay here, dummy!" ordered Max. "Come and sit back down on the corner of my desk and I'll tell you what I think of your theory. I might have been wrong. I don't much like the idea of the student outdoing the teacher, but I should've continued teaching, I suppose. It's possible that the word 'zenith' is a mistranslation in your text; what may've been meant was 'hypogeum,' which obviously changes the meaning completely. Hypogea are burial places – precursors to tombs – built by the Egyptians and the Chinese that differ in one way: although they too are funeral chambers accessed by a corridor, hypogea were constructed underground and not inside a pyramid or any other building. I'm sure I'm not teaching you anything new, but that interpretation would fit for at least one reason. This Ge'ez manuscript probably dates from the fourth or fifth millennium BC, which puts it right in the middle of protohistory – the period when the Asianic peoples first appeared."

"But the Semites who supposedly produced the text in Ge'ez weren't an Asianic people. At least, if my memory of my university lectures serves me right."

"You paid more attention in class than I thought. No, you're right. Their language was Afro-Asian, similar to that of the Berbers and the Egyptians. They appeared in the Syrian desert in the sixth millennium BC. But they most probably came into contact with each other, so could've passed on each other's history. The ones you're interested in for your theory belong to a people I didn't say much about in my lectures, the Pelasgians of the Hypogea. In the early part of the fourth millennium, some Pelasgians left Greece and settled in southern Italy: Sardinia to be precise. They then continued their journey to Anatolia, where they took to the sea and founded a new civilisation on the islands and coasts of the Mediterranean. There's no reason to think they didn't continue their crossing towards Egypt via Crete. What I'm trying to tell you is that in this text, the Semites and their ancestors could easily have been recounting an event that belonged to the history of the Pelasgians of the Hypogea."

"Do you think one of these Pelasgians could have travelled up the Nile as far as the Blue Nile?"

"As far as Ethiopia? I doubt it. In any case, such a journey couldn't have been undertaken by an individual – only by a group, over the course of two to three generations.

Having said that, I'd be inclined to think it would have been made in the opposite direction, from the source to the delta. Perhaps someone brought your mysterious object to the Pelasgians. If you really want me to help you, Keira, you have to tell me more."

Keira started pacing to and fro.

"Four hundred million years ago, five fragments formed a single object with astounding properties."

"Which is ridiculous, Keira, admit it. No human being was evolved enough at that stage to craft any kind of material. It would've been impossible. You know that as well as I do," protested Max.

"If Galileo had claimed that one day we'd send a radio telescope to the ends of our solar system, he'd have been burned alive before he'd even finished his sentence. If Clément Ader had claimed that man would walk on the moon, his aircraft would've been reduced to matchsticks before he'd even left the ground. Only twenty years ago, everyone said Lucy was our oldest ancestor, and if you'd have voiced the idea back then that the mother of humanity was ten million years old, you'd have been fired from your university job!"

"I was still a student twenty years ago!"

"Whatever. If we were to make a list of all the things that have ever been declared impossible yet have become a reality, it would take us several nights."

"Just one night with you would fill me with happiness."

"Don't be crude, Max. What I do know for sure is that someone discovered the object in the fourth or fifth millennium BC. For reasons I've still to understand myself, except perhaps because of the fear its properties instilled in them, the person or people who found it decided, since they couldn't completely destroy it, to break it into pieces. And that's exactly what the first line of the manuscript seems to be telling us: *I have split up the table of memoranda, and entrusted the parts it combines to the magisters of the colonies.*

"Sorry to interrupt you, but 'table of memoranda' very likely refers to a body of knowledge. If I go along with your idea, I'd say that the object was perhaps split up so that each of its fragments carried a piece of information to the far reaches of the world."

"Possible, but that's not what the end of the document suggests. For it to be completely clear, we need to know where these fragments have been scattered. We have two in our possession and a third has been found, but there are more still. Listen, Max, I didn't stop thinking about the Ge'ez text while I was in prison, especially a word in the second part of the first sentence: *entrusted...to the magisters of the colonies.* Who were these magisters in your opinion?"

"Scholars. Tribal chiefs probably. A magister is a master, if you prefer."

"So you were my magister?" asked Keira ironically.

"Something like that, yes."

"Well, that's my theory, dear magister," Keira continued. "A first fragment reappeared in a volcano in the middle of a lake on the border between Ethiopia and Kenya. We found another one, also in a volcano, this time on Narcondam Island in the Andamans. So, one in the south and one in the east. Both were located a few hundred kilometres from the source or the estuary of major rivers. The

Nile and the Blue Nile for the first, and the Irrawaddy and the Yangtze for the second."

"So?" interrupted Max.

"Let's accept, for a reason I haven't understood yet, that this object was deliberately split into four or five pieces and each one left at a different place on the globe. One was found in the east, another in the south, and the third – which was in fact the first to be discovered twenty or thirty years ago…"

"Where is it?"

"I've no idea. Stop interrupting me all the time, Max, it's irritating. I'm prepared to bet the two remaining objects are in the north and the west."

"I certainly wouldn't want to irritate you – I sense I'm annoying you enough as it is – but the north and the west, that's pretty vast."

"Look, if you're just going to make fun of me, I'd rather go home."

Keira jumped up and headed for Max's office door for the second time that evening.

"Don't go, Keira! And stop acting so bossy, you're being annoying too, dammit! Is this a monologue or a conversation? Come on, carry on your reasoning; I won't interrupt you anymore."

Keira went and sat back down next to Max. She took a sheet of paper and drew a rough planisphere showing the continental land masses.

"We know the major routes taken during the first human migrations that populated the planet. A first colony left Africa and made its way towards Europe, while a second went towards Asia," Keira said, drawing a big arrow on the paper, "and split up north of the Andaman Sea. Some of them continued to India, others went through Burma and then crossed Thailand, Cambodia, Vietnam, Indonesia, the Philippines, New Zealand and Papua New Guinea, before arriving in Australia; yet others," she said, drawing another arrow, "headed north, crossing Mongolia and Russia, and travelling up the Yana River towards the Bering Strait. This third colony travelled along the frozen coastlines of Greenland during the ice age before reaching Alaska via the Beaufort Sea fifteen to twenty thousand years ago. From there, a fourth colony descended the North American continent and arrived in Monte Verde twelve to fifteen thousand years ago.[1] Perhaps these are the same routes taken by the people carrying the fragments five to seven thousand years ago: a tribe of messengers left for the Andamans and ended their journey on Narcondam Island, and another headed towards the source of the Nile, as far as the border between Kenya and Ethiopia."

"And you've come to the conclusion that another two of these 'messenger peoples' may have reached the west and the north in order to transport the other fragments?"

"The text reads: *I have…entrusted the parts it combines to the magisters of the colonies.* Since such a journey couldn't have been accomplished by one generation, each group of messengers went to take a piece similar to my pendant to the magisters of the first colonies."

---

1 *Sources*: Susan Anton, New York University; Alison Brooks, George Washington University; Peter Forster, University of Cambridge; James F. O'Connell, University of Utah; Stephen Oppenheimer, University of Oxford; Spencer Wells, National Geographic Society; Ofer Bar-Yisef, Harvard University.

"Your hypothesis holds together, but it isn't necessarily right. Do you remember what I taught you at university? Just because a theory seems logical, it doesn't mean it's proven."

"And you also told me that just because something hasn't been found, it doesn't mean it doesn't exist."

"What are you expecting from me, Keira?"

"To tell me what you'd do in my place," she answered.

"I'll never possess the woman you've become, but I see I'll always keep a part of the student you once were. That's something at least."

Max stood up and took over pacing up and down his office.

"You're a pain with your questions, Keira. I don't know what I'd do in your place. If I'd been good at these kinds of riddles, I'd have abandoned teaching and dusty university halls to carry out my profession."

"You were frightened of snakes, you hated insects and you dreaded being without your creature comforts. That's got nothing to do with your powers of reasoning, Max. You were just a bit too middle class, it's not a sin."

"When it comes to pleasing you it is, apparently."

"Do stop it and answer me! What would you do in my place?"

"You told me about a third fragment discovered thirty years ago. I'd start by trying to find out exactly where it was found. If it was in a volcano a few dozen or hundred kilometres from a major river in the west or the north, then that information would back up your reasoning. If, however, it was found in a sugar beet field in France or a potato field in England, you can bin your hypothesis and start all over again. That's what I'd do before going

EUROPE

ASIA

AFRICA

RIFT
VALLEY

INDIAN
OCEAN

AUSTRALIA

- 40 000
YEARS AGO

- 40 000 /
- 30 000
YEARS AGO

- 70 000 /
- 50 000
YEARS AGO

- 200 000
YEARS AGO

- 50 000
YEARS AGO

(Source : *National Geographic*)

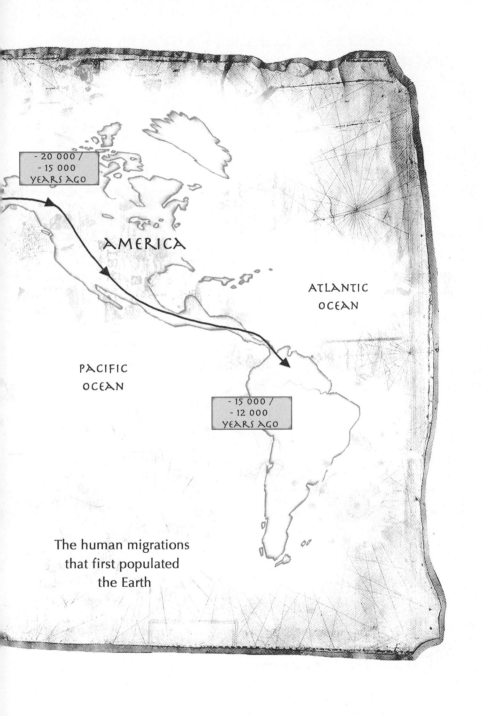

- 20 000 /
- 15 000
YEARS AGO

AMERICA

ATLANTIC
OCEAN

PACIFIC
OCEAN

- 15 000 /
- 12 000
YEARS AGO

The human migrations
that first populated
the Earth

off I don't know where. Keira, you're looking for a stone hidden somewhere on the planet – that's completely un-realistic!"

"Isn't it unrealistic to spend your life in the middle of an arid valley looking for bones hundreds of thousands of years old with nothing but your intuition to guide you? Or to look for a pyramid buried under the sand in the middle of the desert? Our profession is just one big Utopia, Max. But for each of us, it's also a dream of making discoveries that we try to turn into reality."

"There's no point getting so worked up. You asked me what I'd do in your place and I replied. Find out where that third fragment was unearthed and you'll know if you're on the right track."

"And if I am?"

"Come back and see me and we'll think about the route you should take to pursue your dream. Now, I have to say something that might annoy you again."

"What?"

"Time obviously flies by for you when you're in my company, which I'm delighted about. But it's 9.30pm and I'm very hungry. Shall I take you out to dinner?"

Keira looked at her watch and leapt up.

"Jeanne, Adrian – shit!"

It was nearly ten o'clock when Keira rang her sister's doorbell.

"Aren't you planning on eating this evening?" Jeanne questioned her as she opened the door.

"Is Adrian here?" Keira asked, looking over her sister's shoulder.

"Unless he's got the power to teleport himself, I don't see how he could be."

"I told him to meet me here."

"And did you give him the entry code for the main door?"

"Didn't he call?"

"Did you give him my number?"

Keira said nothing.

"In that case, perhaps he left a message for me at work. But I left quite early to prepare you a meal, which you'll now find in the bin. Overcooked – don't hold it against me!"

"But where's Adrian?"

"I thought he was with you. I thought you'd decided to have a romantic evening together."

"No, we didn't. I was with Max."

"It gets better and better. And can I know why?"

"For our research, Jeanne. Don't start. But how am I going to find him?"

"Call him!"

Keira rushed to the phone and got through to my voice-mail (I had a minimum of self-esteem!). She left me a long message: "I'm sorry, time flew. It's unforgivable of me, but it was fascinating. I've got some fantastic things to tell you. Where are you? I know it's past ten, but call me back. Call me back!" Then she left a second one giving me her sister's home phone number. And a third saying she was really worried by me not calling back. Then a fourth in which she was a bit annoyed. And a fifth in which she accused me of being nasty. Then a sixth at around three o'clock in the morning, and a last one where she hung up without saying a word.

*

I'd slept in a small hotel on Ile St-Louis. As soon as I'd eaten breakfast, I got a taxi over to Jeanne's, whose building still required an entry code that I didn't have. I went and sat down on a bench on the pavement opposite and read my newspaper.

Jeanne came out of her apartment building shortly afterwards. She recognised me and crossed over the road.

"Keira was sick with worry."

"Well, that makes two of us."

"I'm sorry," Jeanne said, "I'm furious with her too."

"I'm not furious," I answered straight back.

"Well, you should be!"

Jeanne said goodbye, started walking off, and then turned back to me.

"Her meeting with Max last night was strictly professional, but mum's the word!"

"Would you be so kind as to give me the entry code to your apartment building?"

Jeanne scribbled it on a piece of paper and left for work.

I stayed on the bench and read my newspaper right to the last page. Then I went to a little baker's shop on the street corner and bought a few French pastries.

Keira opened the door for me, her eyes still clouded with sleep.

"Where were you?" she asked, rubbing her eyes. "I was worried to death!"

"Croissant? Pain au chocolat? One of each?"

"Adrian!"

"Eat your breakfast and get dressed. There's a Eurostar leaving at noon; we can still make it."

"I have to go and see Ivory first, it's very important."

"Actually, there's a Eurostar every hour, so let's go and see him."

Keira made us some coffee and gave me the same presentation she'd given Max. While she was explaining her theory, I thought about that interesting thing the antiques dealer had said regarding armillary spheres. I didn't know why but I felt like calling Erwin to discuss it with him. Keira noticed my attention had wandered and called out to me.

"Do you want me to come and see the old professor with you?" I said, picking up her conversation again.

"Would you like to tell me where you spent the night?"

"No. I mean, I could, but I'm not going to," I replied with a big smile on my face.

"I really couldn't care less."

"Well, let's not mention it anymore then. Back to Ivory – that's where we were, isn't it?"

"He hasn't come back to the museum, but Jeanne has given me his home phone number. I'm going to call him."

Keira headed towards her sister's room, where the telephone was, then turned to me and said, "So where did you sleep?"

Ivory agreed to see us at his place. He lived in an elegant apartment on Ile St-Louis, a stone's throw from my hotel. When he opened his door, I recognised the man I'd watched getting out of a taxi the day before as I leafed through my book on the café terrace. He invited us into his sitting room and offered us tea or coffee.

"It's a pleasure to see you both again. What can I do for you?"

Keira went straight to the point and asked him if he knew where the fragment he'd told her about at the museum had been discovered.

"Perhaps you could tell me first why that interests you."

"I think we've made some progress in interpreting the text written in Ge'ez."

"How extremely intriguing. What have you learned?"

Keira explained her theory about the people of the hypogea to him. In the fourth or fifth millennium BC, people had found the object when it was still whole, and split it up. According to the manuscript, groups had formed to take the different pieces to all four corners of the globe.

"It's a wonderful theory," exclaimed Ivory, "that might well make sense. Except you have no idea what could have motivated those journeys, which would have been as perilous as they are unlikely."

"I do have an idea actually," answered Keira.

Borrowing what she'd learned from Max, she suggested each piece carried a piece of knowledge that needed to be revealed.

"I don't agree with you on that. I'd even be inclined to say the opposite were true," retorted Ivory. "The end of the text gives every reason to think they carried a secret to be kept. Read it for yourself: *…may the shadows of infinity remain concealed.*"

While Ivory debated with Keira, the "shadows of infinity" made me think about the antiques dealer again.

"What's intriguing about armillary spheres is not so much what they show, but what they don't show and what we can nevertheless guess," I muttered.

"I beg your pardon?" asked Ivory, turning to me.

"The void and time," I said.

"What are you on about?" enquired Keira.

"Nothing, an idea that isn't related to your conversation, but just sprang to mind."

"And where do you think you'll find the missing pieces?" continued Ivory.

"The ones we have in our possession were both discovered in a volcano crater a few dozen kilometres from a major river. One in the east, the other in the south. So I suspect the others are hidden in similar places in the west and the north."

"Do you have the two fragments on you?" asked Ivory insistently, his eyes sparkling.

Keira and I glanced sideways at each other. She took off her pendant, I pulled out the one I kept safely in my inside jacket pocket and we laid them on the coffee table. Keira put them together and they turned that bright blue that never failed to amaze us. Except that this time, I noticed they sparkled less brightly, as if the objects were losing their brilliance.

"That's astonishing!" exclaimed Ivory. "Even more so than anything I'd imagined."

"What had you imagined?" asked Keira, intrigued.

"Nothing, nothing in particular," spluttered Ivory, "but you have to admit it's an incredible phenomenon, especially when we know how old the object is."

"Now please will you tell us where your fragment was discovered?"

"It isn't mine, sadly. It was found thirty years ago in the Peruvian Andes, but unfortunately for your theory, it wasn't in a volcano crater."

"Where then?" enquired Keira.

"About a hundred and fifty kilometres northeast of Lake Titicaca."

"In what circumstances?" I asked.

"During a mission conducted by a team of Dutch geologists. They were travelling up towards the source of the Amazon River and spotted the object because of its unusual shape in a cave where they had taken shelter from the bad weather. They wouldn't have paid it any special attention, but the mission leader witnessed the same phenomenon as you. That stormy night, lightning flashes caused the famous projection of luminous dots on the side of his tent. The episode made even more of an impression on him when he realised at daybreak that the canvas had become permeable to the light: thousands of little holes had been made in it. As there are frequent storms in that region, the explorer experienced the same thing several times, which made him realise it wasn't just any old stone. He brought the fragment back and had it examined more closely."

"Is it possible to meet this geologist?"

"He died a few months later – a silly fall during another expedition."

"Where's the fragment he discovered?"

"Somewhere safe, but I'm not at all certain where."

"So the volcano idea isn't right, but it was definitely found in the west."

"You can say that all right."

"And a few dozen kilometres from a tributary of the Amazon."

"That's right too," Ivory continued.

"Two out of three theories confirmed. That's not so bad," Keira said.

"I'm afraid it won't help much with discovering the other pieces. Two of them were uncovered by accident. And you were just very lucky with the third."

"It involved my hanging above a two-thousand-metre drop, flying over Burma practically skimming the ground in something with wings that passed for a plane; I nearly drowned, and Adrian nearly died of pneumonia. Not forgetting three months spent in prison in China. I don't really see how you think luck comes into any of that!"

"I didn't mean to play down your respective talents. Let me think about your theory for a few days. I'll bury myself in my reading again and if I find the slightest piece of information that could help your investigation, I'll call you."

Keira noted my telephone number down on a piece of paper and held it out to Ivory.

"Where are you planning to go?" he asked as he showed us out.

"London. We have some research to do too."

"Have a good trip to England then. One last thing before you go: you were right a moment ago when you said that luck hadn't really been with you on your travels. Consequently, I advise you to take the greatest care. For a start, don't show the phenomenon you've just let me see to anyone else."

We left the elderly professor, picked up my bag from the hotel, where Keira made no comment about the previous evening, and I accompanied her to the museum so she could kiss Jeanne goodbye before we left.

London

I hadn't paid much attention to the bizarre-looking couple when they jostled me on the platform at the Gare du Nord without so much as an apology, but I ran into them again in the buffet car. At first glance they looked like your average badly dressed English youth and his equally scruffy girlfriend. The boy stared at me strangely as they continued on up the aisle towards the front of the train. We were due to stop at Ashford in about fifteen minutes, so presumably they were going to fetch their luggage before getting off. The employee at the fast food counter (though "fast" seemed a misnomer, considering the endless queue to get to him) let out an audible sigh as he watched the shaven-headed young couple move off.

"Don't judge them by their haircuts," I told him, ordering a coffee. "They're probably very nice once you get to know them."

"Could be," he replied doubtfully, "but that fellow's spent the whole trip filing his nails with a cutter and the girl just sat there watching him. It hardly makes you want to strike up a conversation with them!"

I paid for my coffee and started walking back to my seat. As I entered the carriage where I'd left a sleepy Keira, I bumped into the two oddballs loitering around near the luggage compartment where we'd left our bags. I went up to them. The youth made a sign at the girl, who turned around and barred my way.

"It's being used," she said arrogantly.

"I can see that," I replied, "but what for?"

The youth stepped between us. He took his knife out of his pocket and told me he didn't like the way I'd spoken to his girlfriend.

I'd spent quite a bit of my adolescence in Ladbroke Grove, where my best friend at school used to live. I knew all about the pavements some gangs claimed as their territory, the crossroads we weren't allowed to use, and the cafés you wouldn't want to play foosball in. I could tell these two characters were looking for a fight. If I moved, the girl would jump me from behind and pin my arms to my side while her friend beat me up. Once they'd knocked me flat, they'd be kicking my ribs in to finish me off. It wasn't all gardens with green lawns in the England of my childhood, and things hadn't changed much since then. It's never easy to act on instinct when you've got principles, but I gave the girl an almighty slap that sent her flying into the luggage, clutching her cheek. The astounded youth jumped into my path, switching his knife from one hand to the other. It was time I let the adult I'd supposedly become take over from my inner teenager.

"Ten seconds," I said to him. "You've got ten seconds before I take that knife away from you. And if I get hold of it, you'll be climbing off this train naked. Is that what you want? Or are you going to put it back in your pocket, and we call it quits?"

The girl got up, furious, and came back to challenge me. Her boyfriend was looking increasingly nervous.

"Slash the bastard," she screamed. "Stab him, Tom!"

"You really should show your girlfriend who's the boss, Tom. Put that knife away before one of us gets hurt."

"Will someone tell me what's going on?" Keira asked, coming up behind me.

"A little argument," I replied, forcing her back.

"Want me to call for help?"

The two youngsters weren't about to hang around waiting for reinforcements to arrive. The train was slowing down; I could see Ashford Station platform looming up. Tom pulled his girlfriend along, still making threatening gestures with his knife. Keira and I stood stock-still, our gaze fixed on the blade he was waving around in front of us.

"Shove off!" he snarled. He jumped on to the platform as soon as the train came to a standstill, and the two of them took off at top speed.

Keira stood there, speechless, until the disembarking passengers forced us to move aside. We went back to our seats and the train jerked forward again. Keira wanted me to call the police, but it was much too late. Our two thugs must have made a break for it, and my mobile was in my bag. I got up and went to check it was still there. Keira and I looked through our bags. The contents had been messed up a bit, but there didn't seem to be anything missing. I shoved my mobile and my passport into my jacket pocket. By the time we reached London we'd forgotten the whole incident.

*

A feeling of sheer happiness flooded through me as I stood at the door of my little house. I was fidgeting with impatience at the thought of going in. I rooted fruitlessly through my pockets for my keys. I was sure I'd had them when I left Paris. Luckily my neighbour caught sight of me from her window. Old habits die hard, and she offered to let me go through her garden again.

"You know where I keep the ladder," she told me. "I'm busy ironing. Don't worry, I'll put it away when I'm done."

I thanked her, and was jumping over her fence a few seconds later. I still hadn't got my back door fixed – maybe I should give up on it altogether – so I gave the handle a sharp yank and finally got inside. I went to open the door to Keira, who was waiting for me in the street.

We spent the rest of the afternoon doing our grocery shopping in the neighbourhood. A fruit and veg stall caught Keira's eye, and she filled up her basket with enough provisions to last us through a siege. Unfortunately, as it turned out, we didn't have time for dinner that evening.

I was in the kitchen dicing courgettes on Keira's orders while she made up a sauce she refused to give me the recipe for, when the phone rang. Not my mobile – the land line. Keira and I exchanged an intrigued look. I went to the living room to pick it up.

"So it's true. You're back!"

"We arrived a little while ago, my dear Walter."

"Thanks for letting me know – really too kind of you."

"We've only just got off the train."

"I can't believe I heard you were back through a FedEx courier. You're not exactly the world-famous Tom Hanks, as far as I know."

"A courier let you know we were back? That's weird."

"It so happens a letter addressed to you was delivered to the Academy. Well, not you, actually. It's got your friend's name written on the envelope, care of you. Tell them they should address your correspondence to me next time. It also has 'Extremely Urgent' on it. So, since I seem to have become your personal postman, do you want me to bring it over?"

"Hold on – let me ask Keira about it."

"An envelope addressed to me and delivered to your Academy? What's all this about?" she asked.

I was as much in the dark as she was. I asked if she was okay with Walter's kind offer to drop off the envelope. Her expressive gestures made it amply clear that it was the last thing she felt like. I found myself in an awkward position, with Walter breathing in my left ear and Keira rolling her eyes to my right. A decision had to be made, so I asked Walter if he could wait for me at the Academy. I told him I couldn't expect him to come all the way across London; I'd drive over and pick up the letter. I hung up, relieved I'd hit on this excellent compromise, but when I turned round I realised Keira didn't share my enthusiasm. I promised her I'd be back within an hour, tops. I pulled on a raincoat, got my spare keys out of the desk drawer and walked up my road to the small garage where my car lived.

I sniffed the familiar intoxicating smell of old leather as I got in. But as I drove out of the garage I found myself having to brake sharply so as not to run over Keira, who was standing ramrod straight in front of my headlights. She ran round and slipped into the passenger seat.

"That letter could've waited till tomorrow, couldn't it?" she said, slamming the door shut.

"Walter said it had 'Urgent' written on it in red letters. But I can go on my own, don't feel obliged to come."

"I'm the one it's addressed to and you're dying to see your pal, so let's get going."

Monday evenings are about the only time you can get through London traffic at any speed. It took us barely twenty minutes to reach the Academy. It started raining on the way – one of those heavy showers the city gets so often. Walter was waiting for us in front of the main door. The bottoms of his trousers were soaked and so was his jacket, and he was wearing his "I've had a terrible day" face. He bent down to the car window and handed us the envelope. I couldn't even offer him a lift home, my coupé being a two-seater. We decided to at least wait until he'd got a taxi. As soon as one stopped, Walter coldly took his leave of me, not looking at Keira, and went off. We sat there in the car with the rain beating down on the roof and the envelope on Keira's knees.

"Aren't you going to open it?"

"It's Max's handwriting," she murmured.

"That man must be psychic!"

"Why do you say that?"

"I suspect he saw us preparing our romantic dinner and waited till your sauce was cooked to perfection to send you a letter and screw up our evening."

"That's not funny."

"Maybe not, but you have to admit you wouldn't think it was funny if one of my ex-girlfriends had interrupted us."

Keira ran a hand over the envelope.

"And which of your ex-girlfriends would be writing to you?" she asked.

"That's not what I said."

"Answer me."

"I don't have any ex-girlfriends."

"You mean you were a virgin when we met?"

"I mean *I* don't have any ex-girlfriends who were my university lecturers."

"Very sensitive, that little remark."

"Are you going to open that envelope or not?"

"I did hear you say 'romantic dinner,' didn't I?"

"I may have said it."

"Are you in love with me, Adrian?"

"Open that envelope, Keira!"

"I'll take that as a 'yes.' Drive us back to your house and let's go straight up to bed. I'd much rather have you for dinner than fried courgettes."

"I'll take that as a compliment. What about the letter?"

"It can wait until tomorrow. And so can Max."

That first night in London brought a lot of memories flooding back. You fell asleep after we'd made love. The bedroom windows were ajar; I sat looking at you, watching your steady breathing. I could see the scars on your back that time would never heal. I traced them with my fingertips. The warmth of your body made my desire for you surge up as strongly as it had at the start of the evening. You moaned in your sleep and I took my hand away. You pulled it back, your sleep-thickened voice asking why I'd stopped caressing you. I moved my lips over your skin, but you'd fallen asleep again. So I told you I loved you. "Me too," you murmured. Your voice was barely audible, but those two words were enough to carry me away into your night.

We were both so dead tired we slept through the morning. It was nearly midday when I woke. Your side of the bed was empty. I found you in the kitchen wearing one of my shirts and a pair of socks you'd found in a drawer. Our confession to each other the previous night had sparked a sudden shyness, and made us awkward and distant with each other. I asked if you'd read Max's letter. You jerked your head towards the unopened envelope on the table. For some reason, at that instant, I didn't want you to ever open it. I would've happily put it away in a drawer for us to forget about. I didn't want that crazy chase to start again. I dreamed of spending time with you, just you and me, in this house; we'd only go out to stroll along the Thames, have a browse in Camden Market or a feast of scones in a Notting Hill café, but you opened the envelope and none of it ever happened.

You unfolded the letter and read it out to me. Maybe you wanted to show me you had nothing to hide from me after last night.

Keira,
Your visit to the print works made me unhappy. Seeing you again at the Tuileries has reawakened feelings I'd thought were dead.

I've never told you how painful our separation was for me and how much your leaving, your long silences and your absence made me suffer. Perhaps the hardest thing to bear was knowing you were happy, without a thought for our time together. But I've had to face up to facts: you're a woman whose mere presence is enough to make a man happier than he could ever hope to be, but your self-centredness and absences create a permanent emptiness. I ended up realising that it's no use trying to hold on to you, no one can do that; your love is sincere, but it doesn't last. I had a few seasons of happiness and that's something, though the scars take a long time to heal for the people you love and leave.

I'd rather not see you again. Don't tell me how you're getting on, don't come and see me when you're in Paris. This isn't an order from your former teacher; it's a request from your friend.

I've thought about our conversation a lot. You were an awful student but as I've already told you, you have instinct – a precious quality in your line of work. I'm proud of what you've achieved, even if I can't take any credit for it – any teacher would have detected the potential of the archaeologist you've become. The theory you set out to me isn't implausible; I want to believe it, and perhaps you're getting close to a discovery that we can't quite understand yet. Follow the trail of the Pelasgians of the Hypogea – who knows where it will lead you.

As soon as you left the works, I went back home, opened books I hadn't read for years, took out my archived notebooks and read through my notes. You know how obsessively tidy I am, how everything is filed away and well-ordered in my den, where we spent such happy times. In one of my notebooks, I found the details of a man whose research you might find useful. He has devoted his life to studying the great human migrations and written several papers on the Asianic peoples, although he's published hardly anything – he just gave a few talks at a few obscure venues such as the one where I heard him speak many years ago. He too had some innovative ideas about the journeys undertaken by the early civilisations of the Mediterranean basin. He had several detractors, but in our field, who doesn't? There's so much jealousy among our colleagues. This man is a very learned scholar and my respect for him is unbounded. Go and see him, Keira. I've been told he retired to Yell, a small island in Shetland off the northern tip of Scotland. Apparently he lives there as a recluse and refuses to speak to anyone about his work – he's a wounded man; but maybe your charm will draw him out of his lair and make him talk.

The famous discovery you've always aspired to, the one you dream of giving your name to, is perhaps finally within your reach. I believe in you; you'll achieve what you've set out to do.

Good luck.

Max

Keira folded the letter and put it back in the envelope. She got up, stacked her breakfast dishes in the sink and turned on the tap.

"Shall I make you some coffee?" she asked, her back to me.

I didn't reply.

"I'm sorry, Adrian."

"Because that man's still in love with you?"

"No, because of what he says about me."

"Do you see yourself as the woman he makes you out to be?"

"I don't know, maybe not anymore. But he's being sincere, so there must be some truth to it."

"He's saying that hurting the man who loves you comes easier to you than to question your self-image."

"Do you think I'm selfish too?"

"I wasn't the one who wrote that letter. But it does seem a bit cowardly to get on with your life and tell yourself that because you're fine the other person will be too, and that it's all just a question of time. I hardly think I need tell you, the anthropologist, about the wonderful human instinct to survive."

"Don't be cynical. It doesn't suit you."

"I'm English, it must be in my genes. Let's change the subject, shall we? I'm going to walk to the travel agency – I'd like to get some fresh air. You want to go to Yell, don't you?"

Keira decided to come with me. We arranged to depart the next day. We'd be landing at Sumburgh Airport on the main island of Shetland after a stopover in Glasgow. A ferry would take us to Yell from there.

After picking up our tickets at the travel agency, we went for a stroll down the King's Road. I'm a regular in this area; I like to walk all the way up the long shopping street, then turn off into Sydney Street for a meander through the lanes of Chelsea Farmers Market. We'd arranged to meet Walter there, and our long walk had made me hungry.

Walter scrutinised the menu and ordered a double hamburger. He bent over to whisper in my ear. "The Academy's given me a cheque for you – the equivalent of six months' salary."

"What for?" I asked.

"That's the bad news. Because of your repeated absences, you're being made an honorary professor. You no longer have tenure."

"You mean they've fired me?"

"No, not exactly. I did my best to plead your cause, but we're in the thick of budgetary restrictions and the board of directors have been ordered to cut all unnecessary costs."

"Should I infer that I'm an unnecessary cost as far as the board is concerned?"

"Adrian, the board members don't even know what you look like – you practically haven't set foot in the Academy since you got back from Chile. You have to understand them."

Walter's face grew even gloomier.

"What now?"

"You'll have to clear your desk. I've been asked to send your things to your home address. Someone else needs the desk from next week on."

"They've already hired my successor?"

"No, not exactly. Let's just say they've assigned the class you were meant to teach to a thoroughly reliable colleague of yours, and he needs a place to prepare his lectures, correct papers and meet students. Your office would suit him perfectly."

"May I know the name of this charming colleague who's kicking me out of my office behind my back?"

"You don't know him. He only joined the Academy three years ago."

Walter's last sentence made me realise that the board was making me pay for taking advantage of the freedom I'd been given. Walter was mortified, and Keira wouldn't look at me. I took the cheque, firmly resolving I'd cash it that very day. I was furious. But I had no one to blame but myself.

"The Shamal has blown as far as England," Keira murmured.

Her bittersweet allusion to the wind that had chased her away from her Ethiopian site proved that the tension underlying our conversation that morning hadn't completely subsided.

"What will you do?" Walter asked.

"Well, since I'm now unemployed, we'll be able to go travelling."

Keira was battling with a particularly recalcitrant slice of meat. I got the impression she'd have tried to cut her plate up if it kept her out of the conversation.

"We've heard from Max," I told Walter.

"Who's Max?"

"An old friend of my girlfriend's."

The slice of roast beef skidded out from under Keira's

knife and travelled a fair distance before landing between a waiter's legs.

"I'm not all that hungry," she explained. "I had a late breakfast."

"Was it the letter I gave you yesterday?" Walter asked.

Keira took a gulp of beer. It went down the wrong way and made her cough noisily.

"Carry on, carry on," she said, wiping her mouth. "Just pretend I'm not here."

"Yes, that was it."

"Does it have something to do with your travel plans? Are you going far?"

"To northern Scotland – the Shetland Islands."

"I know the area very well. I used to holiday there as a child. My father would take the whole family to Whalsay. The landscape's barren, but it's wonderful in summer – never gets hot. Dad hated the heat. The winters are harsh, but Dad loved winter, though we never went there at that time of year. Which island are you going to?"

"Yell."

"I've been there too. Britain's most haunted house is at the northern end of Yell. The Windhouse, it's called – it's a ruin, and it really is wind-battered. Why are you going there?"

"We're going to pay a visit to one of Max's acquaintances."

"I see. What does he do?"

"He's retired."

"I get it. You're off to the north of Scotland to meet a retired friend of an old friend of Keira's. There must be some logic to it. There's something very peculiar about the two of you this morning. You're not hiding anything from me, are you?"

"You do know Adrian's got a terrible character, don't you, Walter?" Keira suddenly asked.

"Yes, I'd noticed," he replied.

"Then you know everything there is to know."

Keira asked me for the house keys and said she'd rather walk back and leave us men to finish this fascinating conversation. She said goodbye to Walter and left the restaurant.

"Have the two of you argued? What have you gone and done now, Adrian?"

"I don't believe this. Why would it be my fault?"

"Because she's the one who left the table, not you – that's why. So. I'm all ears. What is it you've done now?"

"Nothing at all, for God's sake, apart from stoically listening to the lovelorn prose of the fellow who wrote her that letter."

"You read a letter addressed to her?"

"She read it out to me."

"Well, at least that proves she's being honest. Anyway, I thought this Max was a friend?"

"A friend who was naked in her bed a few years ago."

"You weren't exactly a virgin either when you met her, my dear chap. Would you like me to remind you of all the women you told me about? Your first marriage, your doctor, your redheaded barmaid… shall I go on?"

"I've never gone out with a redheaded barmaid!"

"Oh, you haven't? That must have been me then. Never mind. Don't tell me you're stupid enough to be jealous of her past?"

"Fine, I won't tell you that."

"Honestly, you should be thanking this Max, not hating him."

"I really don't see why."

"Because if he hadn't been idiotic enough to let her go, the two of you wouldn't be together now."

I looked at Walter intently. His reasoning wasn't totally off the mark.

"All right, buy me dessert and then you can go and apologise to her. What a bungler you are."

The chocolate mousse must have been delicious; Walter begged me to stay long enough for him to eat another one. I think he was probably trying to extend our time together to talk to me about Aunt Elena, or rather to get me to talk about her. He was planning to invite her to come and spend a few days in London and wanted to know if I thought she'd agree. I couldn't remember my aunt ever having travelled any further than Athens, but nothing surprised me anymore. For some time now, everything had begun to seem possible. Even so, I told Walter to take it slow. He listened to the copious advice I gave him and then confessed, almost blushing, that in fact he'd already invited her, and that she'd told him she'd always dreamed of visiting London. They'd decided she would come out at the end of the month.

"If you already know her answer, why are we having this conversation?"

"Because I wanted to make sure you wouldn't be offended. You're the only man in the family, so I obviously want your permission to go out with your aunt."

"I didn't get the impression you were really asking for my permission, but maybe I missed something."

"Let's say I was sounding you out. If I'd heard the slightest hint of hostility in your reply when I asked if you thought I stood any chance with her…"

"…you'd have shelved your plans?"

"No," Walter admitted, "but I'd have begged Elena to convince you not to resent me for it. Adrian, we barely knew each other only a few months ago. I've grown attached to you since then. I wouldn't want to risk upsetting you in any way. Our friendship is very precious to me."

"Walter," I said, looking him straight in the eye.

"What? You think my relationship with your aunt is inappropriate, don't you?"

"I think it's fantastic that my aunt has finally found with you the happiness she's been looking for all these years. You were right when you said in Hydra that if you were twenty years older than her no one would think twice about it, so let's not worry about hypocritical provincial middle-class prejudices."

"It's not just the provinces. I think people in London would take a dim view of it too."

"Nobody's saying you should get into a passionate clinch with her right under the window of the Academy's board of directors. Though it wouldn't be a bad idea, come to think of it."

"So do I have your consent?"

"You don't need it."

"I do, actually. Your aunt would much rather have you talk to your mother about her little trip – if you agree, that is."

My mobile vibrated in my pocket. My home number showed up on the display. Keira was probably getting impatient. She should have stayed with us then.

"Aren't you going to answer that?" Walter asked, concerned.

"No. Where were we?"

"The little favour your aunt and I were hoping you'd do us."

"You want me to tell my mother about her sister's indiscretions? I have a hard enough time telling her about mine. But I'll do my best. I owe you that much."

Walter took my hands in his and squeezed them warmly.

"Thank you, thank you, thank you," he said, shaking me as if I were a fruit-laden plum tree.

The mobile vibrated again. I left it on the table where I'd placed it, and turned to find the waitress to order a coffee.

Paris

Ivory was sitting at his desk updating his notes by the light of a small lamp. The telephone rang. He took off his glasses and picked it up.

"I wanted to inform you that I've delivered your package to the person it was addressed to."

"Has she read it?"

"Yes, this very morning."

"And how did they react?"

"It's too soon to say."

Ivory thanked Walter. He called another number and waited for the man at the other end to pick up.

"Your letter has arrived safe and sound and I wanted to thank you. You did write everything I told you to?"

"I copied what you said word for word. I merely took the liberty of adding a few lines."

"I'd told you not to change any of it."

"So why didn't you send it yourself, or tell her all of it in person? Why use me as your go-between? I don't understand what you're playing at."

"How I wish it were just a game. She takes you far

more seriously than me – more than anyone else, in fact. I'm not trying to flatter you, Max. You were her teacher, not me. When I call her in a few days to confirm the information she'll be given on Yell, she'll be all the more convinced. Don't they say it's always a good idea to get a second opinion?"

"Not when both opinions are held by the same person."

"But we're the only ones who know that, aren't we? If you're not comfortable with it, remember I'm doing this for their safety. Let me know as soon as she calls you back. She'll call – I'm sure of it. And when she does, make sure she can't reach you, as we agreed. I'll give you a new number to call me at tomorrow. Goodnight, Max."

London

We left first thing in the morning. Keira was groggy and unsteady on her feet. She went back to sleep in the taxi and I had to shake her awake when we reached Heathrow.

"I'm becoming less and less fond of flying," she said as the plane took off.

"That's a little inconvenient for an explorer. Are you planning to walk all the way to the Arctic?"

"There are ships."

"In winter?"

"Let me sleep."

We had a three-hour stopover in Glasgow. I'd have liked to take Keira around the city, but the weather was hardly encouraging. Keira worried our plane wouldn't take off because of the increasingly foul weather. The sky was turning black and large clouds obscured the horizon. A voice over the PA system announced one flight delay after another and thanked the passengers for their patience. A spectacular thunderstorm had left the runway waterlogged and most of the flights were cancelled, but ours was one of the few still displayed on the departure board.

"What do you think of our chances of getting the old man to talk to us?" I asked, watching the refreshment bar staff shutting up shop.

"What do you think of our chances of getting to Shetland in one piece?"

"I shouldn't think they'd make us take unnecessary risks."

"I'm fascinated by your faith in the human race," Keira replied.

The storm was moving away, and a hostess took advantage of a short calm spell to hurry us along to the departure gate. Keira trailed unwillingly along the gangway.

"Look," I said, pointing out of the window, "there's a clear patch there – we're going to fly through it and avoid the storm clouds."

"Is your clear patch going to follow us all the way to where we'll be landing?"

The good thing about the turbulence that shook us throughout the fifty-five minute flight was that Keira clung to me the whole time.

We reached the Shetland Islands amid driving rain in the middle of the afternoon. The travel agency had suggested we rent a car at the airport. We drove through ninety-odd kilometres of open plains where herds of sheep were grazing. The sheep are kept outside, so each local farmer dyes his herd to distinguish it from the livestock of neighbouring farms. As a result, the countryside is dotted with pretty colours that contrast with the greyness of the sky.

At Toft we got on a ferry sailing to Ulsta, a small village on the east coast of Yell; the rest of the island is made up of scattered hamlets. I had booked us a room at a bed and breakfast in Burravoe – possibly the only tourist accommodation on the island. It turned out to be a farm where the owners rented one of the rooms to the odd visitor who came all the way out here.

Yell is an island at the ends of the earth – an expanse of moorland thirty-five kilometres long and barely twelve kilometres wide. Nine hundred and fifty seven people live on the island. The head count is precise – every birth or death has a significant impact on the place's demographics. Otters, grey seals and terns definitely outnumber humans here.

The farmer and his wife came out to greet us. They seemed like a very pleasant couple, although their accent made it impossible to understand everything they said. Dinner was served at 6pm, and an hour later Keira and I went up to our room, where the only light came from two candles. A gusty wind was blowing outside, making the shutters rattle. The blades of a rusty wind turbine creaked in the darkness, and rain was hammering at the windowpanes. Keira snuggled up to me, but neither of us was up to making love that night.

I had fewer regrets about our early night the next morning, when we were woken at an unearthly hour by the sounds of sheep bleating, pigs grunting and various breeds of poultry cackling – the only thing missing was a cow mooing. That said, the eggs, bacon and sheep's milk we were given for breakfast tasted wonderful. I've never come across such flavour since, unfortunately. The farmer's wife wanted to know what had brought us to Yell.

"We've come to see a retired anthropologist who lives on the island – a man named Jan Thornsten. Do you know him?" Keira asked.

The woman gave a shrug and walked out of the kitchen. Keira and I looked at each other, surprised.

"Remember I asked you yesterday about the chances of this chap agreeing to see us?" I said in a low voice. "I've just revised my expectations downwards."

I went to the stables after breakfast to try my luck with the farmer. When I asked about Jan Thornsten, the man grimaced.

"Is he expecting you?"

"Not exactly, no."

"Then he'll fire his gun at you by way of greeting. That Dutchman's a nasty fellow – never so much as a 'hello' or 'goodbye.' He's a loner. He doesn't talk to anyone when he comes into the village once a week to buy provisions. Two years ago, the family on the farm next door to him ran into trouble. The woman started to give birth in the middle of the night and it wasn't looking good. They had to go for the doctor, but the husband's car wouldn't start. The man walked a kilometre across the moors in the pouring rain and the Dutchman fired his rifle at him. The baby died. I'm telling you, he's a nasty piece of work. The priest and the carpenter will be the only people at his funeral."

"Why the carpenter?" I asked.

"Because he's the one who owns the hearse and the horse that pulls it."

I repeated what he'd told me to Keira, and we decided to go for a walk along the coast to work out our strategy.

"I'll go on my own," Keira announced.

"What? No way."

"He won't fire at a woman – he's got no reason to feel threatened by me. Listen, neighbour-from-hell stories are a dime a dozen on these islands. I'm sure this man isn't the monster they're making him out to be. I know plenty of people who'd fire off their gun if they saw a shape approaching their house in the middle of the night."

"You keep some very strange company."

"Leave me in front of his property. I'll walk the rest of the way."

"No, you won't."

"He won't shoot me, believe me. I'm more scared of the flight back than I am of meeting this man."

We kept arguing as we walked along the foot of the cliffs, discovering unspoilt little coves on the way. Keira took a fancy to an otter. It wasn't at all shy and followed a few metres behind us, appearing to find us most entertaining. We wandered along for more than an hour watching the otter's antics. An icy wind was blowing, but it wasn't raining, and the walk was a pleasant one. We ran into a man on his way back from fishing and asked him for directions.

He had an even stronger accent than our hosts. "Where are you going?" he growled into his beard.

"To Burravoe."

"It's an hour's walk, behind you," he said as he walked away.

Keira left me standing and scurried after the man. "It's a beautiful region," she told him.

"If you say so," he replied.

"The winters must be harsh," she continued.

"Spare me the platitudes. I've got to get home and cook lunch."

"Mr. Thornsten?"

"I don't know anyone by that name," the man said, walking faster.

"I find it hard to believe that. There aren't many people on this island."

"Believe whatever you want to – just stop bothering me. You asked me to tell you the way and I've told you it was behind you. Now turn around and you'll be heading in the right direction."

"I'm an archaeologist. We've come a long way to meet you."

"I couldn't care less whether or not you're an archaeologist. I've told you I don't know your Thornsten."

"All I'm asking for is a few hours of your time. I've read your work on the great migrations of the Palaeolithic Age and I need to ask you some questions."

The man stopped and looked Keira up and down.

"You look like a troublemaker, and I don't want to be troubled."

"And you look like a sour, hateful man."

"I couldn't agree more," the man replied, cracking a smile. "That's all the more reason for us not to get to know each other. What language do I have to use to get you to understand the words 'leave me alone'?"

"Try Dutch! There can't be too many people in the area with an accent like yours."

The man turned his back on Keira and set off again.

She followed, catching up with him almost immediately.

"All right, be pig-headed. I don't care. I'll follow you all the way to your house if I have to. What are you going to do when we come to your front door – shoot at us to chase us off?"

"Is that what the farmers in Burravoe told you? Don't believe all the crap you hear on this island. People are so bored they have to resort to making things up."

"I'm only interested in hearing what you can tell me. Nothing else," she said.

The man looked my way for the first time. Ignoring Keira, he took a step in my direction.

"Is she always this much of a pain in the butt, or have I been singled out for special treatment?"

I wouldn't have put it exactly like that, so I merely smiled and confirmed that Keira could be very determined.

"What about you? What do you do, apart from trailing around after her?"

"I'm an astrophysicist."

His face suddenly changed and his deep blue eyes widened.

"I like stars," he breathed. "They've guided me in the past…"

Thornsten looked at the tips of his shoes and sent a pebble flying with his foot.

"I suppose you like them too, if that's your job?" he said.

"I suppose so," I replied.

"Follow me. I live at the end of this path. I'll offer you a drink, you talk to me about the sky and then you leave me alone. Is that a deal?"

We shook hands to seal our agreement.

The main room of his small house was furnished with a worn carpet on the wooden floor, an old armchair in front of the fireplace, two dusty bookshelves groaning under the weight of books along a wall, a wrought-iron bed covered with an old patchwork quilt in a corner, a lamp and a bedside table. We sat around the kitchen table and our host served us black coffee. It turned out to be as bitter as it looked. He lit up a cigarette rolled in corn paper and stared at the two of us.

"What exactly have you come looking for?" he asked, snuffing out his match.

"Information on the earliest human migrations across the Arctic and into America."

"Those migratory flows are very controversial. The peopling of the American continent is a lot more complex than it seems. But it's all in the books. There was no need for you to come here."

"Do you think it's possible that a group could have left the Mediterranean basin and reached the Bering Strait and the Beaufort Sea via the North Pole?" Keira asked.

"That would've been one hell of a journey," Thornsten sniggered. "I suppose you think they travelled by plane?"

"There's no need to act all superior. I'm just asking you to answer my question."

"And when do you say this epic journey would have taken place?"

"During the fourth or fifth millennium BC."

"I've never heard of such a thing. Why that era in particular?"

"Because that's the one I'm interested in."

"Ice would have covered much more of the Earth's surface than in our day, and the ocean would have been smaller. If they travelled in periods of favourable weather, yes, it would have been possible. Now, let's put our cards on the table. You say you've read my work. I don't know how you'd have managed that feat. I published hardly any of it, and you're far too young to have attended one of the few talks I gave on the subject. If you really have studied my papers, you'd have known the answer to the question you've just asked me before you came here, because that was precisely the theory I put forward, and the reason why I was banned from the Archaeological Society. So it's my turn to ask a couple of questions. What is it you really want from me, and why?"

Keira downed her coffee in one go.

"Fine," she said. "Let's play it straight. I've never read anything you've written. I didn't know anything about your work until last week. A lecturer friend of mine suggested I come and see you. He said you could tell me about these great migrations our colleagues can't agree on. But I've always kept looking when others have given up. And right now I'm looking for a passage that people might have used to cross the Arctic in the fourth or fifth millennium BC."

"Why would they have undertaken the journey?" Thornsten asked. "What would have pushed them to risk their lives? That's the key question for anyone who claims to be interested in migrations, young lady. People migrate solely out of necessity – because they're hungry or thirsty, or being persecuted. It's our survival instinct that drives us to leave. Look at you. You left your cosy little home and came to this old heap because you needed something, didn't you?"

Keira looked at me, seeking an answer to her silent question: could we take this man into our confidence, show him our fragments, put them together again for him to witness the phenomenon? I had noticed that the intensity diminished each time we did it. I preferred to save its energy and ensure that as few people as possible knew about our search. I moved my head slightly and she understood. She turned back to Thornsten.

"Well?" he asked.

"They left to deliver a message," she replied.

"What kind of message?"

"Important information."

"Who to?"

"The magisters of the civilisations that had settled on each of the great continents."

"And how would they have known about the existence of other civilisations so far away from theirs?"

"They couldn't have been sure. Then again, I can't think of a single explorer who's set out on his journey knowing what he'll find. But the people I've got in mind had come across a large enough number of civilisations different from their own to presume that there were yet others living in faraway lands. I have proof that three similar journeys were undertaken at around the same time, over considerable distances – one southward, one eastward, all the way to China, and one westward. The northern journey is all that remains to prove my theory."

"Do you really have proof that these journeys took place?" Thornsten asked suspiciously. The tone of his voice had changed. He moved his chair closer to Keira's and placed his hand on the table, scraping its wooden surface with his nails.

"I wouldn't lie to you," said Keira.

"Not twice in a row, you mean."

"I was trying to win you over earlier. We'd been told it was hard to get anywhere near you."

"I may be a recluse, but I'm not an animal!"

Thornsten stared at Keira. He had deep wrinkles around his eyes, and his piercing stare was hard to hold. He got up, leaving us on our own for a minute. "We'll talk about your stars next," he shouted from the living room. "I haven't forgotten our deal."

He came back holding a long tube. He slipped a map out of it and unrolled it over the table, weighing down the curling-up edges with our coffee cups and an ashtray.

"There," he said, pointing to the north of Russia. "If that journey did take place, your messengers would have had more than one route to choose from. One would have taken them up through Mongolia and Russia to reach the Bering Strait, as you suggested. By that stage the Sumerians already possessed boats strong enough to sail through the icebergs and up into the Beaufort Sea, though there's no proof they ever went there. Another possible route would have been through Norway, past the Faroe Islands and Iceland, then across or around the coast of Greenland and through Baffin Bay into the Beaufort Sea. They'd have had to survive freezing temperatures, fish for their food and manage not to be devoured by bears, but anything is possible."

"Possible or plausible?" Keira asked.

"My theory was that people of Caucasian origin had undertaken such journeys before 20,000 BC. I also maintained there was no certainty the Sumerian civilisation appeared on the banks of the Euphrates and the Tigris merely because they had learned to store the spelt they cultivated. No one believed me."

"Why are you telling me about the Sumerians?" Keira asked.

"Because they were one of the first civilisations – if not the first – to have invented writing; one of the first to have come up with a tool for men to inscribe their language. Together with writing, the Sumerians invented architecture and built boats worthy of the name. You're looking for proof of a great journey that took place thousands of years ago, and you're hoping to stumble on it by chance? You think Tom Thumb has laid a trail of stones for you to follow? You're being pathetically naive. If whatever it is you're really looking for had existed, you'll find its traces in the texts. Now, should I continue, or are you planning to interrupt me again for no reason?"

I took Keira's hand and squeezed it, silently imploring her to let him go on with his story.

"Some scholars believe that the Sumerians settled along the Euphrates and the Tigris because spelt grew abundantly in the area, and they had learned to store the grain. They could preserve their harvest and feed themselves in winter, when the fields lay dormant. They no longer had to move from place to place in search of food. That's what I was explaining earlier – settlements are proof of people's progression from merely surviving to living. And, as soon as they settle in one place, they began to improve their everyday living conditions. It is then, and only then, that civilisations began to evolve. When a geographical or climate-induced event destroyed this order and makes it impossible for people to find a daily supply of food, they immediately took to the road again. An exodus or a migration is the same thing, and it happens for the same reason – for the eternal survival of the species. But the Sumerians' skills were far too sophisticated for them to have been merely farmers who had suddenly settled. I put forward a theory stating that the Sumerians' remarkably advanced civilisation had resulted from the meeting of several groups, each bearing its own culture – one coming from the Indian subcontinent, another from the sea, via the Persian Gulf, and a third from Asia Minor. The Sea of Azov, the Black Sea, the Aegean and the Mediterranean are geographically close, even contiguous. All these migrants came together to give rise to this extraordinary civilisation. They would have been the only ones capable of undertaking the journey you've described. And if they had done that, they would have written about it. Find those tablets and you'll have proof that what you're searching for really exists."

"*I have split up the table of memoranda…*" Keira intoned in a low voice.

"What's that you say?" Thornsten asked.

"We found a text starting with that sentence: *I have split up the table of memoranda.*"

"What text?"

"It's a long story, but it was written in Ge'ez, not Sumerian."

"God, but you're obtuse!" Thornsten exclaimed,

thumping his fist on the table. "That doesn't mean it was written in the same period as the journey you're talking to me about. You've been to college, haven't you? Then you should know that stories are transmitted from one generation to the next. They cross borders. People transform and make them their own. Don't you know that a number of these borrowed stories have been found in both the Old and the New Testament? Judaism and Christianity stole pieces of history from far more ancient civilisations, and adapted them. The Anglican prelate James Ussher, who was archbishop of Armagh and primate of all Ireland between 1625 and 1656, published a chronology that established the date of the creation of the universe as Sunday 23 October of the year 4004 BC. What absolute rubbish! God created time and space, the galaxies, the stars, the sun and the earth, animals, men and women, heaven and hell. Woman was created from the rib of man!"

Thornsten burst out laughing. He stood up and went to get a bottle of wine. He opened it, filled three glasses and put them on the table. He threw back his wine in one swallow and refilled his glass.

"If only you knew how many morons still believe that men have one less rib than women, you'd be laughing all night. And yet that fable was inspired by a Sumerian poem; it was the result of a simple bit of wordplay. The Bible is stuffed with these borrowings, including the famous story of the flood and Noah's Ark – that was another Sumerian tale. So forget about your people of the hypogea – you're on the wrong track. They would have been mere intermediaries or storytellers. Only the Sumerians could have constructed boats capable of undertaking the journey you're describing; they invented it all. The Egyptians copied everything from them – writing, which inspired their hieroglyphics, and how to build sailing vessels and towns with houses made of brick. If your journey did take place, that's where it started!" Thornsten said, pointing to the Euphrates on the map.

He rose to go into the living room. "Don't move. I'm going to hunt out something for you. I'll be right back."

When we were alone in the kitchen, Keira bent over the map and traced the river's course with her fingertip. She smiled and said to me in a low voice: "The Shamal – it originates there, in the very place Thornsten pointed to. It's funny to think it chased me away from the Omo Valley, only for me to come back to it in the end."

"The butterfly effect..." I mused. It was true: if the Shamal hadn't blown, we wouldn't be here now.

Thornsten reappeared in the kitchen bearing another map, which showed the Northern Hemisphere in greater detail.

"Where exactly were the ice sheets positioned at the time?" he asked. "Which of the routes had become impassable, which other ones had opened up? This is all hypothetical. But the only way you can confirm your theory is to find proof of your messengers' passage – if not their place of arrival, at least the place where they abandoned their journey. We can't be sure they reached their destination."

"Which of these two routes would you take if you wanted to follow in their tracks?" Keira asked.

"I doubt there are any traces left. Unless…"

"Unless what?" I asked.

It was the first time I'd ventured to join the conversation. Thornsten turned to me as if he hadn't noticed me until then.

"You said a journey had been successfully accomplished all the way to China. The people who arrived there could have continued on to Mongolia. In that case, the most logical route would have taken them up to Lake Baikal. From there, they'd have been carried along by the Angara River to the point where it flows into the River Yenisei, at the mouth of the Kara Sea."

"So it *was* do-able!" Keira enthused.

"I recommend you take a trip to Moscow. Go to the Archaeological Society and try and get them to give you the address of a man named Vladenko Egorov. He's an old soak, and a recluse like me. I think he lives in a shack somewhere near Lake Baikal. If you tell him I sent you, and give him the hundred dollars I've owed him for the past thirty years, he should be willing to see you."

Thornsten rummaged in his trouser pocket and fished out a rolled-up ten-pound note. "You'll have to lend me the rest. Egorov is one of the few living Russian archaeologists – at least I hope he's still alive – who was authorised to carry out his research under government protection at a time when everything was forbidden. In Khrushchev's time it wasn't a good idea to be too clever, let alone spout your own theories about how the Motherland was originally populated. If any excavations have revealed traces of the passage of your migrants near the Kara Sea in the fourth or fifth millennium BC, he'd know about it. He's the only person I can think of who'll be able to tell you whether you're on the right track."

Thornsten slammed the table with his fist once again. "Right, now it's dark, I'm going to lend you some clothes so you don't freeze, and we're going out. It's a clear night and there are a few stars I'd like to finally be able to put a name to after all the time I've spent gazing at the damn things."

He took a couple of parkas off the coat rack and threw them in our direction. "Put these on. When we're done, I'll open a few jars of pickled herring and you can tell me what you think of it."

You can't go back on a promise, especially if you're stuck in the back of beyond and the only living soul within a ten-kilometre radius is walking alongside you with a loaded gun.

"Stop looking at me as if I was about to stuff your backside with buckshot. These moors are wild – you never know what beasts you might come across at night. You'd better stay close to me. Now take a look at that one twinkling away up there and tell me what it's called."

We walked along in the night for quite a while. From time to time, Thornsten would stretch out his arm and point to a star, constellation or nebula and I would name them for him, including a few that were invisible to the naked eye. He seemed genuinely happy – he was a different man to the one we'd met in the late afternoon.

The herrings weren't all that bad, and the potatoes he'd cooked in the fireplace ash took off their salty edge. Thornsten didn't take his eyes off Keira during the meal. It must have been a long time since he'd had such a pretty woman in his house – if indeed he had ever had a woman guest of an evening in this isolated spot. A little later, as we sat in front of the fire taking cautious sips of some home-brewed whisky that scorched our palates and throats, Thornsten once again bent over the map he'd spread out on the carpet and beckoned Keira to come and sit on the floor next to him.

"Tell me what you're really looking for."

Keira didn't answer. Thornsten took her hands in his and gazed at her palms.

"The soil hasn't spared them."

He turned his hands palms upward and showed them to her.

"These hands did a lot of digging too, a long time ago."

"Whereabouts did you dig?"

"It doesn't matter. It was a really long time ago."

Late in the evening he led us to his barn and we climbed into his pick-up truck. He dropped us off two hundred metres from the farm where we were staying. We tiptoed up to our room, lighting our way with the flame of an old Zippo he'd sold us for a hundred dollars. He'd sworn a Zippo of that vintage was worth at least twice as much, and wished us a good trip.

I'd blown out the candle and was trying to get warm under the damp, icy sheets when Keira turned around in bed to face me and asked me an odd question.

"Did you hear me ask him about the people of the hypogea?"

"I can't remember. I might have. Why?"

"Because before he asked us to go to Russia and pay off his debt to his old friend, he said: *Forget about your people of the hypogea, you're on the wrong track.* I keep going over our whole conversation, but I'm pretty sure I never mentioned them."

"You must have mentioned them without realising it. The two of you talked for a long time."

"Were you bored?"

"No, not at all. He's an odd bird – quite a fascinating man. What I'd like to know is why a Dutchman's exiled himself on such a remote island in the north of Scotland."

"Me too. We should've asked him."

"I'm not sure he'd have answered."

Keira shivered and scooted closer to me. I was thinking about her question. However carefully I reviewed her conversation with Thornsten, I couldn't remember her mentioning the people of the hypogea either. But the question didn't seem to be bothering her anymore. Her breathing had turned regular. She'd fallen asleep.

Paris

Ivory was walking along the riverbank. He spotted a bench near a large willow and went to sit on it. An icy breeze was blowing along the Seine. The elderly professor pulled up the collar of his coat and rubbed his arms. His mobile vibrated in his pocket. It was the call he'd been waiting for all evening.

"It's done!"

"Did they find you easily?"

"You spoke to me very highly about your friend and I don't doubt she's a brilliant archaeologist, but if I'd waited for those two to find my house, I'd have waited all winter. I made it my business to bump into them."

"How did things go?"

"Exactly the way you wanted."

"And you think…"

"That I convinced them? Yes, I do."

"Thank you, Thornsten."

"Not at all. As far as I'm concerned, we're quits now."

"I've never said you owed me anything at all."

"You saved my life, Ivory. I've wanted to pay back that

debt for a long time now. I can't say I've been living an action-packed life in this forced exile, but at least it's not as boring as being six feet under."

"Come, come, Thornsten. There's no point rehashing all that old business."

"Oh yes there is, and I haven't finished, you're going to hear me out to the end. You pulled me out of the clutches of those fellows who wanted me dead when I found that cursed stone in the Amazon. You saved me from an attempt on my life in Geneva. If you hadn't warned me; if you hadn't found a way for me to disappear…"

"That's all ancient history," Ivory said sadly.

"Not all that ancient – otherwise you wouldn't have sent me your two lost sheep so I could guide them back on the right track. But have you weighed up the risks you're making them run? You're sending them to the slaughterhouse, as you know only too well. The people who went to all that trouble to try and kill me will do the same with them if they get too close to the mark. You've made me your accomplice and I've been feeling sick to my stomach ever since I left them."

"Nothing will happen to them, I assure you. Times have changed."

"Is that so? Why am I still rotting here, then? And when you've got what you want, will you help them change their identity too? Will they have to bury themselves in some backwater so that they won't ever be found? Is that your plan? Whatever you've done for me in the past, we're quits now – that's all I wanted to say to you. I don't owe you anything anymore."

Ivory heard a click. Thornsten had hung up. He sighed and threw his mobile into the Seine.

London

Back in London, we had to wait a few days to get our
Russian visas. The cheque the administrators had gener-
ously given me as full and final payment for my services
was at least letting me finance the trip. Thanks to Walter,
I'd held on to my access to the Academy's library and
Keira was spending most of her time there. My job was
basically to trawl the shelves for the books she wanted
and put them back in their places when she'd finished
with them. I was beginning to find it very boring. I took an
afternoon off and sat down at my computer to re-establish
contact with two dear friends I hadn't been in touch with
for a long time. I sent Erwin an e-mail in the form of a
riddle. I knew he'd utter a stream of expletives at the mere
sight of a message from my address. He'd probably refuse
to open it, but by the evening, knowing him, his curiosity
would get the better of him, and he'd take his computer
off stand-by and wouldn't be able to resist pondering the
question I'd asked.

As soon as I'd hit Send, I picked up the phone and
called Martin at Jodrell Bank Observatory. I was surprised

by his offhand tone when he heard my voice. It wasn't like him at all to speak to me that way. In barely polite terms, he said he was very busy, and practically hung up on me. The abrupt end to the conversation left a bad taste in my mouth. Martin and I had always been on very cordial, even friendly terms, and I couldn't understand his attitude. Maybe he was having personal problems and didn't want to talk about them.

By five in the afternoon, having sorted through my post, paid outstanding bills and dropped off a box of chocolates at my neighbour's to thank her for the many favours she did me all year round, I decided to make a trip to the grocer's at the end of my road to stock up the fridge.

I was wandering through the aisles when the owner came up alongside me, ostensibly wanting to restock a nearby shelf with tinned food. "Don't look now, but there's a fellow watching you from across the road," he whispered.

"Sorry?"

"It's not the first time. I saw him last time you were here too. I don't know what kind of trouble you've got yourself into, but trust me, that one's a fake."

"Meaning?"

"Meaning he looks and acts like a cop, but he's not a cop. Take it from me, he's an out-and-out thug."

"How can you be sure?"

"Got a few cousins in the slammer. Nothing serious, just bad luck shifting stuff that fell off the back of a lorry."

"I think you must be mistaken," I said, looking over his shoulder.

"Whatever you say. But if you change your mind, the storeroom in the back of the shop's open. There's a door into the courtyard. Just go through the next building from there and you'll be out on the street behind."

"That's very kind of you."

"You've been shopping here a long time. I wouldn't want to lose a regular customer."

The shopkeeper went back behind his counter. I casually walked over to a revolving stand near the window, picked up a newspaper and pretended to leaf through it, glancing out into the street as I did so. The shopkeeper was right. A man sitting at the wheel of a car parked along the pavement across the road did seem to be keeping an eye on me. I decided to make sure. I went out of the shop and walked straight towards him. As I crossed the road, I heard the engine of his saloon car start up with a roar and he drove off.

The shopkeeper, who was watching me from the other side of the road, gave a knowing shrug. I went back to pay for my purchases.

"I have to say it's quite strange," I said, handing him my credit card.

"Done anything illegal lately?" he asked.

It seemed an inappropriate question, but it was asked with such benevolence that I wasn't at all offended. "Not as far as I know," I replied.

"Leave your shopping here and run back home."

"Why?"

"Looked to me like that weirdo was on a stakeout – maybe providing cover."

"What cover?"

"As long as you're here they're sure you're not elsewhere, if you know what I mean."

"Elsewhere where?"

"Your place, for example!"

"You think…?"

"That if you keep standing here gabbing you'll get there too late? Yes, I do!"

I picked up my bag of groceries and walked home fast. The house looked exactly as I'd left it – no trace of breaking and entering and nothing odd inside to confirm the shopkeeper's suspicions. I left the groceries in the kitchen and decided to go and pick up Keira at the Academy.

*

Keira stretched, yawning, and rubbed her eyes – a sign she'd worked enough for the day. She shut the book she was reading and went to put it back on the shelf where she'd found it. She left the library after stopping by Walter's office to say goodnight, and rushed into the nearest underground station.

*

Grey skies, a steady drizzle, wet pavements – it was a classic London winter evening. The traffic was horrendous. It took me forty-five minutes to navigate the traffic jams and another ten to find a place to park. I was locking my car door when I saw Walter coming out of the Academy. He'd spotted me too; he crossed the street and came over to me.

"Have you got time for a drink?" he asked.

"Just let me get Keira at the library and we'll join you at the pub."

"Ah, I thought that was why you were here. She left at least half an hour ago, maybe longer."

"Are you sure?"

"She came to my office to wish me a good evening and we chatted for a few minutes. So how about that beer?"

I glanced at my watch. It was the worst time of day for driving through London. I'd call Keira as soon as we were in the pub to tell her I'd be back later.

The pub was packed, and Walter had to elbow people out of the way to reach the bar. He ordered two pints and handed me one over the shoulder of a man who'd managed to squeeze in between the two of us. Walter dragged me to a just-vacated table at the back of the room. We sat down. The noise level was deafening.

"So did you have a good trip to Scotland?" Walter shouted.

"It was great – if you like herring. I'd thought the Atacama was cold, but it's even icier on Yell, and really damp."

"Did you find what you were looking for?"

"Keira seemed enthusiastic, so that's something. I'm afraid we might be leaving again soon."

"This whole business is going to end up costing you a fortune," Walter yelled.

"It already has."

My mobile vibrated deep in my pocket. I pulled it out and clamped it to my ear.

"Have you been going through my things?" Keira asked, her voice barely audible.

"Of course not. Why would I?"

"Are you sure you didn't open my bag?" she hissed.

"You've just asked me that. I said no."

"Did you leave the bedroom light on when you went out?"

"No, I didn't. What's going on?"

"I don't think I'm alone in the house…"

My blood suddenly ran cold. "Get out of there, Keira!" I shouted. "Clear off right now – run straight to the grocer's at the end of Old Brompton Road and wait for me there, okay? Keira, can you hear me?"

The line had gone dead. Before Walter could make head or tail of things, I leaped up, rushed across the pub, shoving people out of the way, and raced outside. A taxi was stuck in traffic and a motorcycle was about to overtake it; I flung myself practically under its wheels, forcing the biker to stop. I explained that it was a question of life or death and promised to pay him if he'd drive me right away to the corner of Old Brompton Road and Cresswell Garden. He told me to hop on, put the bike in gear and accelerated.

We whizzed along Old Marylebone Road and Edgware Road to Marble Arch. The huge crossroads was heaving, buses and taxis seemed inextricably locked in a game of dominoes. My driver veered his bike up on to the pavement. I hadn't been on the back of many motorbikes, but I did my best to lean with him each time we hit a bend. Ten interminable minutes went past as we crossed Hyde Park in the pouring rain, rode up Carriage Drive between two lines of cars, our knees occasionally scraping their bodywork, hurtled up Exhibition Road and around the South Kensington tube station roundabout. I could finally see Old Brompton Road up ahead; it was even more traffic-choked than the other roads. At the intersection

with Queens Gate Mews, the biker opened up the throttle
once more to speed through the crossroads as the light
was changing from yellow to red. A van coming from the
opposite direction had anticipated the light turning green,
and it looked as if we were going to crash straight into
it. The bike toppled over with its rider hanging on to the
handlebars and I spun off it like a top, my back heading for the pavement. For one fleeting moment I saw the
stricken faces of passers-by – horrified witnesses to the
scene. Luckily, my flight ended against the wheels of a
parked truck, with no great harm done. I got up, shaken
but still in one piece. My chauffeur was already on his
feet, trying to lift his bike. I sent him a hasty wave of
thanks – my street was still a few hundred metres away.
I yelled at people to get out of my way; I bumped into a
couple and heard them shout insults at me. At long last I
glimpsed the grocer's and dived in, praying I'd find Keira
waiting for me there.

The owner started when he saw me appear – I was
panting and dripping sweat. I had to repeat myself before
he understood what I was trying to say. No point waiting
for him to answer; there was only one client, a woman,
in the back of the shop. I raced up the aisle and took her
tenderly in my arms. The young woman screamed and
gave me two hard slaps, or maybe three – I didn't have
time to count. The owner picked up his phone, and as I
ran out I asked him to call the police and tell them to get
to 24 Cresswell Place as fast as they could.

I found Keira sitting on my doorstep.

"What's wrong? Your cheeks are all red. Did you bump
into something?" she asked.

"Into someone – who looked a bit like you from the back."

"Your coat's in shreds. What on earth happened to you?"

"I was going to ask you the same thing."

"I think someone paid us a visit when we were out," Keira said. "I found my bag open in the living room. The burglar was still there when I came in. I could hear him walking about on the first floor."

"Did you see him leave?"

A police car stopped in front of us and two officers got out. I explained that we had good reason to think there was a burglar in the house. They ordered us to step aside and went in for a look.

They came out empty-handed a few minutes later. If a burglar had been there, he'd since made his escape through the garden. The first floor in these old houses isn't very high up – only about ten metres – and the thick stretch of lawn under the window would have cushioned his fall. I thought about the door handle I'd never got around to repairing. He must have got in through the back door.

We were asked to make a list of the things that had been stolen and go to the police station to lodge a complaint. The policemen promised to patrol the area and let me know if they caught anyone.

Keira and I inspected each room. My camera collection was intact and the wallet I always left in the odds-and-ends tray in the hall was still there – none of it had been touched. As I was looking around the bedroom, Keira called out to me from the ground floor.

"The garden gate is locked," she said. "I was the one who shut it last night. So how did he get in?"

"Are you sure someone really was here?"

"I'm absolutely certain. Unless your house is haunted."

"So how did this mystery burglar get in?"

"I've not the slightest idea, Adrian!"

I promised Keira nothing would come in the way of the romantic dinner we'd been deprived of the previous evening. She was fine and that was all that mattered, but I was worried. Bad memories of China resurfaced. I rang Walter to tell him about my fears. His line was busy.

Amsterdam

Each time Vackeers walked through the state room of the Royal Palace, he marvelled afresh at the beauty of the maps carved into the marble floor. His favourite one was the third engraving, a huge celestial chart. He emerged into the street outside and crossed the square. Night had already fallen; the street lamps had just been switched on, and their halo was reflected in the calm waters of the city's canals. He went up Hoogstraat, heading homewards. A big motorbike was parked on the pavement outside number 22. A woman pushing a pram smiled at Vackeers, who smiled back before continuing on his way.

The biker lowered his visor and so did his passenger. The engine growled to life and the bike swerved into the service road.

A young couple was leaning against a tree, locked in a kiss. A double-parked van was holding up traffic; only bicycles were managing to wind their way through.

The rider on the back of the bike grasped the bludgeon concealed up the sleeve of his jacket.

The young woman pushing the pram turncd around.

228

The couple stopped kissing.

Vackeers was walking across the bridge when he suddenly felt the terrible bite of a blow across his back. His breath went out of him in a rush; he couldn't seem to get air down his lungs. He dropped to his knees, attempted unsuccessfully to grab hold of a street lamp and slumped face down on the ground. He felt the taste of blood in his mouth and thought he'd bitten his tongue when he fell. He had never felt such pain. Each time he drew breath, the air burned his lungs. Blood was flowing from his mauled back and internal bleeding was compressing his heart further with every passing second.

A strange silence surrounded him. He marshalled his little remaining strength and lifted his head. Passers-by were rushing to help, and he could hear the wail of a siren in the distance.

The woman with the pram was nowhere to be seen. The lovers had disappeared. The passenger on the back of the bike gave him the finger, and the bike turned the corner of the street and vanished.

Vackeers fumbled to get his mobile out of his pocket. He pressed a button, painfully lifted the phone to his ear and left a message on Ivory's answering machine.

"It's me," he whispered. "I'm afraid our English friend didn't appreciate the trick we played on him."

A coughing fit made it impossible for him to continue. Blood was flowing from his mouth; he felt its warmth, and it did him good. He was cold and the pain was growing sharper every second. Vackeers grimaced.

"We won't be playing together anymore, alas. I'll miss our games, my friend. I hope you will too."

Another coughing fit and an unbearable burning sensation. The phone started slipping from his grasp; he caught it at the last minute.

"I'm delighted with the little gift I offered you the last time we saw each other. Make good use of it. I'll miss you, old friend, much more than our games. Be very careful. Look after yourself..."

Vackeers felt his strength fading away. He deleted the number he had just dialled. His grip on the mobile loosened. He could no longer hear or see anything. His head fell back down on the tarmac.

Paris

Ivory walked into his apartment in Paris after an evening spent watching a prodigiously boring play. He hung up his coat in the hall and went to the refrigerator to look for something to eat. He took out a plate of fruit, poured himself a glass of wine and carried his tray into the living room. He sank into the sofa and kicked off his shoes, stretching his aching legs. As he cast about for the remote control, his eye fell on the blinking light on his answering machine. He got up, intrigued, and pushed the button. He recognised his old friend's voice instantly.

Ivory felt his knees buckle as he came to the end of the message. He groped at a nearby bookshelf for support, dislodging a few old books in the process. They thudded onto the polished wooden floor. He regained his balance and clamped his jaw shut as tight as he could, but it was no use – the tears were flowing down his cheeks. He kept wiping them away with the back of his hand, but he found his body shaking with sobs as he held on to the bookshelf.

He grabbed an old treatise on astronomy, opened it to the frontispiece, which featured a watermarked

seventeenth-century celestial chart, and re-read the dedication to him.

*I know you'll enjoy this book. There's nothing
missing because it's got everything, including the
proof of our friendship.*

Your devoted chess partner,
Vackeers

At dawn, Ivory finished packing and locked his suitcase. He pulled the door of his apartment to behind him
and left for the station to take the first train to Amsterdam.

London

The agency had called me first thing in the morning. Our visas were finally ready, and I could go and pick up our passports. Keira was fast asleep. I decided to go on my own, and buy some milk and fresh bread on the way home. It was a cold morning, and the cobblestones on Cresswell Place were slippery. When I reached the end of the road I waved at the grocer, who returned my greeting with a wink. Just then my mobile rang. Keira must not have seen the note I'd left her in the kitchen. To my astonishment, it was Martin's voice I heard.

"I'm really sorry about the other day," he said.

"Don't be. I was just wondering what had happened to make you so bad-tempered."

"I nearly lost my job because of you, Adrian, or rather because of that time you came to the observatory, and the research I did for you using our equipment at Jodrell."

"What on earth do you mean?"

"They threatened to fire me for serious professional misconduct because I'd let someone who isn't part of the staff – your friend Walter – inside."

"Who's 'they'?"

"The people who finance the observatory. Our government."

"But Martin, that was a completely routine visit and besides, Walter and I are both members of the Academy. It doesn't make any sense!"

"Yes it does, Adrian. That's why I haven't called you back before now, and also why I'm calling from a telephone booth this morning. I was clearly given to understand that I'm no longer allowed to respond to any of your requests, and that you are strictly forbidden to visit our premises. I didn't hear about your being laid off until yesterday. I don't know what you've been up to, but good Lord, Adrian, they can't fire someone of your calibre just like that. Or if they can, then my job's hanging by a thread. You're ten times more qualified than I am!"

"It's very kind of you to say so, Martin, and thanks for the compliment, but if it's any consolation, you're the only one who thinks so. I don't know what's happening – I wasn't told I was being dismissed, just that I'd temporarily lost tenure."

"Wake up and smell the coffee, Adrian. They've chucked you out good and proper. I've had two calls about you – I'm not even allowed to talk to you on the phone anymore. Our superiors have gone crazy."

"Yes, eating roast chicken every Sunday and fish and chips all year round will do that to you," I quipped.

"It's not at all funny, Adrian. What are you going to do?"

"Don't worry, Martin. I've had no other job offers and I've got practically no money left in the bank, but I've been waking up recently next to the woman I love. She surprises me, she makes me laugh, she shakes me up, and I'm crazy about her. I marvel at her enthusiasm all day long and at night when she gets undressed, she makes me very… How can I put it? She stirs me. So you see, there's no need to pity me. Not to boast or anything, but I can honestly tell you I've never been happier."

"I'm thrilled for you, Adrian. I'm your friend, and I've been feeling guilty about giving in to the pressure and cutting off all contact with you. I hope you'll understand. I can't afford to lose my job. I've got no one in my bed at night – my passion for my work is all I've got in life. If you ever need to talk to me, leave me a message at the office – just say it's Gilligan calling. I'll call you back as soon as I can."

"Who's Gilligan?"

"My dog, a wonderful basset hound. Unfortunately I had to have him put to sleep last year. I'll talk to you soon, Adrian."

I'd hung up after my conversation with Martin, feeling pensive, when a voice right behind me made me jump.

"Do you really think all that about me?"

I turned around and saw Keira. She'd borrowed another one of my sweaters and hung my coat around her shoulders.

"I found your note in the kitchen," she said. "I wanted to join you at the agency so you could take me somewhere for breakfast. There's nothing but vegetables in your refrigerator, and I don't really fancy courgettes for breakfast. You seemed really absorbed in your conversation, so I came up behind you quietly expecting to catch you chatting with your mistress."

I led her towards a café that did delicious croissants. The passports could wait.

"So I get you all excited when I undress at night, huh?"

"Haven't you got any clothes of your own, or is there something particularly attractive about mine?"

"Who were you talking to about me in such great detail on the phone?"

"An old friend. I know you'll find it strange, but in fact he was worried about me losing my job."

We went into the café. As Keira devoured her second almond croissant, I wondered if it would be wise to tell her about my fears – and they had nothing to do with my work situation.

We'd be on a plane to Moscow the day after next. I couldn't say I'd be sad to leave London.

Amsterdam

There was practically no one in the cemetery that morning, and hardly anyone following the hearse transporting a long, varnished wooden coffin. A man and a woman walked slowly behind the hearse. There was no priest to conduct the funeral service. Four municipal employees lowered the coffin into the tomb with long ropes. When it reached the bottom, the woman threw a white rose and a handful of earth in after it, and the man accompanying her did likewise. They bid each other goodbye and walked off in opposite directions.

London

Sir Ashley gathered up the series of photographs spread out on his desk. He slipped them into an envelope and closed the flap.

"You're looking very beautiful in these photos, Isabel. Mourning suits you wonderfully well."

"Ivory wasn't fooled."

"I should hope so. The whole point was to send him a message."

"I don't know if you…"

"I asked you to choose between Vackeers and the two young scientists and you chose the old man, so don't start complaining to me now."

"Was it really necessary?"

"I can't understand why you're still asking that question. Am I the only one capable of weighing up the consequences of his actions? Do you realise what would happen if his two protégés found what they're looking for? Don't you think it was worth sacrificing the last few years of an old man's life considering what's at stake?"

"I know, Ashley, you've already told me."

"I'm not a bloodthirsty old madman, Isabel, but I won't hesitate when it comes to the national interest. Our decision could save several lives, including the lives of these two explorers – if Ivory finally decides to give up, that is. Don't look at me like that, Isabel. I've always acted in the interest of the majority. I probably won't end up in heaven with the career I've had, but…"

"Please, Ashley. Don't be sarcastic. Not today. I was genuinely fond of Vackeers."

"I valued him too, even if we didn't always see eye to eye. I respected him, and I'd like to think that this sacrifice, which is costing me as much as it's costing you, will have the desired result."

"Ivory seemed really downcast yesterday morning. I've never seen him in such a state. He looked as if he'd aged a decade overnight."

"If he could age another ten and pass on altogether, that would suit us fine."

"So why didn't you sacrifice him then, instead of taking it out on Vackeers?"

"I have my reasons."

"Don't tell me he's managed to protect himself from you? I thought you were all-powerful."

"If Ivory were to die, the archaeologist would be all the more motivated. She's impetuous, and far too smart to believe in an accident. No, I'm sure you made the right choice; we took out the right pawn. But I warn you, if events prove you wrong, if the search continues, I won't need you to name the next two people to find themselves in our sights."

"I'm certain Ivory will have understood the message," Isabel sighed.

"If not, you'll be the first to know – you're the only one he still trusts."

"Our little number in Madrid went like clockwork."

"I made it possible for you to chair the committee. You owe me this."

"I'm not acting out of gratitude towards you, Ashley; if I'm doing this it's because I share your point of view. It's too soon for the world to know – much too soon. We're not ready."

Isabel picked up her bag and got ready to leave. She turned around at the door. "Do we need to recover the fragment that belongs to us?" she asked.

"No, it's perfectly safe where it is – perhaps even more so now Vackeers is dead. Anyway, no one knows how to get in, and that's exactly what we want. He's taken his secret to the grave. It's perfect."

Isabel nodded and left Sir Ashley alone. As his butler escorted her to the door of the mansion, Sir Ashley's secretary went into his office bearing an envelope. Ashley opened it and looked up.

"When did they get these visas?"

"The day before yesterday, sir. They must be on the plane right now. Actually, no," the secretary said, looking at his watch, "they've already landed at Sheremetyevo Airport."

"Why weren't we notified earlier?"

"I don't know, sir. I could make enquiries if you wish. Would you like me to call your guest back? She's still in the grounds."

"Don't do anything. But let our men in Russia know. Those two birds must by no means fly any further than

Moscow. I've had more than enough. Tell them to shoot the girl; the astrophysicist is harmless without her."

"Are you sure you want to do this, after our unfortunate experience in China?"

"If I could get rid of Ivory I wouldn't hesitate one second, but that's impossible, and I'm not sure it would solve our problem once and for all. Do what I've told you to and tell our men not to cut corners – this time I prefer efficiency to discretion."

"In that case, should we tip off our Russian friends?"

"I'll take care of it."

The secretary left the room.

Isabel thanked the butler, who had opened her taxi door for her. She glanced back at the majestic facade of Sir Ashley's London residence, then turned around and asked the driver to take her to City Airport.

Seated on a bench in the little park facing the Victorian house, Ivory watched the car leave. A fine drizzle had started falling. He leaned on his umbrella for support as he got up and went away.

Moscow

The room at the Intercontinental reeked of stale tobacco. Keira flung open the window as soon as we went in, even though the outside temperature was hovering around zero.

"I'm sorry, it was the only room they had."

"It stinks of cigars. It's disgusting."

"And cheap ones at that," I added. "Do you want to change hotels? Or I could ask them for extra blankets, or a couple of anoraks."

"Let's not lose any time. Let's go to the Archaeological Society right away. The sooner we track down this Egorov, the sooner we can get out of here. God, how I miss the perfumes of the Omo Valley."

"I promised you we'd go back there one day, as soon as this whole business is over."

"I sometimes wonder if this whole business, as you call it, will ever be over," Keira grumbled, shutting the door behind us.

"Do you have the address for the Archaeological Society?" I asked her in the lift.

"I don't know why Thornsten keeps calling it that. The

Archaeological Society was renamed the Academy of Sciences in the late 1950s."

"Academy of Sciences? That's a nice name. Who knows, maybe I could get a job there."

"In Moscow? Whatever next?"

"I could easily have been part of a Russian team in the Atacama, you know. The stars couldn't care less."

"Of course you could have. And it would've been really practical for typing out your reports. You must show me how you use a Cyrillic keyboard."

"Is having the last word a need or an obsession with you?"

"The two are not incompatible! Shall we go?"

An icy wind was blowing and we dived into a taxi. Keira attempted to explain our destination to our driver, but since he didn't understand a word she was saying, she unfolded a map of the city and pointed to the address. People who complain about Paris taxi drivers being unfriendly have obviously never been to Moscow. The streets were already icing over, which didn't seem to deter our driver. His old Lada kept fishtailing, but he righted it each time with a quick turn of the steering wheel.

Keira went up to the guard at the Academy, identified herself and said she was an archaeologist. He directed her to the secretary's office. A young research assistant who spoke perfectly understandable English gave us a very friendly reception. Keira explained that we were trying to get in touch with a Professor Egorov who had headed the Archaeological Society in the 1950s. The young woman looked surprised. She had never heard of any such Society, and the archives of the Academy of Sciences only went as far back as 1958, the year it was founded. She asked us to wait and returned half an hour later with one of her superiors, a man well into his sixties. He introduced himself and asked us to accompany him to his office. The young woman, whose name was Svetlana and who happened to be absolutely gorgeous, said goodbye to us and walked away. Keira kicked my shin and asked if I needed her help to get Svetlana's number.

"I don't know what you're talking about," I sighed, rubbing my shin.

"Sure, do I look like an idiot?"

The office we were shown into would have turned Walter green with envy. Light flooded in through a large window, and we could see fat snowflakes falling outside.

"It's not the best time of year to visit us," the man said, inviting us to take a seat. "They've forecast a bad snowstorm for tonight, tomorrow morning at the latest." He opened a thermos and served us cups of smoked tea.

"I think I've tracked down your Egorov," he said. "May I know why you wish to meet him?"

"I'm researching human migrations in Siberia in the fourth millennium BC and I've been told he knows a lot about the subject."

"It's possible," the man said, "though I must say I have a few reservations."

"Why is that?" Keira asked.

"The Archaeological Society was a pseudonym attributed to a very particular branch of the secret services. Scientists weren't any less closely watched than other people in the Soviet era – on the contrary. Under cover of its charming name, that cell was responsible for recording all the archaeological digs in the country, and specifically for inventorying and confiscating any finds that came out of them. Many finds just vanished. Corruption and the lure of financial gain," the man added, noting our astonished expressions. "Life was hard in this country, it still is, but you should realise that unearthing a gold coin at a dig could guarantee its finder months of survival in those days. Similarly, fossils crossed the border more easily than people. Since the reign of Peter the Great, the first to encourage archaeological research in Russia, our heritage has been continuously plundered. The big organisation Khrushchev set up to protect it ended up, alas, becoming one of the biggest antiques trafficking set-ups ever seen. No sooner had they been excavated than the treasures buried in our lands were shared out between the apparatchiks and immediately went off to add to the collections of wealthy Western museums, or were sold to private collectors. Everyone along the line helped themselves, from the lowliest archaeologist to the head of the mission, not to mention the Archaeological Society agents who were supposed to supervise things. Your Vladenko Egorov was probably one of the biggest fish in these murky networks where anything went, including murder – that goes without saying. If we are indeed talking about the same person, the man you're planning to meet is a former criminal who owes his freedom to a few influential people who are still in power – some very good customers who must have been very sorry when he retired. If you want to antagonise every honest archaeologist of my generation, you only have to mention his name. So before I give you his address, I'd like to know what kind of object you're hoping to smuggle out of Russia. I'm sure the police will find it most interesting – unless you'd rather tell them yourself?" the man asked, picking up his telephone.

"You're mistaken. It certainly can't be our Egorov, it must be someone with the same name," Keira cried out, placing her hand over the telephone dial.

"I couldn't believe a word of what you were saying either." Our host smiled and began to redial the number.

"Stop! For heaven's sake, do you think I'd come to the Academy of Sciences to ask for my supplier's address if I were dabbling in antiques trafficking? Do I look that stupid?"

"I have to admit it's not a very subtle approach," the man said, putting the telephone receiver back in its cradle. "Who recommended you meet him, and why?"

"An elderly archaeologist, for the reasons I truthfully explained to you."

"Well, he's certainly had a good laugh at your expense. But perhaps I could give you the information you need, or put you in touch with one of our specialists. Several of our colleagues have studied the human migrations that populated Siberia. We're even organising a conference on the subject to be held next summer."

"I need to meet this man, not go back to college," Keira replied. "I'm looking for evidence that might have wound up in your pseudo-trafficker's net."

"May I see your passports? If I'm going to help you to get in touch with a rogue of that ilk, I want to at least report your names to Customs. Don't be offended – I'm just protecting myself. Whatever you've come here seeking, I have no desire to be associated with it, let alone be accused of complicity. So, quid pro quo – you give me your ID to photocopy and I'll give you the address you're looking for."

"I'm afraid we'll have to come back," Keira said. "We left our passports at the hotel when we checked in earlier and we haven't got them back yet."

"It's true," I said, joining the conversation. "They're at the Metropol Intercontinental. Call the hotel reception if you don't believe us. Maybe they can fax you copies."

There was a knock on the door. A young man came in and exchanged a few words with the older gentleman we'd been talking to.

"Excuse me," he said. "I'll be back in a minute. Meanwhile, please use the telephone on my desk to have copies of your passports faxed to me here."

He scribbled a fax number on a sheet of paper and handed it to me before going out, leaving us on our own.

"That Thornsten – what a bastard!" Keira swore.

"Well," I said, standing up for him, "there was no reason for him to blow the gaff on his friend's past to us. And there's no proof he was involved in the trafficking."

"And you think the hundred dollars was for us to buy sweets with? Do you know what a hundred dollars would have amounted to in the 1970s? Make that call and let's get out of here – this office is giving me the creeps."

When I didn't budge, Keira picked up the phone herself. I took it back from her and replaced it on its base.

"I don't like this one bit. I really, really don't," I said. I got up and walked over to the window.

"What do you think you're doing?"

"Remember that ridge two thousand five hundred

metres high on Mount Hua? Do you think you could do it again if we were just two floors up?"

"What are you talking about?"

"I think our host has gone to meet the cops on the front steps of the Academy, and I'm pretty sure they'll be coming in to arrest us any minute now. There's a police car parked in the street below – a Ford with a nice set of flashing lights on the roof. Lock that door and follow me!"

I placed a chair against the wall, opened the window and evaluated the distance separating us from the fire escape at the corner of the building. The snow would make the surface of the ledge slippery to negotiate, but we'd have a better grip on the freestone facade of this building than on the smooth rock face of Mount Hua. I helped Keira up to the windowsill and followed her. We had just started walking along the parapet when I heard drumming on the door. It wouldn't be long before they discovered we'd done a bunk.

Keira was moving forward along the wall with disconcerting agility; the wind and snow were slowing her progress, but she was managing to hang on, and so was I. A few minutes later, we were helping each other to swing a leg over the railing of the fire escape. We still had to climb down the fifty-odd wrought-iron stairs, which were covered in ice. Keira slipped and fell flat on the first-floor platform. She caught hold of the railing and pulled herself up, swearing. A cleaning service employee who was busy mopping the large corridor of the Academy watched dumbfounded as we appeared on the other side of the window. I sent her a reassuring little wave and caught up with Keira. The bottom bit of the fire escape was a collapsible ladder that unfolded to street level. Keira tugged on the chain to free the hooks keeping it up, but the mechanism was jammed. There we were, stuck three metres above ground – much too high up to try anything, unless we wanted to break our legs. I remembered a college friend who'd jumped from the first floor to go over the wall – he'd ended up flat on the tarmac with his shinbones sticking out at right angles. That fleeting memory made me rule out the temptation to pretend I was James Bond, or one of his stunt doubles. I hammered with my fists at the ice holding the ladder closed while Keira jumped on it with both feet, screaming: "Give way, bitch! Give way!" It worked – the ice shattered all of a sudden and I watched as Keira tumbled down to the street at dizzying speed, hanging on to the ladder for dear life.

She picked herself up at the bottom, complaining loudly. Our host had just popped his head out of his office window. He looked furious. I hastily slid down the ladder to join Keira, and we bolted like a couple of burglars on the run towards the entrance of a metro station a hundred metres away. Keira ran through the underground tunnel and up some steps that lead to the other side of the avenue. Moscow motorists often moonlight as taxi drivers to supplement their income – you just hold up a hand for a car to stop, and if you can agree on a price, it's a done deal. The driver of a Zil agreed to give us a ride for twenty dollars.

I tested his English by giving him a big smile and telling him his car stank of goats, that he was a dead ringer for my great-grandmother and that it couldn't have been easy to pick his nose with hands as stubby as his. Since he nodded each time and said "Da," I decided Keira and I could talk openly.

"What do we do now?" I asked her.

"We pick up our stuff at the hotel and try to get on a train before the police get their hands on us. After that Chinese prison, I'd rather kill than go back to jail."

"So where are we heading?"

"Lake Baikal. Thornsten mentioned it."

The car stopped in front of the Metropol Intercontinental. We raced to the reception desk, where a pretty hostess gave us back our passports. I asked her to prepare our bill, apologising for cutting our stay short, and asked if she could possibly book us two sleeper berths on the Trans-Siberian. She leaned closer and informed me in a low voice that two policemen had just made her print out the names of all the British guests staying at the hotel. They were sitting in the lobby going through it. She added that she had a British boyfriend who was going to take her to London to live. They would be getting married there next spring. I congratulated her on the happy news and she whispered "God Save the Queen" in reply, giving me a conspiratorial wink.

I pulled Keira along to the lift, assuring her twice on the way that I hadn't been flirting with the receptionist, and explained why we had to make ourselves scarce in a hurry.

We'd hastily packed our bags and were just about to leave the room when the telephone rang. The young woman at reception told me we had two confirmed berths in carriage 7 of the Trans-Siberian, which was scheduled to leave from the main station at 11.24pm. She gave me our booking number. We'd just have to collect our tickets at the station – she'd added them to our bill and debited my credit card. And if we went through the bar, we could leave the hotel without having to cross the lobby.

London

Ivory switched off the television when the late-night news began. He went to the window. It had stopped raining. A couple was coming out of the Dorchester. The woman climbed into a taxi. The man waited for the car to drive away before returning to the hotel. An old lady walking her dog along Park Lane greeted the doorman as she passed him.

Ivory left his observation post, opened the minibar, took out a small box of chocolates, undid the wrapping and placed it on the coffee table. He went to the bathroom, rummaged in his sponge bag and found the tube of sleeping tablets. He shook one out into his palm and looked at himself in the mirror.

"You old fool. You knew the score, didn't you? You knew what you were playing at."

He swallowed the pill, poured himself a glass of water from the bathroom tap and returned to the living room to sit down in front of the chessboard.

He gave each of the enemy pawns a name – Athens, Istanbul, Cairo, Moscow, Beijing, Rio, Tel Aviv, Berlin,

Boston, Paris and Rome. He baptised the king London and the queen Madrid, then swept all his own pieces away on to the carpet, except the one he'd named Amsterdam, which he rolled up in his handkerchief and delicately slipped into the bottom of his pocket. He moved the black king back a square, leaving the knight and the pawn where they were, and moved the two bishops forward to the third row. He contemplated the chessboard. Then he took off his shoes, lay down on the sofa and switched off the light.

Madrid

The meeting had just finished, and the participants were gathering around the buffet. Isabel's hand covertly brushed Sir Ashley's. He had been particularly persuasive that evening. At the last meeting, the majority had voted for the search to continue. But this time the English lord had managed to swing the opinion of a majority of the participants in his favour, and the most precious ally of the moment had agreed to cooperate fully. Moscow would use all the means at his disposal to locate and intercept the two scientists. They would be put on the first flight back to London and no longer be granted tourist visas. Ashley would have preferred more drastic measures, but his colleagues weren't prepared to adopt a motion to that effect. To salve everyone's conscience, Isabel had put forward an alternative suggestion that had been unanimously approved. If the use of force hadn't so far dissuaded the two researchers, why not divert them from their quest by making each of them an offer they couldn't refuse – offers that would effectively separate them? Coercion wasn't always the best method. The chairwoman escorted her guests out of the tower where a convoy of limousines would take them away from the Plaza de Europa and to the Barajas Airport. Moscow had offered Sir Ashley the use of his private plane, but the English lord still had some business to take care of in Spain.

Moscow

It seemed to me there were far too many policemen at Yaroslavsky Station for things to be considered normal. Whichever direction we went – towards the platforms, the rows of itinerant stalls, the left-luggage office – there they were, in clusters of four, scrutinising the crowds. Keira sensed my anxiety and tried to reassure me.

"It's not as if we've robbed a bank or anything," she said. "It's one thing for the police to make enquiries at our hotel, but to go as far as thinking they've sealed off stations and airports, as if we were two notorious criminals – let's not get carried away, all right? And anyway, how would they know we were here?"

I was regretting having asked the Intercontinental to book our train tickets. If the inspector following us had obtained a copy of our bill, and I had good reason to think he had, he'd have got the receptionist to spill the beans in less than ten minutes. This was why I didn't share Keira's optimism, and feared the police were there because of us. We were only a few metres from the row of ticket machines. I took a quick look at the ticket counters; if I was right, the employees would already be on the alert, ready to notify the police as soon as a foreigner showed up.

A shoeshine man was shuffling along in front of us, his equipment slung over his shoulder, looking out for someone who wanted their shoes polished. He'd passed me several times, eyeing my boots. I beckoned him over and offered him a different kind of deal.

"What are you doing?" Keira asked.

"There's something I want to check."

The shoeshine man pocketed the dollars I gave him as an advance payment. I told him I'd pay him the rest of the promised amount as soon as he'd collected our tickets from the machine and given them to us.

"It's disgusting of you to get that guy involved by making him run your errands for you."

"We're not notorious criminals, so he's in no danger."

The minute our shoeshine man tapped our booking reference number into the screen, I heard the crackle of several police walkie-talkies and a voice shouting instructions – I guessed exactly what they meant. Keira realised what was going on too and couldn't stop herself yelling at the shoeshine man to get out of there. I barely had time to grab her arm and push her into an out-of-the-way corner. Four uniformed men passed us and ran towards the ticket machines. Keira was paralysed. There wasn't much we could do for the shoeshine man – they were already handcuffing him. I reassured her he'd be in police custody for a few hours at most. On the other hand, he'd be pointing them in our direction in a matter of minutes.

"Take your coat off," I told Keira, slipping out of mine. I shoved our coats into our bags, handed her a pullover and yanked one on myself. Then I slipped an arm around her waist and propelled her along to the left-luggage office. I kissed her and asked her to wait for me behind a pillar. Her eyes grew wide as she watched me return to the ticket machines. But that was exactly where the police were least expecting us to be. I slipped through, courteously asking a policeman to let me pass, and went up to a machine. Fortunately for me, it had instructions for tourists in English. I booked two seats on a train, paid in cash and went back to get Keira. The staff monitoring ticketing transactions in the station's control room would pay no attention to the purchase I'd just made.

"What are we going to Mongolia for?" Keira enquired, looking at the ticket I was holding out to her.

"We're getting on the Trans-Siberian as planned. Once we're on the train I'll tell the ticket inspector we made a mistake and pay him the difference if necessary."

We weren't home and dry, though – we still had to try and get on the train. The policemen probably only had a simple description to go on – at the very worst they'd have a copy of our passport photos – but the noose would tighten around us as soon as we got anywhere near the train. There was no point attracting attention; the police were looking for a couple, so Keira started walking fifty metres ahead of me. The Trans-Siberian No. 10 to Irkutsk was scheduled to leave at 11.24pm. We didn't have much time left.

The bustle on the platform gave it the feel of a country village on market day. Crates full of chickens and stalls selling cheese, dried meat and all kinds of other food were parked alongside the suitcases, trunks and packages cluttering up the platform. The passengers of the old train that would soon be setting off on its six-day journey across the Asian continent were fighting their way through the chaotic jumble of hawkers selling their wares. People squabbled and shouted abuse at each other in a medley of tongues – Chinese, Russian, Manchurian and Mongolian. A few children were peddling packs of essential items – hats, scarves, razors, toothbrushes and toothpaste. A policeman spotted Keira and began making his way towards her. I stepped up my pace and bumped into him, apologising politely. The policeman began reproving me. When he turned back to the crowd, Keira had vanished from his sight – and mine.

A voice over the PA announced the train's imminent departure and the passengers still on the platform began jostling each other even harder. The ticket collectors were struggling to keep up. There was still no sign of Keira. I had let myself be swept along by the crowd into the queue in front of carriage 7. I could see the overcrowded corridor through the carriage window, and people hunting for the seat number they'd been assigned, but I couldn't see Keira's face among them. It was my turn to climb the steps. I threw one last glance at the platform and then had no choice but to let myself be heaved upward by the crowd pressing into the carriage. If Keira wasn't on the train, I'd get off at the first stop and find some way to return to Moscow. I wished we'd given each other a meeting point in case we lost each other, and started trying to guess which part of the train she would think of as a likely place.

As I walked up the corridor I saw a policeman coming

my way, and ducked into a compartment. He barely glanced at me. Everyone was settling in, and the two railway employees in charge of the carriage had their hands too full for the moment to start checking people's tickets. I sat down next to an Italian couple. There were some French people in the next compartment, and I would bump into a number of other British travellers on the journey. The Trans-Siberian attracted a number of foreign tourists all year round, which was entirely to our advantage.

The train jerked slowly into motion. A few policemen were still patrolling the deserted platform. Central Moscow soon disappeared, giving way to a landscape of cheerless grey suburbs. My fellow travellers promised to look after my bag and I left them to go and look for Keira. I didn't find her in the next carriage, or the one after that. The train was chugging rapidly along and the suburbs were already giving way to the plains. Third carriage – still no Keira. I had to be patient as I made my way through the congested corridors. Things were already getting very lively in second class, where the Russians had opened bottles of beer and vodka and were toasting each other with much shouting and singing. The dining car was equally animated. I spotted a group of six solidly built Ukrainians raising their glasses and shouting "Vive la France!" I went up to them and discovered a pretty tipsy Keira in their midst.

"Don't look at me like that!" she said. "They're really sweet." She scooted up to make a place for me at the table and explained that her new travel companions had helped her into the train, using their bodies to shield her from a policeman who was taking an over-inquisitive interest in her physique. If they hadn't been there, he would have questioned her. So the least she could do was buy them a round of drinks. I'd never seen Keira in this state. I thanked her new friends and tried to convince her to come with me.

"I'm hungry and we're in the dining car and besides, I'm fed up with running, so sit down and let's eat!" She ordered a dish of potatoes and smoked fish and downed another two glasses of vodka, slumping down on my shoulder a quarter of an hour later. With the help of the six strapping Ukrainians, I carried her to my compartment, where the Italians seemed to find the situation highly amusing. Keira stretched out on a berth, muttered a few inaudible words and fell asleep again almost immediately.

I spent part of that first night aboard the Trans-Siberian gazing out of the window at the sky. There was a tiny cabin at one end of each carriage where an attendant, a *provodnista*, dispensed hot water and tea from a samovar round the clock. I went to help myself and asked the attendant when we would be reaching our destination. She told me it would take us three days and four nights, including this one, to travel the four thousand five hundred kilometres to Irkutsk.

Madrid

Sir Ashley put his mobile back on the living-room table, loosened the belt of his dressing gown and walked towards the bed.

"What's the latest news?" Isabel asked, folding her newspaper shut.

"They've been spotted in Moscow."

"In what circumstances?"

"They went to the Academy of Sciences to ask for information about a former antiques trafficker. The director got suspicious and notified the police."

Isabel sat up in bed and lit a cigarette.

"Have they been arrested?"

"No. The police tracked them down to their hotel, but arrived too late."

"Have we lost them?"

"I don't know, actually. They tried to board the Trans-Siberian."

"Tried?"

"The Russians have been questioning a man who was trying to collect the tickets booked in their names."

"So they're on the train?"

"The station was swarming with policemen, but no one saw them getting on."

"If they were feeling hunted, they might have tried to send their pursuers off on the wrong track. It's not a good idea for the Russian police to get mixed up in our business. It'll only make our task harder."

"I doubt our scientists are as cunning as you think they are. I'd say they're on the train. The fellow they're looking for lives near Lake Baikal."

"Why do they want to meet that antiques smuggler? What a strange idea. Do you think he…"

"…has one of the fragments in his possession? No – we'd have known about it a long time ago if he had. But if they're prepared to go to all that trouble to meet him, the man must have information they need."

"In that case, my dear, all you have to do is silence this man before they reach him."

"It's not that simple. He's a former Party member. And, considering his background, if he's enjoying a golden retirement in a lakeshore dacha, it means he's got some powerful protectors. Our only option is to send out our own people – we're not likely to find anyone prepared to touch a hair on his head in Russia."

Isabel stubbed out her cigarette in the ashtray on the bedside table, slid another one out of the packet and lit it up.

"Have you got another plan to make sure they don't meet each other?"

"You smoke too much, my dear," Sir Ashley said, opening a window. "You know more about my projects than anyone else, Isabel, but your alternative suggestion to the committee is costing us time."

"Well, can we intercept them?"

"Moscow promised me they would be intercepted. We agreed it's better for our prey to feel they don't need to remain on their guard. Intervening on a train isn't as easy as it seems, and a forty-eight-hour respite should give them the impression they've slipped through the net. Moscow will send a team to take care of them when they reach Irkutsk. But in line with the committee's resolution, Moscow's men will merely question them and put them on a plane back to London."

"At least my proposal to the committee swung the votes in favour of stopping their research, not to mention that it put you completely in the clear as regards Vackeers. So things don't necessarily have to go as planned..."

"Are you giving me to understand you wouldn't be opposed to more radical measures?"

"You can understand whatever you like, but please stop pacing up and down like that. You're making my head spin."

Ashley shut the window, took off his dressing gown and slipped under the sheets.

"Aren't you going to call your men back?"

"There's no need. The required steps have been taken. I'd already made my decision."

"What decision?"

"To step in before our Russian friends do. It'll all be sorted tomorrow when the train leaves Ekaterinburg. I'll notify Moscow afterwards as a matter of courtesy, so he doesn't send his men for nothing."

"The committee will be furious when they find out you've ignored the resolutions we voted last evening."

"I'll let you play it any way you like at the next meeting. You could denounce me for going ahead and using my initiative, or for my inability to respect the rules. You'll harangue me and I'll apologise and swear my men took matters into their own hands. Believe me, in fifteen days' time no one will be talking about it anymore. Your authority will remain intact, and our problems will be solved – what more could we ask for?" Ashley switched off the light.

Trans-Siberian

Keira spent the whole day lying on her berth, laid low by a migraine. I refrained from the slightest criticism of her overindulgence on the previous day, even when she begged me to finish her off to stop the pain. I went along to the end of the carriage every half hour, and each time the woman tending the samovar kindly handed me a warm compress that I rushed back to place on Keira's forehead. When she fell asleep again, I pressed my face up against the window and watched the countryside go by. From time to time the train passed a village of houses built from birch logs. When it stopped at small stations, the local farmers hurried onto the platform to sell the passengers their specialities – potato salad, *tvorog* cottage cheese pancakes, jams, cabbage rolls and meat dumplings. The stops never lasted long, and the train would start moving again through the vast, barren plains bounded by the Ural Mountains.

Keira perked up a little towards the end of the afternoon. She drank a few mouthfuls of tea and nibbled on some dry fruit. We were approaching Ekaterinburg, where our

Italian travel companions would leave us to get another train to Ulan Bator.

"I'd love to visit the city," Keira sighed. "I hear the Church on the Blood is magnificent."

The strangely named church had been built on the ruins of Ipatiev House, a merchant's home where Nicholas II, Tsarina Alexandra and their five children were held before being executed in July 1918. We would have no time for sightseeing, unfortunately – our carriage attendant had told me the train only stopped at Ekaterinburg for half an hour for a locomotive change. Still, at least we could get out to stretch our legs and buy something to eat; that would do Keira good.

"I'm not hungry," she moaned.

The suburbs came into view; they looked no different from the outskirts of any other large industrial city. The train drew into the station and stopped.

Keira agreed to leave her berth to go for a short walk. Night had fallen and the platform was full of babushkas crying out their wares. A fresh set of passengers was getting on the train. Two policemen were patrolling the station in a leisurely way, which reassured me. We seemed to have left our problems behind in Moscow. We were already more than one thousand five hundred kilometres from the capital.

There was no whistle blown to announce the train's departure; only the movement of the crowd made us realise that it was time to get back into our carriage. I'd bought a case of mineral water and a few *piroshki*, which I ended up eating all by myself. Keira had lain down on her berth and fallen asleep again. When I'd finished my meal I lay down too. The swaying of the train and the regular clickety-clack of its wheels lulled me into a deep slumber.

It was two in the morning Moscow time when I heard an odd noise at the door. Someone was trying to enter our compartment. I got off my berth, pulled open the curtain and poked my head out, but there was no one to be seen. The corridor was deserted – abnormally deserted. Even the *provodnista* had abandoned her samovar.

I put the latch back on and decided to wake Keira. Something wasn't quite right. She started; I covered her mouth with my hand and signalled for her to get up.

"What's up?" she whispered.

"I don't know yet, but get dressed quick."

"To go where?"

The question wasn't entirely devoid of sense. We were shut in a compartment six square metres in size. The dining car was six carriages away and I wasn't too keen on us making our way there. I emptied out my bag, stuffed our berths with our things and covered them with sheets. Then I helped Keira climb onto the luggage rack, switched off the light and slid in beside her.

"What are we supposed to be playing at?"

"Don't make any noise – that's all I'm asking."

Ten minutes later, I heard the latch click once more. The door to our compartment slid open. Four quick shots rang out, then the door closed again. We stayed huddled up against each other for a long moment until Keira warned me she'd start screaming with pain any minute because of the cramp in her leg. We left our hiding place. Keira wanted to switch the ceiling light back on, but I wouldn't let her; instead, I twitched the curtain half open to let in the moonlight. The colour drained from our faces when we saw our bedding pierced by four holes where our bodies should have been. Keira knelt in front of her berth and pushed her finger through one of the circular rips in the sheet. "Terrifying," she murmured.

"Yes, I should think the bedding's had it."

"Why the hell are we being hounded like this? We don't even know what we're looking for, let alone whether we'll find it one day."

"The people who have something against us probably know more than we do. We'll have to keep calm if we want to escape this trap. And we'd better think fast."

Our killer was on the train and he'd stay on it at least until the next stop, unless he decided to wait for our bodies to be discovered to ensure he'd accomplished his mission. In the first case our best bet was to stay holed up in our compartment; in the second, it would be wiser to get off before he did. The train was slowing down. We were probably approaching Omsk. The stop after that, Novosibirsk, was scheduled for early morning.

My first reaction was to try and find a way to make sure the door couldn't be opened from the outside, which I did by slipping my trouser belt around the handle and tying it to the rail of the ladder going up to the luggage rack. The leather was strong enough to prevent anyone sliding the door open. Then I asked Keira to crouch down beside me so we could both watch the platform without anyone noticing us.

The train stopped. From our position, it was hard for us to see who was alighting, and the little we did glimpse gave us no reason to hope the killer had left the train.

We repacked our bags and sat patiently for the next few hours of the journey, ears cocked for the slightest sound. At six in the morning we heard people screaming, and passengers from nearby compartments came spilling out into the corridor.

Keira jumped up. "I've had it with being cooped up in here!" she said, freeing the door handle. She opened the door and threw me my belt. "Let's go out," she said. "There are too many people out there for us to risk anything at all."

A passenger had discovered the carriage attendant lying lifeless in front of her samovar with a nasty wound on her forehead. Her day-shift colleague ordered us to go back to our compartments and stay there until the police got on the train at Novosibirsk.

"Back to square one!" Keira complained.

"If the cops inspect the compartments, we'd better hide our sheets," I said, putting my belt back on. "This is not the time to be drawing attention to ourselves."

"Do you think that man's still lurking on the train?"

"I don't know, but he can't try anything now."

At Novosibirsk station, two police inspectors interrogated the passengers one by one. No one had seen anything. The body of the young *provodnista* was taken away in an ambulance, and another railway employee took her place. There were plenty of foreigners on the train, so we didn't attract special attention from the authorities. There were Dutch, Italian and German passengers in our carriage alone, and even a Japanese couple – we were just two British tourists. The inspectors got off after noting

everyone's passport details, and the train started moving
again.

We were travelling through tracts of frozen marshland
dotted with snow-capped mountains, which gave way
once again to the Siberian plains. Towards midday the
train crossed a long metal bridge spanning the majestic
Yenisei River. It stopped at Kranoyarsk for half an hour.
I'd have preferred to stay in the compartment, but Keira
was getting fidgety. The temperature must have been
around minus ten on the platform. We took advantage of
our little outing to buy some food.

"I don't see anything suspicious," Keira said, chomp-
ing on a vegetable fritter.

"Let's hope it stays that way till tomorrow morning."

The passengers were getting back on the train. I cast a
final glance around us and helped Keira up the steps. The
new *provodnista* hurried us along, and the door slammed
shut behind me.

I suggested to Keira that we spend our last night aboard
the Trans-Siberian in the dining car. Russians and tourists
sat there drinking all night; the more people around us,
the safer we'd be. Keira agreed, relieved. We sat down at
a table next to four Dutch tourists.

"How are we going to find our man once we reach
Irkutsk?" Keira asked. "Lake Baikal is more than six
hundred kilometres long."

"Once we're there we'll try and find an Internet café
and Google him. With any luck we'll be able to track him
down."

"Oh, so now you know how to do a search in Cyrillic?"

I looked at Keira. Her mocking smile reminded me

how beautiful I found her. She was right; we'd probably need an interpreter.

"We'll go and see a shaman in Irkutsk," she said teasingly. "He'll teach us a lot more about the region and its inhabitants than any of your search engines!" Over dinner, Keira explained why Lake Baikal had become a mecca for palaeontologists. Palaeolithic encampments discovered in the Transbaikal region in the early twentieth century provide evidence of human habitation in Siberia around 25000 BC. These people could use a calendar and had already begun performing religious rites.

"Asia is the birthplace of shamanism," continued Keira. "In these parts, shamanism is regarded as humankind's earliest religion. Local lore has it that shamanism emerged when the universe was created, and the very first shaman was the son of heaven. So as you can see, our two professions have been connected since the beginning of time. There are many Siberian legends about the origin of the universe. A bone sculpture dating from the fifth millennium BC was found in the Oleni Island necropolis on Lake Onega. The sculpture represents a shamanic headdress decorated with an elk's muzzle. The headdress was worn by a priest, who is shown rising towards the heavens with two women at his side."

"Why are you telling me all this?"

"Because here, as in all Buryat villages, if you want to know something you go and see a shaman. Why are you feeling me up under the table?"

"I'm not feeling you up."

"What are you doing, then?"

"I'm looking for the guidebook you must be hiding

somewhere. Don't tell me you already knew all this stuff about shamans – I won't believe you."

"Don't be silly," Keira said, giggling as I slid my hands behind her hips. "I haven't got a book under my bum. There are good reasons why I know all this – no, there's nothing in my cleavage either; that's enough, Adrian!"

"What reasons?"

"I went through a very mystical phase when I was in college. I was mad about shamanism. Incense, magnetic stones, dances, trances, shamanic ecstasy – the works. It was my New Age phase, if you see what I mean. And don't you dare make fun of me. Adrian, stop, you're tickling me, no one would go hiding a book there."

"And how are we going to find a shaman?" I asked, straightening up.

"The first kid you see in the street will tell us where the local shaman lives. Trust me. I'd have loved to make this trip when I was twenty. Some people thought the road to heaven led to Kathmandu, but this was where *I* dreamed of coming."

"Really?"

"Yes, really. Look, I've got nothing against your in-depth frisking, but let's go back to the compartment."

I needed no further encouragement. By dawn I'd inspected every inch of Keira's body – and I hadn't found the slightest trace of a crib sheet on her.

London

Sir Ashley was sitting at the dining-room table reading his morning newspaper and sipping his tea. His personal secretary entered the room and proffered a mobile phone on a silver tray. Ashley took the phone, listened to what the person on the other end had to say and handed the phone back. The secretary would customarily have left the room immediately, but he hovered there, seeming to want to say something to Sir Ashley.

"What now? Can't I have breakfast in peace?"

"The head of security wishes to speak to you as soon as possible, sir."

"Tell him to come and see me this afternoon."

"He's waiting in the corridor, sir. It appears to be an urgent matter."

"What's the head of security doing here at 9am? What's all this about?"

"I think he'd rather speak to you in person, sir. He didn't want to tell me anything, except that he had to see you immediately."

"Then ask him to come in instead of wittering on – it's

most annoying. And get me some tea at the proper temperature, not this tepid dishwater I've been drinking. Go
on then, since it's urgent!"

The secretary left the room and showed the head of
security in.

"What do you want?"

The man handed Sir Ashley a sealed envelope. He
opened it to find some photographs of Ivory sitting on a
bench in front of his house.

"What's that fool doing here?" said Ashley, going over
to the window.

"They were taken late afternoon yesterday, sir."

Ashley dropped the curtain and turned back to the head
of security. "If that old loony wants to feed the pigeons
on the street across from my house, that's his problem. I
hope you haven't disturbed me at this early hour for such
a stupid reason."

"It seems the operation in Russia was carried out according to your wishes."

"Well, why didn't you start with that excellent bit of
news? Would you like a cup of tea?"

"Thank you, sir, but I must be off. I have a lot to do."

"Wait a minute. Why did you say 'It seems'?"

"Our emissary had to get off the train sooner than expected. However, he is certain he fatally wounded his two
targets."

"In that case, you can leave."

Irkutsk

We were relieved to get off the Trans-Siberian. We wouldn't have very good memories of our journey, except for our last night on board. I looked around carefully as we made our way out of the station, but nothing seemed suspicious. Keira spotted a young boy hawking cigarettes and offered him ten dollars to take us to the shaman. The boy hadn't understood a word Keira was saying, so he led us to his house instead. His father owned a small tannery on a narrow little street in the old town.

I was struck by the ethnic diversity of the place. A multitude of communities lived together here in perfect harmony. Irkutsk was a city with a singular past and sagging old wooden houses sinking ever lower into the ground before crumbling altogether for lack of upkeep. Its old tram stopped in the middle of the street because there were no stations, and elderly Buryat women all wore a woollen headscarf tied under their chin and carried a bag over their arm. Every valley and mountain had its own spirit there; the sky was worshipped, and people would not partake of alcohol before spilling a few drops on the table first as a toast to the gods.

The boy's father ushered us into his modest home and told us in broken English that his family had lived there for three centuries. His grandfather had been a furrier back in the day when the Buryats still bought and sold furs in the city's trading posts, but that was all in the past. The sables, ermines, otters and foxes were long gone, and his little tannery a short distance from the Chapel of St. Paraskeva no longer made anything but leather satchels, which he was hard put to sell in the nearby bazaar.

Keira asked him if he knew how we could get a shaman to grant us an audience. He told us that as far as he knew, the best shaman was to be found in Listvyanka, a town on the shores of Lake Baikal. We could save money by taking a minibus there. The taxis were overpriced, he told us, and only marginally more comfortable. He offered us a meal; hospitality is an enduring tradition in these lands so often ravaged by demented oppressors. Some stringy boiled meat, a few potatoes, a slice of bread, and tea with butter. I can still remember that winter lunch at the tannery in Irkutsk.

Keira had winkled the shy little boy out of his shell and they were giggling as they repeated words in English and Russian to each other. The craftsman looked on fondly. In the early afternoon the boy led us to the bus stop. Keira wanted to give him the ten dollars she'd promised him, but he wouldn't take the money. So she unwound her scarf and gave it to him. He wrapped it around his neck and scampered off, stopping at the end of the street to turn and wave goodbye. I knew that Keira's heart was heavy and that she was missing Hari terribly. I realised she must be seeing his gaze in the eyes of every child we met along our journey. I took her clumsily into my arms and she rested her head on my shoulder. I felt her sadness and whispered the promise I'd made into her ear. We would return to the Omo Valley, however long it took us, and she would see Hari again.

The minibus ran along the river, skirting a landscape of steppes. Women walked on the roadside carrying their sleeping children in their arms. During the journey, Keira told me more about shamans and the visit awaiting us.

"A shaman is a healer, a sorcerer, a priest, a magician, a fortune-teller – a man possessed. His job is to heal certain illnesses, attract game and bring rainfall, and sometimes to find lost objects."

"Can't you get your shaman to direct us straight to our fragment? That way we could avoid going to see this Egorov, and save time."

"All right, I'll go on my own!"

It was obviously a sensitive topic and not to be joked about. I listened attentively to her explanation.

"The shaman puts himself into a trance to come into contact with the spirits. His convulsions show that a spirit has entered his body. When his trance is over, he collapses and has a cataleptic fit. It's an intense moment for the people gathered around; there's never any certainty that the shaman will come back to life. When he comes to, he recounts his journey. One of his journeys should appeal to you – the one where he travels into the universe. It's known as his magical flight. The shaman travels through the pole star – the 'nail' that fixes the heavens in place."

"All we need is an address, you know. Could we just ask for his no-frills finding service?"

Keira turned to look out of the window of the bus and refused to say another word to me.

Listvyanka

Like many other towns in Siberia, Listvyanka is made up entirely of wooden buildings. Even the Orthodox Church is built of birch. The shaman's house was no exception. We weren't the only ones paying him a visit that day. I'd been hoping for the sort of brief exchange you'd have with the mayor of a small village on the subject of a local family you were trying to track down, but it turned out we'd have to sit through the ceremony that was getting underway when we arrived.

We took our places in a circle of about fifty people sitting on rugs spread out inside a room. The shaman came in, wearing ceremonial dress. The gathering was silent. A young woman who couldn't have been older than twenty was lying on a mat, obviously burning up with fever from some illness. Sweat was dripping off her forehead, and she was moaning. The shaman picked up a drum. Keira, who was still in a huff, explained without any prompting on my part that the drum was an indispensable part of the ritual, and that it represented both genders: the skin was male and the body female. I made the mistake of laughing and immediately got a whack on the head for it.

The shaman began by passing the flame of a torch over the drum skin to warm it up.

"You have to admit it's a little more complicated than calling directory enquiries," I whispered in Keira's ear.

The shaman lifted his hands and his body began swaying to the beat of the drum. His chanting was hypnotic, and I soon lost any desire to be flippant. Keira was totally caught up in the scene unfurling before our eyes. The shaman went into a trance and his body began shaking violently. The sick woman's face underwent a transformation during the ceremony – the fever seemed to be dropping, and the colour returned to her cheeks. I was as fascinated by it as Keira.

The drumbeats stopped, and the shaman collapsed. You could have heard a pin drop in the room. All eyes stayed riveted on the shaman's inert body for a long moment. When he came to, he rose, went over to the young woman, laid his hands on her face and asked her to stand up. She got shakily to her feet, apparently cured of the illness that had laid her low only a little while ago. The gathering applauded the shaman. His magic had worked.

I've never been able to figure out what the man's powers really were. The scene I witnessed that day in the shaman's house in Listvyanka will forever remain a mystery to me.

The crowd scattered after the ceremony and Keira went up to the shaman to request an audience. He gestured for her to sit down and listened while she asked her questions. He told us the man we were looking for was a prominent local figure – a benefactor who gave a lot of money to the poor and paid for schools to be built. He'd even financed the conversion of a dispensary into a small hospital. The shaman wouldn't tell us where the man lived until we explained why we wanted to see him. Keira assured him we were merely looking for some information. She described her job and told him why she thought Egorov could help us: her search was purely scientific.

The shaman looked intently at Keira's pendant and asked her where it had come from.

"It's an extremely old object," she replied truthfully. "It's a fragment of a celestial chart, and we're looking for the missing bits."

"How old is it?" the shaman wanted to know, and asked if he could take a closer look.

"Millions of years old," Keira replied, handing it to him.

The shaman stroked the pendant and his face immediately clouded over. "You should not continue your journey," he said solemnly.

Keira turned to look at me. What was it that had alarmed the man all of a sudden?

"Do not keep wearing it," he said. "You do not know what you are doing."

"Have you already seen something like this?" Keira asked.

"You do not understand its implications!" the shaman said. His face had darkened.

"I don't know what you mean," Keira said, taking back her pendant. "We're scientists."

"You are fools! Do you have any idea how the world turns? Do you wish to take the risk of upsetting its balance?"

"What on earth are you talking about?" Keira snapped.

"Go away! The man you want to meet lives two kilo-metres from here, in a pink dacha with three turrets. You cannot miss it."

A few youngsters were skating on Lake Baikal some dis-tance from the shore, where the waves had been frozen into terrifying-looking sculptures. An old cargo boat with a rusted hull lay on its side, held prisoner by the ice.

"What was that man trying to tell us?" Keira wondered, thrusting her hands deep into her pockets.

"I don't have the slightest idea. You're the expert on shamanism. He's probably just afraid of science."

"His fear didn't appear irrational to me, and he seemed to know what he was talking about. It's as if he wanted to warn us about some danger."

"Keira, we're not dabbling in black magic. There's no room for anything supernatural or esoteric in either of our fields. Our approach is purely scientific. We have two frag-ments of a map we're trying to complete, and that's it."

"A map that according to you was drawn up four hun-dred million years ago, and we have absolutely no idea what it would reveal to us if we completed it."

"When we've completed it, we'll be able to scien-tifically envisage the possibility that a civilisation had knowledge of astronomy at a time when we didn't think civilisation existed on Earth. Such a discovery would put quite a few things about the history of humanity into per-spective. Isn't that what you've always been fascinated by?"

"What about you? What are you hoping for?"

"I'd be happy if this chart showed me a star whose existence I was unaware of. Why the long face?"

"I'm scared, Adrian. I've never encountered violence in the course of my research, and I still don't understand the motives of the people who've got it in for us. That shaman knew nothing about us. The way he reacted when he touched my pendant… it was really scary."

"Do you realise what you told him, and what it means for him? The man's an oracle; his power and aura are based on his knowledge and the ignorance of the people who look up to him. We turn up at his place and brandish proof of knowledge far greater than his right under his nose. You're putting him in danger. Not that I would expect the members of the Academy to react any differently if we were to make a similar disclosure to them. If a doctor arrived in a remote village untouched by modernity and treated a sick person with his medicines, the other villagers would think he was some kind of magician with unlimited powers. People venerate anyone whose knowledge exceeds their own."

"Thanks for the lecture, Adrian. But it's not the local people's ignorance that frightens me – it's ours."

We had come to the pink dacha. It looked exactly the way the shaman had described it, and he'd been right; it was so ostentatious that there was no way we could have mistaken any other house for it. The owner had made no attempt to conceal his wealth – on the contrary, he was showing it off as proof of his success and power.

Two men with Kalashnikovs slung over their shoulders were guarding the entrance to the property. I introduced myself and asked to meet the master of the house. I said we'd come on behalf of his old friend Thornsten, who'd sent us to pay off a debt. The guard ordered us to wait at the gate. Keira began jumping up and down in an effort to keep warm under the amused gaze of the second guard, who was eyeing her in a way I found extremely unpleasant. I took her in my arms and rubbed her back. The first guard returned a few moments later. We were thoroughly frisked and finally allowed into Egorov's palatial residence.

Our host greeted us in his living room, where, as he was quick to point out, the floors were made of Carrara marble and the wood panelling on the walls had been imported from England. The carpets were from Iran – very expensive ones, he added.

"I thought that old bastard Thornsten died a long time ago," he chuckled, pouring us some vodka. "Drink!" he urged. "It'll warm you up."

"Sorry to disappoint you," Keira said, "but he's fit as a fiddle."

"Good for him," Egorov replied. "So you've brought me the money he owes me, have you?"

I opened my wallet, took out a hundred-dollar bill and showed it to our host.

"There you go," I said, placing the banknote on the table. "It's all there, you can check."

Egorov looked scornfully at the greenback.

"I hope this is a joke."

"It's the precise amount he asked us to give you."

"It's what he owed me thirty years ago! If you adjusted that amount for inflation you'd still have to multiply it by a hundred for us to be quits – and that's not even counting interest. I'll give you two minutes to get the hell out, or you'll be sorry you came here to make a fool of me."

"Thornsten said you could help us," Keira said. "I'm an archaeologist, and I need your help."

"Sorry, I stopped dealing in antiquities a long time ago. Raw materials are far more lucrative. If you've come here hoping to buy something from me, you've had a wasted trip. Thornsten's pulling a fast one on both of us. Take that hundred-dollar bill and get out."

"I don't understand your hostility towards him. He spoke of you very respectfully. He seems to admire you."

"Really?" Egorov said, flattered by Keira's words.

"Why did he owe you money?" Keira asked. "A hundred dollars would've been a fair amount in these parts thirty years ago."

"Thornsten was only a go-between. He was acting on behalf of a buyer in Paris – a man who wanted to acquire an old manuscript."

"What kind of manuscript?"

"An engraved stone that had been found in a frozen tomb in Siberia. I suppose you know as well as I do that several of those tombs were discovered in the 1950s. They were all stuffed with treasures perfectly conserved by the ice."

"And they were all thoroughly looted."

"Yes, unfortunately," Egorov said, sighing. "Human greed's a terrible thing, isn't it? As soon as there's money involved, people lose all respect for the treasures of the past."

"And of course you spent all your time tracking down those tomb raiders," Keira said sarcastically.

"You've got a cute behind and a certain charm, but don't abuse my hospitality, Miss."

"Did you sell Thornsten that stone?"

"I palmed off a copy on him. His buyer was completely taken in. I knew he wouldn't pay me, so I gave him a copy – a really top quality one, though. Take back that money. Buy yourselves a good meal and tell Thornsten we're quits."

"And do you still have the original?" Keira asked, smiling.

Egorov looked her up and down, his eyes lingering on her curves. He smiled back and stood up.

"Well, since you've come all the way here... Follow me, I'll show it to you."

He walked over to the bookcases lining the walls of his living room and picked up a box covered in soft leather. He opened it and then replaced it on the shelf.

"It's not in this one. Now where could I have put it?"

He opened three similar boxes, then a fourth, and finally took an object wrapped in cotton voile out of the fifth box. He undid the string around it and showed us a stone measuring around twenty square centimetres. He placed it gently on his desk and asked us to come closer. The stone's surface had acquired a patina of age and was engraved with writing that looked like hieroglyphics.

"It's in Sumerian," he explained. "This stone is more than six thousand years old. Thornsten's buyer should have paid me for it back in the day – the price was entirely affordable. Thirty years ago I'd have sold Sargon of Akkad's coffin for a few hundred dollars. These days, this stone is priceless. Strangely enough, it's also unsellable, except to a private collector who'd keep it hidden. This kind of object can no longer circulate freely. Times have changed – antiquity smuggling has become much too dangerous. As I was saying, trading raw materials is far more profitable, and a lot less risky."

"What do these engravings mean?" Keira asked, fascinated by the stone's beauty.

"Not much. It's probably a poem or an old legend, but the man who wanted to buy it seemed to think it was very important. I should have a translation of it somewhere," he said, feeling around in the box. "Here, I've got it."

He handed the piece of paper to Keira, who read it out to me: "*There is a legend which says that a child in the womb knows the whole mystery of Creation, of the origins of the world, until the end of time. When the child is born, a messenger passes over its cradle and puts his finger on its lips so it will never reveal the secret that was entrusted to it – the secret of life.*"

I couldn't hide my astonishment when I heard those words – they resounded in my head, bringing back memories of an unfinished journey. They were the last few words I'd read on a flight to China, before I lost consciousness and the plane turned around. Keira had stopped reading, worried by my troubled expression. I groped in my pocket for my wallet, took out a sheet of paper and unfolded it. I read out the end of the strange text.

"*This finger, which erases the child's memory forever, leaves a mark. We all have this mark above our top lip, except for me. On the day I was born, the messenger forgot to pay me a visit, and I can remember everything.*"

Keira and Egorov stared at me, their faces mirroring

my astonishment. I explained the circumstances in which I'd come by the text: "It's your friend Professor Ivory who had it delivered to me just before I left for China to look for you, Keira."

"Ivory? What's he got to do with it?" she asked.

"That's the name of that son of a gun who never paid me!" Egorov exclaimed. "I thought *he* died a long time ago too."

"You're obsessed with sending everyone to their grave, aren't you?" Keira said. "And I doubt he's got anything at all to do with your loathsome tomb-raiding business."

"I'm telling you – that irreproachable professor of yours is the very man who bought the stone from me, and I'd thank you not to challenge me. I'm not in the habit of having some silly little goose doubt my word. Apologise, if you please!"

Keira crossed her arms and turned her back on him. I grabbed her shoulder and ordered her to apologise immediately. She sent me a scathing look and muttered "sorry" to our host. Fortunately he seemed to find it acceptable, and agreed to tell us more.

"That stone was found in northwestern Siberia during a dig to uncover frozen tombs. The area is full of them. The tombs had been protected by the cold for thousands of years, and were remarkably well preserved. You must understand the circumstances. All research at the time was carried out under the authority of the Party's central committee. Archaeologists were paid a measly salary to work in extremely difficult conditions."

"We're no better off in the West, but we don't go about plundering our dig sites."

I did wish Keira would keep that kind of remark to herself.

"Everyone smuggled things to make ends meet," Egorov went on. "Because I was fairly high up in the Party hierarchy, I approved reports, authorisations and funding allocations, and I decided which discoveries were sufficiently interesting to be transferred to Moscow and which would remain in the region. The Party was the first to plunder the Russian Federation's republics of their rightful treasures; all we did was take a small interme-diary's cut. Some objects never reached Moscow – they wound up in the collections of Western buyers. That's how I met your friend Thornsten. He was acting on behalf of Professor Ivory, who was fascinated by anything to do with the Scythian and Sumerian civilisations. I knew I'd never get paid and I had a talented epigraphist on our team, so I had him make a reproduction of the stone from a block of granite. Now, why don't you tell me what's brought you here? I don't suppose you've crossed the Ural Mountains to pay me back a hundred dollars."

"I'm following the tracks of nomads who would have undertaken a long journey around 4000 BC."

"Where would they have started from, and where were they going?"

"I have proof that they left from Africa and got as far as China. We can only hypothesise about what happened after that. I'm guessing they turned off towards Mongolia, crossed Siberia and sailed up the River Yenisei to the Kara Sea."

"Quite a trip. And why would your nomads have trav-elled all that distance?"

"To reach the American continent via the Arctic."

"That doesn't really answer my question."

"To carry a message."

"And you think I can help you to prove this journey happened? Who gave you that idea?"

"Thornsten. He claims you're a specialist in the Sumerian civilisation, and I suppose the stone you've just shown us bears out what he says."

"How did you meet Thornsten?" Egorov asked, a puckish glint in his eye.

"Through a friend who recommended we go and see him."

"That's very amusing."

"I don't see what's so amusing about it."

"And your friend isn't acquainted with Ivory?"

"Not as far as I know."

"Would you like to wager they've never met?" Egorov handed his phone to Keira, challenging her with his gaze. "Either you're a fool or the pair of you are amazingly naive. Call this friend and ask him."

Keira and I looked at Egorov, not quite sure what he was trying to prove. Keira took the phone, dialled Max's number and moved to the other side of the room – which, I must admit, really annoyed me. She came back a couple of minutes later. Her face had crumpled.

"You've got his number off by heart," I remarked.

"This is definitely not the time for that, Adrian."

"Did he ask after me?"

"He lied. I asked him straight out and he swore to me he didn't know Ivory, but I could tell he was lying."

Egorov went over to his bookcases, cast his eye over

the shelves and pulled out a big book. "If I've understood correctly," he said, "this old Professor Ivory of yours sent you to a friend who sent you to Thornsten who, in turn, sent you to me. And by coincidence, thirty years ago that same Ivory was trying to buy this stone of mine with its Sumerian inscription, and he's already given you a translation of that text. And of course this is all a pure fluke."

"What are you implying?" I asked.

"The two of you are puppets and Ivory's pulling your strings any which way he pleases. He's sending you off in every direction he wants – north, south, east, west. If you still haven't realised he's using you, you're even stupider than I thought."

"I think we've realised you take us for a couple of idiots; you've made that abundantly clear," Keira hissed. "But why would he do such a thing? What does he stand to gain?"

"I don't know what exactly it is you're looking for, but I suppose he must be extremely interested in the outcome. You're carrying on a task he left incomplete. It doesn't take much intelligence to figure out that you're working for him without even realising it."

Egorov opened the big book and unfolded an ancient map of Asia.

"This proof you're hoping to find is under your nose," he said. "It's the stone on which the Sumerian text is inscribed. Your Ivory was hoping I still had it, and he's fixed things to get you to come all the way to me."

Egorov sat at his desk and gestured for us to take the two large armchairs facing it.

"Archaeological research in Russia began in the

eighteenth century, on the initiative of Peter the Great. Until then, the Russians had absolutely no interest in their past. When I was in charge of the Siberian branch of the Academy, I tore my hair out trying to convince the authorities to safeguard priceless treasures – I'm not the common trafficker you think I am. Of course I had my contacts, but thanks to them I saved thousands of pieces and had at least as many restored. If it hadn't been for me, they would've been destroyed. Do you think that Sumerian stone would still exist if I hadn't been around? It would probably have been used, like hundreds of others, to shore up the wall of a barracks or fill in a road. I'm not saying my little trading business never earned me any perks, but I always knew what I was doing. I didn't sell the vestiges of our Siberia to just anyone.

"In any case, the professor hasn't wasted your time. I have indeed studied the Sumerian civilisation in greater depth than anyone else in Russia, and I've always been convinced that they travelled much further than anyone thinks they did. No one was prepared to accept my theory. I was told I was incompetent, and a crank. The artefact you're looking for to prove that your nomads did reach the Arctic is under your nose. And do you know how old the text engraved on it is? It goes back to 4004 BC. See for yourselves," he said, indicating a smaller line than the others at one end of the stone, "it's positively dated. Now why do you think they'd have tried to reach the American continent? If you're here, I suppose you must know why."

"I told you," Keira said. "They were carrying a message."

"I'm not hard of hearing, you know. What message?"

"I don't know. It was a message for the magisters of ancient civilisations."

"Do you think your messengers reached their destination?"

Keira bent over the map and pointed at the Bering Strait. Then she traced the Siberian coast with her forefinger.

"I don't know," she said again in a low voice. "And that's exactly why I need to follow their tracks."

Egorov took Keira's hand and moved it slowly over the map.

"Manpupuner," he said, placing her hand east of the Urals, in the northern section of the Komi Republic. "The site of the Seven Giants of the Urals. That's where your messengers to the magisters made their last stop."

"How do you know that?" Keira asked.

"Because the stone was found in that exact spot in Western Siberia. The river your nomads sailed down wasn't the Yenisei, it was the Ob, and they were sailing to the White Sea, not the Kara Sea. The Norway itinerary would have been a shorter, more accessible route to their destination."

"Why do you say it was their last stop?"

"Because I have good reason to think their journey ended there. I'm going to tell you something my colleagues and I have never revealed to anyone. We were digging in that area thirty years ago. There are seven stone pillars from thirty to forty-two metres high jutting out of the vast, wind-battered plateau of Manpupuner – seven enormous standing stones. Six of them are grouped into a semi-circle, and the seventh one appears to be facing the others. The Seven Giants of the Urals are an unsolved mystery. No one knows why they're there. Erosion alone can't have been responsible for these formations. The site is the Russian equivalent of your Stonehenge, except that these rocks are incomparably high."

"Why weren't your finds disclosed?"

"Strange though it may seem to you, we covered everything and left the site looking exactly as we had found it. We purposely erased all traces of our presence. The Party had no interest in our work at the time. Incompetent civil servants in Moscow would have ignored our finds. At best, they would have archived our extraordinary discoveries without analysing them or making any effort at conservation. They would have ended up gathering dust in boxes in the basement of some government building."

"What did you find?" Keira asked.

"A substantial number of human remains dating from 4000 to 3000 BC – around fifty bodies perfectly preserved by the ice. The Sumerian stone was buried in one of their tombs. The people whose tracks you're following were trapped by the onset of winter and the snow. They all died of hunger."

Keira turned to me in a fever of excitement. "This is a major discovery!" she exclaimed. "No one's ever been able to prove that the Sumerians travelled such a distance. If you'd published your discovery with all that evidence to back it up," she told Egorov, "you'd have been acclaimed by the international scientific community."

"You're very sweet, but you're far too young to know what you're talking about. If our superiors had got wind of the possible impact of our discovery, we would have immediately been deported to a gulag, and the Party apparatchiks would have taken all the credit for our work. There was no such word as 'international' in the vocabulary of the Soviet Union."

"Is that why you buried it all again?"

"What would you have done in our place?"

"Buried nearly all of it again, if I may say so," I interjected. "I don't suppose this stone is the only thing you brought back in your luggage."

Egorov gave me a dirty look.

"There were also some of the travellers' personal effects. We only took a few things. It was imperative we all keep quiet about it."

"Adrian," Keira said, "if the Sumerians' journey ended in those circumstances, it's very likely the fragment is somewhere on the Mapupuner plateau."

"*Man*pupuner," Egorov corrected. "What fragment are you talking about?"

Keira looked at me and, not waiting for a reply to her unasked question, took off her necklace, showed Egorov her pendant and told him practically everything about our search.

Egorov was fascinated by our story and invited us to stay for dinner. As the evening wore on, he offered us a room for the night into the bargain – which was just as well, since we'd totally forgotten about finding ourselves a place to stay.

Egorov kept firing questions at us during the meal, which was served in a dining room large enough to hold a badminton court. When I told him what happened when the fragments were joined, he begged us to let him see it for himself. We could hardly refuse. Keira and I put the two fragments together and they immediately gave out their bluish light, though it seemed even paler than the last time. Egorov's eyes widened, and his face suddenly looked much younger; our self-possessed host had become as excited as a child on Christmas Eve.

"What do you think would happen if all the fragments were reunited?"

"I have absolutely no idea," I replied before Keira could say anything.

"Are you both sure that these stones are four hundred million years old?"

"They're not stones," Keira replied, "but yes, we're certain they really are that old."

"Their porous surface is dotted with millions of tiny holes," I said. "When the fragments are exposed to a very strong light source, they project a map of the stars precisely as they would have appeared in the sky four hundred million years ago. If we had a powerful enough laser, I could demonstrate it for you."

"I would have loved to see that, but unfortunately I don't have that kind of equipment here."

"I must admit I'd have been worried if you did," I replied.

After dessert – a sponge cake soaked in large quantities of alcohol – Egorov got up and started pacing around the room.

"Do you think one of the missing fragments might be found on the site of the Seven Giants of the Urals?" he asked. "Yes, of course you do – what a stupid question."

"How I wish I knew the answer," Keira said.

"Naive *and* optimistic – you really are charming."

"And you…" she began. I gave her knee a warning nudge with mine under the table.

"We're in the depths of winter," Egorov said, "when the cold, dry winds sweeping the Manpupuner plateau barely give the snow a chance to settle. The ground will be frozen. How do think you're going to conduct your dig – with two small spades and a metal detector?"

"Stop being so condescending – it's really irritating. And for your information, the fragments aren't made of metal," she snapped.

"What I'm about to propose is not a metal detector for amateur treasure hunters sweeping beaches for stray coins," Egorov retorted. "It's something on a far bigger scale."

He led the way into a drawing room as huge as the dining room. The marble floor was replaced here by oak parquet, and the furniture was all French or Italian. We settled down on comfortable sofas facing a gigantic fire-place where an over-stoked fire was crackling, its flames leaping to impressive heights.

Egorov offered to place around twenty men and all the equipment Keira would need for her dig at our disposal. He promised her more resources than she'd ever been given. There was just one condition if we accepted this heaven-sent offer: he was to be associated with all her discoveries.

Keira pointed out that there would be no financial gain involved. The object we were longing to find had no market value, only scientific interest. Egorov looked offended.

"Who said anything about money?" he asked angrily. "You're the ones obsessed with it. Did you hear me mention money?"

"No," Keira replied, seeming genuinely confused. "But we both know the equipment you're offering to provide is extremely expensive, and I haven't come across too many philanthropists in the course of my career." She sounded almost apologetic.

Egorov opened a humidor and held it out to us. I was tempted to reach for a cigar, but Keira sent daggers at me so I didn't.

"I've spent most of my life on archaeological digs," Egorov said, "in far worse conditions than you'll ever experience. I've risked my neck both physically and politically. I've saved any number of treasures – I've already told you how – and all I get by way of recognition from those bastards at the Academy of Sciences is to be considered a common smuggler. As if things had really changed! What hypocrites. They've been sullying my reputation for close to three decades. If your dig is a success, I stand to earn much more than money. The times when the dead were buried with all their worldly goods are long gone. I won't be taking either the Persian carpets or the nineteenth-century paintings that adorn the walls of my house with me when I die. What I'm saying is that I want to restore my respectability. Thirty years ago, if we hadn't been afraid of our superiors, we would have published our discovery and, as you rightly pointed out, I would have become a recognised and respected scientist. I'm not going to let this second chance I've been offered pass me by. So, if you agree, we'll go on this expedition together. And if fortune smiles on us and we find anything to back up your theory, we'll jointly present our discovery to the scientific community. Does that little bargain suit you?"

Keira hesitated. Considering our circumstances, we could hardly afford to turn our backs on such a powerful ally. I pondered the full extent of the protection this partnership could give us. If Egorov could be persuaded to take the two gun-toting goons we'd met at his gate along, we'd have back-up next time someone made an attempt on our lives. Keira and I sent each other interrogative glances. It was a shared decision, but I chivalrously left it to her to speak first.

Egorov smiled at Keira. "Give me back the hundred dollars," he said solemnly.

Keira took out the dollar bill and Egorov promptly pocketed it.

"There. That's your contribution to financing the expedition. We're in business. Now we've sorted out the money aspect you seemed so worried about, can we put our heads together, as two scientists, and focus on the organisational details to ensure we make a success of this extraordinary dig?"

They sat down at the coffee table and spent the next hour drawing up a list of all the equipment they'd need. I felt excluded from their conversation. Since they were ignoring me, I seized the opportunity to inspect the books lining the walls. I found several books on archaeology, a seventeenth-century alchemist's manual, an equally ancient tome on the human anatomy, the collected works of Alexandre Dumas and a first edition of Stendhal's *The Red and the Black*. The collection of books I was browsing must have been worth a small fortune. I pored over an amazing fourteenth-century treatise on astronomy while Keira and Egorov got on with their preparations.

Keira finally noticed – at nearly 1am – that I wasn't with them, and came over to me. She actually had the nerve to ask me what I was doing. I caught the note of reproach in her question and accompanied her back to her place in front of the fire.

"It's fantastic, Adrian. We'll have all the equipment we need – we'll be able to do some really large-scale excavation. I don't know how long it'll take us, but if the fragment really is somewhere in the middle of those giant pillars, we stand a very good chance of finding it with all this gear."

I went through the list she'd drawn up with Egorov – trowels, spatulas, plumb lines, brushes, GPSs, measuring tapes, grid pegs, drawing grids, sifting screens, weighing scales, anthropometric instruments, compressors, aspirators, generators and flares to work at night, tents, markers, cameras – there seemed to be nothing missing from this extravagant list worthy of an archaeological supplies shop. Egorov lifted the receiver of a phone sitting on a side table, and two men came into the room a few moments later. He gave them the list and they immediately withdrew.

"Everything will be ready by midday tomorrow," Egorov said, stretching.

"How are you going to have it all transported?" I ventured to ask.

Keira turned to Egorov, who looked at me with a triumphant air.

"That's a surprise. Meanwhile, it's late and we need to get some sleep. I'll see you at breakfast. Be ready – we'll be off before midday."

A bodyguard led us to our quarters. The guest room wouldn't have looked out of place in a luxury hotel. Not that I'd ever been in a luxury hotel, but I doubted any bedroom could be larger than the one we'd be sleeping in that night. The bed was big enough for both of us to stretch out either lengthwise or sideways. Keira flung herself on to the thick, fluffy quilt and invited me to join her. I hadn't seen her this happy since… come to think of it, I'd never seen her this happy. I'd risked my life several times and travelled thousands of kilometres to find her. If I'd known, I'd have just given her a spade and a sieve. I was a lucky man – it didn't take much to make the woman I loved ecstatically happy. She stretched luxuriously, took off her pullover, unhooked her bra and gave me a sultry look that said I shouldn't dawdle. I didn't intend to.

Kent

The Jaguar sped along the narrow country lane leading to the manor. Sir Ashley was sitting in the back seat with the roof light switched on, leafing though a file. As he shut it, yawning, the car phone rang. The driver informed him it was a call from Moscow and passed him the phone.

"We failed to intercept your friends at Irkutsk Station. I don't know how they managed it, but they gave our men the slip," Moscow explained.

"That's unfortunate!" Ashley said, irritated.

"They're currently in the home of an antiquities trafficker on the shores of Lake Baikal."

"So why haven't you picked them up? What are you waiting for?"

"For them to come out. Egorov has connections in the region, and there's a small army guarding his dacha. I don't want a routine arrest turning into a bloodbath."

"You weren't always this cautious."

"I know you find it hard to believe, but we do have a few laws in this country. If my men go in and Egorov's guards retaliate, we'll have a hard time explaining to the federal authorities why we mounted an attack in the middle of the night without a warrant. After all, there are no legal grounds on which we can arrest the two scientists."

"Isn't being in the house of an antiquities smuggler good enough reason?"

"No, it's not a crime. Be patient. We'll snap them up without anyone being the wiser as soon as they emerge from their lair. I promise I'll have them on a plane to you tomorrow evening."

The Jaguar swerved sharply, making Ashley slide along the seat and nearly drop the phone. He caught hold of the armrest, straightened up and rapped on the glass partition to convey his annoyance to the driver.

"Just one thing," Moscow said. "You wouldn't have tried anything without notifying me, by any chance?"

"What do you mean?"

"There was a little accident on the Trans-Siberian. A railway employee received a brutal blow to her head. She's still in hospital."

"I'm sorry to hear that, my dear fellow. It's despicable to hit a woman."

"I wouldn't doubt your sincerity if it wasn't for the fact that your archaeologist and her friend were also on that train. It so happens this unspeakable attack took place in their carriage. I suppose I should see it as a mere coincidence? You would never have taken the liberty of doing something behind my back, let alone on my territory, right?"

"Of course I wouldn't," Sir Ashley replied. "I'm offended you'd even suggest it."

The car swerved violently once more. Ashley adjusted

his bow tie and banged on the glass partition again. When he put the phone back to his ear it was to find that Moscow had hung up.

Ashley pressed a button to lower the glass panel. "Have you finished shaking me up?" he barked. "And why are you driving so fast? We're not on a race circuit, as far as I know."

"No, sir, but we're going down a steepish slope and the brakes have stopped working! I'm doing the best I can, but perhaps you should fasten your seat belt – I'm afraid I may have to steer us into a ditch as soon as I can to stop this damn car."

Ashley rolled his eyes and did as he had been told. The driver managed to negotiate the next bend, but then had no choice but to veer off the road and plough into a field to avoid an oncoming truck.

The car shuddered to a halt and the driver opened Ashley's door, apologising for the inconvenience. He couldn't understand it – the car had just been serviced. He'd gone to the garage to pick it up before this trip. Ashley asked if there was a flashlight in the car. The driver immediately took one out of the tool kit and handed it to him.

"Get under the car and see what's gone wrong, dammit!" Ashley ordered.

The driver took off his jacket and obeyed. Squeezing under the low-slung car was no easy task, but he managed to wriggle in from the back. He reappeared a few minutes later covered in grime from head to foot, and sheepishly reported that the brake hoses had been perforated.

Ashley experienced a moment's doubt. It was

unthinkable that someone would make such a crude and deliberate attempt to get back at him. Then he remembered the photographs the head of security had shown him. Seated on his bench, Ivory had seemed to be looking straight at the camera. And he'd been smiling.

Paris

Ivory was leafing for the umpteenth time through the book his late chess partner had given him. He returned to the frontispiece to re-read the dedication.

> *I know you'll enjoy this book. There's nothing missing because it's got everything, including the proof of our friendship.*

> *Your devoted chess partner,*
> *Vackeers*

He didn't understand it at all. He looked at the time on his watch and smiled. He put on his coat, wound a scarf around his neck and went down for his nightly walk along the Seine.

When he reached the Pont Marie bridge he called Walter.

"Did you try to call me?"

"Several times. I was starting to lose all hope of talking to you. Adrian called me from Irkutsk. It seems they had a problem on the way."

"What sort of problem?"

"Quite an upsetting one. Someone tried to kill them."

Ivory stared at the river, forcing himself to stay calm.

"We've got to bring them back," Walter said. "Something will end up happening to them and I would never forgive myself if it did."

"I wouldn't forgive myself either, Walter. Do you know if they've met Egorov?"

"I suppose so. They were going to look for him after our phone call. Adrian seemed terribly worried. If Keira hadn't been so determined he'd have surely come back."

"Did he tell you he meant to?"

"Yes, he said he wanted to several times, and I was very hard put not to encourage him to do so."

"Walter, it's only a question of days, a few weeks at most. We can't back off. Not now."

"Have you no way of protecting them?"

"I'll contact Madrid first thing tomorrow. She's the only one with any influence over Ashley. I don't doubt for an instant that he's behind this latest barbaric attack. I managed to get a little message to him earlier this evening, but I don't think it'll be enough."

"Then let me tell Adrian to come back to England. Let's not wait for it to be too late."

"It's already too late, Walter. I've told you – we can't back off now."

Ivory hung up. Lost in thought, he slipped his phone into his coat pocket and walked back home.

Russia

A butler came into our room and opened the curtains. It was a sunny day, and we were dazzled by the glare of the morning light.

Keira buried her head under the sheets. The butler placed a breakfast tray at the foot of the bed and informed us that it was nearly eleven. He told us we were expected to be in the hall with our bags packed by midday, and went out.

I watched the top of Keira's head emerge from under the sheets, and her sidelong glance at the basket of Viennese pastries. She reached out and grabbed a croissant, dispatching it in three bites.

"Can't we stay here for a day or two?" she pleaded, sipping the tea I'd poured out for her.

"Let's go back to London. I'll treat you to a week in a luxury hotel and we'll never leave our room."

"You don't want us to go on, do you?" she asked, starting on a brioche. "We're safe with Egorov, you know."

"It seems to me you've been very quick to trust this guy. Yesterday we didn't know him from Adam, and now we're associates. I don't know where we're going, or what's in store for us."

"Me neither, but I just feel we've almost reached the end."

"What end, Keira? The Sumerians' graves, or our own?"

"Fine," she said, throwing off the sheets and bounding up. "Let's go back. I'll tell Egorov we're giving up, and if his bodyguards let us out of here we'll hop into a taxi, go to the airport and catch the first flight to London. I'll just stop off in Paris first to apply for unemployment benefits. You should be able to sign on for those in the UK too, right?"

"There's no need to be cynical. All right, we'll go on, but promise me first – if we run into the slightest danger, we stop everything."

"Define 'danger,'" she said, sitting back down on the bed.

I took her face in my hands and replied: "When someone tries to kill us, we're in danger. I know your thirst for discovery is stronger than anything else, but you should be aware of the risks we're running before it's too late."

Egorov was waiting for us in the hall wearing a long white fur cape, with a chapka on his head. If I'd ever dreamed of meeting a real-life version of Michael Strogoff, courier to the tsar, my wish had come true. He gave us stocking caps, gloves and two fleece-lined parkas that made our coats look like poor cousins.

"It'll really be freezing cold where we're going, so wrap up warm. We're leaving in ten minutes. My men will get your bags. Follow me – let's go to the garage."

The lift stopped at the second level of the basement,

where there was a neat line-up of cars ranging from sports coupés to a presidential limousine.

"I see you don't only trade in old stuff," I told Egorov.

"Quite right," he replied, opening the car door.

There were two sedans in front of ours, with another two bringing up the rear. The convoy swept out into the street and along the road skirting the lake.

"Western Siberia is three thousand kilometres away, if I'm not mistaken," I said a little while later. "Have you planned on a rest stop, or are we doing it in one stretch?"

Egorov signalled to the driver and the car screeched to a halt. He turned to look at me.

"Are you going to be bugging me the whole time? If this trip bores you, it isn't too late to get out."

Keira shot me a look blacker than the waters of the lake and I apologised to Egorov, who held out a hand to me. How could I refuse a gentlemanly handshake? The car started up and we drove on in silence for the next half-hour. The road plunged into a snow-covered forest. When we reached the picturesque little village of Koty shortly afterwards, the convoy slowed and turned off onto a track. There were two hangars that couldn't be seen from the road at the end of the track. The cars came to a halt and Egorov asked us to follow him. Inside were two of the huge helicopters used by the Russian Army to transport troops and cargo. I'd seen machines like these in documentaries about the Soviet war in Afghanistan, but I'd never seen one up close.

"I know you're not going to believe me," Egorov said, walking towards the first helicopter, "but I won these in a card game."

Keira shot me an amused glance and started climbing the ladder into the cabin.

"Who are you really?" I asked Egorov.

"An ally," he replied, slapping me on the back, "and I haven't given up hope of convincing you it's true. Are you boarding, or would you rather stay in the hangar?"

The cockpit was as large as that of any commercial airliner. Forklift trucks were driving up the rear loading ramp and dropping large crates into the hold, where Egorov's men lashed them down securely. The cabin had seating for up to twenty-five passengers. The Mil Mi-26's proprietor seemed as proud of its twin 11,240-shaft horsepower engines as any thoroughbred breeder. We would be making four refuelling stops. The helicopter had a range of six hundred kilometres with the payload we were carrying, and Manpupuner was three thousand kilometres away. It would take us eleven hours flying to cover the distance. The trucks retreated, Egorov's men checked the ropes securing the crates of equipment one last time, then the rear cargo door was pulled up and the helicopter was towed out of the hangar.

The turbines started up with a whistling sound. The noise became deafening as the eight rotor blades turned faster and faster.

"You'll get used to it," Egorov shouted. "Enjoy the view – you're going to see Russia in a way few people ever have."

The pilot turned and gave us a quick wave, and the heavy flying machine lifted off. The nose of the helicopter dipped when it was fifty metres above the ground, and Keira pressed her face to the window.

*

We'd been flying for about an hour when Egorov pointed to the town of Ilanksy in the distance, to our left. Then we passed Kansk and Krasnoyarsk, keeping well clear to stay off the air traffic control radars. Our pilot appeared to know what he was doing; all we were overflying was a seemingly endless white expanse. From time to time we'd see a frozen river – a silver thread winding across the landscape like a charcoal line across a blank sheet of paper.

We stopped to refuel for the first time along the Uda River. The two tankers pumping fuel into the helicopter's tanks had come from the town of Atagay, a few kilometres from the place where we'd landed.

"It's all a question of organisation," Egorov said, watching his men swarming around the helicopter. "There's no room for improvisation when the outside temperature is minus twenty. If we were grounded because we couldn't refuel, we'd die here in a matter of hours."

We took advantage of the stop to stretch our legs. Egorov had been right: it was unbearably cold.

We were asked to re-board, the tanker trucks already disappearing down a track leading into the forest. The turbines whistled and we lifted off. The wind would soon erase our footprints in the snow.

I'd experienced turbulence in planes, but never in a helicopter. It wasn't my first time in one – in the Atacama, I'd often taken a helicopter to return to the valley, but not in these weather conditions. We were flying into a snowstorm. The helicopter pitched and rolled and we were thrown around in our seats for quite a while, but since Egorov didn't seem worried, I decided we weren't running any risks. A little later, however, as the machine juddered even harder, it occurred to me that perhaps Egorov wouldn't show his fear in the face of death if he could help it.

The sky turned calm again after the second fuel stop, and Keira dropped off on my shoulder. I put my arms around her to settle her more comfortably and caught Egorov looking at us tenderly – I was surprised by the benevolence in his gaze. I smiled at him but he turned to look out of the window, pretending he hadn't noticed.

Third fuel stop. This time there was no question of us getting off; the storm had started up again and we couldn't see a thing. It was too risky to move even a few metres away from the helicopter. Egorov got up and went over to the cockpit, looking worried. Leaning closer to the glass partition, he spoke to the pilot in Russian. I couldn't understand what they were saying. He came back a few seconds later and sat down facing us.

"Is there a problem?" Keira asked.

"If the tankers can't spot us in this whiteout, yes, we'll have a serious problem."

I bent to peer out of the window. Visibility was near zero. There was a gusty wind blowing, and each new flurry lifted a pile of snow.

"Any chance of the helicopter icing up?" I asked.

"No," Egorov replied. "The engine air intakes are fitted with a de-icing system to fly missions in extreme cold."

A yellow light swept across the cabin. Egorov got to his feet, relieved to see the powerful headlights of the tanker trucks. The entire crew was called on to help with the refuelling. The pilot started up his machine as soon as the tanks had been filled; he had to do a warm-up procedure before taking off. The storm continued for another two hours. Keira wasn't feeling well. I did my best to comfort her, but we were trapped in this sardine can, tossed about worse than we'd have been on a trawler navigating a rough sea.

The sky finally cleared. "It's often like this when you overfly Siberia in this season," Egorov told us. "The worst is behind us. Get some rest. We've another four hours of flying and once we're there we'll need all hands on deck to set up camp."

We were offered a meal, but our stomachs had been subjected to too much churning to want even a morsel of food. Keira put her head on my knees and fell asleep again. It was the best way to kill time. I leaned towards the window again.

"We're only six hundred kilometres from the Kara Sea," Egorov said, pointing northwards. "But believe me, it would have taken our Sumerians rather longer than us to get there!"

Keira sat up and peered out in an attempt to see something. Egorov encouraged her go to the cockpit. The co-pilot got up and offered her his seat. I went and stood just behind her. She looked fascinated, dazzled and happy, and seeing her like this swept away all my reluctance to go on with this trip. This adventure we were experiencing together would leave us some fabulous memories, and I told myself that made the risks well worth taking.

"If you tell your kids about this one day, they won't believe you!" I shouted to Keira.

She answered without turning, in that little voice I'd become so familiar with: "Is that your way of telling me you'd like us to have children?"

Hotel Baltschug Kempinski, Moscow

Moscow was enjoying afternoon tea with a young lady who wasn't his wife in the crowded lobby bar of a luxury hotel at the Red Square end of the bridge spanning the Moskva River. Uniformed waiters zigzagged between the tables carrying tea and pastries to the tourists and businesspeople who were mingling in the elegant surroundings of one of the city's most sought-after venues.

A man sat down at the bar and stared at Moscow, trying to catch his eye. When Moscow noticed him, he asked his guest to excuse him and made his way to the bar.

"What the hell are you doing here?" Moscow asked, perching himself on the next stool.

"I'm sorry to disturb you, sir. It was impossible to intervene this morning."

"You're a bunch of good-for-nothings. I promised London it would all be taken care of this evening. I thought you'd come to tell me they were on a flight to Heathrow."

"We couldn't do anything because they came out of Egorov's house with an escort and then flew off in a helicopter with him."

Moscow knew his hands were tied, and it made him furious. As long as the scientists were under the protection of Egorov and his men, it would be impossible for him to intercept them without sparking off a massacre.

"Where are they going in this helicopter?"

"Egorov filed a flight plan this morning. He was supposed to be landing at Lesosibirsk, but the helicopter veered off course and disappeared from radar a short time later."

"If only we could be sure they crashed!"

"It's not impossible, sir. There was a very bad snowstorm."

"They might have been able to land and wait for the snowstorm to move away."

"It did move away, and the helicopter didn't reappear on the radar screens."

"Which means the pilot managed to fly under the radar and we lost them."

"Not exactly, sir. I did think of that possibility. Two tanker trucks carrying twelve thousand litres of fuel left Pyt-Yakh in the early afternoon and only returned to their base four hours later. If they'd refuelled Egorov's helicopter it would have been at a spot halfway to Khanty-Mansiysk, precisely two hours away by road from Pyt-Yakh."

"That doesn't tell us where the helicopter was flying to."

"No, but I worked it out. They'd have been flying into headwinds along the way, and the Mil Mi-26 would have a range of six hundred kilometres at most in those conditions. After departure, they must have travelled as the crow flies to reach their refuelling spot when they did. If they continue along the same route, and considering their range, they'll arrive just before nightfall in the Komi Republic, somewhere around Vuktyl."

"Any idea why they're going there?"

"Not yet, sir, but it must be for a very good reason if they're willing to fly for eleven hours and travel nearly three thousand kilometres. If we get a Sikorsky to take off from Ekaterinburg tomorrow morning, we can start circling the area from midday onwards to locate them."

"No, let's do it differently. It's vital they don't see us, or they'll slip away immediately. Find out where they could have landed. Have the local police interrogate people in the area so we'll know whether anyone has seen or heard the helicopter. Call me on my mobile when you've got more information, even if it's the middle of the night. And get a special ops team ready. If those fools are hiding in an isolated enough spot we can go in, no holds barred."

Manpupuner

The pilot announced that we were on our final approach. We went back to our seats and the co-pilot returned to his, but Egorov recommended we stand up again and peer through the cockpit to see the sight looming up in the distance.

Seven stone behemoths rose up on a high plateau merging with the horizon to the north of the Urals, looking like seven giants frozen in their tracks. Nature is said to have shaped them over a period of two hundred million years, and the result is one of the most amazing geological formations on the planet. They are impressive because of their sheer size, as well as their positions – six of the pillars stand in a semi-circle facing the seventh. Winter had clothed them in a thick white coat, as if to protect them from the cold.

I turned to Egorov, who was visibly moved. "I never thought I'd be back one day," he breathed. "I have so many memories of my time here."

The helicopter was descending, dislodging large puffs of snow as it neared the ground.

"Manpupuner means 'the little mountain of the gods' in the Mansi language," Egorov explained. "In former times, the Mansi shamans were the only ones allowed on the site. There are many legends about the Seven Giants of the Urals. The most popular one tells of a quarrel breaking out between a shaman and six giants who had sprung up from hell to cross the mountain range. The shaman transformed them into these stone monsters, but his own fate was sealed in the process – he's trapped inside the seventh stone, the one facing the others, or so the story goes. You can't reach this plateau in winter unless you've had very advanced fitness training, or come by air."

The helicopter landed and the pilot shut down the turbines. All we could hear was the whistling of the wind as it lashed the fuselage.

"Let's go," Egorov ordered. "We've no time to lose."

His men unfastened the ropes securing the crates in the hold and began to open them up. The first two contained snowmobiles; they could each carry three people. Other boxes had sled hitches covered in thick waterproof canvas. An icy wind blew into the cabin when the loading door was opened. Egorov beckoned us to hurry up; we all had to get down to our tasks if we wanted to set up camp before nightfall.

"Can you drive a snowmobile?" he asked me.

I *had* ridden across London on a motorbike – on the back, but still. And this bike had had a ski and tracks, so surely it was more stable. I nodded yes. Egorov must have had his doubts about my riding skills. He rolled his eyes as I searched in vain for the kick starter on the side, and pointed out the electric start.

"There's no neutral gear and no clutch on these things, and when you want to accelerate you don't twist the handlebar grip, you push this lever under the brake. Sure you know how to drive it?"

I nodded again, and asked Keira to get on behind me. While I skidded around on the ice trying to get the hang of this new vehicle, Egorov's teams were busy installing track lighting to mark off our camp boundary. When they started up the two generators, a large section of the plateau was flooded with light as bright as full daylight.

Three men were walking around carrying gas bottles on their backs; the bottles were equipped with nozzles spraying large jets of fire. They looked like the flamethrowers used in wartime, but Egorov called them "heaters." The men swept the ground with these powerful torches. Once the ice had softened, they set up a dozen perfectly aligned canvas tents covered in a greyish insulated material that made the place look like a base camp on the moon.

Keira had gone into archaeologist mode, even though the environment was totally unfamiliar. She had set up her laboratory in one of the tents and was already hard at work arranging all her tools and implements, while the two men who'd been assigned to her emptied out crates containing more equipment than she'd likely ever seen. I was given the task of sorting. All the labels on the boxes were in Cyrillic, but I got on with it to the best of my ability, ignoring Keira's scolding when I put a trowel into the drawer meant for spatulas.

At 9pm Egorov came into our tent and took us off to the mess tent. My self-esteem took a blow when I realised the cook had managed to set up a mobile kitchen worthy of a military camp in the time it had taken me to put away the contents of barely a dozen boxes.

We were served a hot meal. Egorov's men talked among themselves, not paying us the slightest attention. We ate at the boss's table – the only one with a fine red wine on it instead of beer. Work began again at 10pm. A dozen men marked out the excavation site under Keira's command. A bell rang at midnight to signal the end of the first stage of operations. Now the camp was operational we were all allowed to go to bed.

Keira and I had been allotted two camp beds set off to one side at the end of a large tent where ten other people were sleeping. Egorov was the only one entitled to a tent of his own.

The silence was broken only by the snoring of the men, who'd fallen asleep immediately. Keira got off her bed and came over to mine.

"Move over," she whispered, wriggling into my sleeping bag. "We can keep each other warm."

She fell asleep, exhausted by our tiring evening. Our canvas tent billowed as the wind blew more and more strongly.

Hotel Baltschug Kempinski, Moscow

A blue light was flashing on the bedside table. Moscow picked up his mobile and slid it open.

"We've located them."

The young woman lying next to Moscow turned over in her sleep and her hand landed on his face. He pushed it off, got out of bed and went into the small sitting room of the suite he had booked into with his mistress.

"How do you wish to proceed?" said the man on the other end.

Moscow picked up the packet of cigarettes lying on the sofa, lit one and went to the window. The water in the river would normally have frozen over by now, but this year winter hadn't yet caught the Moskva in its icy grip.

"Organise a rescue operation," Moscow replied. "Tell your men the two Westerners who are to be freed are valuable scientists, and that their mission is to recover them safe and sound. Tell them to show no mercy with the kidnappers."

"Clever. What about Egorov?"

"If he survives the attack, good for him. If he doesn't,

have him buried with the small fry. Don't leave any traces. I'll join you as soon as our two subjects have been taken to safety. Treat them considerately, but make sure no one talks to them before I get there. And I mean no one."

"We'll be intervening on extremely hostile terrain. I'll need some time to put together an operation of this scale."

"Cut that time in two, and call me back when it's all over."

Manpupuner

It was sunrise. The storm had blown over during the night. Keira and I emerged from our tent dressed like two Eskimos setting out on a jaunt and found that the ground was covered in snow. The mess tent was only a few metres away, but by the time we reached it I felt as if I'd already burned up all the calories I'd accumulated during the night. It was freezing outside. Egorov assured us that in a few hours' time the air would be drier and we'd feel the biting cold less keenly. After breakfast Keira got down to work and I helped her. She had to get used to working in these conditions. One of Egorov's men spoke reasonably good English, and was doubling as her dig supervisor and translator. The dig site had been marked off. Keira's glance swept the surroundings and paused at the stone giants. They really were impressive. I wondered whether nature alone was responsible for the shapes they had acquired after two hundred million years of being incessantly sculpted by the rain and the wind.

"Do you really think there's a shaman trapped in there?" Keira asked me, walking up to the one standing off by itself.

"Who knows?" I replied. "One can never tell how much truth there is to these legends."

"I feel as if they're observing us."

"Who, the giants?"

"No, Egorov's men. They seem to be paying us no attention, but I can tell they're taking it in turns to keep an eye on us. It's stupid – where do they think we'd go?"

"That's exactly what's worrying me. We've been given conditional freedom in the middle of this unwelcoming landscape and we're totally dependent on your new pal. If we find our fragment, what's the guarantee he won't spirit it away and leave us here?"

"It wouldn't be in his interest to do that. He needs our scientific cachet."

"That's if he's genuinely here for the reason he told us."

We changed the subject. Egorov was making his way towards us.

"I've re-read my notebooks from the last time. We should find the first tombs in this area," he said, pointing to the space between the last two stone giants. "Let's start digging. Time's short."

Egorov either had a remarkably sharp memory or he'd taken very detailed notes. By midday we'd already stumbled on our first discovery, and it left Keira speechless.

We'd spent the morning digging and clearing away the ice and soil to a depth of around eighty centimetres when the vestiges of a tomb were suddenly exposed. Keira scraped at the ground, revealing a swatch of black fabric. She pulled out a few threads with a pair of tweezers and put them in three glass tubes that she closed up immediately. Then she continued working, carefully moving away the ice. Egorov's men were doing the same thing a short distance away.

"If they really are the Sumerians, it would be quite simply fantastic!" she exclaimed, sitting up. "A whole group of Sumerians northeast of the Urals – do you realise the significance of this discovery, Adrian? And they're exceptionally well preserved. We'll be able to learn how they dressed and what they ate."

"I thought they'd died of hunger."

"Their desiccated organs will show traces of bacteria from their diet and their bones will have marks of the diseases they suffered from."

I fled her unappetising explanations and went to find us a thermos of coffee. Keira warmed her hands on the cup – she'd been digging in the ice for the past two hours. Her back was hurting, but she knelt and set to work once more.

Eleven tombs had been unearthed by the end of the day. The bodies in them were mummified by the cold, and we wondered how to preserve them. Keira asked Egorov about it over lunch.

"How are you planning to protect them?"

"Nothing's likely to happen to them in these temperatures. We'll store them in an unheated tent. I'll have watertight containers brought here by helicopter in two days' time to transfer two of the bodies to Pechora. I think it's important they stay in the Komi Republic. I see no reason why we should let the members of the Academy in Moscow get their hands on the remains. If they want to see them, they can make the trip here."

"What are we going to do with the other bodies? You said there were fifty tombs. How do we know there aren't more of them on the plateau?"

"We'll film the ones we've opened, and close them up again until we've announced our spectacular discovery to the scientific community, with evidence to prove it. Then we'll get official permission for the dig from the relevant authorities, and take the necessary steps together with them. I don't want to be suspected of looting anything whatsoever. But let me remind you it's not the only thing we've come looking for. It's not the number of tombs under the ice we're interested in – what we really want is to find the one that has your fragment. We'll have to spend less time on each body. You should be focusing on the area around them."

Keira looked pensive. She pushed her plate away, staring into space.

"What's up?" I asked.

"These men died of cold and hunger. It was the forces of nature that buried them. There's no way they would've had the strength to dig the graves of the ones who'd died before them. Anyway, apart from the children and the oldest among them, they must all have died within a short time of each other."

"What are you trying to say?" Egorov asked.

"Think about it. You've travelled thousands of kilometres to carry a message – a journey undertaken over several generations. Now, imagine you're the last survivors of this incredible adventure. You realise you're trapped and won't be able to finish the journey. What would you do?"

Egorov looked at me as if he thought I knew the answer. It was the first time he'd shown any interest in me. I helped myself to some more stew. It was pretty disgusting, but it helped me play for time.

"Well," I said, thinking hard as I chewed my mouthful, "in any event…"

"If you'd travelled all those thousands of kilometres to carry a message," Keira interrupted, "and sacrificed your life, wouldn't you do everything you could to make sure the message got to the people it was meant for?"

"In that case, it wouldn't be a good idea to bury it," I said, with a triumphant look at Egorov.

"Exactly!" Keira exclaimed. "And so you'd use the last of your strength to display it in a place where it would be seen."

Egorov and Keira jumped up; they pulled on their parkas and raced outside. Still unsure what she meant, I followed them.

The teams were already back at work.

"Where, though?" Egorov asked, his gaze sweeping the landscape.

"I'm not an archaeology specialist like the two of you," I ventured humbly, "but if I were dying of cold, which I am, actually, and if I wanted to make sure an object wouldn't get buried… well, the only possible place is staring us right in the face."

"The stone giants," Keira said. "The fragment must be embedded in one of them."

"I swear I don't want to be a killjoy," I said, "but since these blocks of stone are approximately fifty metres high and ten metres in diameter, that is to say pi times ten times fifty, that gives us a surface area of one thousand five hundred and seventy one square metres per pillar to search, not counting the crevices, presuming we've first managed to melt the snow covering them and found a way to hoist ourselves up, in which case I would describe this endeavour as mind-bogglingly difficult."

Keira looked at me strangely.

"What? What'd I say?"

"You're a killjoy."

"He's not entirely wrong," Egorov said. "We don't have the equipment to free the giants of their coating of ice. We'd have to put up huge scaffolding, and we'd need ten times as many men. It's impossible."

"Wait," Keira said. "Let's think some more."

She began pacing along the grid.

"I'm the one carrying the fragment," she said, thinking out loud. "My fellow travellers and I are trapped on this plateau we were foolhardy enough to climb up to because we wanted to look far out into the distance and see which direction to take. The sides of the mountain have frozen over, and we can't go back down. There's no game, no vegetation, nothing to eat, and I realise we're going to die of hunger. The snow has already covered up the bodies of our dead. I know it'll soon be my turn to die, so I decide to use the little remaining strength I have to climb one of these giants and embed the fragment I'm responsible for in the stone, in the hope that someone will find it some-day, and continue the journey."

"That's a very vivid description," I told Keira, "and I'm full of compassion for this hero who sacrificed his life, but it doesn't tell us which of the giants he chose, or which side of it he climbed up."

"We have to stop digging in the middle of the plateau and devote all our efforts to digging at the foot of the giants. If we find a body, we'll be almost there."

"What makes you think so?" Egorov asked.

"I'm full of compassion for that man too," Keira replied, "and if I'd run out of strength after carrying out my mission and embedding the fragment in the stone, and if I saw all my friends lying dead, I'd have just let myself fall into the void to cut my suffering short."

Egorov decided to trust Keira's instinct. He ordered his men to abandon their search and gather round – he had new instructions for them.

"Where do you want us to start?" Egorov asked Keira.

"Do you know the legend of the seven wise men?" she asked.

"The Abgal? The Seven Sages, half-man, half-fish, are found in several ancient civilisations in the form of civilising gods. They were the seven guardians of the sky and the Earth, who brought knowledge to human beings. Are you testing my knowledge of the Sumerian civilisation?"

"No, but what do you think? If the Sumerians had believed these seven giants were the Abgal…"

"Then," he interrupted her, "they'd certainly have chosen the first one – the one leading the way."

"The giant facing the others?" I asked.

"Yes," Egorov replied. "They called him Adapa."

Egorov ordered his men to gather at the foot of the huge pillar and start digging. I began to hope that the heroic Sumerian had broken his neck climbing the giant stone and fallen to the ground clutching the fragment. There was nothing scientific about my hypothesis, but if it was true we'd save a lot of time. And anyway, luck can strike when you least expect it. I suspected Keira of thinking along the same lines, because she was urging Egorov's men to go slowly and explore the ground more carefully.

As things turned out, we would have to wait. The snow was falling faster than we could clear it away, and the weather conditions were worsening by the hour. A storm bigger than the previous one began raging, and forced us to break off our search. I was totally exhausted; all I could think of was a hot bath and a comfortable mattress. Egorov sent us all off to get some rest and said he'd call us back to work as soon as the storm blew over, even if it was the middle of the night. Keira was very keyed up and complained bitterly about the storm hampering her progress. She wanted to leave our tent and go to the laboratory to study the first finds. I had to reason with her to persuade her otherwise. We couldn't see five metres in front of us, and it would be reckless to go outside in these conditions. She finally gave in and agreed to come and lie down beside me.

"I think I'm cursed," she said.

"It's only a snowstorm in the middle of winter in deepest Siberia, so I hardly think it's a curse. I'm sure the weather will be better tomorrow."

"Egorov told me the storm could last several days," Keira fumed.

"You look like death warmed over. You should get some rest. And even if the storm lasts for forty-eight hours, it's not the end of the world. The finds you unearthed this morning are priceless."

"Why do you always exclude yourself? We'd never

have got here or experienced the things we have if it hadn't been for you."

I thought back to the events of the past few weeks and was hard put to find any basis for her generous remark. Keira snuggled up to me. I stayed awake for a long time listening to her breathing. Outside, the assaults of the wind were getting stronger. I secretly blessed the bad weather for the respite it had given us, and these moments of intimacy.

The next day dawned almost as dark as night. The storm had worsened. There was no question of leaving the tent without being roped together. We walked to the mess tent by the light of a powerful flashlight, battling to stay upright as we were knocked back by incredibly violent gusts of wind. Towards the end of the afternoon, Egorov told us the worst was over. The area of low pressure was restricted to this region, and it wouldn't be long before the north winds chased it away. He was hoping we could start work again the next day. Keira and I tried to gauge the amount of snow we'd have to clear away before we could carry on. We played cards; there was no other way to while away the hours. Keira left the game several times to go and check on the storm's progress, and returned each time looking unsure.

At six in the morning I was woken by the sound of footsteps just outside our tent. I got out of bed noiselessly, gently opened the double-zipped flap of our tent and poked my head through the opening. The storm had subsided and thin snow was falling under a grey sky. My gaze travelled to the stone giants, which were finally visible again in the dawn light. But something else caught my eye – something I'd much rather not have seen. At the foot of the solitary stone giant that supposedly contained the body of an ancient shaman, the body of one of our own was lying in a pool of blood that stained the snow.

Around thirty men in white overalls were surging up over the mountainside with surprising agility. I watched as they advanced upon us and encircled the camp. One of our guards stepped out. I saw him freeze, stopped in his tracks by a bullet that had hit him right in the chest. He barely had time to fire a shot before collapsing.

The alert had been given. Some of Egorov's men rushed out of their tents and were mowed down with near-military precision. It was carnage. The ones who'd stayed inside had taken up position and were firing back with pump-action shotguns, but the targets were too far away for them to be effective. The battle continued. Our assailants were gaining ground, crawling closer and closer. I saw two of them get hit and fall.

The shots had woken Keira. She sat straight up in bed and saw my haggard face. I ordered her to get dressed immediately. I evaluated our situation as she pulled on her shoes. There was no hope of escape. It would be impossible to sneak out through the back; our canvas tent was too solidly fixed. I gave in to panic, picked up a spade and started digging. Keira went over to the peephole I'd left open. I turned around and yanked her back inside.

"They're shooting point blank at anything that moves. Stay away from the walls and help me!"

"Adrian, the ice is hard as wood, you're wasting your time. Who are these people?"

"I've no idea – they didn't have the courtesy to intro-duce themselves before opening fire on us."

There was a fresh round of shots – bursts of machine-gun fire this time. I hated feeling so powerless, and did exactly what I'd forbidden Keira to do. Poking my head outside again, I came to witness a massacre: the men in white approached a tent and fed in a cable along the ground that allowed them to see inside. Moments later, they emptied their magazines into the canvas and went on to the next pitch.

I zipped up our tent flap, went over to Keira and curled up over her to shield her as best as I could.

She lifted her head, smiled sadly and placed a kiss on my lips.

"That's terribly chivalrous of you, my darling, but I'm afraid it won't help much. I love you and I have no re-grets," she said, kissing me again.

There was nothing left to do but wait for it to be our turn. I held her close and whispered that I had no regrets either. Our declarations of love were interrupted by the brutal intrusion into our tent of two men holding assault rifles. I tightened my grip on Keira and shut my eyes.

Luzhkov Bridge, Moscow

Vodootvodny Canal had frozen over. A dozen or so people were skating rapidly along the thick coat of ice. Moscow was walking to his office, a black Mercedes following a short distance behind. He took out his mobile phone and called London.

"The raid is over," he said.

"You're sounding odd. Did everything go the way we hoped?"

"Not really – the conditions were extremely difficult."

Ashley held his breath, waiting for his colleague to tell him what had happened next.

"I'm afraid I may be called to account sooner than I thought," Moscow went on. "Egorov's team fought bravely, and we lost some of our men."

"I don't give a damn about your men," Ashley snapped. "Tell me what happened to our scientists."

Moscow hung up and waved his driver over. The Mercedes drew up beside him and his bodyguard got out to open the door. Moscow climbed into the back seat and the car sped off. The onboard telephone rang several times, but he refused to take the call.

He made a quick stop at the office and then had his driver take him to Sheremetyevo Airport, where a private plane was waiting for him in front of the corporate aviation terminal. The car zipped through the traffic jams, siren wailing, as it crossed the city. Moscow sighed and looked at his watch. It would take him another three hours to reach Ekaterinburg.

Manpupuner

The men who had burst into our tent dragged us swiftly outside. Blood-soaked bodies were strewn over the plateau of the Seven Giants of the Urals. Egorov alone seemed to have survived the attack. He lay face down on his belly, wrists and ankles handcuffed. Six rifle-toting men were guarding him. He lifted his head for a farewell glance at us and was immediately given a hard kick in the neck.

We heard the muffled sound of a rotor and loose snow began blowing about in front of us. A powerful helicopter appeared over the cliff face and landed a few metres away. The two attackers escorting us gave us a friendly tap on the back and led us to the helicopter. As we were being pulled on board, one of them gave us a thumbs-up sign, as if to congratulate us. The door closed and the helicopter took off. The pilot circled the camp and Keira bent to the window to take a final look at it.

"They're destroying everything," she said as she sat back, her face crumpling.

I looked out too and witnessed a frightful scene. A

dozen men in white overalls were sliding the lifeless bodies of Egorov's men into the Sumerian tombs and closing them back up, while others were busy dismantling the tents. Keira was inconsolable.

Not one of the helicopter's six-man crew would say a word to us. We were offered hot beverages and sandwiches, but we weren't hungry or thirsty. I took Keira's hand and held it firmly in mine.

"I don't know where they're taking us," she told me, "but this time I really do believe we've come to the end of our search."

I took her by the shoulder and hugged her close, whispering that the important thing was that we were still alive.

After two hours of flying, the man facing us asked us to fasten our safety belts. The helicopter was preparing to land. The door opened as soon as the wheels touched the ground. We found ourselves in front of a large hangar at the far end of a mid-sized airport where a twin-engined jet with a Russian flag on the tail and no tail number was parked. A stairway was lowered from it as we approached. Two men in navy blue suits were waiting for us inside the plane. The slimmer one got up and greeted us with a wide smile.

"I'm glad to see you made it safe and sound," he said in perfect English. "You must be exhausted. We'll be taking off immediately."

The engines started up. A few seconds later, the plane taxied onto the runway and took off.

"Ekaterinburg – a very pretty city," the man said as the plane climbed. "We'll be landing in Moscow in an hour and a half, and you'll be put on a plane to London. We've booked you two seats in business class. Don't thank me – it was the least we could do considering the ordeal you've had to endure these past few days. Two scientists of your calibre deserve the highest consideration. Meanwhile, I must ask you to hand over your passports."

The man put the passports away in his jacket pocket and opened a baggage compartment containing a minibar. He poured us some vodka. Keira downed hers in one shot and held out her glass for a refill. She threw the second one back equally wordlessly.

"Could you explain what's going on?" I asked our host.

He refilled our glasses and raised his in a toast.

"We're delighted to have been able to free you from your kidnappers."

Keira spat out the mouthful of vodka she'd been about to swallow.

"Our kidnappers? What kidnappers?"

"You were lucky," the man said. "The men holding you prisoner were reputed to be extremely dangerous. We got there in time. You should be feeling indebted to our teams, who took quite some risks on your behalf. We've had heavy losses among our ranks, unfortunately. Two of our best agents lost their lives to save yours."

"But no one was holding us prisoner!" Keira exploded. "We were there of our own free will. We'd got started on an incredible dig and your men ruined it. It was a genuine slaughter. It was unspeakably cruel. How dare you…"

"We know you were taking part in an illegal dig," the man cut in, "organised by criminals with the sole aim of shamelessly looting Siberia's treasures. Didn't you know Egorov is a member of the Russian mafia, Miss? Two scientists with reputations such as yours could only have been forced into being accessories to these crimes. No doubt your kidnappers threatened you with summary execution if you made any attempt to rebel. Your visas show you entered Russia purely for tourism purposes. We're flattered you chose our country as your leisure destination. I'm sure you would have acted within a legal framework if you'd had the slightest intention of working on our territory. You are certainly well aware of the risks that looters face. The punishment ranges from ten to twenty years in jail, depending on the seriousness of the crime. Do we now agree on my version of events?"

I unhesitatingly told him we had no objection. Keira remained silent, but only for a short time. She couldn't stop herself asking what would happen to Egorov. The question made our host smile.

"That, my dear young lady, will depend entirely on his willingness to cooperate with our investigation. But don't have any regrets about him. I can assure you he's a most disreputable character."

He then said he had some work to be getting on with, and apologised for cutting our conversation short. He pulled a file out of a case and buried himself with it for the rest of the flight.

The plane began its descent into the Russian capital. When we'd landed, the man led us to a car and drove us to the foot of a gangway attached to a British Airways plane.

"Two things before you leave. Don't come back to Russia – we can no longer guarantee your safety. Now listen carefully. I'm breaking a rule, but I like the two of you a lot more than the person I'm betraying. There's a reception committee waiting for you in London, and I fear the outing in store for you will be far less pleasant than the little trip we've just had. So if I were you, I wouldn't hang around at Heathrow. Once you've passed through customs, I'd get away as soon as I could. In fact, it would be even better if you could find a way to avoid going through customs altogether."

The man gave us back our passports and gestured towards the gangway. A hostess led us to our seats. Her unmistakably English accent was music to my ears, and I thanked her profusely for her kind welcome.

"Want me to get you her telephone number?" Keira asked as she buckled up.

"No, but it'd be great if you could convince that man sitting on the other side of the aisle to lend you his mobile."

Keira gave me a surprised look but obligingly turned to her neighbour, who was tapping out a text message on his phone. She unleashed a thoroughly indecent charm offensive and handed me the phone a couple of minutes later.

London

The Boeing 767 landed at Heathrow four hours after taking off from Moscow. It was 10.30pm local time. Perhaps night would be on our side. The plane taxied to a stop in a parking bay some distance from the terminal. Through the window, I saw two shuttle buses waiting at the foot of the airstairs. I told Keira to take her time; we'd disembark with the second lot of passengers.

We got on the bus and I asked Keira to stay close to the door. I wedged my foot in it to keep the safety latch from locking. The bus moved along the tarmac and entered a tunnel under the runways. The driver braked to allow a tractor towing luggage trailers to go past. It was now or never. I pushed open the folding door, took Keira's hand and pulled her out. Once we were outside, we raced through the dark tunnel after the departing luggage trailers and jumped up on the last one. Keira landed against two large suitcases and I found myself lying on some bags. The passengers who'd witnessed our escape from the bus were staring open-mouthed and I suppose they must have said something to the driver, but our convoy was already moving off in the opposite direction. It entered the basement of the terminal a few moments later. There was hardly anyone in the baggage handling area at this late hour. Only two teams were at work, but they were a fair distance away and couldn't see us. The tractor wound its way amid the conveyors.

I spotted a goods lift a few metres away and decided it was time to abandon our hiding place. But when we reached the lift I saw that the call button was locked; it couldn't be operated without a key.

"Any idea how we can get out of here?" Keira asked.

I looked around. All I could see was a network of mostly immobile conveyor belts crisscrossing the area.

"There!" Keira exclaimed, pointing to a door. "An emergency exit."

I was worried it would be locked, but luck was on our side and we pushed it open to find ourselves at the foot of a staircase.

"Stop running," I told Keira. "Let's walk out pretending everything's normal."

"We don't have badges," she pointed out. "If we run into someone, we'll look out of place."

I glanced at my watch: 11pm. The shuttle bus must have reached the terminal by now. There wouldn't be too many people at customs, and the last passenger off our flight would soon be going through immigration control. I didn't think we had much time before the people waiting for us realised we'd given them the slip.

There was another door blocking our way at the top of the staircase. Keira pushed the bar to open it and a siren went off. We emerged into the terminal between two moving conveyor belts, one of them empty. A maintenance worker saw us and looked taken aback. Before he could give the alert, I grabbed hold of Keira's hand and we took to our heels. Someone blew a whistle. *Whatever you do, don't turn back*, I told myself. *Just keep running.* We had to make it to the sliding doors leading to the pavement outside the terminal. Keira stumbled and cried out. I helped her up and yanked her along. *Faster.* I could hear the sound of thudding footsteps behind us, and the whistle blowing ever closer. *Don't stop. Don't panic. Freedom is only a few metres away.* Keira was gasping for breath.

A taxi was parked at the curb outside the terminal. We scrambled in and begged the driver to start the engine.

"Where to?" he asked, turning to look at us.

"Just go! We're late," Keira panted.

The driver started up the car. I forbade myself to look back, imagining our furious pursuers stranded on the pavement watching our black cab drive away.

"We're not safe yet," I breathed to Keira.

"Could you take us to Terminal 2, please," I told the driver.

Keira gave me an astonished look.

"Trust me. I know what I'm doing."

At the second roundabout, I asked the driver to stop. I pretended my wife was pregnant and had started feeling terribly nauseous. He braked immediately. I handed him a twenty-pound note and told him we were going to get some fresh air on the verge of the road. There was no need to wait – I was used to these turns of hers, it could last a while. We'd walk the rest of the way.

"It's dangerous to go walking around here," he told us.

"Watch out for the trucks, they're all over the place."

He drove off with a little wave, thrilled with the amount he'd pocketed for the short run.

"Right, now the baby's born, what do we do?" Keira asked.

"We wait," I replied.

"What for?"

"You'll see."

Kent

"What do you mean, they got away? Weren't your men waiting to pick them up at the plane?"

"Yes, sir. But your two scientists weren't there."

"What are you saying? My contact assured me he'd personally put them on that flight."

"I don't intend to doubt his word, but the two subjects we were supposed to take in didn't go through passport control. There were six of us watching for them – there's no way they would have got past us."

"I suppose you're going to tell me they did a parachute jump over the English Channel?" Sir Ashley shouted into the telephone.

"No, sir. The plane should have been attached to an air bridge, but at the last minute it was directed to a parking bay, and we weren't informed. The two individuals escaped from the shuttle bus taking them to the terminal where we were waiting for them. There was really nothing we could do. They escaped through the basement."

"You can tell the security people at Heathrow from me that heads will roll!"

"I'm sure they will, sir."

"Pathetic fools! Hurry to their house this instant instead of blathering on. Go through the city with a fine-tooth comb; check all the hotels. Sort it out anyway you like, but make sure you arrest them tonight if you have any hopes of holding on to your job. I'm giving you until tomorrow morning to find them for me, do you hear?"

The man on the other end apologised once again, and promised to make up for the miserable failure of the operation he'd been put in charge of.

Concord Roundabout, Heathrow

The Fiat 500 drew up alongside the pavement. The driver leaned over to open the passenger door.

"I've been going round in circles for an hour," Walter grumbled, folding down the front seat so I could climb into the back.

"Couldn't you find a smaller car?"

"You've got some nerve, I must say! You ask me to come and pick you up at a roundabout in the middle of nowhere at an outlandish hour and then you complain?"

"I was just saying it's a good thing we haven't got any luggage."

"I suppose if you did you'd have asked me to pick you up in front of the terminal like any normal person would, instead of making me drive around ten times waiting for you."

"Are you two going to keep squabbling for long?" Keira broke in.

"I'm delighted to see you again," Walter said, extending a hand for her to shake. "How did your little trip go?"

"Badly," she replied. "Shall we go?"

"Certainly – but where?"

I was about to ask Walter to take us to my house, but two police cars sped past us with their sirens wailing loudly, and I decided it wasn't such a good idea after all. Whoever our enemies were, I was quite sure they knew my home address.

"Well?" Walter asked. "Where do we go?"

"I've no idea."

Walter joined the motorway.

"I'm quite happy to drive all night," he said. "We'll just have to fill up at some point."

"Is this little car yours?" Keira asked. "It's sweet."

"I'm very glad you like it. I've just bought it."

"What's the deal?" I asked. "I thought you were broke."

"It was a very good deal, actually. Since your delightful aunt is arriving on Friday, I used up the last of my savings to buy it so I can take her around the city in style."

"Elena's coming to see you this weekend?"

"Yes, I told you about it, don't you remember?"

"We've had quite a hectic week," I told him, "so don't hold it against me if I seem distracted."

"I know where we can go," Keira said. "Walter, you'd better stop at a gas station to fill up."

"Could I enquire as to which direction I should be going?" he asked. "I warn you, I'll have to be back tomorrow at the latest. I have an appointment at the hairdresser's."

Keira cast a glance at Walter's bald pate.

"Yes, I know," he said, rolling his eyes. "But I must get rid of this ridiculous tuft of hair, and besides I read in an article in *The Times* this morning that bald men have a higher sex drive."

"If you've got a pair of scissors, I could take care of it for you right away," Keira offered.

"Absolutely not. I would only entrust my last few strands of hair to a professional. Are you going to tell me where I should drive you?"

"St. Mawes, in Cornwall," Keira replied. "We'll be safe there."

"Who with?" Walter asked.

Keira didn't answer. I guessed the reply to his question and asked if he'd let me drive.

During the six-hour drive, I told Walter about our adventures in Russia. He was appalled to hear what had happened to us on the Trans-Siberian and the Manpupuner plateau. He asked me several times if I knew who'd tried to kill us, but I told him his guess was as good as mine. My only certainty was that their desire to harm us was somehow related to the object we were looking for.

Keira remained silent throughout the drive. When we arrived in St. Mawes at daybreak, she made us stop in front of a small inn on a narrow street leading up to the graveyard.

"This is it," she said.

She said goodbye to Walter, got out of the car and started walking away.

"When will I see you again?" Walter asked me.

"Enjoy your weekend with Elena and don't worry about us. I think a few days' rest will do us a world of good."

"This is a peaceful place," Walter said, looking at the Victory Inn's facade. I'm sure you'll be fine here."

"I hope so."

"She's had quite a shock," Walter said, nodding

toward Keira, who was walking up the street.

"Yes, these past few days were really tough, and she was very affected by the sudden stop to our research. We were really close to our goal."

"But you're alive, and that's all that counts. To hell with those fragments. It's time you stopped this business; you've taken far too many risks. It's a miracle you've managed to escape."

"Things would be a lot easier if it was just a treasure hunt, Walter, an adolescent game. But it's not. If we'd reunited all the fragments, we'd have probably made an unprecedented discovery."

"You're not going to tell me about your first star again, are you? Well, may it stay up there in the sky, and you here on Earth in good health – that's all I ask."

"It's very kind of you to say so, Walter, but we might actually have found a way to glimpse the very first instants of the universe's existence, and finally learn where we come from, and who the first people on our planet were. Keira's cherished that hope all her life. And now she's crushed."

"Then don't stay here talking to me, run and join her. If things are as bad as you say, she needs you. Look after her and forget about your crazy research."

Walter hugged me goodbye and started up his Fiat 500.

"I hope you're not feeling too tired to drive back," I said, leaning down to the window.

"Tired? No, I managed to get some sleep on the way here."

I watched the car drive off along the coast road and its rear lights disappear from view behind a house at the far end of the village.

*

Keira had vanished. I looked for her as I climbed the slope. The gate leading into the graveyard at the top was ajar. I went in and walked down the central path. The place wasn't very big – there couldn't have been more than a hundred souls residing in St. Mawes graveyard. Keira was kneeling at the end of a row, near a wisteria-draped wall.

"It produces lovely purple flowers in spring," Keira said without looking up.

I glanced at the tombstone. The gold lettering had all but disappeared, but the name "William Perkins" was still visible.

"Jeanne will be upset with me for bringing you here without telling her first."

I put my arm around her and remained silent.

"I've gone around the world trying to show him what I was capable of, and all I've managed is to come back here empty-handed and with a heavy heart. I think he's the one I've always been searching for."

"I'm sure he's proud of you."

"He never said that to me."

Keira dusted off the tombstone and took my hand.

"I wish you could've met him. He was such a retiring man, such a loner towards the end of his life. When I was a little girl I used to bombard him with questions and he would always try and answer them. When it was a particularly tricky question, he'd just smile and take me for a walk along the shore. At night I'd tiptoe out of bed and find him sitting at the kitchen table deep in his encyclopaedia. The next day at breakfast he'd turn to me and casually say: *You asked me a question yesterday; we must have started talking about something else and I forgot to give you the answer, so here it is…*

Keira shivered. I took off my coat and wrapped it around her.

"You've never told me about your childhood, Adrian."

"Because I'm as retiring as your father was, and besides, I don't much like talking about myself."

"You'll have to make an effort," Keira said. "If we're going to be together, I don't want us to keep secrets from each other."

Keira took me to the inn. The dining room of the Victory was still deserted at this hour. The owner led us to a table near the bay window and served us a hearty breakfast. Keira and he seemed to get along. Then he accompanied us to a room on the first floor with a view over the little port of St. Mawes. We were his only customers. The place was delightful, even in winter. I went to the window. It was low tide, and the fishing boats had been pulled up and turned on their sides. A man was walking along the shore holding his little boy by the hand. Keira came to lean on her elbows at the window next to mc.

"I miss my father too," I told her. "I missed him even when he was still alive. We couldn't communicate. He was a man of many qualities, but he was too absorbed in his work to take much notice of his son. When he finally became aware of my existence, I'd just left home. We were like two ships passing in the night without ever meeting. But I can't complain – my mother gave me all the love and affection I could have hoped for."

Keira stared at me for a long time and then asked why I'd wanted to become an astrophysicist.

"When I was a child, every time we went to Hydra my mother and I had a bedtime ritual. We would stand side by side at the window, like the two of us right now, and look at the sky together. Mum would invent names for the stars. One evening I asked her how the world had been created, why day broke each morning, and if night would always fall. Mum looked at me and said: *There are as many different worlds as there are lives in the universe. My world began the day you were born, the moment I held you in my arms.* Since childhood I've dreamed of knowing where the dawn begins."

Keira turned to me and slipped her arms around my neck.

"You'll make a wonderful father," she said.

London

I'll sell my car on Monday, I'll pay you back and buy myself a pair of walking boots. To hell with my office roof. I'm not going any further. I refuse to do anything else to convince them to continue. Don't count on me to help you anymore. Every morning when I look at myself in the mirror, I feel dirty for betraying Adrian's trust. No, don't insist – nothing you can say will make me change my mind. I should have sent you packing a long time ago. And if you do anything at all to encourage them to take up their travels again, I'll tell them everything, even though I actually hardly know anything about you.

"Are you talking to yourself, Walter?" Elena asked.

"No, why?"

"You really looked as if you were murmuring something – your lips were moving."

The light went red. Walter braked and turned to Elena.

"I have an important call to make this evening and I was rehearsing what I'd say."

"Nothing serious?"

"No, no, I assure you – on the contrary."

"You're not hiding anything from me? If there's someone else in your life, someone younger, I mean, I'd understand. But I'd rather you told me."

Walter moved closer to Elena.

"I am hiding absolutely nothing from you – I wouldn't dare. And I couldn't possibly find any woman more desirable than you."

Walter went crimson as soon as the words were out of his mouth. "I like your new hairstyle very much," Elena said, changing the subject. "I think the light's green and someone behind us is honking. You should start the car. I'm so happy to be visiting Buckingham Palace. Do you think we'll be lucky enough to see the Queen?"

"Perhaps," Walter replied. "You never know, she might step out onto the balcony."

St. Mawes

We slept for most of the day. When I reopened the curtains the sky was already taking on twilight hues.

We were starving. Keira knew of a tearoom a few streets away from the inn and showed me around the village on our way there. As I gazed at the little white houses perched on the hillside I caught myself dreaming of living here one day. I'd spent my life rushing around the world, but perhaps I'd end up settling in this little Cornish village. I wished Martin and I hadn't grown apart – I was sure he'd enjoy coming to see me here from time to time. We'd have a beer on the port and reminisce about the good old days.

"What are you thinking about?" Keira asked.

"Nothing in particular," I replied.

"You looked miles away. We said there'd be no secrets between us."

"If you really want to know, I was wondering what we'd be doing next week, and the ones after that."

"And?"

"I've no idea."

"I do."

Keira faced me, tipping her head to one side. When she did that it meant she had something important to say to me. Some people adopt a serious tone when they want to give you a momentous piece of news. Keira cocks her head.

"I want us to go and see Ivory and demand an explanation. But I need you to help me tell a small lie."

"What kind of lie?"

"I want to let him believe we managed to leave Russia with the third fragment."

"What for? How would that help us?"

"It would make him reveal where the one found in the Amazon is."

"He told us he didn't know."

"He told us lots of things, and he hid a lot of other things too, that canny old bird. Egorov wasn't totally off the mark when he accused Ivory of manipulating us like two puppets. If we make him believe we have three fragments in our possession, he won't be able to resist the desire to complete the puzzle. I'm sure he knows more than he's willing to admit."

"I'm starting to think you're even more manipulative than he is."

"He's far more talented at it than I am, and I wouldn't mind getting my little revenge on him."

"Fine, let's say we manage to convince him we're telling the truth, and he tells us where the fourth fragment is. We'd still be missing the one that's somewhere on the Manpupuner plateau, and the celestial chart would remain incomplete. So why go to all that trouble?"

"Just because one piece of the puzzle is missing, it doesn't mean we can't visualise the entire image. When we unearth fossilised remains they're hardly ever complete – practically never. But if we find a large enough number of bones we can guess which are the missing bits, and piece together the skeleton and even the entire body. So if we add Ivory's fragment to the two we have, maybe we'll be able to understand what this map is supposed to show us. Anyway, I don't see what else we can do – unless of course you tell me you want to pass the rest of your life here in this little village and spend your days fishing."

"What a laughable idea!"

Back at the inn, the first thing Keira did was to call her sister. They spent a long time on the phone. Keira didn't tell Jeanne anything about our adventures in Russia, she merely said we were both in St. Mawes and that she might be coming to Paris soon. I preferred to let them chat in peace, so I went down to the bar and ordered a beer while I was waiting for her. She joined me there an hour later. I put down my newspaper and asked if she'd talked to Ivory.

"He denies influencing our research in any way. He nearly got offended when I suggested he'd been using me since that first day I met him at the museum. He seemed sincere, but I'm not totally convinced."

"Did you tell him we brought the third fragment back from Russia?"

Keira picked up my glass of beer and drained it, giving an affirmative nod.

"Did he believe you?"

"He immediately stopped reproaching me and said he's impatient to see us."

"How will you keep up the pretence when we meet him?"

"I told him we'd put the fragment in a safe place, and that I would only show it to him after he'd told us more about the fragment found in the Amazon."

"What did he say?"

"He said he thinks he knows where it is, but he doesn't know how to get at it. He suggested we help him solve a riddle."

"What sort of riddle?"

"He didn't want to talk about it on the phone."

"Is he coming here?"

"No. We're to meet him in Amsterdam in forty-eight hours' time."

"How do you think we're going to get to Amsterdam? I'm in no hurry to return to Heathrow. If we try and leave the country again there's every chance we'll be arrested."

"I know. I told him what happened to us. He's advised us to get a ferry to Holland. He says we'll run fewer risks of checks on a ship out of England."

"And where do we get a ferry to Amsterdam?"

"Plymouth. It's an hour and a half away by car."

"But we haven't got a car."

"We can take the bus. Why are you being so reluctant?"

"How long is the crossing?"

"Twelve hours."

"That's what I was afraid of."

Keira looked contrite. She patted my hand.

"What is it?" I asked.

"In fact," she said, looking embarrassed, "they're not actually ferries – they're cargo ships. Most of them accept passengers. But anyway, whether it's a ferry or a cargo ship, we don't mind, right?"

"As long as there's a foredeck where I can die of seasickness during the twelve-hour crossing, no, we don't mind!"

The bus left at seven in the morning. The owner of the inn had made us sandwiches for our journey. When we said goodbye, he promised Keira he would go and clean her father's grave as soon as spring returned. He said he hoped to see us again, and that he'd keep the same room for us if we gave him sufficient notice.

On reaching Plymouth we went to the port and sought out the harbour master. The port official informed us that a bulk carrier flying the British flag would be casting off for Amsterdam in an hour's time. Its cargo had nearly finished being loaded. He sent us to wharf 5.

The captain asked us to pay him a hundred pounds each in cash. When we'd handed over the money he told us to go along the gangway to the wardroom. There was a free cabin we could use in the crew's quarters. I explained that I'd rather stay on deck, either forward or aft, wherever I would be the least bother.

"As you wish, but it'll be bloody freezing once we've put out to sea, and the crossing takes twenty hours."

I turned to Keira.

"I thought you said twelve hours at most?"

"On an ultra-fast vessel, maybe," the captain said with a roar of laughter, "but this old tub barely ever goes over twenty knots, and that's if we have a favourable wind. If you're prone to seasickness, stay outside. I don't want you throwing up all over my boat. And cover up."

"I swear I didn't know," Keira said. I could tell she had her fingers crossed behind her back.

The ship lifted anchor. There was minimal swell in the Channel, but the rain had invited itself along for the trip. Keira kept me company on deck for more than an hour before going inside – it was teeth-chatteringly cold. The first mate took pity on me and got his bridge lieutenant to bring me an oilskin and some gloves. The man took the opportunity for a smoke and started chatting to me to take my mind off things.

There were thirty men on board – officers, mechanics, cooks and deck hands. The lieutenant explained that loading bulkers was an extremely complex operation, and that the ship's safety depended on it being done properly. In the 1980s, a hundred ships like this one had sunk so fast that not one seaman had escaped. Six hundred men had perished at sea. The biggest danger we faced was the cargo shifting, which would make the ship list and keel over. I could see excavators pushing the ship's cargo of grain to the centre of the holds; their job was to make sure it didn't happen. And that wasn't the only possible danger, he added, taking a long drag on his cigarette. If a very high wave sent water sloshing in through the large hatches, the extra weight in the holds could split the hull in two, and the ship would sink in a matter of minutes. The Channel was calm tonight, so unless there was an unexpected gale we didn't risk anything of the kind. The lieutenant chucked his cigarette butt overboard and went back to work, leaving me to mull over what he'd said.

Keira came to see me several times and begged me to join her in the cabin. She brought me sandwiches, which I refused, and a thermos of tea. Towards midnight she went to bed after repeatedly telling me it was ridiculous to want to stay above deck, and that I was risking death. Wrapped up in my oilskin, I curled up at the foot of the mast under the beam of the masthead light and dozed off, lulled by the sound of the ship's bow ploughing through the water.

When Keira woke me in the early morning, I was lying on the foredeck with my arms crossed over my chest. I'd started to feel the pangs of hunger, but my appetite fled as soon as I stepped into the storeroom and smelled the mingled odour of fish, rancid oil and coffee. I retched and raced back outside.

"That's the Dutch coast you can see in the distance," Keira said, coming up next to me. "Your ordeal's nearly over."

Her estimate was approximate to say the least; we had to wait another four hours before the foghorn blared and I felt the engines slowing down. The ship moved towards dry land and entered the channel leading to the port of Amsterdam shortly afterwards.

We got off the ship as soon as it had docked. A customs officer was waiting for us at the foot of the gangplank. He gave our passports a cursory examination, went through our bags, which contained only a few things we'd bought at a shop in St. Mawes, and let us through.

"Where are we going?" I asked Keira.

"To have a shower."

"And then?"

She looked at her watch.

"We're meeting Ivory at 6pm in a café..." She paused to take a scrap of paper out of her pocket."...on the square in front of the Royal Palace."

Amsterdam

We got a room at the Grand Hotel Krasnapolsky. It wasn't exactly the cheapest hotel in town, but it was a mere fifty metres from the place where we were to meet Ivory. Towards the end of the afternoon Keira led the way to Dam Square, where we mingled with the crowd. There was a long queue stretching from Madame Tussaud's and a few tourists having a meal under patio heaters on the terrace of the Europub. Ivory wasn't among them. I finally spotted him and he joined us at our table by the restaurant window.

"I'm so happy to see you," he said, sitting down. "What a journey you've had!"

Keira was giving him the cold shoulder and the elderly professor immediately realised he wasn't in friendly territory.

"Are you angry with me?" he said archly.

"Why should I be angry with you? We almost fell into a ravine, I nearly drowned in a river and spent a few weeks all expenses paid in a prison in China, someone shot at us on a train, and we were thrown out of Russia by a bunch of commandos who slaughtered twenty men before our very eyes. I'll spare you the details of the extreme conditions in which we've travelled over the past few months – faulty planes, battered old cars and ramshackle buses, not forgetting the little tow tractor on which I found myself squeezed between two suitcases. And I suppose you were sitting pretty in your comfortable apartment while you shuttled us around as you pleased and got us to do all the dirty work. Did you start making a monkey out of me the day we met in your office, or did that happen a little later?"

"Keira," Ivory said pompously, "we already had this conversation on the phone the day before yesterday. You're mistaken. All right, so I haven't had a chance to explain everything, but I've never manipulated you. On the contrary – I've never stopped trying to protect you. You're the ones who decided to go off on this search. I didn't need to convince you – all I did was to bring a few facts to your attention. As for the risks the two of you have run, you should know that I myself took several risks to bring Adrian back from China and get you out of prison. And I lost a very dear friend, who paid for your release from prison with his life."

"What friend?" Keira asked.

"His office was in the palace in front of us," Ivory said sadly. "That's why I asked you to meet me here. Have you really brought back the third fragment from Russia?"

"Let's do a trade-off," said Keira. "I told you I'd show it to you after you'd told us everything about the one found in the Amazon. I know you know where it is – don't try and convince me you don't."

"It's in front of you," Ivory sighed.

"Stop talking in riddles, professor. You've been playing me along too long, and I've had enough of playing. I don't see any fragment on the table."

"Don't be a fool. Look up – what do you see?"

Our gaze turned to the palace on the other side of the square.

"It's in that building?" Keira asked.

"Yes, I've every reason to think so, but I don't know where exactly. My friend had it in his custody, but he's taken the answer to the riddle that would let us get our hands on it to the grave with him."

"How can you be so sure?" I asked.

Ivory bent to the bag at his feet, took out a big book and placed it on the table. The cover immediately caught my eye – it was a very old astronomy manual. I picked it up and leafed though it.

"It's magnificent."

"Yes," said Ivory, "it's a first edition. It was a cherished gift from my friend. Take a look at his dedication."

I went back to the first few pages and read out the handwritten message on the frontispiece: "*I know you'll enjoy this book. There's nothing missing because it's got everything, including the proof of our friendship. Your devoted chess partner, Vackeers.*"

"Those words contain the key to the riddle. I know Vackeers was trying to tell me something. It's definitely no ordinary sentence. But I don't know what it means."

"How do you expect us to help you? We never even met this Vackeers."

"Believe me, I'm sorry you didn't. You would have

liked him very much. He was an unusually intelligent man. Since the book is a treatise on astronomy, I thought perhaps you might understand something, Adrian."

"It's nearly six hundred pages long," I pointed out. "I'm not going to be able to find something in it in just a few hours. It'll take me several days to give it at least one proper read. Don't you have any clues at all, anything that could guide us? We don't even know what we're looking for in this book."

"Follow me," Ivory said, getting to his feet. "I'll take you to a place no one has access to – practically no one. Only Vackeers, his personal secretary and I are aware of its existence. Vackeers knew I'd found his hiding place, but he pretended he didn't know. I suppose that sensitivity was proof of friendship on his part."

"Isn't that precisely what he says to you in his dedication?"

"Yes," Ivory sighed, "and that's exactly why we're here."

He paid the bill and we followed him through Dam Square. Keira wasn't paying any attention to the traffic and nearly got run over by a tram, even though the driver had rung the warning bell several times. I only just managed to pull her back in time.

Ivory led us into the New Church through a side door and we walked up the magnificent nave to the transept. I was admiring the tomb of Admiral de Ruyter in a small apse when a man in a dark suit joined us.

"Thanks for coming to meet us," Ivory said, talking in a whisper so as not to disturb the few worshippers in the church.

"You were his only friend, and I know Mr. Vackeers

would have wanted me to accept your request. I'm counting on your discretion. I would be in serious trouble if anyone were to find out."

"Have no fear," Ivory said, patting his shoulder. "Vackeers held you in very high regard. He genuinely liked you. When he talked about you his voice took on a tone that was… how can I put it… friendly. Yes, that's exactly it. Vackeers thought of you as a friend."

"Really?" the man said, a touching note of sincerity in his voice.

He took a key out of his pocket and turned it in the lock of a small door at the far end of the chapel. We went down a staircase just behind the door. Fifty steps down, we came to a long corridor.

"This corridor runs under Dam Square and goes straight to the Royal Palace," the man told us. "It's quite dark and it gets worse as we go along, so keep close to me."

All we could hear was the echoing sound of our footsteps. The further we went along the corridor, the darker it got, until it turned pitch black.

"Another fifty steps and we'll see light again," said our guide. "Keep to the central gutter and be careful not to stumble. It's not a very pleasant place, I know; I really dislike having to use it."

Another staircase appeared before us.

"Watch out, the steps are slippery – hold on to the hemp rope along the wall."

At the top of the steps we found ourselves in front of a wooden door reinforced with heavy iron bars. Vackeers' secretary turned two large knobs and a mechanism opened the bolt. We emerged into an antechamber on the ground floor of the palace. Three gigantic maps were engraved into the white marble floor of the state room. The first two represented the western and the eastern hemisphere respectively. The third was an astonishingly precise celestial chart. I walked up to take a closer look. I'd never had the opportunity to go from Cassiopeia to Andromeda in a single stride, and I started jumping from one galaxy to the next for the fun of it. Keira gave a little cough to remind me where we were. Ivory and our guide were staring disapprovingly at me.

"It's this way," the man in the dark suit said. He opened another door and we went down another staircase leading to the palace basement. It took a few moments for our eyes to get used to the gloom and make out a network of walkways positioned just above the waters of an underground canal.

"We're directly under the state room," the man said. "Watch your step – the canal water is icy cold and I don't know how deep it is."

He went up to a beam and pressed a wrought-iron retaining plate. Two planks pivoted to reveal a passage leading to the back wall. It was only when we got closer that we saw a door in the brickwork, previously invisible in the darkness. The man led us into a room and switched on the light. A metal table and an office chair were the only furniture in it. A flat screen hung on the wall, and there was a computer keyboard on the table.

"There," Vackeers' secretary said. "I can't be of any further help. As you can see, there's hardly anything here."

Keira switched on the computer and the screen lit up. "It's password protected," she said.

Ivory took a slip of paper out of his pocket and handed it to her. "Try this code. I stole it when I went to his house for a game of chess."

Keira tapped on the keyboard and pressed Enter. We were granted access to Vackeers' computer.

"Now what?" she asked.

"I've no idea," replied Ivory. "Take a look at the contents of the hard disk; maybe we'll find something to lead us to the fragment."

"The hard disk is empty. All I can see is a communications program. This computer must have been used exclusively for videoconferencing. There's a little camera above the monitor."

"No, that's impossible," said Ivory. "Look again. I'm sure the key to the riddle is in there."

"Sorry to contradict you, but there's nothing, no information."

"Go to the root and copy the dedication: *I know you'll enjoy this book. There's nothing missing because it's got everything, including the proof of our friendship. Your devoted chess partner, Vackeers.*

The screen displayed an error message: "Unknown command."

"That's funny," said Keira. "Look. The hard disk's empty, but the disk space is reading half-full. There's a hidden partition. Do you have any idea what the other password is?"

"No, I can't think what it could be," Ivory replied.

Keira looked at the elderly professor. She bent over the keyboard and typed "Ivory." A new window opened on the screen.

"I think I've found the proof of his friendship, but we're still missing a password."

"Which I don't have," Ivory sighed.

"Think. What did the two of you have in common?"

"We had so many things in common. There are so many memories to choose from. I don't know – try 'chess.'"

The words "Unknown command" re-appeared on the screen.

"Try again," said Keira. "Think of something more complicated – something that would only have occurred to the two of you."

Ivory began pacing up and down the room with his hands behind his back, mumbling to himself.

"There was that game we once played."

"What game?" I asked.

"A famous match between two great eighteenth-century players, François-André Danican Philidor and Captain Smith. Philidor was a masterly chess player, probably the finest player of his day. He published a book titled *Analysis of the Game of Chess*, which was long considered a chess player's bible. Try typing his name." Keira obeyed. The "Access denied" error message came up again.

"Tell me about this Danican Philidor," said Keira.

"Before going to live in England," Ivory said, "he used to play at the Café de la Regence in France, where all the top chess players could be found."

Keira typed "Regence" and "Café de la Regence," but nothing happened.

"He was a student of Mr. de Kermeur," Ivory added.

Keira typed "Kermeur." No luck. Once again the screen denied us access. Ivory suddenly looked up.

"Philidor rose to fame when he defeated the Syrian chess master Philipp Stamma. No, wait. He became really famous when he won a tournament, playing three blindfolded games simultaneously against three different opponents. He achieved this feat at the chess club in St. James Street in London."

Keira typed "St. James Street." It was another non-starter.

"Maybe we're on the wrong trail," she said. "Maybe we should be going after Captain Smith. Or maybe, I don't know… what were your Philidor's dates of birth and death?"

"I don't really remember," said Ivory. "Vackeers and I were only interested in his career as a chess player."

"When exactly did this match between Captain Smith and his pal Philidor take place?" I asked.

"13 March 1790."

Keira typed "13031790" and we stood there gaping. An ancient celestial chart appeared on the screen. From its degree of precision and the mistakes I could see, it must have dated to the seventeenth or eighteenth century.

"That's absolutely incredible," Ivory exclaimed.

"It's a wonderful engraving," said Keira, "but it still doesn't tell us where we can find what we're looking for."

The man in the dark suit looked up.

"It's the map in the state room on the ground floor of the palace," he said. "It looks a lot like it, anyway, except for a few details."

"Are you sure?" I asked.

"I must have walked over that map thousands of times. I've worked for Mr. Vackeers for the past ten years, and I always took that route to come and meet him in his first-floor office."

"How is this one different?" Keira asked.

"They're not exactly the same drawings," he told us. "The lines connecting the stars aren't placed the same way."

"When was the palace built?" I asked.

"It was completed in 1655," the man replied.

Keira immediately typed in the year. The map on the screen began revolving and we heard a muffled sound that seemed to come from the ceiling.

"What's on the floor above us?" Keira asked.

"The Burgerzaal – the state room with the maps in the marble floor," the man replied.

All four of us raced to the door. The man warned us to be careful as we tore along the wooden walkways positioned a few centimetres above the underground canal. Five minutes later we were in the state room of the Royal Palace. Keira dashed towards the celestial chart engraved on the floor. It was turning slowly in an anticlockwise direction. When it had turned a half-circle, it stopped. Suddenly the central part raised up a few centimetres above the floor. Keira thrust her hand into the opening that had appeared and triumphantly pulled out the third fragment, which looked similar to our two.

"I beg you to put everything back as it was," said the man. "If the state room is found this way when the place opens tomorrow, it would be a disaster for me."

But our guide didn't have to worry for long. The words were barely out of his mouth when the cover of the secret cavity lowered itself back into place. The map turned in the opposite direction, back to its original position.

"And now," said Ivory, "where is the fourth fragment you brought back from Russia?"

Keira and I exchanged a look. We were both horribly embarrassed.

"I don't want to be a spoilsport," the man in the dark suit said, "but I'd be grateful if you could continue your discussion outside the palace. I still have to go and lock up Mr. Vackeers' office. The guards will be starting their rounds any minute; you really should leave."

Ivory took Keira's arm.

"He's right," he said. "We have all night to talk."

Back at the Hotel Krasnapolsky, Ivory asked us to accompany him to his room.

"You lied to me, didn't you?" he said, shutting the door behind us. "Oh, please. Don't think I'm a fool. I saw the way your faces fell earlier. You weren't able to bring back the fourth fragment from Russia."

"No, we weren't," I said, getting angry. "We knew where it was, we were only a few metres away from it, but since no one had alerted us to the danger in store for us, since you'd taken good care not to warn us about the ruthlessness of the people who've been chasing us ever since you sent us off on the hunt for these fragments, we almost got killed. I hope you're not expecting us to apologise on top of it all!"

"You're irresponsible, the pair of you. By making us come here, you've made me advance a pawn that should only have been moved as a last resort. Do you think our visit will have gone unnoticed? The computer we broke into is part of a highly sophisticated network. By now, dozens of computer engineers will have informed their section heads that Vackeers' computer turned itself on in the middle of the night, and I doubt anyone will believe it was his ghost!"

"But who the hell *are* these people?" I shouted.

"Calm down, both of you. This is not the time to settle your scores," Keira interrupted. "Screaming at each other isn't going to get us anywhere. It wasn't all lies we told you. I'm the one who convinced Adrian to play this trick on you. I'm hoping the three fragments will give us enough clues to help us go on with our search, so why don't we try putting them together instead of quarrelling?"

Keira took off her pendant and I took the second fragment out of my pocket and unwrapped the handkerchief I'd put it in. We joined them to the one we'd found under the floor of the Royal Palace.

We were in for a big disappointment. Nothing happened. The blue light we'd had such hopes of seeing didn't appear. What was worse, the magnetic force that had drawn the first two fragments together until then didn't seem to be working anymore. They'd turned into inert objects.

"Well, a long way that's got us," Ivory snorted.

"How can it be possible?" Keira asked.

"I suppose we've handled them so much that we've used up all their energy," I said.

Ivory went into his bedroom and slammed the door shut, leaving the two of us in the small sitting room.

Keira gathered up the fragments and pulled me out of the suite.

"I'm hungry," she told me when we were out in the corridor. "The restaurant or room service?"

"Room service," I replied unhesitatingly.

Keira was soaking in a bath. I'd placed the fragments on the small desk in our room and was staring at them, my head buzzing with questions. Did we have to expose them to a source of bright light to recharge them? What kind of energy could recreate the force that had drawn them to each other? I just knew something was eluding me. I examined the one we'd just found more closely. The triangular fragment looked like the other two, and all three were of identical thickness. I was turning it in my hand when a detail on the side caught my attention. There was a groove – a U-shaped horizontal notch – running along the outside edge. It was so even that it couldn't be accidental. I brought the three fragments closer together on the table and looked at that section more closely. The furrow ran perfectly levelly around all three. A thought occurred to me. I opened the desk drawer and found what I was looking for – a pencil and a scratch pad. I pulled off a sheet of paper, put my fragments on it and brought them together. I began to trace their outline on the paper with the pencil. When I took away the fragments and looked at my drawing, I discovered three-quarters of the outline of a perfect circle.

I ran into the bathroom.

"Put a bathrobe on and come and see," I said.

"What's happening?" Keira asked.

"Hurry up!"

She arrived a few seconds later, wrapped in a towel with another one around her head turban-style.

"Look," I said, showing her my drawing.

"Wow. You can almost draw a full circle. Is that why you got me out of my bath?"

I took the fragments and positioned them on the sheet of paper.

"Don't you notice anything?"

"Yes – there's still one missing."

"Which is an incredibly important piece of information! Until now we never really knew how many pieces this map was made up of, but if you look at that paper – you said it yourself – it's obvious there's only one missing, not two as we thought for so long."

"But there *is* one missing, Adrian, and the ones in our possession no longer have any powers, so can I go back to my bath before the water turns totally cold?"

"Don't you see anything else?"

"Are we going to be playing guessing games much longer? No, all I can see is a line sketched with a pencil, so tell me what it is that my intelligence, which is obviously inferior to yours, isn't picking up."

"The interesting thing about an armillary sphere isn't so much what it shows us as what it doesn't show, and which we can nevertheless guess."

"What does that mean, in plain English?"

"If the fragments aren't reacting anymore it's because they lack an electrical conductor, the fifth missing piece of the puzzle. These fragments were set in a ring – a wire that must have carried a current."

"So why did the first two fragments light up before?"

"Because they'd accumulated energy from the lightning. By joining them so often, we used up their reserves. They work in a rudimentary way, according to a principle that applies to any form of current – an exchange of positive and negative ions that must be allowed to flow freely."

"You're going to have to enlighten me a little more," Keira said, sitting down next to me. "I can't even change a light bulb."

"An electric current is the movement of electrons within a conductive substance. Any current is caused by the transfer of electrons – from the most powerful current to the weakest, like the electrical impulses running through your nervous system. If our objects aren't reacting anymore, it's because there's no conductor. And the conductor is precisely the fifth missing piece I was telling you about – a ring that must certainly have fitted around the object when it was still in one piece. The people who split it up into fragments must have broken it. If we can find a way to make a new one that will adjust perfectly to the outer edges of the fragments, I'm sure they'll regain their light-emitting power."

"And where do we get this ring of yours made up?"

"We'll go to a restorer of armillary spheres. Some of the finest ones were built in Antwerp, and I know someone in Paris who could give us some leads."

"Shall we tell Ivory about this?" Keira asked.

"Absolutely. And we mustn't let that man who was with us at the Royal Palace out of our sight – he could be very useful. I don't speak a word of Dutch."

I had to persuade Keira to make the first move. She called Ivory and said we had something important to tell him. The elderly professor was already in bed, but he agreed to get up and asked us to join him in his suite.

I explained my reasoning to him. At least it dispelled

his bad mood. He said he would rather I didn't call the antiques dealer in the Marais who I'd thought of earlier. We didn't have much time; he feared our troubles would be starting up again very soon. He liked the idea of going to Antwerp – the more we were on the move, the safer we'd be. He telephoned Vackeers' secretary even though it was the middle of the night, and asked him to find us a craftsman who would be able to restore a very ancient astronomical instrument. The man promised to look into it, and said he would get in touch with us the next day.

"I don't want to be nosy," said Keira, "but does this gentleman have a name? If we're going to see him again tomorrow I'd at least like to know what to call him."

"You can call him Wim for now. In a few days' time he'll probably be known as Amsterdam, and we'll no longer be able to count on him."

The next day we met the man we were to call Wim. He was wearing the same suit and tie as the previous day. Over coffee at the hotel, he told us there was no need for us to go to Antwerp. There was a very old watchmaker's in Amsterdam and its owner was reputed to be a direct descendant of Erasmus Habermel.

"Who's Erasmus Habermel?" Keira asked.

"The most famous maker of scientific instruments in the sixteenth century," Ivory replied.

"How do you know that?" I asked.

"I'm a professor, in case you hadn't noticed. Do excuse me for being educated."

"I'm so glad you've brought that up," said Keira. "What exactly were you a professor of? Adrian and I were wondering."

"I'm happy to hear the two of you are interested in my career, but tell me, are we looking for a restorer of ancient astronomical instruments or would you rather we spent the day discussing my résumé? Fine. Now, what were we saying about Erasmus Habermel? Since Adrian seems astonished by my erudition, let's hear what he has to say for himself. We'll see if he paid attention at university."

"The instruments made in Habermel's workshop are unsurpassed for their beauty and the quality of their workmanship," I said, shooting Ivory a furious glance. "The only known sphere to have been designed by him is to be found in Paris – in the collections of the National Assembly, if I'm not mistaken. Habermel would have been in close contact with the greatest astronomers of his day, Tycho Brahe and his assistant Johannes Kepler, as well as the famous Swiss watchmaker Jost Bürgi. He is also said to have worked with Gualterus Arsenius in Louven. They fled the town together after the eruption of the Black Death in 1580. The stylistic similarity between Habermel's instruments and those of Arsenius is so obvious that…"

"Fine, our pupil Adrian knows his lesson off by heart," Ivory broke in curtly, "but we haven't got time to listen to him parade all his knowledge. It's that connection between Habermel and Arsenuis we're interested in. We've learned, thanks to Wim, that one of Habermel's direct descendants lives right here in Amsterdam, so if you have no objections, I suggest we lock up the classroom and go and see him as soon we can. Get your coats. Let's meet in the lobby in ten minutes."

Keira and I left Ivory and went up to our room.

"How come you know all that stuff about Habermel?" Keira asked me as we were going up in the lift.

"From poring over a book I'd bought at an antiques dealer's in the Marais."

"When?"

"The time you so classily stood me up to spend the evening with your Max and I slept at a hotel, remember? I had all night to read the book."

A taxi dropped the four of us off in a lane of the old city. There was a watchmaker's at the end of a cul-de-sac. From the courtyard, through the glass window running the length of the workshop, we could see an old man perched at his workbench, busy repairing a clock. The mechanism he was meticulously assembling was made up of an impressively large number of tiny components, which were all lined up in perfect order before him. A bell jingled when we pushed open the door, and the man lifted his head. He was wearing a curious pair of glasses which made his eyes look abnormally large, like some strange animal. The workshop smelled of old wood and dust.

"What can I do for you?" he asked.

Wim explained that we wanted him to make up a component to complete a very old instrument.

"What sort of component?" the man asked, taking off his funny glasses.

"A brass or copper circle," I replied.

The man turned to me and asked in English with a faint German accent, "What diameter?"

"I couldn't say exactly."

"Could you show me the old instrument you want to repair?"

Keira moved closer to the workbench. The man threw his arms up into the air and exclaimed: "Not there, for heaven's sake! You'll mess everything up. Follow me to this table, here," he said, pointing to the centre of the workshop.

I'd never seen so many astronomical instruments before. My Marais antiques dealer would have gone livid with jealousy. Astrolabes, spheres, theodolites and sextants were sitting on the shelves waiting to be restored to their former beauty.

Keira placed the three fragments on the table the old craftsman had indicated, pushed them together and stepped back.

"What a strange instrument," the old man said. "What is it used for?"

"It's a kind of astrolabe," I said, moving closer.

"In this colour and substance? I've never seen anything like it. You'd almost think it's onyx, but it obviously isn't. Who do you say it was made by?"

"We've no idea."

"You're an odd bunch of customers. You don't know who made it, you don't know what it's made of and you don't even know what it's for, but you want to repair it. How can you repair something if you don't know how it's supposed to work?"

"We want to complete it," said Keira. "If you look at it closely, you'll see there's a groove along the edge of each of these fragments. We're sure it contained a hoop, probably made of a conducting alloy, into which the whole thing was set."

"Could be," said the man, whose curiosity seemed to have been aroused. "Now, let's see," he mused, looking at the multitude of tools hanging from the ceiling on long strings.

"I don't know where to put things anymore, so I've had to improvise. Ah, here's what I was looking for."

The craftsman took hold of a long compass with telescopic arms connected by a graduated arc. He put on his glasses and peered at our fragments.

"That's funny," he said.

"What?" Keira asked.

"The diameter is 31.4115 centimetres."

"What's funny about that?" she asked.

"It's exactly the numerical value pi multiplied by ten. I suppose you know that pi is a transcendental number?" the old watchmaker asked. "Pi is a constant whose value is the ratio of the surface area of a sphere to the square of its radius – or the ratio of the circumference of a circle to its diameter, if you prefer."

"I must have skipped school the day they were teaching that lesson," Keira confessed.

"It doesn't matter," said the watchmaker. "It's just that I've never seen an instrument with precisely this diameter. It's extremely ingenious. You have absolutely no idea what it was used for?"

"No!" I immediately replied, knowing Keira's propensity for being truthful only too well.

"It isn't hard to make a hoop. I should be able to do it for, let's say, two hundred florins, which works out to…" The man opened a drawer and took out a calculator. "…ninety euros. I'm sorry, I still haven't got used to this new currency."

"When will it be ready?" I asked.

"I must finish putting together the clock I was working on when you arrived. It has to be replaced on the main facade of a church, and the priest calls me practically every day to know how I'm getting on. I also have three old watches to repair. I could start working on your piece at the end of the month, if that's all right?"

"A thousand florins if you can start work on it immediately," said Ivory.

"Do you really need it in such a hurry?" the craftsman asked.

"Even faster," Ivory said. "I'll double the amount if the hoop is ready this evening."

No," the watchmaker replied, "a thousand florins is more than enough and anyway, I'm so late with the rest of it that one more day won't matter much. Come back at 6pm."

"We'd rather wait here, if you don't mind."

"Well, if you don't disturb me while I'm working, why not? After all, it'll do me good to have some company."

The old craftsman set to work immediately. He opened one drawer after another and chose a brass rod he seemed to find suitable. He studied it attentively, compared its width to the thickness of the indentation around the fragments and told us it should do the trick. He placed the rod on his work table and began to shape it. Using a wheel-cutter, he dug a furrow on one side; he turned the rod around and showed us the rib that had formed on the other side. All three of us were fascinated by his dexterity. The craftsman checked that it fitted properly into the groove and used the tool once again, moving it to and fro to deepen the line. Then he unhooked a template hanging from a chain. With a tiny hammer he began to curve the brass rod around the outline.

"Are you really Habermel's descendant?" Keira asked.

The man looked up and smiled at her.

"Does that make a difference?" he asked.

"No, but all these old instruments in your workshop…"

"You must let me work if you want me to finish your hoop. We'll have plenty of time to talk about my ancestors later."

We stayed silently in a corner observing the craftsman and marvelling at his skill. He remained stooped over his workbench for two hours, manipulating his tools with a surgeon's precision. All of a sudden he pivoted on his stool to face us.

"I think that's it," he said. "Would you like to come and see?"

We bent over his bench for a look. The circle was perfect. He polished it on a metallic brush mounted on a motorised lathe and buffed it with a soft cloth.

"Let's see if our fragments fit into it," he said, picking the first one up. He positioned the second one and then the third.

"There's obviously one missing fragment, but I've made the hoop tight enough to hold the three fragments together, as long as it's handled gently, of course."

"Yes, there's one missing," I said, hard put to hide my disappointment. Despite my hopes, no electrical phenomenon had resulted.

"What a pity," the craftsman said. "I'd have really liked to see the complete instrument. You did say it's a kind of astrolabe, didn't you?"

"Quite so," said Ivory, lying barefacedly.

He placed five hundred euros on the workbench and thanked the craftsman.

"Who do you think could have made it?" the man asked. "I can't remember ever seeing something like this."

"You've done a wonderful job," Ivory said. "You really are extremely skilled. I will certainly recommend you to any of my friends who want a precious object repaired."

"They'll be welcome, as long as they're not as impatient as you are," the man said, accompanying us to the door.

"And now," said Ivory when we were back in the street, "have you got any more bright ideas for ways I can spend my money? I can't say I've seen anything earthshaking so far."

"We need a laser," I said. "A powerful enough laser would provide enough energy to recharge the whole thing, and then we'd obtain a new projection of the map. Who knows, perhaps what appears through the third fragment will reveal something important."

"A powerful laser – is that all? And where do you suppose we'd find one?" an exasperated Ivory asked.

Wim, who hadn't said a word all afternoon, stepped forward.

"There's one at the Laser Centre at VU University. It's jointly used by the physics, astronomy and chemistry departments."

"The Laser Centre?" Ivory asked.

"Yes. It was set up by Professor Hogervorst. I studied there and I was well acquainted with the professor. He's retired now, but I could call and ask him to put in a word for us so we can have access to the campus equipment."

"Well, what are you waiting for?" said Ivory.

Wim took a little notebook out of his pocket and flipped hurriedly through the pages.

"I don't have his number here, but I'll call the university. I'm sure they'll know how to contact him."

Wim spent half an hour on the phone calling several numbers to try and track down Professor Hogervorst. He came back looking defeated.

"I managed to get his home number, though it was no easy task. Unfortunately his secretary couldn't get me through to him. Hogervorst is away at a conference in Argentina. He won't be back until early next week."

There was no reason why something that had worked once couldn't work again. I remembered Walter's tactic when we'd needed access to a laser in Crete. He'd said he was from the Academy. I borrowed Ivory's mobile and rang Walter. When I got through, he sounded gloomy.

"What's up?" I asked.

"Nothing."

"I can tell there's something wrong, Walter. What is it?"

"Nothing, I told you."

"Forgive me for insisting, but you seem to be out of sorts."

"Have you called me to talk about my mood?"

"Walter, don't be childish. You don't sound like yourself. Have you been drinking?"

"So? I can do whatever I want."

"It's only 7pm. Where are you?"

"In my office."

"You've been getting sloshed at the office?"

"I'm not sloshed, just a bit tipsy. And don't start preaching at me, I'm not in the mood for it."

"I wasn't going to preach. But I'm not hanging up until you've told me what's wrong."

There was a silence. I could hear Walter breathing into the phone, and suddenly made out a choked sob.

"Walter, are you crying?"

"What do you care? I wish I'd never met you."

I didn't know what it was that had got Walter into such a state, but I was deeply hurt by his remark. Another silence and another stifled sob. This time Walter blew his nose loudly.

"I'm sorry. I didn't mean that."

"But you said it. What have I done to make you so angry with me?"

"You, you, you – it's always all about you! Walter do this, Walter do that. I'm sure the reason you're calling now is because you want something. Don't tell me you only telephoned to ask me how I'm doing?"

"Well, that's precisely what I've been trying to do – in vain – since the beginning of this conversation."

There was another silence as Walter thought about what I'd said.

"That's true," he sighed.

"So are you going to tell me why you're so upset?"

Ivory was getting restive and making impatient gestures. I walked away, leaving him with Keira and Wim.

"Your aunt's gone back to Hydra and I've never felt so lonely in all my life," Walter told me with another sob.

"Did your weekend go well?" I asked, praying it had.

"Even better. Every moment was idyllic. We got along beautifully."

"Then you should be wildly happy. I don't understand."

"I miss her, Adrian. You have no idea how much I miss her. I've never felt this way before. Until I met Elena my love life was a desert dotted with the odd oasis that turned out to be a mirage. But with her it's all real, it all exists."

"I promise I won't tell Elena you compared her to a palm grove. It'll be our secret."

The quip must have made my friend smile – I could feel he'd perked up.

"When are you seeing each other again?" I asked.

"We haven't decided anything. Your aunt seemed very troubled when I was driving her to the airport. I think she was crying on the motorway, but you know how self-effacing she is – she looked out at the scenery for the whole journey. But I could tell she was heavy-hearted."

"And you didn't fix a date to see each other again?"

"No. Before getting on the plane, she told me it wasn't sensible for us to have a relationship. She said her life was in Hydra with your mother and she has her shop there. As for me, my life's in London, in this dingy office at the Academy. We're separated by a distance of two thousand five hundred kilometres."

"Come on, Walter. And you say I'm a bungler. Didn't you understand what she meant?"

"She'd rather end our relationship and never see me again," Walter said, weeping.

"Not at all!" I had to shout to be heard above his sobs.

"What do you mean, not at all?"

"You've got the wrong end of the stick. What she meant

was: *Hurry up and join me on my island. I'll be looking out for you every morning when the first boat comes into port.*"

There was yet another silence.

"Are you sure?" Walter asked.

"Positive."

"How can you be sure?"

"She's my aunt, not yours, as far as I know."

"Thank God for that. I'd never flirt with my aunt, even if I was madly in love with her. That would be totally obscene."

"Obviously."

"Adrian, what should I do?"

"Sell your car and buy yourself a plane ticket to Hydra."

"What a brilliant idea!" exclaimed Walter, sounding like himself at last.

"Thanks, Walter."

"Right, I'm going to hang up, go back home, set my alarm for 7am and go to bed, and tomorrow I'm going to the car dealer, then straight to a travel agency."

"Before you do that, I've got a small favour to ask, Walter."

"Anything you want."

"Do you remember our little adventure in Crete?"

"Of course I remember. What a great chase – I still laugh when I think about it. If you'd seen your face when I knocked that guard out…"

"I'm in Amsterdam and I need access to the same kind of equipment. The one I want to use is on the VU University campus. Do you think you can help me get in?"

There was one final silence as Walter put his thinking cap on.

"Call me back in half an hour. I'll see what I can do."

I went back to Keira. Ivory proposed we have dinner at the hotel. He thanked Wim for his help and let him go for the evening. Keira asked me how Walter was. I told her he was doing fine, absolutely fine. During dinner, I left them and went up to our room. Walter's line was busy. I rang back several times until he finally picked up.

"You have a meeting with Dr. Boelelaan in Amsterdam at 9.30am tomorrow. Be on time. You can use the laser for one hour, not a minute more."

"How did you manage that feat?"

"You won't believe me."

"Tell me."

"I called VU University and asked to speak to the duty officer. I said I was the chairman of our Academy and told him I had to speak to their chief executive urgently; I said he should call him at home and have him call me back. I gave him the Academy's number so he could make sure it wasn't a joke, and my extension to make sure he'd reach me. After that it was child's play. The head of the Amsterdam faculty, a Professor Ubach, rang me a quarter of an hour later. I thanked him warmly for calling me back at this late hour and informed him two of our most distinguished scientists were currently in Holland, that they were in the final stages of a potential Nobel Prize–winning project and that they needed to use his laser to check a few parameters."

"And he agreed to see us?"

"Yes. I added that in return for this little favour, the

Academy would double its admission quota for Dutch students, and he accepted. Don't forget he thought he was on the line with the chairman of the Royal Academy of Science. It was great fun."

"How can I thank you, Walter?"

"You should be thanking the bottle of scotch I've polished off this evening, otherwise I'd never have been able to play my role so well. Adrian, take care of yourself. And come back soon. I miss you very much too."

"The feeling is mutual, Walter. In any case, I'll be playing my last card tomorrow. If my idea doesn't work, we won't have any choice but to give it all up."

"That's not what I wish for you, though I won't deny it's what I sometimes hope for."

I hung up and went downstairs to give Keira and Ivory the good news.

London

Sir Ashley got up from the dinner table to take the phone call his butler had just come to announce. He apologised to his guests and withdrew to his office.

"What's the latest?" he asked his caller.

"The three of them are spending the evening together at their hotel. I've got a man parked outside in case they go out again tonight, but I doubt they will. I'm meeting up with them again tomorrow morning and will call you back as soon as I've got more information."

"Don't let them out of your sight, whatever you do."

"You can count on me."

"I'm glad I backed your application – you've done a good first day's work in your new job."

"Thank you, Sir Ashley."

"My pleasure, Amsterdam. Have a good evening."

Ashley hung up, left his office and returned to his guests.

VU University, Amsterdam

Wim met us in front of the entrance to the Laser Centre at VU University at 9.25am. Although everyone here spoke fluent English, he'd interpret for us if the need arose. We were received by the director of the research establishment himself. I was surprised to see how young Professor Ubach was – he couldn't have been more than forty. His firm handshake and down-to-earth manner immediately won him my trust. I hadn't met too many well-meaning people since the start of this adventure and decided to let him in on the purpose of the experiments I was hoping to carry out using his facilities. I explained openly what I was planning to do and the result I was expecting to obtain.

He was astounded. "Are you serious?" he asked. "I must admit I'd have taken you for a crank if you hadn't been personally recommended to me by the president of your Academy. But if what you've described actually happens – well, I'll see why he mentioned a Nobel Prize! Follow me. Our laser is at the other end of the building."

Keira looked at me, intrigued. I signalled to her not

to say anything. We walked down a long corridor. None of the researchers or students we passed along the way seemed to pay the director much attention.

"Here we are," he said, tapping an entry code on a keypad next to a double door. "Given what you've just told me, I'd rather we worked as a very small team. I'll operate the laser myself."

The laboratory's state-of-the-art facilities would have made every other European research centre green with envy, and the piece of equipment put at our disposal was gigantic. I could guess how powerful it must be and couldn't wait to see it in action.

An arm extended out in line with the barrel of the laser. Keira helped me position the sphere of fragments on a stand.

"What beam width do you require?" asked Ubach.

"Pi multiplied by ten," I replied.

The professor bent over his desk and entered the value I'd just given him. Ivory stood close by. The laser began turning slowly.

"What intensity?"

"The strongest possible."

"Your object will melt in an instant. I don't know any material able to withstand maximum charge."

"Trust me."

"Do you know what you're doing?" whispered Keira.

"I hope so."

"Come and stand behind the protective screens, please," Ubach instructed.

The laser started crackling as the energy from the electrons stimulated the gas atoms contained in the glass tube and the resulting photons began resonating back and forth between the mirrors located at either end. The process intensified. It would only be a matter of seconds before the beam was powerful enough to pass through the semi-transparent mirror and I finally found out if I'd been right or wrong.

"Are you ready?" asked Ubach, who was as impatient as we were.

"Yes," Ivory replied, "readier than ever. You've no idea how long we've waited for this moment."

"Wait!" I shouted. "Have you got a camera?"

"We've got something a lot better," answered Ubach. "Six cameras record what happens in front of the laser over a one hundred and eighty degree angle as soon as it's started up. Can we go ahead now?"

Ubach pushed a lever and an extremely intense beam of light flashed out of the machine, hitting the three fragments head on. As the brass ring reached melting point, the fragments turned a more vibrant blue than Keira and I had ever seen. Their surfaces began sparkling and grew increasingly luminous with every passing second. Suddenly, billions of brilliant dots were reflected on the wall opposite the laser. All of us instantly recognised the vast expanse of the night sky and were dazzled by the sight.

Unlike the first projection we'd seen, the universe depicted now began revolving slowly on its axis. Meanwhile, the fragments themselves were spinning at full speed inside the ring.

"Phenomenal!" Ubach whispered.

"That doesn't begin to describe it," said Ivory, his eyes wet with tears.

"What is it?" the professor asked.

"It's playing out the first moments of the universe," I explained.

More surprises followed. The fragments' radiance intensified as they spun around faster and faster. The night sky continued to turn on its axis, then stopped still for an instant. I'd hoped it would complete its course and show us the image of the first star forming, of time zero. I'd yearned for that. But what I saw was completely different. The projected image now started enlarging before our very eyes. Stars began disappearing off the edges of the wall, as if we were moving forwards. The visual effect was startling – we felt like we were travelling through galaxies. Until we approached one I recognised.

"We've entered the Milky Way," I told the others, "and the journey's continuing."

"Where to?" asked Keira, amazed.

"I don't know yet."

The fragments spiralled ever more rapidly on their stand, making a piercing whistling sound as they went. The star the projection was refocusing on was growing bigger and bigger. Our sun appeared in the centre, followed by Mercury.

The fragments were now spinning at dizzying speed. The band holding them together had long melted, but it seemed nothing would split them apart now. Their colour changed from bright blue to indigo. My gaze moved back to the wall and watched us hurtling towards Earth. We could already make out the oceans and three of the continents. The projection began focusing on Africa, then shifted to the east of the continent, the image still enlarging at a breathtaking pace. The noise coming from the spinning fragments was becoming unbearably shrill. Ivory put his hands over his ears. Ubach kept his firmly on the controls, ready to stop everything. Kenya, Uganda, Sudan, Eritrea and Somalia vanished from our field of vision as we closed in on Ethiopia. Suddenly the fragments slowed down and the image started getting sharper.

"I can't keep the laser going at this power!" cried Ubach. "We have to stop!"

"No!" shouted Keira. "Look!"

A miniscule red dot appeared in the centre of the image. The closer we got, the more vivid it became.

"Is everything we're seeing being filmed?" I checked.

"Everything," replied Ubach. "Can I turn it off now?"

"Wait a bit longer," Keira begged.

The whistling ceased and the fragments came to a standstill. The vibrant red dot stopped moving as the image on the wall stabilised. Ubach didn't bother asking; he dropped the lever and the laser beam went out. The projection stayed on the wall for a few seconds, then disappeared.

We were all in shock. Ivory was speechless. He appeared to have aged suddenly. Not that the face I was used to was particularly young-looking, but his features had changed.

"Do you realise I've been dreaming of this moment for thirty years?" he murmured after a while. "If you knew all the sacrifices I've made for these objects. I even sacrificed my only friend to them. It's strange – I ought to feel relieved, freed from an enormous weight, but I don't. I wish

I were a few years younger so I could live long enough to see this adventure through to its conclusion, to find out what that red dot's indicating. This is the first time in my life that I'm afraid of dying. Do you understand what I mean?"

He sighed and went to sit down, not waiting for my reply. I turned to Keira. She was standing in front of the wall, staring at its now-blank surface.

"What are you doing?" I asked her.

"Trying to remember," she said. "Trying to recall what we've just witnessed. It was definitely Ethiopia that appeared. I didn't recognise the landscape of the region I know so well, but I wasn't dreaming; it was Ethiopia. You saw the same thing as me, didn't you?"

"Yes, the last image focused on the Horn of Africa. Were you able to identify the place where the dot was?"

"Not precisely. I've got an idea, but I don't know if it's just wishful thinking on my part or if it's what I really saw."

"Well, we can find that out in a snap," I said, turning to Ubach. "Where's Wim gone?" I asked Keira.

"I think the excitement was too much for him. He didn't feel well. He went out to get some air," she told me.

"Could you project the last few images your cameras recorded?" I asked Ubach.

"Yes, of course," he replied, getting up. "I just have to switch on the projector. Hopefully we won't have to wait too long for the damn machine to start working."

London

"What's the news?"

"What I've just witnessed is nothing short of incredible," answered Wim.

Amsterdam gave Sir Ashley a very detailed description of what had just taken place in the laser room of VU University.

"I'll send some men over," Ashley announced. "It's vital we put a stop to all this before it's too late."

"No, I'm sorry – as long as they're on Dutch territory, they're my sole responsibility. I'm the one who'll step in, when the time is right."

"You're a little new to your post to be addressing me in that tone, Amsterdam."

"Please, Sir Ashley. I intend to perform my role fully, without interference from any allied country or its representatives. You know the rule: united but independent. Each of us handles things on our own territory as we see fit."

"I'm warning you – the minute they're out of your borders, I'll take every step in my power to stop them."

"I presume that's the last thing you'll tell the committee. I owe you, so I won't denounce you. But I won't cover for you either. As you've already pointed out, I'm too much of a new boy to risk compromising myself."

"I wasn't asking you any such thing," Ashley replied curtly. "Don't play God with those scientists, Amsterdam. You have no idea of the consequences if they achieve their goal. They've already gone much too far. What do you intend to do with them then, as they're in your hands?"

"I'll confiscate their equipment and have them deported back to their respective countries."

"What about Ivory? He's with them, isn't he?"

"Yes, he is – I've already told you that. What do you want me to do? We can't accuse him of anything. He's free to come and go as he pleases."

"I have a small favour to ask you. Consider it a way of thanking me for the post you seem so happy to be occupying."

VU University

Ubach had switched on the overhead projector. The high-definition images filmed by the cameras had been stored on the university's server, and we'd have to wait a few hours for the software to finish decompressing the files. Keira and I asked if the computers could be instructed to concentrate on the last sequence we'd watched. Ubach tapped a series of commands on his keyboard and sent them to the central mainframe. We waited while the graphics processors executed their algorithms.

"Be patient," Ubach told us, "it won't be long. The system's a bit slow this morning – we're not the only ones using it."

The projector lens finally came to life and began screening the last seven seconds the fragments had displayed.

"Stop there, please," Keira asked Ubach.

The projection froze on the wall. I'd been expecting the image to lose sharpness, as it usually does with a freeze frame, but it didn't. I now realised why we'd had to wait such a long time to view the final few seconds. The resolution was so high that there must have been a massive amount of information to process for each image. Oblivious to my technical concerns, Keira moved closer to the projection and examined it carefully.

"I recognise these twists and turns," she said. "This meandering line, this shape that looks like a head, this straight line, these four loops. It's a section of the Omo River – I'm almost certain. But something's not quite right. There," she said, pointing to the place where the red dot shone.

"What's not right?" Ubach enquired.

"If that's really the section of the Omo I'm thinking of, we ought to be seeing a lake to the right of this image."

"You recognise this place, then?" I asked Keira.

"Of course I do! I spent three years of my life there. The dot's indicating a small plain enclosed by a wood on the edge of the Omo River. We'd even nearly started our excavations there, but then decided the position was too far north, too far from the Ilemi Triangle. What I'm saying makes no sense though. If it is the place I'm thinking of, Lake Dipa would be featured."

"Keira, the fragments we've found don't just create a map. Together, they form a disk that probably contains billions of pieces of information, although unfortunately for us the missing fragment holds the sequence that interests me the most. But that doesn't matter right now. This memory disk projected a depiction of the evolution of the cosmos from the very first moments of its existence up to the time it was recorded. Perhaps Lake Dipa didn't exist yet in those far-off times."

Ivory joined us by the wall to observe the image up close.

"Adrian's right. What we need now are the exact coordinates. Do you have a detailed map of Ethiopia on your server?" he asked Ubach.

"I should be able to find one on the Internet and download it."

"Please do then, and see if you can superimpose it over this image."

Ubach went back behind his desk. He loaded a map of the Horn of Africa and did as Ivory had asked.

"Apart from a slight deviation in the river bed, it corresponds almost perfectly!" he said. "What are the dot's coordinates?"

"Latitude 5°10'2"67 north, longitude 36°10'1"74 east."

"You know what the next step is," Ivory said, turning to Keira and me.

"I know what *I* have to do next," Ubach cut in. "Vacate this lab. I've already held up two researchers' work to help you out. I'm not sorry I did, but I can't monopolise this room anymore."

Wim came in just as Ubach had switched everything off.

"Did I miss anything?"

"No," replied Ivory, "we were just getting ready to leave."

As Ubach was leading us to his office, Ivory had a dizzy spell. The director wanted to call a doctor but Ivory begged him not to. There was no need to worry, he assured us – it was just tiredness. He asked us if we'd be kind enough to take him back to the hotel so he could get some rest. Then he'd feel better. Wim offered at once to drive us there.

Back at the Krasnapolsky, Ivory thanked Wim and

invited him to come back and have tea with us at the end of the afternoon. He said he'd be pleased to, and left. We took Ivory up to his room. Keira folded back the bedspread and I helped him to lie down.

"Thank you," Ivory sighed, folding his arms across his chest.

"Let me call a doctor. It's ridiculous."

"No. But could I ask you to do me another little favour, please?" he requested.

"Yes, of course," replied Keira.

"Go to the window, twitch the curtain aside discreetly and look out. Tell me if that idiot Wim really has gone."

Keira glanced at me, intrigued, then carried out his instructions.

"Yes, he has. There's nobody in front of the hotel, at any rate."

"And the black Mercedes with two morons inside parked right opposite – is it still there?"

"I can see a black car, but I can't tell from here if there's anyone in it."

"There is, believe me," snapped Ivory, jumping up.

"You shouldn't get out of bed."

"I didn't believe it for a moment when Wim said he was feeling poorly earlier on! And I doubt he believed me, which means we haven't got much time."

"But I thought Wim was our ally," I said, surprised.

"He was – until he got promoted. It was no longer Vackeers' former assistant you were talking to this morning, but his replacement. Wim is their new Amsterdam. No time to explain it all to you now. Hurry back to your room and get your things ready while I sort out your tickets. Come and meet me back here when you're ready. Get a move on – you have to leave the city before the trap snaps shut, if it's not already too late."

"Where are we going?" I enquired.

"Where do you think? Ethiopia, of course."

"No way. It's too dangerous. If the men you still don't want to tell us about are on our tail, I won't put Keira's life in danger again. And don't try to convince me otherwise."

"What time does the plane leave?" Keira asked Ivory.

"We're not going!" I insisted.

"A promise is a promise. If you hoped I'd forgotten about it, you're wrong. Come on, let's hurry!"

Half an hour later, Ivory had us leaving the hotel via the kitchens.

"Don't hang about together at the airport. As soon as you've gone through passport control, have a browse around the shops, but separately. I don't think Wim's smart enough to guess the trick we're playing on him, but you never know. Promise to let me know how you are as soon as you can."

Ivory handed me an envelope and made me swear not to open it before take-off. He gave us a friendly little wave as the taxi drove away.

We boarded the plane without a hitch at Schiphol Airport. We'd ignored Ivory's advice and gone to a café together to spend some time on our own. I'd told Keira about a conversation I'd had with Professor Ubach as we were leaving. In exchange for me promising to let him know how our research was progressing, he'd agreed to keep

silent about it until we published our findings. He'd keep
the recordings made in his lab and send Walter a copy.
Before take-off, I'd called Walter to ask him to lock a parcel he'd soon be receiving from Amsterdam safely away
and not to open it under any circumstances until we were
back from Ethiopia. I'd added that if anything happened
to us, he'd be free to do what he liked with it. Walter had
refused to listen to my last remark, saying it was out of
the question that anything would happen to us, and had
then hung up on me.

During the flight, Keira was overcome with remorse:
she hadn't got in touch with her sister. I promised we'd
call her together as soon as we landed.

Addis Ababa

Addis Ababa's airport was teeming with people. Once we'd gone through customs, I looked for the desk of the small private airline company I'd used before. A pilot agreed to fly us up to Jinka for six hundred dollars. Keira shot me a look of alarm.

"That's way too expensive! Let's go by road. You're broke, Adrian."

"When Oscar Wilde was breathing his last in a hotel room in Paris, he declared, 'Alas, I am dying beyond my means.' Seeing as we're heading towards our worst troubles yet, please let me be as dignified as him!"

I took an envelope containing a wad of dollars out of my pocket.

"Where did that come from?" Keira asked.

"A present from Ivory. He handed it to me just before we left."

"And you accepted it?"

"He made me promise not to open it until we'd taken off. I was hardly going to chuck it out of the window at an altitude of ten thousand metres, was I?"

*

We left Addis Ababa on board a low-flying Piper. The pilot pointed out a herd of elephants migrating northwards. Further on, we saw giraffes gambolling across a vast plain. An hour later, the airplane began its descent. The short airstrip at Jinka appeared before us, the wheels dropped and we bounced onto the ground. The plane slowed down and made a U-turn at the end of the field. Through the window, I glimpsed a group of kids rushing towards us. One boy who looked older than the others was sitting on an old barrel watching the aircraft taxi over to the straw hut that served as the airport terminal.

"I think I recognise that little fella," I told Keira, pointing to him. "He's the one who helped me find you the day I came here looking for you."

Keira leaned over to look out. Her eyes welled up with tears.

"I recognise him for sure!" she exclaimed.

The pilot turned off the propellers and Keira was the first to disembark. She pushed her way through the gaggle of shouting, jumping children. The young boy slid off his barrel and began wandering away.

"Hari!" yelled Keira. "Hari, it's me!"

Hari turned around and stood stock-still. Keira rushed over to him, tousled his messy hair and hugged him tight.

"You see," she said, sobbing. "I kept my promise!"

Hari looked up at her.

"You took your time!"

"I did my best," she answered, "but I'm here now."

"Your friends have rebuilt everything. It's even bigger

than before the storm. Are you going to stay this time?"

"I don't know, Hari. I've no idea."

"When are you leaving then?"

"I've only just arrived and you already want me to leave?"

Hari freed himself from Keira's embrace and walked off. I hesitated for a moment, then ran and caught up with him.

"Listen, little fella. She hasn't gone a day without talking about you, or a night without thinking about you as she fell asleep. Don't you think she deserves a nicer welcome?"

"She's with you now, so why has she come back? For me, or to dig up the ground again? Go back home, I've got things to do."

"Hari, you can refuse to believe it, but Keira loves you. That's just the way it is. She loves you. If you only knew how much she's missed you. Don't turn your back on her. I'm asking you, man to man, don't push her away."

"Leave him alone," Keira whispered as she joined us. "Do what you want, Hari. I understand. Whether you're cross with me or not won't change how much I love you."

Keira picked up her bag and headed for the straw hut without turning around. Hari hesitated for a moment, then ran in front of her.

"Where are you going?"

"I don't exactly know, buddy. I've got to try and join Eric and the others – I need their help."

The young boy thrust his hands into his pockets and kicked a stone.

"Yeah, I see," he said.

"You see what?"

"That you can't manage without me."

"I've known that since the day I met you, sweetheart."

"You want me to help you get there – is that it?"

Keira knelt down and looked him straight in the eye.

"First I'd like us to kiss and make up," she said, holding out her arms to him.

Hari wavered, then held out his hand. But Keira hid hers behind her back.

"No, I want a kiss!"

"I'm too old for that now," he said solemnly.

"*You* might be, but I'm not. Okay, a hug then?"

"I'll think about it. Just follow me for now – you've got to sleep somewhere. I'll give you my answer tomorrow."

"All right," said Keira.

Hari glanced at me defiantly, then led the way. We scooped up our bags and followed him along the path towards the village.

A man in a frayed vest standing in front of his hut remembered me and started waving enthusiastically.

"I didn't know you were so popular around here," Keira teased me.

"Maybe it's because the first time I came, I introduced myself as one of your friends."

The man invited us in and offered us two mats to sleep on and something to eat. During the meal, Hari didn't take his eyes off Keira. All of a sudden, he got up, announced he'd be back the next day and scampered out of the door.

Keira rushed after him. I followed her, but the boy was already in the distance.

"Give him a bit of time," I told her.

"We don't have much time," she replied melancholically as she returned inside.

I was woken at dawn by the sound of an engine approaching. I went out onto the doorstep and saw a 4x4 driving towards us trailing a cloud of dust. The vehicle stopped level with me and I at once recognised the two Italians who'd helped me on my first visit.

"What a surprise! What brings you back here?" called the heftier of the pair as he exited the car.

His friendly tone rang false and made me suspicious.

"Same as you," I answered. "My love of the country. When you've been here once, it's hard to resist the temptation to come back."

Keira joined me on the porch and laced her arm around me.

"I see you've found your friend," said the other man on his way over. "Isn't she pretty? I can see why you went to so much trouble."

"Who are these guys?" whispered Keira. "Do you know them?"

"I wouldn't say that. I bumped into them when I was looking for your camp and they pointed me in the right direction."

"Is there anyone in the area who didn't help you find me?"

"Just don't be aggressive. That's all I'm asking."

"Aren't you going to invite us in?" asked the stocky one as they reached us. "It's damn hot, even this early."

"This isn't our home and you haven't even introduced yourselves," retorted Keira.

"He's Giovanni and I'm Marco. Can we come in now?"

"I've already told you – this isn't our house," Keira repeated in a less than friendly tone.

"Come, come," continued the one calling himself Giovanni. "What about good old African hospitality? You could at least offer us some shade and something to drink: I'm dying of thirst."

Our host appeared on the doorstep and invited everyone into his home. He placed four glasses on a crate, served us coffee, then left for the fields.

Marco, if that was his real name, eyed Keira up in a way that irritated me intensely.

"If I remember rightly, you're an archaeologist, aren't you?" he asked her.

"You're well informed," she answered. "Which reminds me, we've got work to do; we have to go."

"You're really hospitable, aren't you? You could be more friendly – we did help your friend find you a few months ago, after all. Didn't he tell you?"

"Yes. Everyone around here helped him find me. And I wasn't even lost! Now, excuse me for being so direct, but we really must go," she said brusquely, standing up.

Giovanni jumped up and blocked her way. I intervened at once.

"What the hell do you want?"

"Nothing! Just a chat. We don't often come across other Europeans here."

"Well, now that we've exchanged a few words, let me past," insisted Keira.

"Sit down!" ordered Marco.

"I'm not in the habit of taking orders!" she barked back.

"Well, I'm afraid you'll have to change your habits. Now sit down and shut up."

This time the guy had overstepped the mark with his rudeness. I was just getting ready to thump him when he got a gun out of his pocket and aimed it at Keira.

"Don't try to be a hero," he said, flicking off the safety catch. "Stay calm and everything will be okay. A plane's arriving in three hours. The four of us will leave this hut and you'll follow us over to it without doing anything stupid. Then you'll get on it, nice and quiet. Giovanni will escort you. All very straightforward."

"And where's the plane going?" I asked.

"You'll see in good time. Now, as we've got time to kill, why don't you tell me what you've come here to do."

"Meet two assholes with a gun!" exclaimed Keira.

"She's certainly got character, that one!" sniggered Giovanni.

"'She' has a name – Keira," I said. "No need to be offensive."

We sat looking at each other for the next two hours. Giovanni picked his teeth with a match while Marco stared blankly at Keira. The hum of an engine in the distance broke the silence. Marco walked out onto the porch.

"Two 4x4s are coming in this direction," he told us as he stepped back inside. "We're just going to wait sensibly for them to drive by – without attracting any attention to ourselves. Got it?"

We were truly tempted to do something, but Marco kept his gun pointed at Keira. The cars came closer. We heard their brakes screech a few metres from the small house, their engines cut and several doors slam. Giovanni went up to the window.

"Shit! There are about ten guys heading this way."

Marco got up and joined Giovanni, all the while keeping his weapon locked on Keira. The door burst open.

"Eric!" cried Keira. "I've never been so happy to see you!"

"Is there a problem?" her colleague asked.

I hadn't remembered Eric being so burly, but was delighted my memory hadn't served me well. Marco looked away and I seized the opportunity to give him a hard kick in the groin. I'm not a violent person, but when I lose my cool I don't do it in half measures. With his breath knocked out of him, Marco dropped his gun and Keira kicked it to the other side of the room. Giovanni didn't have time to react before I punched him in the face. It hurt my fist as much as it must have hurt his jaw.

As Marco was straightening up, Eric seized him by the throat and pinned him to the wall. "What are you playing at? What's the firearm for?"

But with Eric's vice-like hand around his neck, Marco was unable to utter a reply. The colour was draining from his cheeks. I suggested Eric loosen his grip and stop shaking him to let him get his breath back.

"Stop it! I'll explain!" begged Giovanni. "We work for the Italian Government. Our mission is to escort these two nutcases to the frontier. We weren't going to hurt them."

"What have we got to do with the Italian Government?" asked Keira, dumbfounded.

"I've no idea, Miss. And it's none of our business. We

received instructions last night and we know nothing more than what I've just told you."

"Have you been up to no good in Italy?" Eric asked, turning to us.

"We haven't even set foot there. These men are talking rubbish! And what's to prove they really are who they claim to be?"

"Have we harmed you? Do you think we'd just have hung around like that if our plan was to kill you?" Marco spluttered.

"Like you killed the village chief at Lake Turkana?" I enquired.

Eric looked at each of us in turn, then instructed a member of his team to go and get some rope from the car.

"Tie these two guys up, and let's get out of here," he ordered when the young man came back with some straps.

"Listen, Eric, we're archaeologists, not cops," one of his colleagues protested. "What if these men really are Italian officials? Why get ourselves into trouble?"

"Don't worry," I told him. "I'll take care of it."

Marco made a move to resist the fate that lay in store for him, but Keira picked up his gun and aimed it at his stomach.

"I'm very clumsy with this kind of thing," she told him. "As my friend here pointed out, we're only archaeologists, and handling firearms isn't our strong point."

While Keira kept the weapon trained on our assailants, Eric and I put them back to back and tied their hands and feet together. Keira slipped the revolver under her belt and knelt down by Marco.

"I know it's a nasty thing to do, and I wouldn't blame

you for calling me a coward, but 'she' has one last thing to say to you."

Keira slapped him in the face so hard Marco rolled onto the floor.

"Right. We can go now."

As we were leaving the room, I spared a thought for our poor host: he'd find two rather ill-tempered guests when he returned home.

We climbed on board one of the 4x4s. Hari was waiting for us on the back seat.

"You see. You need me," he told Keira.

"You owe him a thank you. He's the one who came to let us know you were in a spot of bother."

"But how did you know?" Keira asked him.

"I recognised the car. No one in the village likes those men. I looked through the window and saw what was happening, so I went to find your friends."

"And how did you manage to reach the excavations in such a short time?"

"The camp isn't very far from here now, Keira," Eric answered for him. "Once you left, we moved the site. We weren't very welcome in the Omo Valley anymore after the village chief died, as you can imagine. And anyway, we found nothing where you'd been digging. A combination of feeling unsafe and generally fed up made us shift further north."

"Oh, right," said Keira. "I see you've really taken control of operations in my absence."

"Do you know how long you took to even contact us? Spare me the lecture."

"Please, Eric, don't take me for a bloody idiot! Relocating the dig meant you removed all trace of my work and could claim any discovery as your own."

"That idea didn't even cross my mind, Keira. I think you're the one with the ego problem, not me. So, are you going to explain why those Italians had it in for you?"

As Eric drove, Keira recounted our adventures since she'd left Ethiopia. She told him about our trip to China and what we'd discovered on Narcondam Island, missing out the part about her stint in Garther Prison, then about the searches we carried out on the Manpupuner plateau and the conclusions she'd reached about the epic journey undertaken by the Sumerians. She didn't mention the harrowing events leading up to us leaving Russia or our troubles on the Trans-Siberian, but she did describe in minute detail the amazing sight we'd witnessed in the laser room at VU University.

Eric stopped the car and turned to Keira.

"You're saying you saw a four-hundred-million-year-old recording of the first moments of the universe? How can someone as educated as you put forward such nonsense? Who would have recorded this disk of yours – Devonian tetrapods? That's just ludicrous."

Keira didn't try to argue with Eric. Her eyes told me not to bother either.

When we got to the camp, I was expecting Keira's team to celebrate her arrival, be pleased to see her again. But no. It was as if they were still angry with her about what had happened when we went to Lake Turkana. But Keira was a born leader. She waited patiently until the end of the day when the archaeologists had finished their work, then asked her old team to gather around because she had something important to announce. Eric was clearly furious about her taking the initiative. I quietly reminded him that the grant enabling them to carry out these excavations in the Omo Valley had been awarded to Keira, not him, and that if the Walsh Foundation discovered she'd been excluded from her research, the generous benefactors on its committee might reconsider making their monthly payments. Eric let her speak.

Keira had waited until the sun disappeared behind the skyline. As soon as it was dark enough, she took out the three fragments in our possession and placed them together. The effect their breathtaking blue light had on the archaeologists was better than any explanations Keira could have given. Even Eric looked disconcerted. Then, as a murmur ran round the gathering, he began clapping.

"A very beautiful object," he said. "Congratulations on that little magic trick. What your colleague hasn't yet said is she wants to make you believe these luminous toys are four hundred million years old, no less!"

The odd snigger sounded from the group. Keira climbed up on a crate.

"Has anyone here ever seen me behaving in an outlandish way? When you agreed to come on this mission in the heart of the Omo Valley and leave your family and friends for months on end, did you check who you were signing up with? Is there one person among you who doubted my credibility before you got on the plane? Do you really think I've come back to waste your time and make a fool of myself in front of you? Who selected you and approached you? I did!"

"What exactly are you expecting us to do?" asked Wolfmayer, a member of the team.

"This object with astounding properties is also a map," Keira continued. "I know it's hard to believe, but if you'd seen what we've witnessed, you'd be stunned. In the space of a few months, I've learned to question all my certainties – it's been a very humbling experience. Latitude 5°10'2"67 north, longitude 36°10'1"74 east is where it points to. I'm asking you to put your trust in me for one week at the most. I'm suggesting you load up these two 4x4s with the equipment we need and leave with me tomorrow to go and start excavating there."

"To find what exactly?" quizzed Eric.

"I don't know yet," Keira admitted.

"And there you have it! Not content with getting us all chased out of the Omo Valley, our great archaeologist is now asking us to chuck seven working days away – and God knows, our time is precious – to take us I don't know where to look for I don't know what! Who's she trying to kid?"

"Hang on a minute, Eric," Wolfmayer continued. "What do we actually have to lose? We've been digging for months and haven't found anything really conclusive so far. And Keira's right about one thing: she's the one who hired us. I assume she wouldn't risk making herself look ridiculous with all of us in tow if it wasn't for a good reason."

"Maybe. But do you know her reasons?" Eric asked indignantly. "She's unable to tell us what she hopes to find. Do you know how much a week of work costs for our team?"

"If you're referring to our salaries," picked up Karvelis, another archaeologist, "it shouldn't bankrupt anyone. And anyway, as far as I know, she's the one in charge of the money. Since she left, we've all been pretending it's just business as usual, but Keira's the one who got these excavations started. I don't see why we shouldn't grant her a few days of our time."

Normand, one of the Frenchmen in the team, put up his hand to speak.

"The coordinates Keira has given us are very precise. If we concentrated on a grid of around fifty square metres, we wouldn't even have to dismantle our set-up here. And we'd only need a small amount of equipment. One short week away would hardly affect our work in progress here."

Eric leaned towards Keira and asked to speak to her in private.

"Well done! I see you haven't lost your gift of the gab," he said after they'd stepped away from the group. "You've almost convinced them to follow you. And why not? But I haven't had my last word. I could threaten to resign and force them to choose between you and me, or I could back you up."

"Spit it out, Eric. I've had a long journey and I'm tired."

"Whatever we find, if indeed we do find something, I want to share the claim to the discovery. I didn't sweat my guts out all those long months while you were taking it easy on your travels just to see myself relegated to the rank of assistant. I took over when you walked out on us. I'm the one who's been taking care of everything here. If you find the team closely knit and efficient, it's thanks to me. You can't just show up on a site I'm now in charge of and demote me to second-in-command. I won't let you."

"And you were talking to me about egos earlier? You're unbelievable, Eric. If we make a major discovery, the whole team will share the credit – including you, obviously. And Adrian, because he's probably contributed more than anyone else here, believe me. So can I count on your support now you're reassured?"

"One week, Keira. I'm giving you one week. And if we get nowhere, you can take your bags and your boyfriend and get out of here."

"I'll let you repeat that to Adrian. I'm sure he'll be over the moon."

Keira returned to the group and climbed back onto the crate.

"The place I was telling you about is three kilometres west of Lake Dipa. If we set off at dawn tomorrow, we can be there by noon and get down to work straightaway. Anyone who wants to come along with me is most welcome."

A hum of voices rose from the group. Karvelis was the first to step forward and stand in front of Keira. Alvaro, Normand and Wolfmayer joined him. Keira's bet had paid off. Soon the entire team had gathered around her, including Eric, who was now sticking to her like a leech.

We loaded the equipment just before sunrise and headed off in the two 4x4s, Keira behind the wheel of one and Eric the other. After driving along a dirt track for three hours, we arrived at the edge of a wood and left the vehicles. The next stage was on foot through the undergrowth, carrying the equipment on our shoulders. Hari led the way, hacking down branches hanging across our path with a machete. I offered to help, but he told me to leave it to him, saying I might hurt myself.

Not long after, we came to the large round clearing Keira had told me about. Stretching about eight hundred metres in diameter, it sat in a meander of the Omo River and was shaped rather strangely, like a human skull.

GPS in hand, Karvelis guided us to the centre of the plain.

"Latitude 5°10'2"67 north, 36°10'1"74 east. Here it is!" he said.

Keira knelt and ran her hand gently over the ground.

"What an incredible journey! And it's led us right back here," she said. "I can't tell you how nervous I'm feeling."

"Me too," I admitted.

Alvaro and Normand began marking out the perimeter of the dig, while the others pitched the tents in the shade of giant heathers.

"No point making the site too large. Focus on an area of twenty square metres maximum. We'll be digging deep, not wide," Keira told them.

Alvaro rewound his string and followed Keira's instructions. By the end of the afternoon, thirty cubic metres of earth had been removed and a large pit had taken shape. But as the sun set in the evening sky, we still hadn't found anything. The fading light forced us to stop digging.

We started again early the next day. By eleven o'clock, Keira was showing signs of strain.

"We've still got a week ahead of us," I reassured her.

"I don't think it's a matter of time, Adrian. The

coordinates are very precise – they're either right or wrong; there's no in-between. Thing is, we're not equipped to dig beyond ten metres."

"How deep are we now?"

"Halfway there."

"All isn't lost, then. I'm sure the deeper we dig, the greater our chances."

"If I've made a mistake," sighed Keira, "we'll have lost everything."

"I thought I'd lost everything the day our car plunged into the Yellow River," I said, wandering away.

The afternoon's excavations were equally unfruitful. Keira went to have a short rest in the shade of the heather. At 4pm, Alvaro, who'd been digging energetically in the depths of the hole for quite some time, let out a shout that could be heard throughout the camp. Seconds later, Karvelis called out too. Keira jumped up, stood paralysed for a moment, then began advancing slowly towards the pit. Alvaro's head appeared. He was wearing the biggest smile I'd ever seen. Keira quickened her pace to a sprint.

"How many times have I told you not to run on the excavation site!" said Hari, catching up with her.

He took Keira's hand and led her to the edge of the trench, where the whole team had gathered. Alvaro and Karvelis had found bones at the bottom of the hole. They were the fossilised remains of a human, and the skeleton was almost intact.

Keira jumped in beside her two colleagues and knelt down. The bones were barely protruding above ground. It would take many more hours to free the skeleton from the earth it was imprisoned in.

"You've caused me no end of trouble, but I found you in the end," said Keira, gently stroking the skull that was emerging. "We'll have to christen you later. First you have to tell us who you were and, more importantly, how old you are."

"Something's not quite right," said Alvaro. "I've never seen human bones fossilised to this degree. I'm not trying to be funny, but this skeleton's too advanced for its age."

I took Keira by the arm and led her away from the others.

"Do you think the promise I made you has come true and these bones are as old as we think?"

"I've no idea for now. It seems so unlikely, and yet… Only sophisticated tests will tell us if our dream has become a reality. If it has, then this is definitely the biggest discovery about the history of humanity ever made!"

Keira returned to her colleagues. They worked until sunset and picked up again the next morning. Nobody was tracking time anymore.

Our troubles weren't over yet. The third day held an even greater surprise in store for us. I'd watched Keira work with painstaking care since the morning. Handling the brush like a pointillist painter, she'd been slowly freeing the bones from their dirt casing, millimetre by millimetre. Suddenly she stopped; she'd felt a slight resistance at the end of her tool. Her expert judgement told her to continue dusting delicately, following the contours of the protuberance. But this particular object taking shape under her fine brush was a mystery to her.

"That's weird," she said, "it looks spherical – like a

kneecap perhaps. Only it's in the middle of the thorax. Very odd."

The heat was unbearable. From time to time I heard her cursing when a bead of sweat trickled down her forehead and landed in the dust.

Alvaro had come off his break and offered to take over. Keira was shattered so she handed over her tools, imploring him to proceed with the utmost care.

"Come with me," she said, "the river's just through the wood. I need a dip."

Keira undressed on the sandy bank of the Omo and dived in without waiting for me. As soon as I'd stripped off my shirt and trousers, I joined her in the water and took her in my arms.

"The scenery is rather romantic, isn't it? The perfect backdrop for a bit of passion," she whispered. "It's not that I don't want to, believe me... But if you carry on jiggling about like that, it won't be long before we have visitors."

"What kind of visitor?"

"The starving crocodile kind! Come on, we can't hang around in here. I just wanted to cool down. Let's go and dry off on the bank, then get back to the dig."

I never knew if her crocodile story was true or just a sensitively made-up excuse so she could get back to her obsession: work. Alvaro was waiting for Keira when we got back to the trench.

"Just what are we digging up?" he asked her in a hushed tone so the others didn't hear. "Do you have the faintest idea?"

"Why that face? You look worried."

"Because of this," answered Alvaro, holding out what looked like a large marble or ball of agate.

"Is that what I was working on before I went off for a swim?" Keira enquired.

"I found it ten centimetres down from the top vertebrae."

Keira took the ball in her hand and dusted it.

"Give me some water," she asked, intrigued.

Alvaro opened his flask.

"Wait. Not here. Let's get out of the trench first."

"Everyone will see us," Alvaro whispered.

Keira climbed out of the pit, concealing the ball in the palm of her hands. Alvaro followed her.

"Pour slowly," she said.

Nobody paid them any attention. From a distance, they looked like two colleagues washing their hands. Keira delicately rubbed the marble to remove the sediment covering it.

"A bit more," she told Alvaro.

"What is this thing?" he asked, evidently as perturbed as Keira.

"Let's go back into the trench."

Hidden from view, Keira cleaned the surface of the ball then examined it more closely.

"It's translucent. And there's something inside."

"Show me!" exclaimed Alvaro.

He took the object in his fingers and held it up to the sun.

"You can see much better like this. It looks like a kind of resin. Do you think it was a pendant of some sort? I'm completely thrown. I've never seen anything like it. Good God, Keira, how old is this skeleton?"

Keira took back the object and raised it up to the light again.

"I think this little thing is going to answer your question," she told her colleague with a smile. "Do you remember about the shrine of San Gennaro?"

"Refresh my memory, please," asked Alvaro.

"San Gennaro (or St. Januarius) was the bishop of Benevento. He was martyred near Pozzuoli in around 300 AD during the Diocletianic Persecution. Legend has it that Gennaro was condemned to death by Timoteo, the prelate of Campania. After escaping unscathed from being burned at the stake and surviving being thrown to the lions because they refused to devour him, Gennaro was beheaded. The executioner also cut off his finger. As was customary at that time, a disciple collected his blood and poured it into two phials that Gennaro had used when celebrating his last mass. The saint's relics were moved several times. At the start of the fifth century, when they were transferred to Naples, the disciple who'd kept the phials placed them by the body and the dried blood inside them liquefied. The phenomenon reoccurred in 1497 when the remains were moved to Naples Cathedral, which is dedicated to San Gennaro. Since then, the liquefaction of Gennaro's blood has been the subject of an annual ceremony in the presence of the Bishop of Naples. Neapolitans all over the world celebrate the anniversary of his execution. The dried blood, kept in two hermetically sealed ampoules, is held up before thousands of believers, who witness it liquefying and sometimes even boiling."

"How do you know all that?" I asked Keira.

"While you were studying Shakespeare, I was reading Alexandre Dumas."

"And like with St. Januarius, this transparent object may contain the blood of the person buried in your trench?"

"It's possible the solidified red matter we can see inside is blood. If it is, it'll be another miracle. We'd be able to find out almost everything about this man's life, his age and his biological characteristics. If we can get his DNA to talk, he'll hold no secrets from us. We've got to take it to a safe place and get the contents analysed by a specialist laboratory."

"Who are you planning to entrust that task to?" I asked.

Keira fixed her eyes on me, giving away her plan.

"I'm going nowhere without you!" I answered before she'd even opened her mouth. "Out of the question."

"Adrian, I can't ask Eric, and if I leave my team a second time, they'll never forgive me."

"I couldn't give a damn about your colleagues, your research, that skeleton or even this ball! If something were to happen to you, I'd never forgive you either! I won't leave here without you, even for the most important scientific discovery ever made."

"Adrian, please!"

"Listen to me, Keira. What I'm going to tell you is very hard for me to say, and I won't say it again. I've dedicated most of my life to searching the galaxies for the smallest sign of the first moments of the universe. I believed I was the best, most progressive, ballsiest person in my field. I thought I was unbeatable and was proud of it. But when I thought I'd lost you, I spent my nights looking up at the sky, unable to remember the name of a single star. I couldn't care less about that skeleton's age and what it'll teach us about the human race. Whether it's one hundred years old or four hundred million years old is all the same to me if you're no longer there."

I'd totally forgotten about Alvaro, who gave an embarrassed little cough.

"It's none of my business," he said, "but with the discovery you've just given us, you could come back in six months and ask us to do a potato sack race around Machu Picchu and I'm willing to bet everyone would follow you. Me first."

I sensed Keira hesitate. She looked at the bones in the ground.

"For God's sake!" cried Alvaro. "After what this man has just said to you, would you prefer to spend your nights lying next to a skeleton? Get out of here and come back as soon as you can to tell me what's in this resin ball!"

Keira held out her hand and I helped her out of her hole. She thanked Alvaro.

"Go on, scram! Ask Normand to drive you to Jinka. You can trust him – he's discreet. I'll explain everything to the others once you've left."

While I got our belongings together, Keira went to talk to Normand. Luckily, the rest of the group had left the camp to go and take a dip in the river. The three of us crossed the wood. When we arrived at the 4x4, Hari was there waiting for us, arms folded across his chest.

"Were you going to leave without saying goodbye to me again?" he asked Keira, eyeing her distrustfully.

"No. And this time, it'll only take a few weeks. I'll be back soon."

"This time, I won't go and wait for you in Jinka. You won't come back. I know it."

"I promise I will, Hari. I'll never abandon you. Next time, I'll take you back home with me."

"I've got no business in your country. You spend your time looking for dead people – you should know my place is here, where my parents are buried. This is my land. Go away now."

Keira moved closer to Hari.

"Do you hate me?"

"No, I'm sad and I don't want you to see me sad, so go away."

"I'm sad too, Hari. You have to believe me. I've come back once, I'll come back again."

"Perhaps I will go to Jinka then. But only now and again."

"Will you give me a kiss?"

"On the lips?"

"No, not on the lips, Hari!" Keira said, bursting out laughing.

"So I *am* too old for that! I'd really like a hug though."

Keira took Hari in her arms and just had time to plant a kiss on his forehead before he flew off towards the forest without turning back.

"If all goes well," said Normand, "we'll get to Jinka before the mail plane. You'll be able to leave on it – I know the pilot. You should land in Addis Ababa in time to catch the Paris plane. Otherwise there's always the last flight of the day to Frankfurt: you'll definitely get that."

As we were driving along, I turned to Keira to ask her a question that was playing on my mind.

"What would you have done if Alvaro hadn't pleaded on my behalf back there?"

"Why do you ask?"

"Because when I saw your gaze switch from the skeleton to me, I wondered which one of us you liked better."

"I'm in the car with you, aren't I? That should answer your question."

"I guess," I muttered, fixing my eyes back on the road.

"What do you mean, you guess? Did you have your doubts?"

"No, no."

"If Alvaro hadn't said what he did, maybe I'd have acted all proud and stayed. But ten minutes after you'd left, I'd have begged someone to drive me in the second 4x4 to catch you up. Happy now?"

Paris

It was a race against the clock to catch the plane for Paris.
By the time we arrived at the Air France desk, boarding
had nearly finished. Fortunately there were still a dozen
seats available and a sympathetic air hostess agreed to
let us jump the long queue of passengers waiting to get
through security. I managed to squeeze in a couple of
quick phone calls before the plane left the terminal – one
to Walter, who I woke up in the middle of the night, and
the other to Ivory, who wasn't asleep. After breaking the
news that we were on our way back to Europe, I asked
each of them where we could find the best laboratory to
carry out some complex DNA tests.

By 6am, we were crossing the French capital from
Roissy Airport to Ile St-Louis by taxi. Ivory had invited
us to come over as soon as we landed. He opened the door
in his dressing gown.

"I didn't know exactly what time you'd arrive," he
said. "I must have dropped off to sleep very late."

He disappeared into the kitchen to make some coffee,
asking us to wait in the sitting room. A few minutes later,

he came in carrying a tray and sat down on an armchair opposite us.

"So, what did you find in Africa? It's because of you that I couldn't sleep – it was impossible to after your call."

Keira took the ball from her pocket and handed it to the elderly professor. Ivory adjusted his glasses and examined the object closely.

"Is it amber?"

"I don't know yet, but the red spots inside are probably blood."

"It's beautiful! Where did you find it?"

"In the exact place the fragments indicated," I replied.

"On the thorax of a skeleton we've unearthed," Keira continued.

"This is a major discovery!" Ivory exclaimed.

He walked over to his desk, opened a drawer and took out a sheet of paper.

"Here's my final translation of the text written in Ge'ez. Read it."

I took the document Ivory was waving under my nose and read it out loud.

"*I have split up the disk of memories, and entrusted the parts it combines to the masters of the colonies. May the shadows of infinity remain concealed beneath the trigonals of stars. Let none know where the hypogeum is. The night of one is guardian of the origins. Let none disturb that slumber. Our era will end when imaginary times are united.*"

"I think the riddle makes rather more sense now, don't you?" said Ivory. "Thanks to Adrian's repair job at VU University, we got the disk to divulge information and it pointed out the location of a tomb – the famous hypo-geum where it was probably discovered in the fourth mil-lennium. The people who realised how important it was split it into fragments and took them to all four corners of the globe."

"But what for?" I asked. "Why make those journeys?"

"So no one would find the body you've dug up, the very one they discovered holding the disk of memories. *The night of one is guardian of the origins*," whispered Ivory, wincing with pain.

The old professor's face had turned pale and fine beads of sweat were forming on his forehead.

"What's wrong?" asked Keira.

"I've dedicated my whole life to it, and you've found it at last. Nobody would believe me. I'm fine – I've never felt better in my life," he said, grinning.

But Ivory clutched his hand to his chest and lowered himself into his armchair, his face white as a sheet.

"It's nothing," he said. "Just tiredness. So, what's he like?"

"Who?" I enquired.

"The skeleton, for heaven's sake!"

"Completely fossilised and surprisingly intact," replied Keira.

The professor groaned and bent double with pain.

"I'm calling an ambulance," she said.

"Don't call anyone!" ordered Ivory. "It'll pass, I tell you! Listen to me. We don't have much time. The labora-tory you want is in London. I've jotted down the address on the notepad by the front door. Be extra vigilant: if they find out what you've discovered, they won't let you see it through. They'll stop at nothing. I'm sorry I've put you in danger, but it's too late now."

"Who are these people?" I asked.

"I've no time to explain. There are more urgent matters. There's another text in my desk drawer – please take it."

Ivory collapsed on the carpet.

Keira grabbed the phone off the coffee table and dialled the emergency services, but Ivory seized the cord and pulled it out of the socket.

"Please leave!"

Keira knelt beside him and slipped a cushion under his head.

"There's no question of us leaving you, do you understand?"

"I adore you – you're even more stubborn than I am! Just leave the door open when you go and call the emergency services in a little while. My God it hurts," he said clasping his chest. "Please continue what I can't do anymore. The end is in sight."

"What end, Ivory?"

"My dear, you've made the most sensational discovery ever. The one all your fellow archaeologists will envy you for. You've found the first ever human being. And that ball of blood you have will provide the proof. But you'll see – if I'm not mistaken – there are yet more surprises in store for you. Adrian is already familiar with the second text in my desk. Don't forget to take it. You'll both understand it in the end."

Ivory lost consciousness. Keira paid no attention to his last instructions. While I was rummaging through his desk, she called an ambulance from my mobile.

Leaving his apartment building, we were stricken with guilt.

"We shouldn't have left him up there on his own."

"He chucked us out!"

"He was only protecting us. Come on, let's go back up."

We heard a siren wailing in the distance. It was getting closer by the minute.

"Let's listen to him for once," I said to Keira, "and get out of here."

I stopped a taxi coming up Quai d'Orléans and asked it to drive us to the Gare du Nord. Keira looked at me, surprised. I showed her the piece of paper I'd ripped off the notepad in Ivory's hall just before we left. The address he'd scribbled down was in London – the British Society for Genetic Research, 10 Hammersmith Grove.

London

I'd called Walter to let him know our plans and he came to meet us at St. Pancras Station. He was waiting at the foot of the escalators, hands clasped behind his gabardine.

"You don't look in a very good mood," I said when I saw him.

"Funnily enough, I slept badly. I wonder who's to blame!"

"Sorry for waking you up."

"You two don't look very well," he said, inspecting our faces.

"We spent the night in the plane and these past few weeks haven't been particularly restful. Right then, shall we be off?" Keira suggested.

"I've found the address you were after," Walter said, guiding us towards the taxi rank. "At least my sleep won't have been spoiled for nothing. I certainly hope not anyway."

"Don't you have your little car anymore then?" I asked him as I climbed into the black cab.

"I listen to my friends' advice, unlike other people I

could mention," he replied. "I've sold it and I've got a surprise for you. You'll have to wait till later to find out. 10 Hammersmith Grove, please," he said to the driver. "The place you want is the British Society for Genetic Research."

I decided to keep Ivory's note firmly in my pocket and not let Walter know of its existence.

"So?" he asked. "Can I know why we're going there – a paternity test, perhaps?"

Keira held up the ball to Walter.

"Beautiful," he admired. "And what's the red stuff in the middle?"

"Blood," Keira replied.

"Yuck!"

Walter had managed to get us a meeting with Dr. Poincarno, the head of the palaeo-DNA department.

"The Academy's good name opens doors, so why not take advantage?" he said sardonically. "I took the liberty of listing your respective qualities. Rest assured, I didn't expand on the nature of your work, but in order to secure a meeting at such short notice, I had to disclose that you were returning from Ethiopia with some extraordinary things to have analysed. I couldn't say any more than that to them as Adrian made a point of telling me absolutely nothing!"

"The doors of our plane were closing – I hardly had any time. And anyway, I thought I'd disturbed your sleep."

Walter shot me a provocative look.

"So are you going to tell me what you discovered in Africa, or are you going to let me die stupid? With all the trouble I go to for you, I think I've got a right to a little information. I'm not just a courier, chauffeur, postman and what have you."

"We've found an incredible skeleton," Keira revealed, tapping him affectionately on the knee.

"What is it about old bones that gets both of you so worked up? You must have been dogs in a former life. In fact you look a bit like a spaniel, Adrian, with your doleful eyes. Don't you think so, Keira?"

"And what kind of dog am I?" she asked Walter, threatening him playfully with her newspaper.

"Don't put words into my mouth!"

The taxi drew up outside the British Society for Genetic Research. It was a modern, remarkably luxurious building. Long corridors led to a succession of examination rooms stuffed to the hilt with equipment ranging from pipettes and centrifuges to electronic microscopes and cold chambers. Researchers in red lab coats bustled around the state-of-the-art facilities in an impressive atmosphere of calm. Poincarno gave us a tour of the premises and explained how the laboratory worked.

"Our work offers countless scientific opportunities. Aristotle said, 'Anything that nourishes itself, grows and decays is alive.' You could say, 'Anything that contains programs – its own kind of software – is alive.' An organism must be able to develop avoiding disorder and anarchy. In order to build something, a plan is needed. Where does life hide its plan? In DNA. Open any cell nucleus and you'll find strands of DNA carrying all the genetic information about a species in one vast coded message. DNA is the vehicle of inheritance. Thanks to an ambitious cell-sampling campaign carried out among diverse populations around the globe, we've established astonishing relatedness between people, and traced the major human migrations through the ages. Analysing the DNA of thousands of individuals has helped us decode the process of evolution over the course of these migrations. DNA passes on information from one generation to the next. The program evolves and makes us evolve. We're all descended from one human being, are we not? Tracing him means discovering the source of life. We've found that the Inuit are related to the people of northern Siberia. We can tell individuals where their great-great-great-grandparents originally came from. But we also study the DNA of insects and plants. We recently got the leaves of a twenty-million-year-old magnolia to give us information. Nowadays, we can extract DNA from places you wouldn't think there could be a million of a millionth of a gram left."

Keira got the little ball out of her pocket and handed it to Poincarno.

"Is it amber?" he enquired.

"I don't think so. More likely some kind of artificial resin."

"What do you mean, artificial?"

"It's a long story. Could you analyse what's inside, please?"

"As long as we can break through the material surrounding it. Follow me," instructed Poincarno, intrigued by the object in his hand.

The laboratory was bathed in a red half-light. Poincarno flicked a switch and the neon ceiling lights buzzed to life. He sat down on a stool, placed the ball between the jaws of a small vice and tried, in vain, to cut the surface with the blade of a surgical knife. He put the tool away and replaced it with a diamond point, but that didn't even scratch the surface. So we changed room and tactics: this time the doctor attacked the marble with a laser, but the result was just as unsatisfactory.

"Right," he said. "Desperate times call for desperate measures. Follow me!"

We entered an airlock where Poincarno made us put on strange hooded overalls, glasses and gloves so we were completely covered from head to toe.

"Are we going to operate on somebody?" I asked from behind my mouth mask.

"We have to avoid contaminating the sample with any foreign DNA – yours for example. We're going into a sterile chamber now."

Poincarno sat on a stool in front of a hermetically sealed tank. He put the ball in a first compartment and shut it. Then he thrust his hands into two built-in rubber gloves to manipulate the ball from inside the tank, and moved it into a second chamber after it had been cleaned. He then placed the ball on a plinth and turned a small valve. A transparent liquid flooded into the compartment.

"What's that?" I asked.

"Liquid nitrogen," Keira explained.

"Minus 195.79° Celsius," added Poincarno. "The liquid nitrogen's very low temperature prevents enzymes from potentially damaging the DNA, RNA and proteins we want to extract. The gloves I'm using are specifically insulated to be burn resistant. The ball should crack any minute now."

But it didn't. An ever more fascinated Poincarno wasn't about to give up though.

"I'm going to drop the temperature radically using helium-3. It's a gas that lets you get close to absolute zero. If your object resists a thermal shock like that, I'll throw in the towel – there won't be another solution."

Poincarno turned a small tap. Nothing appeared to happen.

"It's an invisible gas," he explained. "Wait a few seconds."

Walter, Keira and I had our eyes glued to the glass wall of the tank, our breath held. After all our hard work, we couldn't accept the idea of being so powerless in the face of the unbreakable outer layer of such a small recipient. Then a minute fracture suddenly began to form on the ball's transparent surface. Poincarno pressed his eyes to the lens of his electronic microscope and manipulated a fine needle.

"I've got your sample!" he exclaimed. "Now we can carry out the tests. It'll take a few hours. I'll call you as soon as we have something."

We left him in his lab and exited via the sterile airlock after removing our gear. I suggested to Keira that we go back to my house, but she reminded me about Ivory's warnings and asked me if it was wise to. Walter offered to put us up, but I wanted a shower and clean clothes. So we said our goodbyes on the pavement outside and Walter took the underground back to the Academy, while Keira and I climbed into a taxi and headed for Cresswell Place.

Dust had settled throughout the house, the refrigerator was depressingly empty and the bedclothes were exactly as we'd left them – unmade. After trying to tidy up a bit, we fell asleep in each other's arms, completely exhausted.

We were woken by the phone ringing. I groped around for the receiver and heard a worked-up Walter at the other end when I picked it up.

"What on earth are you doing?"

"Believe it or not, we were sleeping and you've woken us up. That makes us quits."

"Do you know what time it is? I've been waiting for you at the laboratory for forty-five minutes. I've been trying to call you."

"I can't have heard my mobile. What's the big hurry?"

"That's just it. Dr. Poincarno refuses to tell me without you being here too. He contacted me at the Academy and asked me to come to the laboratory extremely urgently. So get dressed and come on over now," ordered Walter, before hanging up on me.

I woke Keira and told her we were eagerly awaited at the lab. She jumped into her trousers, slipped on a sweater and was out in the street before I'd had time to finish closing the windows. It was about 7pm when we arrived in Hammersmith Grove. Poincarno was pacing up and down the building's deserted foyer.

"You took your time," he grumbled. "Come to my office. We have to talk."

He asked us to sit down opposite a white wall, drew the curtains, turned out the light and switched on a projector.

The first slide he showed us looked like a colony of spiders clustered together on a web.

"What I've seen is downright absurd and I need to

know if all this is a massive fabrication or a hoax in bad taste. I agreed to see you this morning because of your professional standing and the Academy's recommendations. But this is beyond the pale and I won't put my reputation on the line to give any credit whatsoever to two time-wasting impostors."

Keira and I couldn't understand Poincarno's vehemence.

"What have you found out?" asked Keira.

"Before I answer that, tell me where you found this resin ball and in what circumstances."

"At the bottom of a grave in the north of the Omo Valley. It was lying on the sternum of a fossilised human skeleton."

"Impossible. You're lying!"

"Listen, doctor, I'm not wasting your time, or mine for that matter. If you think we're impostors, that's your call. But may I remind you that Adrian is an astrophysicist with an established reputation, and I have a few qualifications to my name too. So please tell us what you're accusing us of!"

"You could cover my office walls with your diplomas, Miss, but that wouldn't change a thing. What do you see on this image?" he asked, forwarding to a second slide.

"Mitochondria and strands of DNA," Keira replied.

"Yes, absolutely right."

"And that's causing you a problem?" I enquired.

"Twenty years ago, we successfully took and analysed a DNA sample from a weevil preserved in amber. The insect came from Lebanon. It had been discovered between Jezzine and Dar al-Baida, where it had got stuck in some resin. The paste had turned to stone, which had kept it intact. The insect was thirty million years old. You can imagine what we were able to find out from that discovery. It's the oldest evidence of a complex living organism to this day."

"I'm really thrilled for you," I said, "but what's that got to do with us?"

"Adrian's right," Walter intervened. "I still don't see where the problem is."

"The problem, gentlemen," continued Poincarno brusquely, "is that our spectroscope seems to think the DNA you've asked me to examine is three times older. It may even be four hundred million years old!"

"But that's a fantastic discovery!" I said enthusiastically.

"That was precisely our reaction at the beginning of the afternoon, even if some of the colleagues I phoned right away were doubtful. But the mitochondria you see on this third image are in such perfect condition that it raised questions. Let's say this special resin, which we still haven't managed to identify, protected them for all that time – although I sincerely doubt it. Now, look closely at this slide. It's an enlargement of the previous photograph using the electronic microscope. Come closer to the wall, please. I don't want you to miss this under any circumstances!"

Keira, Walter and I did as Poincarno asked and went and stood close to the projected image.

"Well? What do you see?"

"An X chromosome! The first man was a woman!" exclaimed Keira, clearly deeply moved.

"Yes. The skeleton you've found is unmistakably that

of a woman and not a man. But don't think I'm angry because of that – I'm not a woman-hater!"

"I still don't understand," Keira whispered to me. "This is fantastic! Can you believe it? Eve born before Adam," she said, smiling.

"Men's egos are going to take quite a bashing because of this!" I added.

"You're right to bring humour into it," Poincarno continued. "Because it gets even more comical. Look closer and tell me what you can see."

"Don't make us play guessing games, Dr. Poincarno. This discovery is incredibly moving. It's the culmination of a decade of work and sacrifices for me. Please just tell us what's making you angry. It'll save us all time, and I was given to understand yours was precious."

"Your discovery would be extraordinary if evolution accepted the principle of going backwards, but you know as well as I do that nature's way is for us to progress, not regress. Yet these chromosomes we're looking at are much more sophisticated than yours or mine!"

"Mine too?" asked Walter.

"More evolved than those of any human being alive today."

"Oh, right! What makes you say that?" Walter went on.

"This little part here, which we call an allele: a form of a gene located on both members of a pair of homologous chromosomes. These ones here have been genetically modified. I doubt very much that was conceivable four hundred million years ago! So now, please explain how you masterminded this hoax. Unless of course you'd prefer me to put my question to the Academy's board of directors instead."

Keira sat down, stunned.

"Why would these chromosomes have been modi-fied?" I asked.

"Genetic manipulation isn't what we're here to discuss today, but I'll answer your question. We're experimenting with this kind of intervention on chromosomes in order to prevent hereditary illnesses and some cancers, to provoke mutations and enable us to address living conditions that are evolving more quickly than we are. Modifying genes is a bit like correcting life's algorithm – putting right certain disorders, including those caused by ourselves. In short, the significance for medicine is infinite. But that's not our concern this evening. This woman you've discov-ered in this Omo Valley of yours can't belong to a distant past *and* contain traces of the future in her DNA. Now, tell me the reason for this prank. Were you both dreaming of the Nobel Prize? Did you hope fooling me in such a crude manner would win you my support?"

"This is no prank!" Keira protested. "I understand your suspicions, but we haven't invented a thing – I swear to you! We dug up the ball you've analysed the day before yesterday and, believe me, the state of fossilisation of the bones buried with it couldn't have been faked. If you only knew what we've been through to find that skeleton, you wouldn't doubt our sincerity for a second."

"Do you realise what it would imply if I believed you?" asked the doctor.

Poincarno's tone had changed and he suddenly seemed prepared to listen to us. He sat down behind his desk and turned the light back on.

"It means," answered Keira, "that Eve was born before

Adam. But most importantly that the mother of human-kind is much older than we all thought."

"No, not just that. If the mitochondria I've studied really are four hundred million years old, then that brings up a number of other theories your astrophysicist accomplice will certainly have explained to you – I imagine the two of you got your little routine off pat before coming here."

"We did nothing of the sort!" I said, standing up. "What theory are you talking about?"

"Come, come. Do you think I'm totally stupid? The research we carry out in our respective professions sometimes overlaps – you know that very well. Many scientists agree that life on Earth could have begun as a result of meteorite impacts. Isn't that right, Mr. Astrophysicist? And that theory was backed up when traces of glycine were discovered in the tail of a comet, as you must know."

"What's glycine?" asked Walter.

"Glycine is the simplest of the amino acids," I explained. "It's a vital molecule – one of life's building blocks. The Stardust probe found samples of it in the tail of the Wild 2 comet while it was passing three hundred and ninety million kilometres above Earth. Chains of amino acids make up the proteins that compose the organs, cells and enzymes of living organisms."

"And to the great delight of astrophysicists," Poincarno butted in, "this discovery backed up the idea that life on Earth could have originated in space, and be more common there than we think. I'm not exaggerating, am I? That theory's one thing, but it's sheer madness to dabble in dubious experiments to try and make us believe the Earth was once inhabited by beings as complex as us."

"What are you suggesting?" enquired Keira.

"I've already told you: this Eve of yours can't belong to the past *and* carry genetically modified cells. Not unless you're expecting us to swallow the idea that the first ever man – woman, in this case – arrived in the Omo Valley from another planet!"

"Not wishing to interfere in what's none of my business," Walter piped up, "but if you'd told my great-grandmother that people would be able to travel from London to Singapore in just a few hours, flying at an altitude of ten thousand metres in a metal tin weighing five hundred and sixty tonnes, she'd have reported you to her village doctor and you'd have been sent to the loony bin in a jiffy! Just imagine how talking about supersonic flight, man landing on the moon and a probe capturing amino acids in the tail of a comet three hundred and ninety million kilometres above Earth would have been received! Why do the most educated of us always lack so much imagination?"

Walter had become angry and was pacing up and down the room. Nobody dared interrupt him. He halted in front of Poincarno and pointed an enraged finger at him.

"You scientists spend your time making mistakes. You're constantly challenging your peers' errors, or your own, and don't try to tell me otherwise. I've pulled my hair out trying to balance budgets so you have the money you need to reinvent everything. And yet, each time an innovative idea is mooted, the same old reaction's trotted out: impossible, impossible and impossible! It really is incredible! Was modifying chromosomes conceivable a hundred years ago? Would your research have been given the least bit of credit as short a time ago as the start of the twentieth century? Certainly not by my trustees. You'd quite simply have been passed off as a crank and nothing but. Mr. Doctor of Genetic Engineering, I've known Adrian for months and I forbid you – forbid you, do you hear – of suspecting him of the slightest deceit. That man sitting in front of you is the model of decency, even if it sometimes verges on stupidity!"

Poincarno glanced from one to the other of us.

"You're in the wrong profession, Mr. Administrator of the Royal Academy of Science: you should have been a lawyer! Very well, I won't say anything to your board of directors. We'll continue our tests on the blood. My report will confirm what we find out, and nothing more. It will mention any anomalies and inconsistencies discovered, but not put forward or support any theory whatsoever. You can then publish whatever you want, but you alone will be entirely responsible for what you write. If I read just one line about your work that implicates me or calls me to witness, I'll get a writ issued against you immediately. Is that clear?"

"I never asked you for more than test results," Keira said. "If you agree to authenticate the age of the cells, to confirm from a scientific point of view that they are four hundred million years old, that will already be a huge contribution. Please be assured it's much too early for us to be thinking about publishing anything at all. And please be aware that we're just as shocked as you by what you've told us, and incapable of drawing any conclusions for the moment."

Poincarno saw us to the door of the laboratory and promised to contact us again in a few days.

*

It was raining in London that evening. Walter, Keira and I found ourselves out in the wet and the cold in Hammersmith Grove, exhausted after the day's events. Walter suggested we go and have dinner together in a nearby pub. We could hardly have left him on his own.

As we sat at a table next to a bay window, he asked us hundreds of questions about our trip to Ethiopia and Keira regaled him with every detail. He was so captivated that he jumped when she recounted the moment they discovered the skeleton. With such a good audience, she played up the drama, and I saw Walter shiver several times. He was like an overgrown schoolboy in some respects, a side of him Keira really liked. Seeing them laugh together that evening made me forget all the trouble we'd experienced in recent months.

I asked Walter what he'd meant earlier on when he'd said to Poincarno, if I remembered the wording correctly, that I was the model of decency, even if it sometimes verged on stupidity.

"That the bill's on you again this evening!" he answered, ordering a chocolate mousse. "Don't get on your high horse! It was for dramatic effect. For a good reason."

I asked Keira to give me her pendant, took the two other fragments out of my pocket and handed the lot to Walter.

"Why are you giving me these? They belong to you," he said, rather embarrassed.

"Because I'm decent sometimes verging on stupid," I replied. "If our work leads to a major publication, I'll be writing in the name of the Academy I belong to and I want your name to be associated. Then maybe you'll be able to get the roof over your office repaired at last. In the meantime, keep them in a safe place."

Walter put them in his pocket. I could see he was touched.

This amazing adventure had spawned a love I'd had no idea was possible, and a true friendship. Having spent most of my life exiled in some of the world's most far-flung countries scanning the universe in search of a distant star, here I was in an old pub in Hammersmith listening to the woman I loved chat and giggle with my best friend. I realised that evening that these two people I was so close to had changed my life.

We all have a little of the Robinson Crusoe in us, with a new world to discover and a Man Friday to meet.

Come closing time, we were the last to leave the pub. A taxi passed by and we let Walter take it. Keira and I felt like walking a bit.

The lights went out behind us. Hammersmith Grove was quiet; there was not a soul in sight. The nearest station was a few roads away so we'd definitely find a taxi around there.

The hum of an engine interrupted the silence as a van left its parking space. It pulled up alongside us, the back door opened and four masked men jumped out. Neither Keira nor I had time to realise what was happening before we were grabbed roughly. Keira cried out, but it was too late. We were thrown into the back of the van and it drove off at top speed.

We tried to put up a fight inside. I managed to knock one of my assailants over and Keira almost scratched out the eye of the man trying to pin her to the floor. But they bound our hands and feet, gagged and blindfolded us, then made us inhale sleeping gas. That was the last thing we remembered about our evening that had started so well.

Unknown location

When I came to, Keira was leaning over me, smiling weakly.

"Where are we?" I asked.

"I haven't the faintest idea."

I looked around the place. Four concrete walls and no opening except a reinforced door. A neon light on the ceiling emitted a pale glow.

"What's going on?" wondered Keira.

"We didn't listen to Ivory's advice."

"We must have been asleep for quite some time."

"What makes you think that?"

"Your beard. You were close shaven when we had dinner with Walter."

"You're right. We've probably been here a while. I'm hungry and thirsty."

"Me too, I'm dying of thirst," Keira said.

She got up and drummed on the door.

"Give us something to drink!" she shouted.

Not a sound.

"Don't tire yourself out. They'll come at some point."

"Or not!"

"Don't be silly! They aren't going to let us die of hunger and thirst in this cell."

"I don't want to worry you, but I didn't get the impression those bullets they aimed at us on the Trans-Siberian were made of rubber. Why on earth have they got it in for us this badly?" she groaned, sitting back down on the floor.

"Because of what you found, Keira."

"Why are human remains, however old, the cause of such a ruthlessness?"

"They aren't any old remains. I don't think you've really understood why Poincarno was so troubled."

"That idiot accused us of forging the DNA we asked him to test!"

"That's what I thought – you haven't completely grasped the implication of your discovery."

"It's not *my* discovery, it's ours!"

"Poincarno tried to make you understand the dilemma the tests faced him with. All living organisms contain cells. The simplest have just one, but humans have over ten billion of them, and all our cells are built on the same model, using two fundamental materials – nucleic acids and proteins. These building blocks of life are made of a combination of elements – carbon, nitrogen, hydrogen and oxygen. Those are established facts about how life works. But how did it all start? Scientists believe two different scenarios: either life appeared on Earth after a series of complex reactions, or material from space kick-started the process of life on Earth. All human beings evolve; they don't regress. If the DNA of that Ethiopian

Eve of yours contains genetically modified alleles, that makes her body more evolved than ours. Which is impossible, unless…"

"Unless what?" Keira interrupted.

"Unless your Eve died on Earth but wasn't born here."

"That's unthinkable!"

"If Walter was here, you'd make him angry saying that!"

"Adrian, I haven't spent ten years of my life looking for the missing link to end up explaining to my peers that the first human came from another planet."

"As we speak, six astronauts are shut up in a facility near Moscow to prepare for a trip to Mars. I'm not making this up. But there isn't a rocket in sight. It's a ground-based experiment organised by the European Space Agency and the Russian Academy of Sciences Institute of Biomedical Problems to test man's ability to travel in space over long distances. The project's called Mars 500 and is scheduled to become a reality in forty years. What's forty years in the history of humanity? Six astronauts will leave for Mars in 2050, just as those who were the first to walk on the moon did nearly one hundred years earlier. Now, picture the following scenario: if one of them died on Mars, what would the others do, in your opinion?"

"Eat his biscuits!"

"Keira, please! Be serious for two seconds."

"Sorry, being in this cell is making me nervy."

"All the more reason to let me take your mind off things."

"I don't know what the others would do. Bury him, I guess."

"Exactly! I doubt they'd want to do the return journey with a decomposing body on board. So they'd bury it. But they'd find ice under the dust on Mars, like the Sumerians did when they dug those graves on the Manpupuner plateau."

"Not exactly," corrected Keira. "Those graves became buried under the ice over time. But there are lots of ice tombs in Siberia."

"Okay then, like in Siberia. Hoping that another mission would come back one day, the astronauts would bury their comrade's body with a tag and a sample of his blood."

"Why?"

"For two distinct reasons: so the burial place could be located regardless of whether storms had drastically altered the landscape, and so the man or woman buried there could be positively identified – like we were able to do. The crew would leave again, just like the first men on the moon did. From a scientific point of view, there's nothing crazy about what I've just said. In the end, all we've learned to do in a century is travel further in space. But there was a gap of only eighty years between Ader's first flight, which merely hovered a few metres above ground, and Armstrong's first steps on the moon. The technical progress made and the knowledge acquired to go from that short flight to ripping a rocket weighing several tonnes out of the Earth's pull are unimaginable.

"Anyway, back to my scenario: our crew has come back to Earth and their colleague has been laid to rest under the ice on Mars. The universe doesn't care about all that and keeps evolving. The planets in our solar system turn around their star and are heated up by it more and more all the time. In a few million years – which isn't much in the history of the universe – Mars will heat up and the underground ice will melt. The frozen body of our astronaut will start decomposing. It takes just a few seeds to make a forest grow. All it takes is DNA fragments belonging to your Ethiopian Eve to have mixed with water when our planet came out of the ice age and the fertilisation process of life would have started on Earth. The program held within each of her cells would have done the rest. Another few hundred million years, and evolution would have produced human beings as complex as the Eve they originated from. *The night of one is guardian of the origins*. People before us had realised what I've just told you."

The neon light above our heads went out, plunging us into complete darkness. I took Keira's hand.

"I'm here, don't be scared. We're together."

"Do you believe what you've just told me, Adrian?"

"I don't know, Keira. If you're asking me if that scenario is possible, my answer's 'yes.' If you're asking me if it's likely, then based on the evidence we've found, my answer's 'why not?' Like with every investigation or research project, you have to start with a theory. Since Antiquity, the greatest discoveries have been made by those humble enough to see things differently. Our science teacher at school used to say: 'If you want to discover things, you have to step out of your own system. You can't see much from the inside – nothing of what's going on outside, anyway.' If we were free and published these kinds of conclusions supported by the evidence we have, we'd arouse a range of reactions: interest and incredulity, but also jealousy – lots of fellow scientists would accuse us of heresy. And yet, so many people have faith, Keira. So many people believe in God without any evidence of his existence. The things we've learned through the fragments, the skeleton unearthed in Dipa and the extraordinary revelations of the DNA tests give us every right to ask all sorts of questions about the way life appeared on Earth."

"I'm thirsty, Adrian."

"Me too."

"Do you think they're just going to leave us to die like this?"

"I really don't know. It's been ages now."

"Dying of thirst is horrible, apparently. After a while, your tongue swells up and suffocates you."

"Try not to think about it."

"Do you have any regrets?"

"About being locked up in here? Yes. But not the slightest regret about all the time we've been able to spend together."

"At least I found her, humanity's grandmother," Keira sighed.

"Humanity's great-great-grandmother you should say. I haven't even congratulated you yet."

"I love you, Adrian."

I wrapped my arms round Keira, sought her lips in the darkness and kissed her. Our strength was fading with every passing hour.

"Walter must be worried," Keira murmured.

"He's got used to us disappearing."

"We've never gone away without telling him."

"You're right. Maybe this time he'll really worry about what's happened to us."

"He won't be the only one. Our research won't have been in vain, I know it," Keira whispered. "Poincarno will continue his tests on the DNA and my team will bring Eve's skeleton back."

"Is that really what you want to christen her?"

"No, I want to call her Jeanne. Walter's put the fragments in a safe place and VU University will study the recording. Ivory opened up a way and we followed. Others will continue down it without us. Sooner or later, they'll put the pieces of the puzzle together."

Keira fell silent.

"Keep talking."

"I'm so tired, Adrian."

"Don't go to sleep. Resist it."

"What for?"

She was right – dying in our sleep would be gentler.

The neon light flickered on. I had no idea how much time had elapsed since we'd lost consciousness. My eyes had trouble adjusting to the brightness.

There were two bottles of water, some chocolate bars and some biscuits in front of the door. I shook Keira, moistened her lips and rocked her in my arms, begging her to open her eyes.

"Have you made us breakfast?" she mumbled.

"Yes, something like that. Don't drink too quickly."

Once her thirst was quenched, she devoured the chocolate and we shared the biscuits. Before long, we'd recovered some strength and got the colour back in our cheeks.

"Do you think they've changed their minds?" she asked me.

"I know as much as you do. Let's wait and see."

The door opened. Two men in face masks entered, followed by a third, unmasked man wearing a well-tailored tweed suit.

"Get up and follow us," he ordered.

We left our cell and walked down a long corridor.

"In there," the man said. "They're the staff showers. Go and have a wash – you need one. My men will escort you to my office when you're ready."

"To whom do we have the honour of speaking, pray tell?" I asked.

"You're arrogant. I like that," the man answered. "My name's Edward Ashley. See you later."

When we were almost presentable again, Ashley's men escorted us through a sumptuous manor house nestling in the English countryside. The cellar we'd been locked in was in the basement of a building close to a large greenhouse. We crossed an impeccably kept garden, climbed up the steps to a porch and were shown into a vast wood-panelled sitting room. Ashley was sitting at his desk, waiting for us.

"You two have made my life very difficult."

"I could say the same thing to you!" Keira shot back.

"I see you have a sense of humour as well."

"I don't see anything funny about what you've put us through."

"You have only yourselves to blame. You were given plenty of warnings, but nothing seemed to convince you to stop your research."

"And why should we have abandoned it?" I asked.

"If it'd only been down to me, you wouldn't be here now asking me that question. But I'm not the only decision-maker in this affair."

Sir Ashley stood up and walked over to the wall behind his desk. He pressed a button and the wood panelling decorating the room's circular walls retracted, revealing about fifteen screens that all flashed on at once. A different person's face appeared on each. I immediately recognised one of them as our contact in Amsterdam. The men and one woman took turns introducing themselves by the name of a city: Athens, Berlin, Boston, Istanbul, Cairo, Madrid, Moscow, New Delhi, Paris, Beijing, Rome, Rio, Tel Aviv and Tokyo.

"Who are you all?" Keira asked.

"Official representatives of our countries. We're in charge of your case."

"What case?" I enquired.

The lone woman of the group was the first to speak to us. She introduced herself as Isabel, then put a strange question to us: "If you had evidence that God didn't exist, are you sure people would want to see it? Have you really weighed up the consequences of spreading that kind of news? Two billion humans on this planet live below the poverty line. Half the world's population has barely enough to live on. Have you ever wondered what keeps this unsteady, unequal world on its feet? The answer is hope. Hope that a higher, compassionate power exists.

Hope of a better life after death. Call that hope what you will – God or faith."

"Excuse me, Isabel, but people continually kill each other in the name of God. Providing them with the evidence that he doesn't exist would free them once and for all from hatred towards others. Think how many lives have been taken by religious wars and how many victims are still claimed today amid religious strife. How many dictatorships are built on religious foundations?"

"People don't just kill each other because they believe in their god," retorted Isabel. "They do it to survive, to follow nature's orders and ensure the continuity of their species."

"As animals do, without believing in God," interjected Keira.

"But humans are the only living things on Earth to be aware of their own death. They are the only ones to fear it. Do you know when the first religious ritual dates back to?"

"A hundred thousand years ago, near Nazareth," replied Keira. "Probably for the first time in the history of humanity, Homo sapiens buried the remains of a woman in her twenties. By her feet lay those of a six-year-old child. The people who discovered their grave also found a large amount of red ochre and some ritual objects around their skeletons. Both the bodies were in the praying position. Out of the pain of losing a loved one had risen the urge to honour the dead," she explained, repeating almost word for word what Ivory had once taught her.

"A hundred thousand years," Isabel recapped. "A thousand centuries of belief. If you gave humankind scientific proof that God hadn't created life on Earth, the world would be destroyed. A billion and a half human beings live in intolerable, unacceptable poverty. What man, woman or child in distress would accept their condition if they were deprived of hope? What would stop them killing their neighbour to obtain what they lacked if their conscience was devoid of any form of spirituality? People have been killed in the name of religion, but faith has saved so many lives, given so much strength to the most destitute. You can't just extinguish that light. For you scientists, death is necessary. Our cells die so that others can live. We die to make way for those who succeed us. Birth and development followed by death is in the order of things. But for most people, dying is merely a step towards a better world where everything that isn't will be, where everyone they have lost will be waiting for them. You haven't experienced hunger, thirst or destitution. You've been lucky enough to pursue your dreams, whatever your talents. But have you thought about those who haven't had that opportunity? Would you be cruel enough to tell them that their suffering on Earth had no other purpose than evolution?"

I strode over to the screens to face our judges.

"This sorry session," I began, "makes me think of the one Galileo had to endure. Humanity ended up discovering what its censors wanted to hide, yet the world didn't stop turning! On the contrary. When people threw off their fear and decided to advance towards the horizon, the horizon receded before their eyes. What would we be today if yesterday's believers had managed to block the truth? Knowledge is part of man's evolution."

"If you divulge your discoveries, on the first day there will be hundreds of thousands of deaths in the least developed countries. In the first week there will be millions of deaths in the developing nations. The following week the biggest human migration ever will begin: a billion starving humans will cross the continents and take to the sea in search of what they need. Every single one of them will try to live out their hopes for the future in the here and now. The fifth week will mark the start of the first night."

"If our revelations are so devastating, why did you release us?"

"We weren't planning to until we learned from your conversation in the cell that you weren't the only ones who knew. Your sudden disappearance would drive the scientists you've been liaising with to complete your work. Only you can stop them now. You're free to leave, and on your own regarding what decision to make. Not since nuclear fission was discovered has a man or woman carried so much responsibility on their shoulders."

The screens shut down one after the other. Sir Ashley stood up and came over to us. "My car is at your service: my chauffeur will drive you back to London."

London

We spent a few days at home. It was the first time Keira and I had ever been so silent. Each time one of us opened our mouth to say a few words – some trite remark or other – we shut up again almost instantly. Walter had left a message on my answering machine. He was furious that we'd vanished without giving him any news. He guessed we were in Amsterdam or had gone back to Ethiopia. I tried to call him back but he was impossible to get hold of.

The atmosphere in Cresswell Place was heavy. I overheard a phone conversation between Keira and Jeanne. She was incapable of making conversation, even with her sister. I decided we needed a change of air. I'd take Keira to Hydra. Some sunshine would do us the world of good.

Greece

The Athens ferry dropped us at the port at 10am. From the quayside I could see Aunt Elena. She was wearing an apron and giving her shopfront a fresh lick of blue paint with sweeping brushstrokes.

I put down our suitcases and was walking over to surprise her when all of a sudden I saw Walter come out of her shop dressed in checked shorts, a ridiculous hat and sunglasses two times too big for his face. He set to work scraping the wood with a trowel, singing the famous tune from *Zorba the Greek* totally off key at the top of his voice. He caught sight of us and rushed over.

"Where have you been, for goodness' sake?" he quizzed.

"We were locked up in a cellar!" Keira replied, giving him a hug. "We missed you, Walter."

"What on earth are you doing in Hydra mid-week? Shouldn't you be at the Academy?" I asked him.

"When we saw each other in London, I told you I'd sold my car and that I had a surprise for you. But you never listen."

"I remember very clearly!" I protested. "But you didn't tell me what the surprise was."

"Well, I've decided to change jobs. I've entrusted the rest of my meagre savings to Elena, and as you can see, we're refurbishing the shop. We're going to increase the shelf space and I'm hoping to help her double her sales figures from next season. Do you have any objections?"

"I'm thrilled my aunt has at last found an outstanding administrator to assist her!" I said, patting my friend on the shoulder.

"You should go up and see your mother. She must already know you're on the island – I can see Elena on the phone."

Kalibanos lent us two donkeys, two of his "fast" ones, he told us as he handed them over. Mum gave us the traditional island welcome: that evening, without consulting us first, she organised a big party at home. Walter and Elena were seated next to each other, which at my mother's table meant they were more than just dining partners.

After the meal, Walter summoned Keira and me to the terrace. He removed a small parcel from his pocket – a handkerchief tied with string – and handed it over to us.

"These fragments belong to you. I've turned a page. The Academy of Science is now part of my past. My future's right in front of you," he said, spreading open his arms towards the sea. "Do with them as you think fit. Oh yes, one last thing!" he added, looking at me. "I've left a letter in your bedroom. It's for you, Adrian, but I'd rather you didn't read it straightaway. Wait a week or two, let's say."

He turned on his heel and left to rejoin Elena. Keira picked up the parcel and went to put it away in her beside cabinet.

The following morning, she asked me to accompany her down to the cove where we'd swum on her first visit. We sat down on the end of the long stone jetty and dangled our feet in the sea. Keira held out the handkerchief-wrapped parcel to me. Her eyes were filled with sadness.

"These are for you. I know what this discovery means for us both. I don't know if what those people said is true – if their fears are well founded. I'm not clever enough to judge. What I do know is that I love you. If the decision to disclose what we know were to lead to the death of one single child, I wouldn't be able to look either you or myself in the face again or live with you, even though I'd miss you like hell. You've said several times over the course of our incredible journey that we have to make decisions together. But I've made up my mind, you must take these fragments and do what you want with them. Whatever you decide, I'll always respect the man you are."

She put the parcel in my hands, then stood up and walked away.

After Keira left, I went over to a small boat lying on the sand, pushed it into the water, clambered in and began rowing out to sea.

About a kilometre and a half from the shoreline, I untied the string wrapped around Walter's handkerchief and stared at the fragments for a long time. Thousands of kilometres rushed before my eyes. I pictured Lake Turkana and its central island, the temple at the top of Mount Hua, the monastery in Xi'an and the lama who saved our lives. I heard the drone of the plane skimming over Burma, and saw the paddy field we landed in to fill up on fuel, the pilot's wink as we arrived in Port Blair, and the boat trip to Narcondam Island. Then I was back in Beijing, in Garther Prison, in Paris, London and Amsterdam, in Russia on the high plateau of Manpupuner, and among the stunning colours of the Omo Valley, where Hari appeared to me. And in every one of these memories, the most beautiful part of the scenery was Keira's face.

I unfolded the handkerchief.

As I was heading back to the cove, my mobile phone rang. I recognised the man's voice.

"You've made a wise decision and we thank you for it," acknowledged Sir Ashley.

"But how did you know? I've only just…"

"We've kept our guns trained on you since you left. Perhaps one day… But it's too early, believe me. We've still got lots of progress to make."

I hung up on him and flung my mobile into the sea. Once I'd regained land, I made my way home on donkey back.

Keira was waiting for me on the terrace. I handed her Walter's empty handkerchief.

"I think he'd appreciate it if you gave it back to him yourself."

She folded it up, then led me to our room.

The first night

The house was still. Keira and I tiptoed out as quietly as we possibly could and padded stealthily towards the donkeys to untie them. But my mother appeared on the porch and came towards us.

"If you're going to the beach – which is crazy at this time of year – at least take these towels. The sand's wet and you'll catch cold."

She handed us two flashlights as well and went back inside.

A short while later we were sitting at the water's edge. The moon was full. Keira laid her head on my shoulder.

"Do you have any regrets?" she asked.

I looked up at the sky and thought about Atacama.

"Each human being is made up of billions of cells. Billions of humans inhabit this planet, and the number is constantly rising. The universe is populated by billions and billions of stars. What if this universe whose boundaries I thought I knew was only a minute part of an even bigger set-up? What if our Earth was only a cell in a mother's womb? The birth of the universe is like the birth of any new life: the same miracle happens, from the infinitely big to the infinitely small. Can you imagine what an incredible journey it would be to travel up to that mother's eye and look through her iris at her world? Life is an amazing program."

"But who developed such a perfect program, Adrian?"

Epilogue

Iris was born nine months later. We didn't christen her, but on her first birthday, on her first ever trip to the Omo Valley to meet Hari, her mother and I gave her a pendant.

I don't know what she'll choose to do with her life, but when she's big, if she comes to ask me what that strange object around her neck represents, I'll read her the lines of a text an elderly professor gave me:

There is a legend which says that a child in the womb knows the whole mystery of Creation, of the origins of the world, until the end of time. When the child is born, a messenger passes over its cradle and puts his finger on its lips so it will never reveal the secret that was entrusted to it – the secret of life. This finger, which erases the child's memory forever, leaves a mark. We all have this mark above our top lip, except for me. On the day I was born, the messenger forgot to pay me a visit, and I can remember everything.

To Ivory, with all our gratitude,
Keira, Iris, Hari and Adrian.

Thanks to

Pauline.
Louis.

Susanna Lea and Antoine Audouard.

Emmanuelle Hardouin.
Raymond, Danièle and Lorraine Levy.

Nicole Lattès, Leonello Brandolini, Antoine Caro,
Élisabeth Villeneuve, Anne-Marie Lenfant, Arié
Sberro, Sylvie Bardeau, Tine Gerber, Lydie Leroy,
Joël Renaudat and all the team at Éditions Robert
Laffont.

Pauline Normand, Marie-Ève Provost.

Léonard Anthony, Romain Ructsch, Danielle
Melconian, Katrin Hodapp, Marie Garnero, Mark
Kessler, Laura Mamelok, Lauren Wendelken, Kerry
Glencorse, Moïna Macé.

Brigitte and Sarah Forissier.

Kamel, Carmen Varela.

Igor Bogdanov.